PHULE ME TWICE

TWICE THE PHULE, DOUBLE THE TROUBLE

D1501028

PHULE ME TWICE

TWICE THE PHULE, DOUBLE THE TROUBLE

NEW YORK TIMES BESTSELLING AUTHOR

ROBERT ASPRIN
AND PETER J. HECK

WordFire Press
Colorado Springs, Colorado

ISBN: 978-1-61475-575-3

Cover design by Janet McDonald

Cover Image by Jeff Herndon

Art Director Kevin J. Anderson

Book Design by RuneWright, LLC
www.RuneWright.com

Published by
WordFire Press, an imprint of
WordFire, Inc.
PO Box 1840
Monument, CO 80132

Kevin J. Anderson & Rebecca Moesta Publishers

WordFire Press Trade Paperback Edition April 2017
Printed in the USA
wordfirepress.com

PROLOGUE

ll right, all right," said Reverend Jordan Ayres, rubbing his hands together. He stepped out from behind the podium in the rented ballroom and made a beckoning gesture. "Who's ready to make himself over in the image of the King? Step right up!"

Rev had been particularly successful in winning converts to the Church of the King, his own denomination, from among the rookie legionnaires. This might have been because the older legionnaires were more jaded, or perhaps the new crop saw him as one of their own in the way the veterans didn't. Or it may simply have been the luck of the draw. In any case, the meeting room in the Landoor Plaza Hotel was nearly half full with those who'd come to pay their homage to the King, many local civilians in addition to the legionnaires.

"Uh, Rev—this isn't gonna hurt, is it?" The quavering voice belonged to Roadkill, one of the new recruits who'd joined Phule's Company at the same time as Rev's assignment as the company chaplain.

"Hurt?" Rev scoffed. "Are you gonna worry about whether it hurts? This is one of the deepest mysteries of the faith. If you don't love the King enough to put up with a little bit of hurtin',

I'm not a-gonna push you, son. You're not doin' this for me, you're doin' it for yourself—and for *him*."

"The King sang about hurtin'," said another of the recruits, Freefall. "*He* wasn't afraid to walk down Lonely Street ..." Her voice carried just enough of a hint of disapproval to suggest that Roadkill was being shortsighted and selfish—that Roadkill's faith might even be open to question.

"*He* asked us not to be cruel," riposted Roadkill. "Besides, I didn't say I wasn't going to do it. I just want to know ahead of time if it hurts, and you don't know any more about that than I do. The only one here who's gone through with it is Rev, and from what he said, I guess it *does* hurt."

"It don't hurt all that much, though," said Rev, stepping forward and smiling. Then he cleared his throat and quickly changed the subject. "Besides, there's another choice you all need to make before you go any further—a choice you might not even realize you have."

"Another choice?" Freefall raised her eyebrows. "Isn't it enough for us to give up our own appearance to take on His? A face none of us was born with?"

"That's right, there's still another choice," said Rev. "'Cause even the King had more than one way he looked. Why don't y'all set down and let me show you some holos? There are a few li'l constraints on account of bone structure and all, but even with all that, you've got a bunch of different models to pick from." He motioned toward the seats, and with only a little confusion, the disciples obediently took their places.

"All right," said Rev. "I'm a-gonna show you what y'all's choices are, and then we'll start. It's pretty quick once we do. And by tomorrow morning, you'll all be livin' testimonials to the power of the King!"

A hush fell over the crowd as Rev picked up the remote control for the holojector.

"Now, here he is when he first started out," said Rev. "This is a good one if you're young and slim. Notice how the sideburns are narrower than mine ..."

The audience stared at the holo, rapt. Rev droned on.

CHAPTER ONE

Journal #474

My employer's company had achieved a very pleasant modus vivendi on Landoor, its most recent station. The company's original responsibility as a peacekeeping team was quickly modified, as my employer decided to turn his efforts to helping the planet realize its potential as a tourist mecca. After considerable investment of time and money—and no little personal effort—he had achieved success.

The planet's climate was gentle, its people easygoing by nature. And the legionnaires of Omega Company were never too busy to sample the entertainments of two Galaxy-class amusement parks. The officers were also pleased to be free of the corrupting influences to which the troops had been exposed on their previous assignment—not that many of them could have become much more corrupt than they already were. Without much question, Landoor was the healthiest place the company had been.

Relatively speaking, of course.

* * *

Sushi stared at his computer, which currently displayed a long list of names—a list that very few eyes other than his had seen. If some of those on the list had known just who was looking at it and why, there would have been interplanetary repercussions. One of those repercussions would undoubtedly have been a serious attempt to liquidate Sushi. Sushi knew this, of course. It didn't bother him. It was just the downside of the gamble he was taking.

Taking over the Yakuza. It had seemed a ridiculous idea when he'd first come up with it, an inspired improvisation to save his hide when the Japanese mob had sent an assassin to punish him for impersonating one of its members. If he'd thought it all the way through when he first came up with it, he might have decided on something less audacious. After all, he already had what was supposed to be a full-time job—although being a legionnaire in Omega Company, even under Captain Jester, was a good bit less demanding than belonging to most military units. But running this conspiracy was more than a full-time job.

The basic idea was simple. He'd invented a phony superfamily that would unite the families on different worlds, allowing them to mediate territorial disputes and to trade useful information. It was an idea whose time had come a good while back; only the inherent conservatism of the criminal mentality had kept it from coming into being. But he'd done it, essentially with no help from anyone except a few of his own family members who had certain useful knowledge and contacts and had used them to slip him information. And it had worked.

The only problem so far was that the entire superfamily consisted of Sushi and his trusty computer, a Legion milspec model, but with lots of custom features installed by Sushi himself. Eventually, he was going to make a mistake, and he just had to hope it wouldn't be a fatal one—especially not to himself. It was probably a shortcoming in a would-be criminal mastermind, but he really didn't want anybody to get hurt if he could avoid it. He didn't even really want to pocket more than a tiny fraction of the Yakuza's income. The whole idea originally had been to keep himself alive, and he'd be perfectly happy if he could continue to achieve that goal over the long term—say, seven or eight decades.

Behind him a door opened, and almost by instinct he blanked the screen. Then a familiar voice said, "Yo, Soosh, Okie tells me

Dunes Park has a new coaster. Wanna go give it the test?"

Sushi looked over his shoulder to see Do-Wop standing hipshot in the doorway of their shared room in the Landoor Plaza Hotel. "Maybe tomorrow," said Sushi wearily. "Right now, I'm up to my ears in this project."

"Ahh, c'mon," said Do-Wop. "You've been busting your hump on that stuff all week. Time for a break, man."

"Believe me, I'd love to take one," said Sushi. "But this business of taking over the Yakuza is a lot more work than I expected. It wasn't really that hard to get control, but keeping it is turning out to be real work."

"And your ass is grass if it gets away from you," said Do-Wop, nodding in sympathy.

"Right. I've got the families in the sector around old Earth playing along with me," said Sushi, leaning back in his chair and stretching. "They recognize the need for a larger organization, and they aren't picky about who's running it, as long as it doesn't cut their profits. That's the good part." He paused, then added, "At least there *is* a good part."

"Can't be all that good if it don't leave you time to goof off," said Do-Wop, sulking. "You're startin' to act like a freakin' officer."

"Who, me? Watch your mouth," said Sushi with an indignant expression. "If I'd wanted to be an officer, I'd have had my father buy me a commission and gone to the academy."

Do-Wop slouched against the doorway and crossed his arms. "All I know is what I see," he said. "You'd think now that we're in the theme park business, we'd get a chance to go on a ride or two. But no. This whole Yazooka thing has you tied up hand and foot."

"Yakuza," corrected Sushi. "Look, I'm sorry. I really have to finish this report, OK? Why don't you get somebody else to go along on the new rides with you this time?"

"Like who?" asked Do-Wop. "Tusk-anini would go along for the ride, but what we gonna talk about while we're waiting on line? He'd just pull out a book and start reading."

"You could take Mahatma or the Gambolts," said Sushi, looking up distractedly.

"Sure, except they'd have to cut out of training, which they wouldn't do. I tell ya, Soosh, this new generation of legionnaires is going straight down the tubes. Ain't a single one of 'em that really appreciates the fine points of goofing off."

Sushi chuckled. "I suppose not," he said with a broad grin. "Remember back on Haskin's Planet, how we rigged the drinks dispenser in the Plaza Hotel to double as a slot machine? You had to push the button for Diet Prunola to get it to take your bet."

"Yeah," said Do-Wop. "Worked like a charm until Chocolate Harry found the machine and complained to the management when he couldn't get a can of the stuff."

"We should've figured there'd be *somebody* who'd drink that god-awful junk," said Sushi, finally looking up from the computer and laughing. "But you're right; none of these rookies would ever think up a trick like that. And none of them would set up a holo of themselves when they had to stand guard duty, so it'd look like they were walking their rounds when Lieutenant Armstrong came checking up on them."

"I don't think Armstrong would ever have found out about that one if I hadn't forgot and left the projector running after I was supposed to come off duty," said Do-Wop. "Yeah, those were the days, all right."

Sushi chuckled. "They sure were," he agreed. "We must have been the champion goof-offs of Omega Company—and if that's not world-class, I don't know what is."

Do-Wop laughed and said, "Yeah, we had it down to a science back in the old days." Then a troubling thought came to him, and he frowned. "So what's wrong with us, Soosh? Why aren't we out raising hell like we used to?"

Sushi's expression was dead serious as he answered. "Maybe we're just growing up, Do-Wop."

"Growing up?" Do-Wop scoffed. "No freakin' way." He paused for a moment, then added, "I couldn't look myself in the mirror if I thought I was growing up."

"That's OK," said Sushi, grinning again. "Nobody else can stand to look at you, so there's no reason you should have to, either."

Do-Wop punched him on the biceps and said, "See? You just proved my point. So don't you think we oughta go check out that new coaster?"

Sushi sighed and turned off the computer. "I guess I'm not going to get any more work done until I agree, am I? OK, then, let's go."

Journal #475

The Omega Company's move to Landoor was not without its complications, primary among them the necessity of vacating the Fat Chance Casino on Lorelei, where the company had become majority stockholders. Leaving such a casino unattended would have been the equivalent of sending engraved invitations to every rustler in the galaxy. Even when the company had been on duty, organized criminal elements had tried to take over the casino. And while their attempts had failed, any sign of weakness would inevitably attract more predators.

My employer's solution was to give the impression that the casino was guarded as closely as ever, with a squad of actors impersonating Legion personnel (and a cadre of trained security personnel for the infrequent cases where real muscle was needed). And that was just the tip of the iceberg.

* * *

The tourist shuttle came to a stop in front of the Fat Chance Casino, disembarking a small crowd of sophonts of assorted shapes, sizes, and colors, with luggage to match. One thing they had in common: all were comparatively affluent. Otherwise, they could not have afforded the spaceship fare to the orbiting pleasure colony of Lorelei, the gambling center of the galaxy. Lorelei was in the business of separating tourists from their money, and it frowned on tourists who had no money to be separated from. This batch, being fresh off the ship and therefore presumably flush, was greeted at the door with the broadest of smiles.

A casino manager, dressed in an outfit that somehow gave the impression of style and sophistication while still remaining unmistakably a uniform, addressed the group. "Welcome to the

Fat Chance, gentlebeings!" she said warmly. "You've chosen the friendliest destination on Lorelei, and we want all our guests to enjoy every minute of their stay with us. So relax, put aside any worries you might have, and get ready for a great time. If you'd like to get to your rooms right away, please step into the hotel lobby to your left, where our clerks will register you and make you feel at home."

She stepped back and gestured toward the elegant doors behind her, modeled after those of a famous resort on old Earth, and continued. "For those who'd prefer to get started having fun, you can step into the casino lobby to your right or go directly ahead to one of our Galaxy-class restaurants. Our staff will take care of your luggage, and if you'd like to have it checked into your rooms, simply give me a copy of your registration letter, and we'll have it done for you while you enjoy yourself. We'll bring your room key to you. Does anyone have any questions?"

A pink-faced human in a shirt that looked as if it glowed in the dark raised his hand and said gloomily, "I don't know about anybody else, but I'm not letting my luggage out of my sight. My brother went to New Baltimore on a vacation last year, and they stole his suitcase right out of the taxi—while it was moving!"

"Oh, Henry!" said the thin woman standing next to him. "This is the Fat Chance. Nobody would dare try something like that here. After all, the guards are from the Space Legion!" She pointed to the casino entrance, flanked by two black-uniformed figures. Both looked trim, fit, and alert.

"That's right, ma'am," said the casino manager brightly. "And not just any Space Legion company—we have Phule's Company standing guard here. And as you may have heard, the legionnaires are all casino stockholders. It's not just a job to them. It's to their personal benefit to see that all of our guests have a safe, enjoyable experience—and come to visit us again."

"And lose plenty of our money," grumbled Henry. "Well, it won't work this time. I've got a way to beat the house, and the Fat Chance is going to be the proving ground for my system!"

"That's the spirit," said a new voice. The crowd of tourists turned and saw an enthusiastic young man dressed in a Legion officer's uniform. He was slim and energetic, with a smile that radiated sincerity. "If there's one casino on Lorelei to test a system at, this is the one! For starters, we won't throw you out if you start winning with it, the way some other houses will."

"Captain Jester!" said the casino employee.

"I was just on my way back to the office from a lunch date," said the smiling figure. "Heard this guest's comment and thought I'd made sure he knew our policy. Carry on, Miss Shadwell; I'm sure you're doing a fine job." He turned to the guests and said, "Welcome to the Fat Chance. If there's any trouble, my office door is always open." He smiled, sketched a bow, and hurried off.

"That's Willard Phule," said one guest to a neighbor, a discreet hand muffling his words. "The munitions heir—richer than the mint and cleaning up at the casino business, too, I hear."

"What's with the uniform?" said the other.

"Oh, he's gone and joined the Space Legion," said the first man with a chuckle. "I hear tell the Legion will never be the same."

"That's the truth," said Miss Shadwell, smiling. "Nor will the Fat Chance Casino—as you'll see when you get to the tables. Now, if there's anyone who'd like to take advantage of our express registration, I'll take your information here." She pulled out a pocket computer and smiled. The tourists obediently got in line, smiling back at her.

But two figures watched the captain's exit with narrowed eyes, then looked at each other and nodded.

*　*　*

First Sergeant Brandy looked at the line of legionnaires with some satisfaction. The new recruits had begun to shape up much more effectively than she'd have been willing to bet a few short months ago. She certainly hadn't had much to work with in the way of raw material—always excepting the Gambolts, those catlike aliens who were reputed to be, as a species, the finest hand-to-hand fighters in the known Galaxy. Her three Gambolts—Dukes, Rube, and Garbo—had lived up to that image without much doubt. Their natural ability had been evident from the day they'd arrived. Even if they'd made no progress at all in their training, they'd have been among the finest troops she'd ever seen.

The rest of the new troops hadn't done too badly either, and she took that as a personal accomplishment. They'd begun as the usual mix of rebels and rejects that enlisted in the Space Legion. Headquarters had culled out any who showed signs of competence and sent the rest to Omega Company. Brandy didn't mind that; years with the Omega Mob had conditioned her to expect nothing better. But somehow this group had managed to rise above expectations. Now she was beginning to think they had the makings of a pretty good unit.

"OK, listen up," she said. "Today we're going to be working on a river assault simulation. How many people here have any experience with small boats?" This exercise was in response to a near fiasco late last summer, when a native guide ran a boat intentionally aground, spilling the legionnaires aboard it into the water, then easily capturing them. The captain hadn't been happy to learn of that debacle. Thus today's exercise …

As Brandy had expected, several legionnaires raised their hands. "Good," said Brandy, looking around the group. "OK, that's Slayer, Mahatma, Roadkill …"

"Sarge, I didn't raise my hand," came Roadkill's voice, a nasal whine with a Parson's Planet accent. The voice came from the opposite end of the line from where Brandy had been looking.

"What?" said Brandy, doing a double take. "Step forward, you two. Let me look at you." The two complied, and sure enough, the two faces were nearly identical. In fact, they both looked a good bit like Rev, the Omega Mob's chaplain, who (Brandy now remembered) belonged to a cult that encouraged converts to undergo cosmetic surgery to make themselves resemble their prophet. "The King," his followers called him, although his real name was Elvish Priestley, if she remembered right.

"I'm not sure I like this," said Brandy, thinking out loud. "How the hell am I going to tell one of you from the other?"

"I don't see where it matters, Sarge," said Roadkill or … she looked at the legionnaire's name badge … no, it was Freefall.

"We're aren't breaking any regulations, are we?"

"Well, I don't know," said Brandy, scowling. "I don't have anything against Rev or his King, but this is going to cause a lot of confusion."

"Legionnaire's Bill of Rights, Article IV, Section 3-A, forbids any interference with religious expression, Sergeant," said a voice from within the group. Brandy groaned. She recognized *that* voice. It was Mahatma, the bright-eyed and bushy-tailed perennial thorn in her side.

"Mahatma, nobody's said anything about interfering with anything," said Brandy wearily. "I'm just thinking that, in a combat situation, not knowing who you're dealing with could be a real pain in the ass." She knew she wasn't going to convince Mahatma of anything with such a straightforward and reasonable argument, but she had to try. In the old days, she could've let her authority as sergeant settle the matter. Nowadays … well, on the whole, things were better nowadays, Brandy reminded herself. Nostalgia lost a lot of its attraction when there were so few things about the old days that any sane person could consider good.

Mahatma stepped forward. As usual, he had a broad smile on his round, bespectacled face. "If that's so important, why do we have to wear uniforms?" he asked. "It'd be even easier to tell us apart if we all dressed differently."

"Mahatma, there's a time and a place for questions like that," said Brandy. "Right in the middle of a training session isn't it."

"It's not in the middle, Sarge; we just got started," said another recruit. Brandy wasn't sure who had spoken. Mahatma's attitude was unfortunately contagious. Equally unfortunately, none of the others who'd picked up his habit of asking awkward questions and taking the answers literally were half as good as Mahatma was when he put his mind to actually doing his job.

"*Quiet!*" roared Brandy at ear-splitting volume. The silence that followed was the most gratifying thing she'd heard all day. She glared at the recruits for a moment, then said, "Now, as I was about to say, we're going to be working with boats today. The three of you who said you have experience are going to be the squad leaders. The rest of you, count off by threes."

"One."

"Two."

"Three."

The legionnaires began counting.

After a few moments, Brandy held up her hands and shouted, "Hold on! Freefall, you aren't supposed to count."

Freefall pouted. "But Sarge, I wanna count. I *like* counting."

Brandy growled, "It doesn't matter; you're a squad leader. You don't have to count."

"I don't see why Freefall can't count," said another voice from the back of the group. "Counting is fun."

"If Freefall counts, it throws the count off," said Brandy, glaring at the recruit who'd interrupted. "Now, everybody count off by threes—except for Freefall."

Freefall sulked but remained silent while the others began to count again.

"One."

"Two."

"Three."

"One."

"Two ..."

Brandy held up her hands again. "Wait a minute! Mahatma, you're a squad leader, too! You don't count, either."

"You said everybody except for Freefall, Sergeant," said Mahatma, with his usual beatific smile. Brandy was convinced he practiced it in front of a mirror. "I was merely following orders."

"OK, you don't count, either," snapped Brandy. "Everybody except the three squad leaders, count off by threes. And get it right this time!"

"One."

"Two."

"Three ..."

The count continued. This time, it came out right. Brandy sighed. It was days like this that made her think about the nice little nest egg she'd been building up since the arrival of Captain Jester (as Phule insisted on being called by his troops). On the other hand, here she was on a Galaxy-class resort planet, housed in a luxury hotel, eating three meals a day in a cordon bleu restaurant, and actually getting paid for the privilege. Crazy as it was to stay in this outfit, she'd be even crazier retiring. It had even crossed her mind that, when the time came around, she just might reenlist … and that *was crazy*.

Journal #480

As attractive as staying on Landoor would have been, my employer was subject to the whims of the Legion's commanders, who had their own priorities. These differed in several crucial details from his. The concept that having achieved success in some endeavor entitled a person to enjoy the fruits of that success seemed foreign to them. This should surprise no one who has had to deal with governments.

At least my employer had managed by now to enlist a few allies among the ruling elements of society. Not that he had any fewer enemies.

* * *

"Wake up, lover boy, there's somebody here to see you," came the saucy voice in Phule's ear. It was Mother, the voice of Omega Company's Comm Central, of course.

Phule looked up from the screen of his Port-a-Brain computer, where he was running a financial spreadsheet showing the company's investments, and said, "Who is it, Mother?" The omni-directional pickup on his wrist communicator picked up his voice at normal volume.

"That cute Ambassador Gottesman," came Mother's voice. "Maybe you could take your time getting here."

Phule laughed. "Tell him I'll be right there, Mother. Sorry to break up your rendezvous." Actually, he was doing Mother—whose original name was Rose—a favor. For all her brassy personality over the comm system, Mother was impossibly shy when dealing with someone face-to-face. Getting the ambassador out of her presence and into Phule's office would let her relax again—no matter how cute she thought he was.

A few steps down a short corridor took Phule into the Comm Center. The handsome, impeccably groomed ambassador had taken a seat and was making himself as unobtrusive as possible behind a news printout so as not to set off Rose's defensive reaction. He was, after all, a diplomat, and he had met Rose before. Gottesman rose to his feet when the captain entered.

"Hello, Ambassador, come right on in," said Phule, shaking the older man's hand.

"It's good to see you again, Captain," said the ambassador with a warm smile. "I hope you're getting a chance to enjoy yourself after all your work getting the park running."

"Thanks," said Phule. "I am, a little bit—in between the usual unrelenting work." He showed the ambassador to a seat, fixed drinks, then settled back behind his desk.

After a few minutes of conversation on general topics, Ambassador Gottesman set down his drink and said, "You've been doing a great job here, certainly from State's point of view."

"Thank you," said Phule. "It's been an interesting experience. I hope some of the other branches share your appreciation for our work."

"Meaning Legion Headquarters in particular, I take it?" Phule gave just the tiniest nod of acknowledgment, and the ambassador shook his head. "I suspect you're no better off there than before," he said. "They have their own way of seeing things, and it doesn't necessarily mesh with what those of us outside the service see. Of course, I suspect the rest of the government would say pretty much the same about State. But being on our good side is definitely an asset, I can promise you. If nothing else, it'll get you on the short list for some very interesting assignments. In fact, that's why I'm here."

"I suspected something like that," said Phule. "Now that we've got the planetary economy on a fairly steady upward course, there's not a whole lot of work for a peacekeeping force here. I'd been wondering how long it'd be before somebody else came to that conclusion."

"Well, that may have occurred to somebody, but it's not why I'm here," said the ambassador. "To get down to it, we've got a pending request from a friendly government for military advisors, and they indicated a strong preference for your company. Before I took definite action on the request, though, I wanted to find out how the assignment looked to you. We don't want to throw you into a situation you don't think your company is prepared to handle."

"I'll be honest with you, Ambassador Gottesman," said Phule, putting his hands behind his head and leaning back in his chair. "I don't think there's anything my people can't handle, if I have sufficient opportunity to prepare them for it. So I appreciate the chance to see what we might be getting into, ahead of time." He paused and leaned forward, his right hand on his chin. "This friendly government you're talking about—is it by any chance the Zenobian Empire?"

"You got it in one, Captain," said the ambassador with a chuckle. "Flight Leftenant Qual's report on his stay with your company must have made a strong impression on his government. If I were you, I'd see this as a chance to make a similar impression on the powers that be in the Alliance. This would be a very good career move."

"I can see that," said Phule, rubbing his chin. He thought for a moment, then said, "But I have to wonder. A government doesn't ask for military advisors when everything is going smoothly, does it? There's some sort of trouble brewing for the Zenobians, or they'd never have put in the request. I'd prefer to have some idea what kind of trouble it is before I put my people in the middle of it. Or is that an undiplomatic attitude for me to take?"

"It's a damned sensible attitude to take, Captain," said the ambassador. "I wish I could answer you, but we're as much in the dark as you are. Our mission to Zenobia is still being organized, so we don't have any useful intelligence presence there. Right now, the timetable has the military mission landing on Zenobia before we diplomats are even in place. I don't like it, but I didn't get a vote. Anyway, I'm afraid I'm offering you the chance to bid on a pig in a poke. Are you interested, on those terms?"

This time Phule didn't hesitate. "Yes, I'm interested. We'd be crazy to pass it up. If we can't handle it by now, I don't think there's an outfit in the Legion that can."

"Great. That's what I was hoping to hear," said Ambassador Gottesman. He raised his glass. "Here's to opportunities and to those who make the most of them!"

"I'll take that as a personal compliment, if you don't mind," said Phule, smiling as he clinked his glass against the ambassador's.

"And why shouldn't you?" said the ambassador. "That's certainly how it was intended." They both drank.

"I'm glad to hear it," said Phule. "But do me a favor. If you find out anything about why the Zenobians really want us, let me know, will you? If there's real trouble there, we could use a little advance warning."

"Don't worry, Captain; the minute I know anything, you'll be the next to hear it," said the ambassador. He sipped his drink again, then added with a wry grin, "But let me tell you this, based on my own experience: you probably won't know you need to duck until the first ray gun beam flashes past your head. So prepare your people for anything and everything—and then expect a few surprises."

Phule grinned. "Ambassador, I think my people can deal out a few surprises of their own. In fact, they do it to me almost every day."

"This is why we at State have such confidence in you, Captain," said the ambassador, swirling his drink. His smile could have meant anything.

CHAPTER TWO

Without intending it, my employer had become a symbol. And in the nature of all such things, that meant that he represented different things to different people.

To one faction in the Space Legion, he was the bright hope for the future; the (literally) fair-haired young captain who would restore the Legion to its former prestige. This image was shared by a number of supporters in the Alliance government, particularly those who had long chafed at seeing progress stalled by Legion Brass. And to his own men and women (and alien members of his company as well) he was a hero, the first CO who'd ever really given them a chance to be something.

But to another faction, a very powerfully entrenched one, he was a threat to everything the Legion had become. He was a boat rocker of the worst sort. Chief among these enemies was General Blitzkrieg.

* * *

"Military advisors? Over my dead body!" roared General Blitzkrieg. He put enough vehemence into the roar that his listeners, veterans of the rough-and-tumble of General Staff infighting, fell back from his wrath for a moment.

But only for a moment. "This is a signal honor to the Legion," growled General Havoc, the Legion's representative to the Joint Chiefs of Staff. His voice was quiet, but there was no mistaking that he meant every syllable. "The Legion doesn't get a whole lot of honors, Blitzkrieg—in case you hadn't noticed. I'll be damned if we're going to turn this one down just because it puts one officer's nose out of joint."

"I'm afraid you don't get it, General," said Blitzkrieg, his brow wrinkled. He'd realized belatedly that he couldn't bully Havoc, but it took him a moment to decide on alternate tactics. He wasn't accustomed to dealing with people he couldn't bully. "It's nothing to do with getting my nose out of joint. Captain Jester is a troublemaker and an incompetent, and his troops are the dregs of the Legion. We can't risk sending him someplace where he could damage relations with an important ally."

"Colonel Battleax tells me he's had a number of remarkable successes," said General Havoc, looking at the officer in question.

"That's correct, General," said Battleax. She hefted a thick portfolio meaningfully. "Not only has his company handled its assignments with complete success, he's gotten the Legion the most positive publicity we've seen in years. It's only fair to send his company on this assignment. They've earned it."

Blitzkrieg pulled himself up to his full height. "Earned it? *Earned* it?" He pointed to the service stripes on his uniform and put all the scorn he could muster into the question. "Their captain has been in the Legion what, three years? And you're telling me that Jester somehow deserves more than an officer who's served the Legion through good times and bad for the better part of four decades?"

"Quite frankly, General, I don't see how this new assignment for Jester in any way diminishes your status," said General Havoc. "It's a feather in the Legion's cap, and that goes to all our credit. As Jester's commanding officer, you have the right to oppose this assignment. But I would very strongly advise against it. Not only does it deprive the Legion of the chance to score points with State—they haven't been our strongest allies in the past—but if you veto State's request for Jester's company, they'll give the assignment to a Regular Army unit—probably the Red Eagles. We can't allow *that* to happen."

Blitzkrieg walked over to his office window, a scowl on his face. He stood staring at the view—the jagged skyline of the old city, with the snowcapped North Rahnsom Mountains as backdrop—for a long moment before answering. "All right, damn it," he said. "Send them on this assignment. But let the record show that I opposed it. When Jester gets himself into the kind of trouble he can't buy his way out of and gets half his company wiped out by hostiles or causes some diplomatic catastrophe, it's his doing, not mine. I want it on record that I opposed the operation from the word go. Is that clear?"

"Perfectly clear," said General Havoc, peering intently at Blitzkrieg. After a pause, he added, "You realize, of course, that if we put that on record, you'll be in no position to claim credit for a successful mission."

"There is no way in hell Jester's luck will hold out that long," snarled Blitzkrieg. "That weasel has gotten out of one fix after another by the skin of his teeth. Sooner or later, class will tell—and Omega Company is the Legion's worst outfit. Oh, they've managed to pull off a couple of coups, but the day of reckoning will come. Send them into a real fight, and there's going to be nothing left but crumbs."

"That's bullshit, General," said Colonel Battleax with a grim smile. "You've been dead wrong about Captain Jester all along, and he's going to prove it again on Zenobia."

"I'll bet you a thousand dollars he falls flat on his face," said Blitzkrieg.

"Done!" said Battleax gleefully. "General Havoc, you're our witness."

"Ridiculous," said General Havoc, pursing his lips. "The bet is much too vague. How do you decide who's won?"

"Phule's orders will include a list of objectives for the mission," said Battleax. "I'll pay up if his company leaves the planet without fulfilling ninety percent of those objectives."

"Hah!" said Blitzkrieg. "Jester will be lucky to get *anything* done. General Havoc, I trust you to make an unbiased decision. Will you be our arbiter?"

"Oh, very well," said Havoc. "But that's a lot of money to ride on one man's decision. I suggest you find at least one more arbiter, preferably someone outside the Legion."

"He's right," said Colonel Battleax. "Why don't we choose a panel of three, two of whom will have to agree on whether Captain Jester has met his objectives? Since the general is your choice, I should choose the second; then let them choose a third, who won't be beholden to either of us."

"Who's your second?" asked Blitzkrieg, frowning.

"As General Havoc suggests, it should be someone from outside the Legion," said Colonel Battleax. "I was thinking of Ambassador Gottesman."

"There's a fine choice," scoffed Blitzkrieg. "State's completely hoodwinked by Jester. Gottesman's likely to give him the win without even bothering to look at the list."

"The ambassador isn't quite as gullible as you paint him," said General Havoc. "I saw him make some very hardheaded decisions when we negotiated the Landoor peace treaty. But even if he does go easy on Jester, there'll be a third judge to convince, and I can promise you it'll be somebody impartial."

"Who did you have in mind?" said Colonel Battleax.

General Havoc shook his head. "The ambassador and I need to decide on that, and when we do, I don't think we ought to tell you. If you know who it is, you may try to influence him. If you'll accept those terms—and if the ambassador agrees to judge—then I'm your man. If not, then find yourself another boy." He smiled at his joke.

"I can live with those terms," said Colonel Battleax.

"I suppose I can as well," said Blitzkrieg. "Very well, then, do we have any other business to attend to today?"

The three officers busied themselves with other details for another half hour, and then Battleax and Havoc took their leave. The general saw them to the door and then closed it behind them with an evil smile upon his lips.

"What's the secret, General?" asked Major Sparrowhawk, his adjutant, who'd been present taking notes during the entire meeting. "I've known you long enough to know you wouldn't offer a bet for that kind of money unless you were sure of winning. How can you be sure the judges will agree?"

"Easy, Major," said Blitzkrieg, rubbing his hands. "Battleax seems to have forgotten that *I'm* the one who makes up the list of mission objectives for any Legion unit under my command. And I'm going to make damned sure that nobody in the galaxy can complete the list—not even their precious Captain Jester."

* * *

Sushi and Do-Wop had called together the original ride-testing squad from the days when Landoor Park was being built with the help and protection of the Omega Mob. With Mahatma, Tusk-anini, and Rube in tow, they'd taken a hoverjeep over to the gates of Dunes Park, where they were met by Okidata, the local friend who'd tipped them off about the new ride.

"Glad you all could make it," said Okidata, shaking Sushi's hand. "This looks like a really triff ride—not as hot as any of ours, but one you'll want to ride a couple of times."

"What's it called?" asked Do-Wop, who was perhaps the most avid connoisseur of thrill rides in the company.

"The Snapper," said Okidata with a shrug. "Dumb name, but you can't judge by that. Dunes Park always has dumb names."

Dunes Park was one of the older and smaller amusement parks on Landoor, a child's playpen in comparison to the gigantic parks that had grown up in more recent years, especially the ones built by the government and by the ex-rebels working with Phule. But the older parks were still popular with many of the locals, and they had made an effort to keep their audience with a string of new rides, of which the Snapper was the latest.

Do-Wop laughed. "Yeah, almost as dumb as some people's Legion names. Who makes 'em up, anyway?"

"Hieronimus Ekanem, the owner," said Okidata, rolling his eyes. "Guess the guy's got no imagination."

"So why doesn't he hire somebody?" asked Sushi. He pointed toward the park entrance. "Hey, we're wasting time. We can talk about this while we're waiting in line, if it's so fascinating."

"Sushi right," said Tusk-anini. "Can talk anywhere. But longer we talk here, longer line keeps getting and we aren't in it. Let's going."

The group headed through the gates, drawing stares from the other customers. The two aliens, Tusk-anini and Rube, were unusual enough to turn heads anywhere, but on Landoor, a world settled almost entirely by humans, a giant warthog and a human-sized cat couldn't walk the streets without being targeted for rubbernecking and finger-pointing by local youngsters. While the aliens in Phule's company were used to being singled out for attention, the humans in the group didn't like seeing their comrades treated as exotic specimens.

"Mommy, Mommy!" cried a small voice to one side. "Look at the monster!"

"Be quiet, Nanci, that's not a monster," said a woman in hushed tones. "It's an alien soldier."

"Hello," said Tusk-anini, waving. With his alien dentition, he couldn't manage anything a human would recognize as a smile, but he made his voice as friendly as he could manage. "Not soldier—we Space Legion. Better than soldiers!"

"Funny mans," said the child, sticking its finger in a corner of its mouth and smiling shyly. The mother smiled too, and the legionnaires relaxed. The Volton couldn't change his fearsome looks, but that didn't mean he thought it necessary to go around frightening babies, either. Tusk-anini had learned that talking to children could let him cross the line from "monster" to "man" and become something to smile at. He waved again, and the group headed on toward the rides.

The line for the new ride was already long. Landoorans considered thrill rides their national art form, and a new one was always an event. It looked as if a fair number of the locals had taken days off from work and pulled the kids out of school as well. There was probably going to be nearly an hour's wait for the ride. But the park's management sent a series of strolling entertainers to work the line—jugglers, clowns, antigrav dancers, musicians, thimbleriggers, and snack vendors—so the crowd wouldn't notice its slow progress. Strategic glimpses of the ride—usually as the cars plunged down a steep incline, bringing excited squeals from the riders—helped build the anticipation.

The legionnaires were nearly to the front of the line when Do-Wop said, "Look, there's Rev. What's he doing in the park?"

"Goofing off, same as you," said Sushi, elbowing his partner.

"Chaplains ain't supposed to goof off; they're brass," said Do-Wop. "I gotta give him a hard time." He grinned and punched Sushi in the arm, then waved to catch the chaplain's attention. "Yo, Rev," he called. "Yo, over here! We caught ya!"

Several passersby turned their heads, but when they saw who was waving, they went about their way. The one who looked like Rev passed within a few paces of them and looked directly at Do-Wop. Becoming aware that he was the one being called, he stopped and spread his hands apart. "Sorry, you must be making a mistake. That's not my name." If his words hadn't been enough, the thick Landooran accent made it perfectly clear this wasn't Rev.

"Whadda ya mean? Cut the jive, Rev," demanded Do-Wop as the passerby turned to leave, but Sushi put a hand on his shoulder.

"Easy, Do-Wop," said his partner. "That's some local guy who looks like Rev, is all."

"I guess you're right," said Do-Wop. "Damn, he's a dead ringer, though."

"Hey, it could be worse," said Sushi.

"How's that?" asked Do-Wop, frowning.

"The guy could look like *you*," said Sushi, grinning. He ducked as Do-Wop threw a punch in mock indignation. Just then, the line moved up, and the laughing group of legionnaires edged closer to their ride.

Journal #492

My employer had thought he was filling an important void in his people's spiritual life by requesting that a chaplain be assigned to the company. But the doctrines of Reverend Jordan Ayres had given him second thoughts. Not that the chaplain had in any way attempted to undermine what he was doing, but the influence of his doctrine on the legionnaires did take one confusing direction.

* * *

"Captain, this has got to stop. It's driving me crazy," said Brandy. "Don't get me wrong—I don't have anything against the chaplain. Rev's done a pretty good job, building morale. But you can't expect me to do my job when I can't tell one of my people from another."

"I can't see any big problem, Captain," said the chaplain. "You know we ask our disciples to emulate the King, on account of he's such an inspiration. A poor boy, climbed right to the top, without no help from anybody … Why, that makes me feel like I can do the same myself. Ain't that exactly the kind of spirit that makes a good legionnaire, now?"

"Maybe it makes a good legionnaire, but if enough of your disciples look alike, you're going to make one crazy sergeant," said Brandy, crossing her arms. She stared at Rev, who had arrived at the company already made over to resemble his sect's prophet: a dark pompadour with long sideburns, a classic profile, full lips with a tendency to an ever-so-slight sneer.

Phule fidgeted with a pencil, looking back and forth between his top sergeant and the chaplain. "I see your point, Brandy," he said. "But the chaplain's got a point, too. The company's morale is the best it's ever been. And there *is* that clause in the Legionnaire's Bill of Rights."

"Why, thank you, Captain," said the chaplain. "I didn't want to have to mention that clause myself. A feller shouldn't haul out the heavy artillery first thing out of the box, y'know. But it certainly fits, if you look into it. We've got plenty of precedents on our side."

"So I've got to train and evaluate a batch of recruits that all look exactly alike?" Brandy put her hands on her hips and leaned over Phule's desk. "Maybe I'm going to have second thoughts about that early retirement option."

"Now, Brandy, don't blow this out of proportion," said Phule, rising to his feet. "How many of our legionnaires have had their appearance altered, anyway? It surely isn't more than three or four, is it?"

"Eleven," said Rev proudly.

"Eleven?" Phule asked, suddenly dubious.

"Eleven," said Brandy. "And two more have applied for it."

"Eleven." Phule drummed the pencil on the desktop for a moment; then, with a start, he put it down and clasped his hands together. "Well, that's a surprise," he said. "You seem to have been getting your message across very effectively, Rev."

The chaplain bowed his head. "I can't take much credit for it, Captain," he said with humility that seemed genuine enough. "My words have fallen on fertile ground, is all."

"What's that supposed to mean?" said Brandy, bristling.

"Easy, Sarge," said Rev. "No criticism implied. Why, all I mean is, the King's an inspiration for anybody what thinks they can better theirselves. I reckon that could be all of us, if we jes' look at it right."

"I don't want to look at it at all," said Brandy with a significant glance at the chaplain's profile. "Besides, you still haven't told me how I'm supposed to tell one of these eleven legionnaires from another when they all look the same."

"Oh, it ain't all that hard, Sarge," said Rev. "You jes' have to value each and everybody as an individual in their own right, you know? Once you get past the surface, there's all kinds of differences between folks. How tall somebody is, or the exact color of their eyes and hair, or the shape of their hands. You learn pretty soon, Sarge, believe me. I've got plenty experience at it."

"Well, that's good," said Phule, rubbing his hands. "I've been saying all along that we need to take advantage of the individual capabilities of our people, and this is a chance to learn even better what those capabilities are. And there may be advantages to having a group of legionnaires an outsider can't tell apart. I'm sure we'll think of a few now that we've got the capability, won't we, Sergeant?"

"I guess so," said Brandy, looking at Rev out of the corner of her eye. "Well, if that's how it's going to be, I guess I can handle it. I'll have the recruits wear extra-large name tags while I'm learning to spot all these subtle differences between them."

"Good thinking, Brandy," said Phule. "I knew we could solve

this if we put our minds to it." His tone and manner made it clear that the matter *was* solved, as far as he was concerned, and the sergeant and chaplain quickly took the hint and left the office. And that, Phule thought, was the end of it.

Journal #497

The robot my employer had gotten to impersonate him at the Fat Chance Casino on Lorelei was a deluxe model from Andromatic, built to his specifications. Its range of behavior was limited but sufficient to convince people that my employer was still on the job. Generally, it would sit behind a desk and appear to be working. But it also walked around the casino, sat down for drinks with customers, carried on conversations—and broke off the minute the topic strayed beyond generalities. If anybody really needed to talk to Captain Jester, there was always the communicator.

What my employer left out of account was that his company had begun to attract attention in its own right. The success of the Landoor amusement parks—several light-years away from Lorelei—had put his picture on holovid screens all over the galaxy. While a certain amount could be explained by rapid travel, there was always the danger that somebody would realize that there had to be two Phules.

The danger had been pointed out to him, but of course he dismissed it. "Nobody takes the news seriously," he had argued when demonstrating the robot to the Fat Chance's board of directors. "Half the time, they just use stock footage of public figures, and nobody notices." What he left out of account was that his enemies were paying particularly close attention to him.

* * *

Two shadowy figures had been lurking in the corridor leading from the Fat Chance Casino's gourmet dining room back toward the Legion quarters for nearly an hour. Luckily for them, nobody had passed during the entire time. Or perhaps it was more than just luck; they'd scouted out the territory carefully in advance and knew the odds were in their favor when they decided to lay their ambush there. But it had been longer than they'd expected, and it was a definite relief when they finally heard footsteps approaching.

"Here he comes," whispered the shorter of the pair, peering out from under the potted plant behind which they were hiding.

"About farkin' time," grumbled her companion. "Any longer, and I was gonna hafta water this here fern."

"Shhh!" warned the other in a barely audible whisper. "We'll blow the whole plan if he hears us."

But their quarry showed no sign of having heard them. The footsteps came closer, neither hesitating nor deviating from their course. The two crouched in anticipation, frozen for a moment; then, as the footsteps came near the plant, the woman stepped quickly out into the corridor. "Captain, you have to help me!" she said.

The captain paused. "Excuse me, ma'am. What sort of help do you need?"

"A man's been following me," she said, looking behind her. The captain's glance followed hers, and as he was distracted, her partner emerged from the shadows behind him, holding a large sack in both hands. He raised his arms, preparing to place it over the captain's head and shoulders, but some slight noise must have given him away. The captain ducked and stepped to the left, and the would-be captor succeeding only in striking him on the shoulder. In an instant, the captain had turned and lashed out with a kick that the captor just barely eluded.

"That's him!" cried the woman, stepping back. The man with the sack cursed and stepped backward. He dropped the sack and turned to run. The captain took a step in pursuit, but then the woman gave out a little cry and collapsed in a heap on the floor. As the captain turned to help her, the attacker escaped around the corner.

"Are you all right, miss?" said the captain. He threw a brief glance over his shoulder to make sure the attacker had not returned, then turned his gaze on her again. Even in the dim lighting, her thick dark hair and flashing eyes would have made a strong impression on any man not entirely devoid of feeling.

"I think so," she said weakly. Her lashes fluttered, and she made a valiant attempt to sit up but slumped against his chest as her energy failed. "I think I'll be safe if you can just take me to my room."

"Yes, miss," he said. "I'll get you there, and I can have security keep tabs on you for the rest of your stay, if you'd like. We don't want our guests to feel unsafe in the Fat Chance. In fact, I feel I should apologize for what's happened so far."

"No apology necessary, Captain," she said. "If you could just help me up ..."

Helping her get up and walking her to her room was a somewhat complicated process. The young woman was evidently weakened by her ordeal, since she continued to lean much of her weight on the captain as he led her down the corridor. At the door to her room, he waited while she found her key card and watched while she opened the door. "Do you need any more help, miss?" he asked.

"No, I should be all right," she said, smiling.

"Good," he said and took a step backward.

The young woman smiled bravely and began to close the door behind her, then suddenly said, "Oh!" and began to slump toward the floor again.

The captain stepped forward and caught her before the door closed. "Are you sure you're all right, miss?" he asked. "I can call the hotel doctor."

"I don't think I need a doctor," she said, leaning her weight on his chest. "But maybe you could help me get to my bed."

"Certainly, miss, and then I think I should call the doctor—just in case." He picked her up in his arms and carried her through the door to the side of the bed.

"Oh, you're so strong," she murmured, her lips close to his ear. Her arms twined around his neck.

The captain put her onto the bed and, gently disengaging himself from her grasp, stepped back and said, "Now I'm going to call the doctor."

She began to protest, but he held a finger to his lips and said, "No—don't say anything. I suspect you need to rest."

He picked up the phone, touched a button, and spoke briefly to the person on the other end. After a few sentences, he nodded and hung up the receiver. "Dr. Gulkova's on duty tonight. She'll be right up. I'll wait until she comes, and then I'll make sure you're not disturbed. If there's anything else I can do for you, please get in touch with me. Any hotel operator can connect you directly to my office."

She lay back on the bed, listening. As he continued to speak, her face changed expression to a sultry pout. "You *know* what else you can do for me, Captain—don't pretend you don't. I'm beginning to think you don't like me."

The captain smiled. "Now, now, miss, don't worry yourself. I know you've been through a lot tonight. We'll make sure nobody annoys you for the rest of your stay with us."

The woman sat up in the bed and barked, "If you don't want anyone to annoy me, I suggest you get out of my room! I've had just about all of your goody-goody act I can stand."

"Of course, miss," said the captain, smiling. "I'll wait outside the door, and when the doctor comes, I'll leave." He turned and started to leave.

With an inarticulate shout, the woman reached down and grabbed one of her shoes off her foot and threw it with all her might at his retreating back. But by then, he had the door almost closed behind him, and the missile bounced harmlessly off onto the floor. She slammed both fists onto the bed in frustration. "You bastard!" she cried. "You'll pay for this when we finally do catch you! You'll pay!"

But the captain was already gone, the door closed behind him. If he had heard her outburst, he gave no sign at all.

* * *

The two local policemen standing in front of Phule's desk were obviously doing their best to stay calm and professional. The complainant, standing unsteadily on crutches between the policeman, wasn't.

Phule massaged the bridge of his nose. It had been a long day, filled with problems that required instant-minute attention, and the burden of command was weighing particularly heavily on his shoulders this afternoon. Especially since, on top of everything else, he'd skipped lunch—not at all his usual routine. And now he had to deal with a civilian who insisted on having one of his men arrested. "Are you absolutely certain that the man who robbed you and damaged your restaurant was one of my legionnaires?" he asked.

"I seen him with these here eyes," said the restaurateur, a small man with a heavy Landooran accent that seemed incongruous in conjunction with his Japanese features and immaculate dress. "He was Legion, all right—wore the same black uniform as yours. And he done more than damage the place. It'll be a miracle if I can open up again any time this week."

"Well, that's serious enough to require some action, if it's the truth," said Phule. "But I can't discipline the whole company for one man's actions. We'll have to see if you can identify the one who did this."

"I'd know him anywhere," said the restaurateur. "That long, greasy haircut and that smirk on his face. Ain't a whole lot of people who'd look that way if they had any choice in it. My security holovid caught the whole thing, and there ain't much mistake."

A warning bell went off in the back of Phule's mind, but he maintained a calm expression. "If that's the case, I think we can take care of this business quickly. There are holo ID pictures of the entire company on file. Why don't you and the officers look through them and see if you can identify the robber? Then we'll call him in and see what he has to say for himself."

"Oh, that'll be just triff," said the restaurant owner sarcastically. "He'll lie and you'll take his word for it, and I'll end up springin' for the doctor bills."

Phule stood up abruptly and said coldly, "You don't know who you're talking to, do you, Mr. Takamine?"

"Sure I do," sneered the restaurateur, drawing himself up to his full height—perhaps four inches shorter than Phule—and standing face-to-face with him. "You're the captain of this here Legion company. And when it comes to a quarrel between Legion and us poor locals, Legion sticks up for its own. Nothin' we can do but eat whatever shit you pile on our plate."

Phule put his finger in the middle of the man's chest. "You won't gain anything by using that kind of language, Mr. Takamine. I've offered to give you a chance to identify and confront the person you claim is responsible for the robbery and damage and for the injuries to yourself. Do you want to go ahead with this, or are you just here to make a disturbance?"

"I'll look," said the man. "But I ain't expecting much, I tell you for a fact."

Beeker led the policemen and Takamine to an outer office, where they could browse through the ID files. But Phule had a sinking feeling. The description of the legionnaire responsible sounded far too familiar. He'd thought the man had finally outgrown his penchant for getting into trouble with the law—at least, this kind of trouble. Well, if he had to teach the legionnaire a lesson, he'd do it, that was all.

Phule was pacing nervously in front of his desk when the door opened and Beeker returned. "I've set the gentlemen up with the viewer and the appropriate files, sir," he said. "I think we'll have an answer soon."

"Good," said Phule. "I assume you disabled all features except the image viewer? We don't want these people looking into the confidential portions of the personnel files."

"I have done so, sir," said Beeker solemnly. "But I'm afraid I know what the restaurateur will find."

"I'm afraid you're right," said Phule, shaking his head. "I'm disappointed, to tell you the truth. I thought Do-Wop had changed his ways. But the man they describe has to be him."

"Perhaps he only got better at concealing his misdeeds," said Beeker implacably. "The young man's code of ethics seems primarily to consist of *Thou shalt not get caught*."

Phule paced a few more steps, then turned and said, "Well, when they spot him, we'll have to decide what to do with him."

"I should think that would be the local authorities' problem, sir," said Beeker.

"No," said Phule. "I can't just turn a legionnaire over to civilian authorities. We take care of our own, and that means we discipline our own, too. But if these people don't have a military tradition, they may not understand that. Why, we—" He was interrupted by the intercom.

"Yes, Mother?" he answered.

"Those two cops and the hash slinger are back, sweetie," came the sultry, mocking voice. "They don't look happy. Shall I send 'em in so you can cheer 'em up?"

"I'm going to have to talk to them eventually," said Phule. "Yes, send them in."

The trio of Landoorans marched in, all three with frowns on their faces. Takamine opened his mouth to speak, but one of the policemen signaled to him to keep quiet and turned to speak to Phule. "Captain, that's the damnedest trick I've ever seen. I thought a holo ID was supposed to be impossible to jigger, but it looks as if your boy's figured it out, just to stall us. But it's not gonna help him. If he sticks his nose outside this hotel, we're hauling him in and asking questions later. I've got the security vids, and I'll make sure everybody on the force knows that face. Now that I think of it, I've seen him around a few times myself."

"What are you talking about?" said Phule. "Nobody's jiggered those files." He was convinced that he was right until a tickle in the back of his mind that reminded him that Sushi, Do-Wop's partner, was the company's leading expert at electronic chicanery. If anybody on Landoor could alter a holo ID picture, it would be Sushi—or somebody he'd given lessons.

He closed his eyes and massaged the bridge of his nose again. "Let's go see these jiggered pictures you're talking about," he said. He already had a very good idea what he was going to find when he got there.

But he was wrong.

CHAPTER THREE

I told you these files had been jiggered with," said the policeman disgustedly. "No such thing as identical eleventuplets, not when they're from eight or nine different planets. That's the face of the guy that robbed this citizen's place and beat him up. I've seen the vids, and they're pretty clear. Somebody's put the same face on all those files. So which one of 'em's the original?" He pointed at the holofiles, showing the faces of the company's converts to the Church of the King.

"It's not that easy," said Phule. "I think the original owner of that face has been dead for several centuries."

Mr. Takamine leapt up and threw his hands in the air. "What, you're tellin' me a dead man robbed me? That's the biggest load of—"

"I said no such thing," said Phule, making shushing motions in hopes of calming the man down. "What I said was—"

"It was just a trick to make me give up," the man shouted. "You're gonna tell me that just because I can't pick the guy out from the picture, I can't get no satisfaction."

"Sir, my employer has no intention of cheating you of your satisfaction," said Beeker. "The fact is, these legionnaires are all members of some bizarre sect—"

"Well, I wouldn't exac'ly call it *bizarre*, sonny," said a new voice at the door.

"That's the man!" shouted Takamine, turning to point to Reverend Jordan Ayres. "He's the thug that robbed me! Arrest him!"

The policemen moved menacingly toward the chaplain, who raised his hands and said, "Hey, easy there, gen'lemen. I ain't done a thing to this little fellow, and I reckon I can prove it. Just when and where is all this supposed to have happened?"

"Four days ago, in my restaurant over on Hastings Street," the man said, still pointing at Rev. He stopped and frowned, then said, "You put on a hell of a lot of weight since then."

"Ain't put on a gram," said Rev, striking a pose. "I've been workin' out with the fellows, gettin' in shape with a little bit of karate, jes' like the King—"

"King?" said the complainant. "To hell with your king. We don't have no kings here on Landoor and ain't about to start—"

"Son, you're makin' a mistake," said Rev, warming to his favorite subject. "The King's comin' to Landoor, no doubt about it. Why, he's already here, if you look around you. Every true follower—"

"I'll warn you, that sounds a lot like sedition to me," said one cop. "Landoor's got its own government, and we aren't about to change."

"That's right, sedition!" said Takamine, his face lighting up. "I knew this man was a troublemaker when I first laid eyes on him. That greasy hair, that sneer—"

"But it weren't me, I tell you," said Rev.

"That's what I've been trying to tell you, too," said Phule. "There are at least eleven legionnaires who resemble this man, plus quite a few of your own citizens—"

"Dozens," said Rev confidently. "Before long, hundreds of thousands will want to follow the King."

"I've heard just about enough of that," said the cop who'd accused Rev of sedition. "Mister, I don't know whether you robbed this man or not, but I'm gonna take you down to the station for questioning."

"One moment, officer," said Phule, whose checkered history in relation to Legion brass had made him a pretty good barracks-room lawyer. He stepped forward between Rev and the policemen. "The Legion will always cooperate with civilian authorities, but I can't stand by and see my company's chaplain hauled away on an unfounded charge. If you file a formal complaint, a Legion board of justice will determine whether or not there's been a breach of local law—"

"What did I tell ya?" screamed Takamine. "The minute you pin one of these occupying goons down for some offense, the rest of them close ranks to protect him. I'm gonna write the governor and have 'em thrown off the planet. My cousin's a big contributor to the Native Landooran Party. A *big* contributor."

"Well, ain't that somethin'?" said the cop, raising an eyebrow. "Look here, Mr. Takamine, the captain here thinks we're trying to railroad his man, and even you seem to have some doubt it's the right guy. What we gotta do—"

The policeman was interrupted by a legionnaire who came into the records room and said, "Rev, Mother told me you were here—oh, hi, Captain. Can I talk to Rev a moment, or is this a bad time?" The legionnaire was one of Rev's converts, and the facial resemblance was uncanny. His large name tag read Roadkill.

"Howdy, son," said Rev, and the thought crossed Phule's mind, *He can't tell the converts apart either.* Rev walked over to the legionnaire and put his arm around his shoulder. "As a matter of fact, you've come at the perfect time. Officer, I'd like you to meet my first line of defense."

The two policemen and the civilian complainant stood openmouthed, staring at Rev and Roadkill, their eyes shifting back and forth between the two. *This is going to be more trouble than I expected*, thought Phule. This time, he was right—but not quite in the way he anticipated.

Journal #500

The attempt to capture the robotic duplicate of my employer should have alerted the Fat Chance Casino's security teams to the danger of a repeat attempt. Considering the value of the robot and the information that close examination of it would give to any of the underworld groups that still lusted to take over the casino, the failure of anyone to realize that such an attempt had taken place was inexcusable.

Looking backward, the main reason for the failure was simple: The attempt had been such an abject failure that the robot itself had no inkling that anyone had even attempted to capture it.

As for the would-be abductors, they were apparently just as clueless as the robot itself.

* * *

"He didn't react at all," said the dark-haired young woman with a noticeable pout. "I tried every trick in the book, Ernie. It was as if he was a damned robot or something."

"Well, Lola, maybe you ain't as hot as you think," said her partner with a sneer. He ducked under the roundhouse punch she threw at him and backed up a half pace, holding up his hands in mock-serious defense. It was an old game; the two of them had been trading insults and half-playful punches ever since they'd become partners. "What if he *is* a robot?" he asked after a moment's reflection.

"Well, of course he *could* be one," she said, nodding. "That's not impossible. But think about it. If Phule's got somebody—or something—impersonating him, is the real Phule going to be running around on some half-jungle planet, getting shot at by the natives, or here in a first-class hotel, keeping tabs on his money? The robot's gonna be the one out in the boonies. Do you know how much money he's got sunk into this casino?"

"I know how much I've sunk into it," said Ernie, scowling. "I've lost enough to feed him and half his soldiers for a couple of days."

"He gets that from you and the same from a couple of thousand other suckers every day of the year," said Lola, pacing the hotel room floor. "So the real Phule's got to be right here, keeping an eye on his money. But I never thought he'd have the discipline to resist me when I put the moves on him. I guess that's what it takes to run a casino and not gamble away the profits."

"His butler's on that other planet, you know," Ernie pointed out. He lowered himself into an armchair facing the holovision and picked up the remote control from a nearby table. "The reports claim he's the brains behind Phule. So why's he there instead of here?"

"Because Phule wants everybody to think he's really there," said Lola, sitting on the bed and watching the holo picture shimmer into visibility. As usual, the default setting when the set warmed up was an advertisement for the Fat Chance's various attractions, beginning with a close-up of Dee Dee Watkins impersonating a damsel in distress in a costume that managed to be revealing and vulnerable at the same time. Ernie let out a low whistle of appreciation, and Lola glowered at him. "Too bad you're not the one I'm trying to kidnap; your hormones outvote the brain every time. I wish it was as easy to get Phule interested in a few square inches of skin."

"Hey, you can't change human nature," said Ernie, grinning. "Some guys are cold fish, like him. Other guys are natural lovers, like me. Which one would *you* rather have, babe?"

"Believe me, you really don't want to know the answer to that," said Lola, staring at Dee Dee's performance on the screen. The diminutive starlet was singing, "Where is my knight in shining armor?" Her dance routine had her pursued by several performers dressed as dragons, ogres, and trolls. The music changed, and onto the stage danced a heroic figure in holochrome armor to rout the evil creatures and carry Dee Dee off in triumph, still singing and smiling brightly at the cameras. "Say, there's an idea," she said. "It just might work, too."

"What might work?" said Ernie.

She sat up and turned her gaze on Ernie. "Captain Phule's a sucker for a damsel in distress. If he thinks I'm in danger, we can lure him off somewhere and nab him. So we have to make it look as if I'm in trouble and set it up so he's the one who has to rescue me. And guess who gets to be the bad guy?"

Ernie frowned. "I ain't so sure I like this," he said.

"Like it?" Lola stretched like a cat waking up from a nap. "I don't know whether you'll like it, but I can guarantee you, you

Robert Asprin and Peter J. Heck

won't like what happens if we don't come up with some way to catch him before long. The guys that hired us don't like spending the kind of money it takes to house us in the Fat Chance without getting some pretty convincing results for their payout. So if you've got any better strategy for catching our little prince, now's the time to tell me."

Ernie frowned but said nothing. After a long moment, Lola nodded and said, "OK, then, here's my plan ..."

After a few minutes of listening, even Ernie had to admit that it looked as if it might actually work.

Journal #502

General Blitzkrieg's animosity toward my employer had become his driving passion. There were rumors that he had passed up several opportunities to take early retirement in hopes of finding a way to "pay off Jester once and for all," as he had been heard to say. But when diplomatic circles began to bandy about the Zenobians' request for Omega Company as military advisors, the general had to acquiesce in what the other Legion commanders saw as the first significant improvement in the Legion's image in decades.

That did not prevent him from trying to find ways to sabotage the mission. As quickly became apparent, he had more than one ace up his sleeve.

* * *

The intercom buzzed. Warily, Major Sparrowhawk answered, "Yes, General Blitzkrieg?" The general already had his coffee, his news printouts, and the other routine items he wanted first thing every morning. That meant he'd come up with a brainstorm, and General Blitzkrieg's brainstorms meant trouble for Major Sparrowhawk. She might have to spend the next few hours carefully convincing him to change his mind.

"Major, I want a search of Legion personnel files," said the general. "I need a captain or a newly promoted major, somebody from an old-Legion, old-money background. Wouldn't hurt if his family were hereditary nobility somewhere. And he's got to be a

38

stickler for regulations. Give me a dozen candidates, with full dossiers, hard copy, pronto."

"Yes, sir," said Sparrowhawk. She thought a beat, then said, "Male candidates only?"

Blitzkrieg grumbled, then said, "I'll consider a couple of females if they fit the other criteria, but I think this is a job for a man. Oh, yes, and the younger and richer, the better."

"Yes, sir," said Sparrowhawk. She waited a beat, and when the general cut the connection, she began entering the search parameters. Idly she wondered what the general was working up this time. The search parameters were just odd enough that he had to have something particular in mind. Well, she'd find out soon enough.

It was too bad she didn't fit the criteria. Despite the general's lip service to considering a female candidate, it was perfectly obvious that he wanted a male. So much for any dreams she might have had of engineering a transfer and getting out from under Blitzkrieg's thumb.

But she knew better by now than to hope for any such escape. Even in the unlikely case that Blitzkrieg approved the transfer, the other ranking Legion commanders would overrule it, knowing they'd have to ruin some other officer's career to replace her. Nobody wanted the "opportunity" to be Blitzkrieg's adjutant. Her chance to move on would have to await Blitzkrieg's retirement— and she knew all too well that she wasn't the only person in the Legion wishing for that particular event to come sooner rather than later.

She entered the final search parameters and checked to make sure she hadn't made any obvious errors. There was next to no chance that the general would notice any problems on his own unless the whole project blew up in his face, at which point, she'd get the entire blame. That was an implicit function of her position, minimizing the extent to which the general could foul things up by sheer laziness and inattention to detail. The general would still foul up plenty of things on his own, of course, but where it could be prevented, she was expected to do so. In five years on the job, she'd managed to prevent more than one disaster. Of course, it would only take one that slipped past her to ruin her career. But thinking about that was likely to give her ulcers, and so she did her best not to.

At last, satisfied that she'd set up the program properly, she launched the search, then called up another window to take a look at her stock portfolio. Eventually, she'd be able to retire, and even if the general went down in flames and took her with him, she intended to have a safety net waiting when she did get out. She had a couple of stocks that had been sluggish of late; maybe it was time to sell them off and reinvest in something that moved faster. Her broker had mentioned a company marketing a mini antigrav unit that might be a good short-term investment. She studied the figures until the computer signaled that the general's search was done, then printed out the results (Blitzkrieg *always* wanted hard copy) and took them into the inner office.

* * *

Typically, once he had the information in front of him, General Blitzkrieg made his decision almost immediately. Sparrowhawk wondered if he thought that having the computer pick a list of candidates exempted him from having to put any real thought into making a selection among them. In any case, he flipped through the printouts, reading a few sentences here and there, and then pulled one candidate's dossier off the pile with an air of triumph. The entire process took perhaps five minutes.

"Major Botchup," purred the general. He handed the dossier to his adjutant and grinned wickedly. "Yes, this is precisely the man for the job."

"What position did you have in mind for him?" asked Major Sparrowhawk, fingering the personnel dossier. She was somewhat surprised at the general's enthusiasm. The officer in question fit all the search criteria, no question about that. But reading between the lines of his performance ratings—of course she'd already read the candidates' dossiers—he seemed consistently to rub his superiors the wrong way. While performing strictly in conformance with regulations and Legion tradition (in its way, more important than any regulation), he'd managed to establish himself as a pain in the arse. Not that that made him different from most male Legion officers … She looked back at the general.

"He's going to Zenobia," said Blitzkrieg, smirking. "A mission of that importance can't have a mere captain in command of it, let alone a humbler like Jester. Botchup is due for an important command of his own. And if anybody can whip Omega company into shape, he's the man for the job. A genuine respect for Legion traditions—you don't see that very often these days, Sparrowhawk."

"No, sir," said Sparrowhawk. Herself, she was just as glad the old Legion ways were starting to die out. But that wasn't something to admit to Blitzkrieg, who fancied himself the last bastion of Legion tradition—and the legacy of ineptitude that went with it. She was pretty sure that was the main reason he'd taken such a hatred of Phule, far beyond any provocation the captain of Omega Company had given his superiors. "Shall I cut orders for Major Botchup to join the company on Landoor, then?"

The general rubbed his chin, musing. "No, I think that'd give Jester too much time to get ready for him. We'll have him join his new command at their destination on Zenobia. And we'll keep it under our hats for now. No point in having somebody try to undercut the plan before it's had a chance to work."

"Yes, sir," said Sparrowhawk. She knew the reasoning behind that one: easier to ask forgiveness than to get permission. It was no surprise to find out that Blitzkrieg operated on that principle. It was probably the oldest of all Legion traditions.

* * *

"Thank you very much, sir," said Phule. He shook Ambassador Gottesman's hand. "I didn't really want to get my hopes up for this assignment. Quite frankly, some of the top Legion commanders can be counted on to oppose anything that looks like a reward for this unit. But I must say, you came through rather quickly."

"I made use of a few connections," said the ambassador with a wink. "And I did point out that, if this assignment is in the nature of a reward, it's by no means a sinecure. There's some probability your people will face combat, Captain."

Phule grinned and said as nonchalantly as possible, "Well, in the Legion we don't necessarily see that as a liability, sir. But perhaps you can brief me on the situation we'll be going into. All I really know is that it's on the Zenobians' home world—"

"Yes, and they say they're trying to repel an alien invasion," said the ambassador, spreading his hands.

"I see," said Phule, leaning his elbow on his desk. "Who are the invaders, sir?"

"I wish I had a good answer to that, and I'm afraid I don't," said Gottesman. "The Zenobians are being close-mouthed about it." He paused and took a sip of his tea, then looked Phule straight in the eye. "I have the distinct impression they're ... well, *embarrassed* might be the best description of how they're acting."

"Embarrassed?" Phule leaned his other elbow on the desk. Now he was frowning. "Can you be more precise? Are they embarrassed because they can't repel the invaders or because they need help or what?"

The ambassador shrugged. "I don't really know. In fact, it's just my interpretation of how they act. And you must know how hard it can be to read a nonhuman sophont's emotions." He set down the teacup with a wry smile and spread his hands. "I have enough trouble with my teenage daughters, half the time."

"I can imagine," said Phule, thinking that even parenting teenage girls might be easier than commanding the motley outfit he'd been put in charge of. "But this puts my people at a serious disadvantage, going into a possible combat situation without reliable intelligence. If we don't know what we're up against—"

"I understand, Captain," said the ambassador. He stood up and put his hand on Phule's shoulder. "We at State have our intelligence branch working overtime on it, believe me. We don't want to send anybody into a booby trap. The minute we get something useful, you'll get it from us. You have my word on that. Until then, just try to be ready for anything—anything at all."

Phule nodded. "I guess we'll have to be ready, then," he said. He stood up and shook Gottesman's hand. Then he added, "That's what we're supposed to do anyhow, isn't it?"

"I have complete confidence in you and your people, Captain," said the ambassador. Then he added darkly, "I wish I had the same confidence in your superiors." He allowed himself a thin smile and left the office.

Beeker, who had sat silently listening to the entire interview, watched the ambassador leave, then said, "Are you quite certain you want to stick your head into this particular noose, sir?"

Phule turned to look at his butler. "Is that how you read it, Beeker?" He placed high value on Beeker's opinions and advice—not that he always allowed them to influence his decisions. If he had, he'd never have joined the Space Legion. But when the butler smelled trouble, it was worth listening to him.

Beeker steepled his fingers. "Consider the evidence, sir. The Zenobians have asked for help against some sort of external threat that they cannot defeat with their own resources. Yet the Zenobians are remarkably competent warriors, both in their basic physical abilities and in their technological accomplishments. What kind of help is a single Legion company going to be able to provide?"

"Well, as much as we can, of course," said Phule. "I suspect most of our role will be in training and in tactical and strategic consultation. After all, we're being brought in as advisors, not to engage the enemy directly."

Beeker's face grew solemn. "Sir, I hope you have not entered into negotiations to purchase any bridges from the Zenobians."

Phule laughed. "I leave that to State, Beeker," he said. "With Ambassador Gottesman on our side, I'm not really worried about any surprises."

"You should be," scolded Beeker. "Ambassador Gottesman has done a great deal for us when it was to his advantage to do so. Now it is to his advantage to send us to Zenobia, but I have no idea whether it is to *our* advantage to go there. The Black Hills undoubtedly looked like a plum assignment to George Armstrong Custer."

"Good old Beeker, always seeing the bright side," said Phule, grinning. "Don't worry, I can take care of myself. And if I can't, I've got a whole Legion company to do it for me."

"Sir, that's exactly what worries me the most," said Beeker.

Journal #505

It did not take long for word of the company's impending move to filter down to the rank and file. Indeed, within a few short hours of Phule's conversation with the ambassador, the tables at the Landoor Plaza's Poolside Bar were buzzing with speculation. As a rule, the better a position a person was in to know what was really likely to happen, the less they were willing to say about it.

However, this rule could definitely be modified in the case of Chocolate Harry.

* * *

Chocolate Harry stared at Do-Wop and shook his head sadly. "Man, if you knew half as much as you think you know, you'd be a mortal danger."

"He's a mortal danger already," said Super-Gnat, deadpan. "Just ask any woman who's gone on a date with him."

"Ahh, I got girls lined up ten deep waitin' for the chance to go out with me," said Do-Wop, swelling up his chest and making a perfunctory grab at Gnat, who ducked away and stuck out her tongue at him. Frustrated in his effort to demonstrate his appeal, he turned back to the supply sergeant. "But I can't let you get away with that, C.H. I got inside info as good as anybody in the company. You don't know who I been talkin' to."

"Don't matter who you talk to, you wouldn't understand it if they told you two and two is four," said Chocolate Harry. "You'd figure it was six, and by the time you got done tellin' the rest of us, it'd be fifteen or twenty."

"And worth absolutely nothin'," added Slammer, one of the new recruits who'd been assigned to the supply depot under Harry's supervision. He'd quickly picked up the supply sergeant's conversational style: half humorous insults, half bragging, and half plain lies. That's three halves, but those who knew Harry were willing to make allowances for a good bit of surplus.

Carefully choosing his target—the whole company knew better than to try to beat C.H. at his own game—Do-Wop looked at Slammer and said, "Hey, Slammer, I been meaning to ask you—did you get that name because that's where you belong, or because people slam doors in your face?"

"It's because if anybody messes with me, that's what I do to 'em," said Slammer, not taking particular offense.

"That's no problem; nobody *wants* to mess with you," said Super-Gnat with a grin that suggested she intended more than one meaning. "Besides, I want to hear where Harry thinks we're going and why. What's the word, Sarge?"

"I don't think, Gnat, I *know*," said Chocolate Harry. "We goin' to Barriere to take on the renegade robots there. They got a big problem with those bots. And the reason they pick us is because they know ol' C.H. has got the know-how when it comes to fixin' robots. Hell, a man that can customize a hawg the way I have ain't gonna have any problem with a bot."

"This is the first I heard about any renegade robots," said Sushi, leaning his elbows on the table. "How long's that been going on?"

"Man, you ain't got my inside sources, that's all," said Harry with a self-congratulatory grin. He took a deep swig of his beer and sighed in satisfaction. "Thing a lot of folks don't realize, the supply lines are what the Legion runs on. Supply don't do its job, you gonna have a bunch of people sittin' on some bare asteroid, SOL."

"What means *SOL*?" asked Tusk-anini, squinting behind his dark glasses.

"Somebody's Obviously Loony," said Super-Gnat with a sly grin. Her partner's command of human slang was tenuous at best, and she enjoyed ribbing him about it. From her, at least, he usually took it in good nature. He wasn't without a sense of humor, although it sometimes seemed very strange to his human companions.

"Nah, it means Salad Oil Liberation," said Do-Wop, horning in on the game.

Tusk-anini's squint narrowed into a frown. "I don't think Do-Wop tells me right," he said. "Salad oil is no part of it. Am I right, Gnat?"

"Hey, do you want to hear what's goin' on or not?" said Chocolate Harry, sensing his audience slipping away.

"We don't wanna hear no crap about renegade robots," said Do-Wop. "Everybody knows robots just follow orders. They got Asimov circuits that make 'em do what people say."

"Yeah, that's what everybody *thinks*," said Harry, taking the cue and launching into a new spiel. "That's what the robot factories *want* you to think, on account of who's gonna buy a machine that, you wake up one morning and it's killed you and taken over your house?"

"*I* wouldn't buy nothin' like that," said Slammer, obviously impressed by his sergeant's logic.

"You got it," said Harry. He slapped his palm on the table, sending splashes out of several drinks. "Thing is, nobody wants their robots to have a mind of their own, 'cause if the bots figure out that us humans have everything and they got nothin', what's to stop 'em from taking over?"

"I no human," said Tusk-anini, irrefutably. "I no scared of robots, either."

"That's 'cause you ain't run across these here renegades," said the supply sergeant. "They'll just naturally wipe out any kind of sophont. You think it matters to them how many legs or eyes you got on you? It's the last thing they care about."

"You sure this is the straight story from the brass?" asked Do-Wop. Almost automatically, not even watching, he slowly peeled the label off his beer bottle with his thumbnail.

"Pure gospel, man," said Harry, holding up a palm as if taking an oath. "Rev himself ain't ever said a word as true as this stuff I'm lettin' you in on."

Some of the listeners—mostly new members of the company unfamiliar with the supply sergeant's ways—nodded and murmured words of approval. They'd been in the Legion a while, but they still had a tendency to believe everything they heard from a veteran, especially from a fast talker like Chocolate Harry. This made them welcome additions to the supply sergeant's poker games and easy marks for his long string of scams.

But Sushi was a veteran and a first-class scammer in his own right. "It's a triff story," he said, grinning. "What I still haven't figured out is how Harry thinks he's going to make a buck out of it. I'll admit he could be telling lies for free, just to keep in practice, maybe. But somewhere down the road, if we buy this line of stuff, it's going to cost us. What's the deal, Harry? Are you selling robot repellent or something?"

"You oughta know me better than that, Soosh," said Harry, managing a hurt expression. "I'd never try to sell something like that. Why, a robot's mechanical. You can't run it off like you would some kinda bug."

"That's true," said Do-Wop. "The robots I've seen, they just don't let anything bother them. Sorta like Mahatma when he gets wrapped up in something. There's no stopping him."

"That's right," said Harry. "That's why something like a repellent won't work. But there is one thing—"

"Here it comes!" said Sushi, and everyone chuckled. Even Tusk-anini leaned forward in anticipation of Chocolate Harry's spiel.

Harry continued as if he hadn't heard Sushi's stage whisper. "The thing is, robots can only see in certain frequencies. So if you're wearing certain colors—stuff in the purple end of the spectrum, for example—they just naturally can't see you, and you can sneak right up on 'em. And it just so happens I've got in a supply of robot-proof camouflage …" He waved toward a large crate, marked Phule-Proof Camo.

"Which you'll make available, at a price, to anyone who wants a little insurance," prompted Super-Gnat.

"Why, sure," said Harry, his face devoid of all guile. "I'd purely hate to see anybody get hurt if we ended up in a bad robot situation and they weren't prepared, y'know? So who wants some?"

"I think I'll pass," said Do-Wop. "But somehow, I don't think you'll have any shortage of takers, Sarge."

"Sushi, I sure hope you're right," said the supply sergeant. "In my job, you've got to think ahead, and I'm just glad I thought of this particular possibility before it turned into a real problem."

"Harry, you're a pure genius," said Sushi, shaking his head with admiration. "I bet we'll see half the squad wearing purple before we leave Landoor."

"I hope it's more than that," said Chocolate Harry. "Why, I'll hardly rest until I know we're all safe from the robots."

"Harry, somehow I know we will be," said Sushi. He nodded in the direction of Slammer, who was already wearing a purple field vest over his fatigues. Slammer, noticing the attention, lifted his chin and favored his comrades with a satisfied smirk. "Yes indeed, Harry," said Sushi, "somehow, I know you'll be able to rest very comfortably."

Harry's broad grin left no doubt of that.

CHAPTER FOUR

Journal #508

Having been ordered to keep confidential the details of the company's impending reassignment, my employer was at some disadvantage in preventing rumors from spreading. While he could put a stop to specific misconceptions and errors of fact, only announcing specific details of the mission could have prevented some of the speculations and outright fabrications that began to spread among the legionnaires of Omega Company.

And, of course, certain questions were bound to pop up, no matter how much accurate information the troops had been given.

* * *

"Sergeant Brandy, may I ask a question?"

Brandy looked wearily up from her clipboard. When Omega Company had gotten its first batch of new recruits back on Lorelei, she had been assigned to run them through basic training. Despite her initial misgivings, they'd turned into a pretty good group—good enough that she'd decided to keep working with them even after they'd reached the point where they could take regular duty assignments. It gave her a sense of day-to-day accomplishment, despite the unique frustrations that were sometimes part and parcel of working with this group.

This particular pattern of events had become almost a ritual. Sometime during the morning formation, Mahatma would ask a question, usually some innocent query that, upon closer examination, opened up a devastating reappraisal of the Legion way of life, exactly the kind of thing basic training was supposed to make recruits forget about. But there was no stopping Mahatma, and Phule had made it clear that simply stomping the impertinent questioner into the ground (as Brandy sometimes felt like doing) was incompatible with his philosophy of command. Brandy sighed. "What do you want now, Mahatma?" she asked wearily.

"I want to ask a question, Sergeant," Mahatma said earnestly—or was there a hint of humor behind that surface? She'd never been able to prove it, but she had a strong suspicion that Mahatma enjoyed pulling her leg, although it was always so subtle that she never detected it until it was too late to call him on it. She also wondered if she'd ever get used to Mahatma's ability to take each and every statement absolutely literally and find meanings in it nobody else had ever suspected of being there. She wondered if he did it all the time or just to sergeants.

"Yeah, you told me you had a question," said Brandy. After an uncomfortably long silence, which anybody else would have taken as an opportunity to ask the question, she sighed inwardly and said, "Go ahead and ask it, Mahatma."

"Thank you, Sergeant," said the smiling legionnaire. "What I wanted to know was, why are we being transferred out? Does it mean we've done a bad job here?"

"No, it means we've done a good job," said Brandy. "Landoor is prosperous and looks like it's going to remain peaceful, so they don't need us anymore."

Mahatma smiled and nodded. That meant Big Trouble, in Brandy's experience. Sure enough, the little legionnaire followed up by asking, "Then shouldn't they reward us by keeping us here so we can enjoy the peace and prosperity?"

"That's not how the Legion works, Mahatma," said Brandy.

"We're in the business of taking care of trouble, so we go where there's trouble brewing. That's our job, and we're pretty damn good at it." She hoped this answer would give the rest of the squad a feeling of pride in their job, deflecting the subversive implications she suspected—no, *knew*—Mahatma would somehow make out of whatever she said.

Mahatma looked up at her over his round glasses. "What happens if we do our job poorly, Sergeant Brandy?" he said beatifically.

She answered him solemnly—there was no other way to answer this kind of question—"We could get in a lot of trouble, Mahatma."

"So if we do our job well, we are sent to a place where there is trouble, and if we do it poorly, trouble comes to us," said Mahatma sweetly. "Please, Sarge, how does this system encourage virtuous conduct and constructive effort?"

As usual after Mahatma had asked one of his follow-up questions, Brandy could hear the other trainees muttering among themselves as they tried to puzzle out what their comrade was getting at. "Quiet!" she barked. She didn't particularly mind their talking, but the order would distract the squad from thinking about Mahatma's question while she came up with an answer.

She was sure she'd be able to come up with one ...

* * *

"I don't want to leave Landoor with this scandal hanging over us, but I don't know how to refute it, either," said Phule, pacing from one side of his office to the other. Beeker, Rev, and Rembrandt sat along the couch, their heads swiveling like spectators at a tennis match.

Beeker raised a hand and said, "Sir, if I may make a suggestion: Why don't you simply repay the complainant the amount he was robbed plus the damages to his restaurant? If you added on a bit more to demonstrate goodwill, I have no doubt that he'd drop the complaint."

"That would make him go away," said Phule. "And I do mean

to see that he doesn't suffer financially, whatever else happens in this case. But giving him money to go away wouldn't clear my people's reputation. People on Landoor would always be able to say that we just bought our way out of trouble. If one of my people has robbed Mr. Takamine, I want him to own up to it and pay an appropriate penalty."

This response was greeted with shocked silence. At one time, buying his way out would have been Phule's natural response to trouble. Now that didn't seem to be enough. Rev finally spoke. "I reckon it's pretty clear that the culprit in this case is a follower of the King, though I doubt anybody who'd do that is still a true believer. And I don't think he's one of my own flock, Captain. Like I said, there are lots of members of the Church of the King on Landoor. Coulda been any one of 'em. A black jumpsuit don't necessarily mean Legion. It ain't that uncommon a garment among the faithful."

"That's true," said Phule, standing still for a moment to look the chaplain in the eye. "But we can't hide behind that, because Mr. Takamine *believes* it's one of us. We've got to prove he's wrong about that, and we've got to do that before we leave the planet. I'm open to ideas. Anybody have one?"

Rev spoke again. "I can get a record of the King's followers on this planet who've had their faces remade. That'll be a start, I reckon."

"Yes, that's a start," said Phule, pacing again. "But how do we sort out which one it was? If we can eliminate our people, fine—but it has to be beyond question. I don't want anybody claiming that I cooked the evidence. Better yet, we have to identify the actual culprit, whoever it is."

"I've checked our duty rosters for the time involved," said Rembrandt. "If all our people were where they were supposed to be—which isn't necessarily so, knowing this outfit—we can eliminate six of our people right away. We're checking to verify that they were actually on duty."

"That's over half," said Phule. "That's good, but it leaves five unaccounted for. Any way to establish their whereabouts at the time?"

"We're working on it," said Rembrandt. "The problem is, not

everybody who saw one of the suspects can say for sure which one it was. When they all have the same face, it complicates things. Which brings us back to where we started."

"Out of curiosity, am I in the clear or not?" asked Rev, with the slight smirk that seemed to be an unavoidable result of the face-remodeling process.

"For robbing the citizen, yes," said Rembrandt, turning a cool stare toward the chaplain. "You aren't the type who'd do that. Besides, the restaurant owner said you were too fat to be the one who did it. For getting us into this fix to begin with …"

"Now, it's a little late for that, Rembrandt," said Phule wearily. "We can't very well make Rev change the tenets of his faith, even if they're inconvenient for the rest of us."

"Let me point out one more thing, Lieutenant," said Rev. "Just because somebody's thrown in with the King, it don't make 'em perfect. If one of the band goes off-key, it's as much my duty as anybody else's to find 'em and bring 'em back in tune. If I find the culprit, I'm gonna turn him in—and I think I've got an inside track on findin' him, too."

"What would that be?" said Beeker. "If you have some way to identify individual members of your faith that the rest of us don't know, perhaps it would be useful to share it in circumstances like these."

"Oh, I don't have nothin' like that," said Rev. "Just access to records, which I promise to share with y'all. And I hope some of 'em will be more willin' to talk to one of their own, if we can narrow the suspects down to two or three."

"Anything of that kind you can do will be a help," said Phule. His nervous energy at last expended, he sat on the edge of his desk and said, "I guess that'll have to do for now. Rembrandt, Rev, if either of you learn anything, report it to me right away. And if the local police tell me something that might help, I'll pass it along. I want to get this solved before we lift off for our next assignment—and we don't have much time. So make it a priority, all right?"

"Yes, Captain," said Rembrandt. Rev added his assent, and the meeting broke up.

But Beeker said, "Well, sir, I suspect you're going to end up repaying the citizen for what he was robbed after all."

"I think I'm going to do that anyway," said Phule. "Even if we do find the guilty party, he's not likely to be able to make restitution. So why shouldn't I? But we've got the company's good name to uphold, too. That's why I want to prove that none of our people did it—or if they did, to show that we don't just sweep our bad eggs under the rug."

"I agree with your sentiments, if not your metaphor, sir," said Beeker. "I just hope you're able to live up to them."

"So do I, Beeker," said Phule. "So do I." He sat musing for a moment, then looked up and said, "You know, I think we're overlooking a resource that might help us. What do you think about this ...?"

Beeker listened, skeptical at first, but after hearing Phule's idea, he nodded. "It's not an entirely bad idea, sir. I'll see to it at once."

* * *

"He's coming." Ernie's voice in Lola's earpiece was quiet, but she sensed its urgency nonetheless. They'd already blown one attempt at snatching Phule and somehow managed to remain free to try again. They couldn't assume that they could get away with a second failure. No matter how oblivious the captain was, he was eventually going to notice that somebody was trying to kidnap him and take steps to prevent further attempts. If the current trap didn't catch him, they might not get another chance.

Lola took a deep breath and tried to center herself. She had to play her part to perfection, or the scheme had no chance of succeeding. She was confident that she could do what she had to. What worried her was, she could hit all her marks one-two-three, just like that, and Ernie could still fumble the game away. Or Phule could get lucky, and none of their careful preparation would make any difference. Phule seemed to get lucky a lot—more than his share, if she was any judge.

She held her breath until she heard the steady rhythm of footsteps approaching down the corridor, then let it out slowly. As the footsteps reached a position just opposite her hiding place, she burst out with a wild shriek. "Help! Oh, please—help me!" Sobbing, she fell to the ground right in front of the passerby, her eyes closed and her limbs as limp as she could make them.

"What's the matter, miss?" said an unfamiliar voice.

Her eyes popped open. Standing over her, a look of concern on his face and a large tray balanced on his right hand, was a room service waiter.

"Nothing's wrong," she snapped, and began to rise to her feet, gathering her carefully ripped dress close around her.

"But, miss, you asked for help," the waiter said, a confused look on his face.

"Oh, shut up," she said, and flounced away. The waiter stared after her for a moment, then shrugged and went about his business.

A few minutes later, Captain Jester strolled past without incident. But a short distance away, beyond the range of his hearing, Lola was explaining to Ernie, in very graphic and detailed terms, exactly how important precise timing was to this plan and just how badly he'd missed his cue. A spectator would have had no doubt, at this point, which of the pair was most in need of rescue. Perhaps, fortunately for Ernie, there were no spectators.

Journal #511

By taking on the task of convincing the Yakuza's leadership that he represented a superfamily, Sushi had in effect elected himself an officer. By this, I mean that he had taken on a level of decision-making responsibility well above that of an ordinary legionnaire. Like the officers, he could no longer afford to "goof off" when there was no immediate task in front of him. There was always something that needed doing, something that couldn't wait. And there was always somebody asking him to do one more thing he hadn't planned on.

* * *

Sushi leaned back in his chair and closed his eyes. He'd been staring at the computer screen ever since he'd come off duty, and it felt as if the images on the screen were beginning to burn themselves into his retinas. The tension in the back of his shoulders was another sure sign that he'd been working too hard—or, more precisely, worrying too hard. He wasn't used to this. The fact that he'd brought it on himself didn't make it any better.

It had been at least an hour—no, nearly two hours, he realized when he checked the time display—since Do-Wop had tried to get him to go down to the bar for a round or two with the guys. He'd told his buddy he'd be right along, "As soon as I get this one detail cleaned up." He was still nowhere near finished. It was tempting just to let things slide and go down for a drink. The only thing that kept him from doing exactly that was the realization that he was playing a life-and-death game, and that it was his own life on the line if he screwed up. That was enough to keep anybody's nose to the grindstone. He hadn't bargained for this. But there wasn't any going back, either.

A rap on the door jolted him into the present. He walked over and said, "Who's there?" There'd been a time when he would just have opened it. Now he thought twice about that kind of thing.

"It is I, Beeker," came the familiar voice from the other side. Sushi opened the door, and Phule's butler entered.

"Have a seat," said Sushi, indicating the hotel suite's couch and matching easy chairs. "What's the occasion?"

"The captain is concerned about a situation involving a member of Reverend Ayres's sect," said the butler. "The difficulty is that many members have had their faces altered so as to resemble their master. This entails obvious difficulties in telling one from another."

"Yeah, I know what you mean," said Sushi, lowering himself into a chair opposite the butler. "A couple of guys I know had the operation done, and now I can't recognize 'em until they start talking. What do you want me to do about it?"

"The police have surveillance camera coverage of an incident in which they believe one of our people is the guilty party," said

Beeker, steepling his fingers. "The camera clearly shows a member of the Church of the King robbing and damaging a local restaurant and beating the owner. The Rev. Ayres points out that a large number of civilians also belong to his sect and suggests that one of them could be the responsible party."

"Makes sense to me," said Sushi. "But what do you think I can do about it?"

"The captain has asked to review the surveillance footage," said Beeker. "It occurs to us that minute computer analysis of the voice and movements of the criminal could provide as good an identification as the face."

"Sure, if you had similar footage of all the possible suspects to compare it to," said Sushi. "You already mentioned the main objection: there are a lot of those King's men out there. Unless we have all of them on tape, there's no way we can pinpoint which one is the robber."

"We can do one thing fairly quickly," said Beeker. "You're our most accomplished computer user. The captain wishes you to compare the surveillance footage to archival footage of our company. There are several holovid disks available, including the entire company at some point or another. Eliminating the possibility that it is one of ours would be of use."

"What if the opposite happens?" asked Sushi, frowning. "What if the robber *is* one of our guys?"

"That leaves us no choice," said the butler with a long face. "You must turn him in, and the captain will see to it that he pays the appropriate penalty for his crime. There is no other course of action compatible with the honor of the Legion, as he puts the question. However, I doubt it will come to that event. More likely, the culprit's identity will be revealed in the operation's second phase."

"Second phase?" Sushi leaned forward in his chair, his chin on the fingers of his right hand. "OK, I'll bite. What's the second phase?"

Beeker said, "You are, for all practical purposes, the head of a large quasi-criminal organization. This position gives you access to a large body of information, should you ask for it."

"Yeah, I guess I am the head of the Yakuza," said Sushi. "And sure, they have plenty of information. But what makes you think they have the information the captain needs? There are a lot of petty crooks on this planet, and most of them aren't Japanese."

"No, but the owner of the restaurant is," said Beeker. "He is undoubtedly paying your organization for protection. In return, they should be making an effort to find the man who robbed him."

"Japanese? What's the name of the place?" asked Sushi.

"The restaurant is the New Osaka Grill on Hastings Street. A Mr. Takamine is the owner."

"Yeah, I've eaten in there. Good food, even if it is a bit expensive," said Sushi. "But how does this involve me? If the Yakuza can't find the guy that robbed the place without me …"

"*You* are the head of that organization," said Beeker. "It necessarily involves you, if someone under their protection is robbed without justice being done. Surveillance information from other businesses under their protection is likely to show the culprit: If he ate in one Japanese restaurant, he probably ate in more than one. You are in a position to obtain and analyze the information, and this will undoubtedly reveal the culprit."

"It'll take a lot of work," said Sushi. "Just getting in all those vids, let alone setting up a program to analyze them …"

"I suggest you make it a priority," said Beeker. "It works to your benefit on two fronts. First, to show that the superfamily you have invented can, in fact, deliver benefits to a local family. And second, you convince the captain that the time you spend on this project does, after all, benefit his company."

"OK, I see what you mean," said Sushi. "I guess I'd better get on it." He sighed. So much for his hopes of joining the gang in the bar tonight—or anytime soon.

"You will, in time, see the rewards for this hard work," said Beeker, standing up.

"I guess I will," said Sushi. "But a nice cold beer was looking good, too."

Beeker raised an eyebrow. "I can assure you, young man, that the beer in the bar will be just as cold when you have finished this task as it is now, and the satisfaction of a job well done will greatly enhance its flavor."

"Oh, I know that," said Sushi. "I just wish I didn't have to be so damned mature all of a sudden."

Beeker gave just the hint of a smile. "Maturity may not be the most attractive way of life, but speaking only for myself, I am just as happy to be able to take part in it. Perhaps, upon reflection, you will feel the same. Good day, young man."

* * *

This time it was going to work. This time it had *better* work, Lola told herself. All things considered, she and Ernie had been lucky to get away with two failed attempts to kidnap the captain. Their luck couldn't hold out much longer. If it didn't work this time, she was going to call it off and deal with the consequences. As long as her bosses didn't decide to lock her and Ernie in the same room, she figured she could deal with anything less annoying.

"He's coming," said the voice in her ear.

"Are you sure?" she hissed.

"Yeah, I'm sure, babe. Ball's in your court." Ernie sounded calm, assured. That didn't fool her. Ernie had been just as sure of himself the last time, when she'd prostrated herself in front of the wrong target, a room service waiter. She hoped the befuddled waiter hadn't reported the incident—or, if he had, that it had been written off as a drunken prank by a customer. If the captain was alerted to the possibility of trouble, the odds of success dramatically dropped. And they were already low enough, as far as Lola was concerned.

After the previous debacle, she had decided that the best way to prevent any warning from reaching the captain was to set the ambush for first thing in the morning, as the captain was on his way to his office. With any luck, he would still be groggy from sleep—or so Lola hoped. There had to be *some* advantage to getting up at the crack of dawn.

She peered between the fronds of the potted plant as she heard the footsteps nearing. Yes, here came the captain. Lola leapt out into the corridor to sprawl in front of the (hopefully) unsuspecting Legion officer. "Captain! Help me!" she whimpered. She was starting to get good at this act, she realized. Maybe if this caper didn't come off, she could get a job in the Casino's entertainment division, in the chorus behind Dee Dee Watkins.

"What's the matter, miss?" asked Captain Jester, bending over, a concerned look on his face.

Yes! thought Lola, doing her best to keep from smiling. At last, things were working on schedule. "That horrible man's been following me again," she said, doing her best to appear pathetic and intense at the same time.

"He has?" The captain peered around in all directions. "Where is he?"

"He ran back that way," she said, pointing down the cross corridor. It lay on the way to the casino's health club, a facility rarely visited by customers, although the legionnaires made good use of it. This early in the morning, the corridor would be deserted—a perfect spot for their ambush.

"Show me," said the captain, and again she had to bite her lip to keep from breaking out into a grin.

"Yes, but please stay close to me," she said, allowing him to help her to her feet. "I don't want him finding me alone."

"Don't worry," said the captain. "You'll be all right. He's probably run away by now, but we'll catch him if he hasn't." He began walking quietly—almost supernaturally quietly, and very confidently—down the corridor. It occurred to Lola that he was most likely highly trained at one or more martial arts. It was a good thing their plan didn't require them to engage the captain in unarmed combat. She allowed herself to shudder at the notion—it would add a touch of verisimilitude to her "maiden in distress" act.

The captain stopped and looked down at her. "Don't be afraid now, ma'am," he said, misinterpreting the shudder exactly as she'd hoped he would. "The Legion's in charge here, and we're not going to let anything happen to you."

"Oh, thank you," she said, doing her best to make it sound sincere. "I'll just stay right behind you, if you don't mind."

"That's probably best," he said, and he turned to peer down the corridor again. Lola tensed; somewhere not far away, Ernie should be waiting, ready to play his part in their little charade. The captain edged forward, quietly; he was being careful. Would Ernie be able to bring it off?

The captain stopped and peered down a side corridor leading to an emergency exit. He nodded, took a step forward, and then ...

Lola let out a piercing shriek. "Over there!" she cried, and as the captain turned to look, Ernie struck.

They'd chosen their weapon to incapacitate their victim as quickly as possible without undue risk of injury, particularly to themselves. The Zenobian stun ray wasn't in the civilian arsenal yet, but the goo gun was a good second best. Firing a huge gob of incredibly sticky material, it enveloped its victim in a viscous mass of goo and trapped him as surely as a fly on flypaper. Police departments throughout the settled worlds used it for riot control. It wasn't foolproof; inexperienced users sometimes got themselves stuck in the goo when they tried to secure their victim or got a sound thrashing from an incompletely immobilized victim.

But Ernie had practiced. As soon as the goo had enveloped Phule, he flipped a lever on the gun and fired a burst of a clear liquid, setting the goo so that someone attempting to grasp the victim could do so without getting caught.

"Hey, what are you doing?" said the captain—but too late. A moment later, Lola whipped out a gag and threw it over the captain's mouth, while Ernie darted down the hall a few paces and grabbed a laundry cart just outside the gym. They tipped their victim into it, threw a layer of dirty towels over him, and quickly wheeled him into a service elevator and away.

CHAPTER FIVE

Journal #514

Even the most punctual worker is sometimes late. Some are more punctual than others, but even they can sometimes be thrown off schedule by the vagaries of weather, transportation, and sheer chance. Bosses and coworkers will fidget, sigh, look out the window, and (depending on factors too various to enumerate) go about their business without the tardy person or await his arrival with some mixture of anxiety and annoyance. If the worker does not appear by some reasonable time, attempts will be made to get in touch, with greater or lesser degree of urgency.

But when a robot is late, that is in itself an occasion for urgency. When the robot is a custom-built facsimile of one's employer, bought at an exorbitant price and put on duty for reasons of utmost security, panic is likely to ensue. It is to the credit of the staff of the Fat Chance Casino that the panic was kept to a minimum on this occasion.

* * *

"Disappeared?" Gunther Rafael Jr.'s jaw couldn't have dropped farther if there'd been a 100-G gravity field underneath it. "Why, that's impossible."

"I keep hearing about things being impossible, usually right after they happen," said Doc, who had become the Fat Chance Casino's security chief after the departure of Phule's Company. His black Space Legion staff sergeant's uniform was a perfect fit. Only someone with an insider's familiarity with the Legion's insignia and badges would have been able to tell that it was a complete fraud, as were the "Legion" guards Doc commanded. "If it's impossible for the android to disappear, maybe you can tell me what it's done instead of disappearing?"

"OK, Doc, you've made your point," said Rex, who headed up the Casino's entertainment division. "If you're done with the sarcasm, maybe I can interest you in our current problem, which is that the Andromatic Phule *has* disappeared. The most likely explanation is, the thing's been abducted—or maybe that should be *stolen.*"

"Who could've done it?" wailed Rafael. "How? Why?" He began to pace nervously around the table.

"Those are all good questions," said Doc. "A better one is, what are we going to do about it?"

"You're the damned security chief," said Rafael, pointing an accusing finger. "Why don't you know what to do about it?"

Doc bristled. "You know the answer to that as well as I do, Gunther: I'm about as much a security chief as you are a casino manager. I'm just an actor who got put in charge of the guard detail because everybody figured the bad boys would be so scared of us they wouldn't start trouble. Now, with our mechanical boss missing, they're bound to figure out we've been bluffing all along."

"And when they do, they'll swoop down on us like wolves," said Rafael, wringing his hands.

"Wolves don't swoop," barked Tully Bascomb. He headed up the gambling operations, and his years of casino experience had been invaluable to Phule when he agreed to run the Fat Chance. "Pull yourselves together, both of you. We've got to come up with an answer to the missing captain before the bad boys *do* figure out how vulnerable we are. And that means everything's got to look as if nothing's changed. Doc, is there anybody on board you'd trust to play the role of Phule until we can get the bot back?"

"Maybe," said Doc, rubbing his chin. "I've got a couple of kids who're about the right physical type and who are quick studies. With a little makeup …"

"Makeup's no problem," said Rex. "With what we've got here, I could make Dee Dee look like the captain. What I'm worried about is whether your kids can carry off the stunt when they have to talk to customers—and whether they can be trusted keep the secret."

"Well, there's no reason they have to know the whole story," said Doc. "Outside the board of directors, nobody knows that Phule's been replaced by an android. The actor replacing the android doesn't need to know, either. We just tell him the captain's been called off-station on urgent business."

"Or maybe he's sick," said Tully. "That'll do for the short run, sure."

"And as far as the lines, I bet they can do better than the android," said Doc. "They can have a much wider range of permitted responses without getting in over their heads. And they can handle a lot more random situations than the android could."

"I don't know about that," said Raphael. "I was once in a group the android came up to, and somebody started a discussion of the gravball playoffs. I swear, that droid could talk about the sports and weather better than I could! I doubt anybody could have figured out they weren't interacting with a real person."

"Only danger would be if somebody in the group knew the real Phule and spotted the android—or the actor—talking about something Phule didn't know or care about," said Doc. "But with the right direction, even that wouldn't be a problem. Just order the actor to break off the conversation before there's any chance of getting in over his head. We can handle it, believe me."

"OK," said Tully decisively. "We let Doc pick a couple of doubles, coach them to play Phule, and turn them loose as soon as they're ready. We're trusting you on this one, Doc."

"I won't let you down," said Doc. "But this only solves half the problem, y'know."

"Do I ever," said Tully. "Somebody out there's got the android, and it's not going to be very long before they figure out what they've got and what it means. And then we're going to be a target again."

"I hope not. People could get hurt," said Rex. "We need to notify the captain as soon as possible. I'm not anxious to put my actors in the way of that kind of danger. Besides, he's the majority stockholder. We can't deal with a situation of this importance without his input."

"Second the motion and call the question," said Doc. "I don't think we can afford to delay even a moment."

"No argument here," said Tully. "Give me a moment to place the call, and we'll see what advice Captain Phule has to offer." The others sat in silence as he reached for the comm unit and entered a code. The tension was as thick as a high-stakes poker showdown. None of them were sure just who they were playing against, but everyone knew that the stakes were the entire casino.

Journal #515

Preparations for the company's move to its new assignment had begun almost as soon as the ambassador had left my employer's office. While the ambassador had instructed the captain not to reveal the company's exact destination, it soon became clear to all who paid attention to such matters that it was not to be another planet with a first-rate hotel designed for human occupancy. To the officers' surprise, this discovery did not set off a round of griping about having to abandon the luxurious conditions to which the company had become accustomed. Indeed, the legionnaires seemed to look forward to the change as a sort of adventure.

The major exception was, predictably, the mess sergeant.

* * *

"Captain, you got to let me know where we're going," said Sergeant Escrima, leaning forward over Phule's desk. His clenched fists rested on the desktop, and his eyes gleamed. "I got to know what kind of supplies we can get there."

"Sergeant, I sympathize entirely with your viewpoint," said Phule, doing his best to calm down the mess sergeant. "In fact,

I'm trying to find out the same thing, not just for food stocks but for the whole company. What I can tell you is, we're going to a planet without any previous human settlement. A lot of things we've taken for granted won't be available. You'll have to make do—at least at first—with what we can bring in ourselves. Of course, there are bound to be a fair number of local items you can use …"

"Water and what else?" demanded Escrima. "Can we eat the local meat? I can't do anything without fresh meat, or fresh vegetables, either. What about power? I can't even cook without power."

"Power's not going to be a problem," said Phule.

"Hallelujah. I can boil water," Escrima sneered. "Lots of nice hot tea and reconstituted soups, hah?" He pantomimed spitting out something foul tasting. "You got to do better than that, Captain."

Phule stood up. "Escrima, I know for a fact that the natives of this world can eat some of our food, so I'm sure we can eat some of theirs, too. I think you should look on it as a stimulating challenge to find out which of their things our people can use, and ways to prepare them—"

"A challenge?" Escrima's eyes widened. "You don't want to challenge me, Captain. No, not unless—"

"Maybe *challenge* is the wrong word," Phule cut in quickly. "A chance to prove how good you really are. We've all tasted what you can do when you've got a cordon bleu–quality kitchen to work with. I'll guarantee you, there's not a chef on the planet who could top you." This was true; Phule occasionally had reason to eat a meal off-base, and he knew that Landoor's best restaurants served as good a meal as he'd find anywhere in the Galaxy. But the food Escrima put out daily for the legionnaires of Omega Company was even better.

Escrima wasn't in a mood to be flattered. "I make the finest food in the Legion, and now you tell me I got to rough it, cook over a campfire for all I know. How long you think it'll be before everybody starts cracking wise about the food? Captain, you gonna drive me crazy!"

"No, no," said Phule, raising both hands in protest. "We'll have an up-to-date kitchen for you, don't worry about that. As long as I'm in charge of this outfit, you'll never have to settle for anything less than the newest, finest equipment. You have my word on that, Sergeant."

Escrima raised his eyebrows, and for the first time since he'd entered the office, he lowered his voice to something like a civil tone. "I got to give you credit for that, Captain," he said after a moment's thought. "You said you were going to do just that and did it, no fooling around. OK, then, I'll take your word on the equipment. But that's not the whole game. You give me rotten eggs to cook, and I don't care what kind of stove I got."

"No rotten eggs, Escrima. I promise," said Phule, smiling. "Not even powdered eggs, which as far as I'm concerned are even worse."

"At least a rotten egg used to be an egg," agreed Escrima, wrinkling his nose. "That powdered stuff, maybe it came out of a vat in some chemical plant. About all it's good for is you can use it to kill bugs, if you got bugs."

"Kill bugs?" Phule's brow wrinkled. "How do you kill bugs with powdered eggs? I didn't think even bugs would eat the stuff."

"No," said Escrima, a sly grin now on his face. "The way you kill bugs, you take a whole big box of the crap and drop it right on top of the bug. Kills him real good, you bet."

Phule laughed. "I promise, Escrima, you'll get the best ingredients," he said. "If you ever get anything that isn't good enough for you to feed the troops, feed it to me first."

"What?" said Escrima, mortally offended. "You want me to feed you trash?"

Phule nodded. "Yes, absolutely," he said. "That way I know when we're being cheated, and I'll get mad enough to do something about it. You know I'm behind you all the way, Escrima. Look here: On this new assignment, if you want something, let me know, and I'll figure out a way to get it. If I have to put a fleet of private transports on the job, I'll get it. But believe me, we should be able to use the local stuff, too. Just wait and see."

Escrima nodded. "If you tell me that, I believe you. All right then, Captain. We got a deal."

"Good," said Phule. "Now, I told you I'd get you the best equipment available. I've got a new field kitchen ordered—a prototype, designed to allow you to prepare anything you could do in a five-star restaurant under field conditions. We're going to give it a test here on Landoor before we get out somewhere where we can't get it replaced. It arrives day after tomorrow, if everything goes right. I want you to give it a full test and let me know anything it needs to meet your specifications. OK?"

"Yes, sir!" said Escrima. Like half the men in the legion, he loved the chance to play with new toys. Now he was going to get his hands on a brand-new one. It would keep him busy for a while, Phule knew, figuring out ways to get the most out of it. The results would be well worth the effort.

* * *

"All right, so I was wrong," said Lola, not sounding in the least contrite. She turned off the hotel room's built-in computer screen, which had been displaying *Do-It-Yourself Turing Test* by Minsky & Hofstadter Enterprises. "We've gone and stolen the damned robot dupe instead of kidnapping Willard Phule. Now what?"

They'd realized something wasn't right almost as soon as they'd dissolved the goo gun bonds they'd used to capture their prey. The captive's response to the situation had been thoroughly inappropriate, unless one assumed that a total idiot had been running a Legion company and a major Casino Hotel—not only running them, but running them successfully. Their suspicions aroused, they'd called up the Turing test, and the robot had failed it miserably.

Ernie shook his head miserably. "We've blown it for sure," he said. "The bosses send us here to snatch a guy and all we get is a stupid bot. They're gonna wale on our butts for this."

Lola paced back and forth in short steps, thinking furiously. "I think it's time we stopped thinking about the bosses and started looking after ourselves," she said. "We can still make something out of this if we don't panic."

"Panic?" said Ernie, his voice squeaking. "You ever seen what the bosses do to guys who stiff 'em?"

"That's the ones they catch," said Lola. She stopped and pointed at Ernie, and continued, "If we play our cards right, who says they're going to catch us? Especially if we can get Phule to pay to get his robot back. These things can't be cheap. It ought to be worth enough to him to give us enough of a nest egg to run off and hide someplace safe."

"Yeah, I guess the bot's gotta be worth somethin' to him," Ernie said, scratching his head. "I wonder what he'll pay to get it back."

"We need to know the going price for an Andromatic dupe, for starters," said Lola. She flopped onto the bed and stared at the ceiling a moment before continuing, "I guess he'll pay that much just to avoid waiting for the factory to turn out a new one for him. This thing's gotta be a custom model—nobody else would want one that looked like *him*."

"Yeah, I guess we can get replacement value, whatever that is," said Ernie. He looked once more at the replica of Phule sitting, with an expression of seeming unconcern, cross-legged in a chair by the window. It might have been waiting for a dinner date.

Or, more likely, looking for a chance to escape. But the two kidnappers weren't betting that their captive would remain docile. The robot's left leg was shackled to the heavy chair, and even with its superhuman strength, it wouldn't make much progress dragging such an awkward impediment. Still, if it managed to escape the building, it was a good bet that it would find its way back to the Fat Chance, and that shortly thereafter, the two botnappers would be in the hands of unsympathetic security guards, learning firsthand about the penal system of Lorelei Station.

"One thing hasn't changed," said Lola. "We have to get off-station with this thing as quick as we can. The heat's going to be turned way up. We've still got a chance to turn a profit. The bot's worth something. Let's get someplace where we can cash it in."

Ernie looked her in the eye for a long moment, then shrugged. "OK, you're running the game," he said. "But first things first. What do we do to keep the Fat Chance security from beating down our door?"

She stood and moved quickly to the computer terminal she'd signed off from only a few minutes before. "Like I said, we have to get off-station—and take the bot with us—pronto. Tell you what; you go to the public 'puters in the lobby and do some research on the going price of these robots. Meanwhile, I'll see if I can get us a berth on something headed out—and right now, I'm not particular about destinations. Don't take too long, OK? 'Cause I'm grabbing the first thing I can find, even if we have to leave without our luggage to make it. Got it?"

"Got it," said Ernie. He walked over and patted the robot on the head. "You just rest, ol' boy; you're gonna be our ticket to Rich Man's Row before it's all over." The robot, still gagged, said nothing.

"Be careful, it might grab you," said Lola, wrinkling her brow.

"Nah, the Asimov circuits won't let it," said Ernie. "Be back in a bit."

"Make it half a bit," said Lola, but Ernie was already out the door. She turned to the terminal and began searching for a ship headed out—out to anywhere.

* * *

"Andromatic stands behind its product without reservation, Captain Jester," said the customer service representative with an audible sniff. A name badge, which read Stanton, was visible on his chest. "However, if you will examine your purchase agreement, you will see that customer negligence is excluded. It appears that the android's automatic theft alarms have been turned off by you or your agents."

"The factory default settings on the theft alarms prevented us from using the android as intended," said Phule. "With my initial order, I specified that the robot had to be able to mingle freely with customers in the casino. It was your factory-recommended installation consultant that suggested disabling the alarms in that environment so they wouldn't go off every time some unfamiliar person got too close."

"I am afraid that your consultant—who, I should point out, is an independent contractor and not one of our employees—has given you bad advice," said Stanton. "That is not an authorized modification. If you had read the documentation—"

Phule cut him off. "I did read the documentation," he said. "So did a couple of pretty talented engineers. We all agreed that it was nearly useless. Just for starters, the index is completely inaccurate, and the illustrations look as if they were drawn by somebody who'd never laid eyes on the product."

"Of course," said the customer service rep with an insulted expression, "you can't expect the standard manual to cover all the custom features you ordered. Why, we'd have to write a new manual for every order we filled."

"For what I paid, that doesn't seem an outlandish service to expect," said Phule.

"For what you paid, I'd think you could have detailed one of your soldiers to stay with it and guard it," sneered Stanton.

"My men are legionnaires, not soldiers," Phule corrected the Andromatic representative somewhat testily. "More to the point, my whole reason for acquiring an android double was to convince various people that I was still on Lorelei instead of several parsecs away. I've never found it necessary to walk around with a bodyguard, and if I suddenly appeared to change my routine, it would attract attention. That's exactly what I didn't want."

Stanton shook his head slowly. "Nonetheless, I think we have a clear-cut case of customer negligence here. You must understand, Andromatic cannot take responsibility for unintended uses of our products." He made hand-washing gestures.

"I think I need to speak to the manager of customer service," said Phule.

"I am pleased to be able to accommodate you," said Stanton, with a mock bow. "As it happens, *I* am the manager of customer service."

Phule glared at the vidscreen. "I see," he said. "Let me see if I understand this, then. None of your stock units would do what I wanted a robot double for, so I had to custom-order one that would. But the custom modifications I paid extra for aren't covered in the manual, and the warranty doesn't extend to the uses for which I specifically requested the modifications. My failure to follow instructions I didn't receive constitutes negligence or misuse of the product. Is that about right?"

"That covers most of it, yes," said Stanton with a smirk. "Is there anything else that I can help you with today?"

"Evidently not," said Phule. He'd fallen into very precise diction, which anyone who knew him would have recognized as a very dangerous sign. "However, you might save yourself considerable trouble if you started clearing out your desk as soon as this call is over. I'm going to make sure that Andromatic cleans house, and the first department to get swept out will be customer disservice." He cut the connection abruptly and slumped into his chair.

"Shall I begin acquiring Andromatic shares, sir?" said Beeker, who had watched the entire conversation.

"Check the profitability first," said Phule. "If they're running as sloppy an operation as it looks from here, the shares might be overpriced. I suspect the company can turn a decent profit if it's managed right, but I don't see any reason to pay more than we need to for the privilege of turning it around."

"Perhaps it would be advisable to start rumors to get the price down to a reasonable level," noted Beeker.

"If we have to, sure," said Phule. "But don't put a lot of effort into it. We've got bigger fish to fry—among them, figuring out just who's got the robot and how to get it back."

"I should expect they'll give us the courtesy of a ransom call before long, sir," said Beeker. He opened the cover of his Port-a-Brain computer and began calling up his mail program.

"Possibly," said Phule. "That depends on their reasons for the robbery in the first place. If they're looking to make the most possible mischief for me, they can do a lot better by holding onto the thing than by selling it back to me."

"I fear you're right, sir," said Beeker. He looked at the screen, then continued, "At any rate, there's no word on the android at present. We shall have to pursue other channels."

"Well, pursue away," said Phule. "I'm going to go see how Sushi's coming along with his search for the man who robbed that Japanese restaurant. Give me a buzz if there's any useful news."

"Immediately, sir," said Beeker. He turned back to the Port-a-Brain and began his search.

Journal #520

Crises never choose a convenient time to manifest themselves. Of course not; otherwise, they would hardly qualify as crises. So it did not in the least surprise me that the theft of the robot coincided with an impending move by the company. In comparison, the contretemps with the local citizen convinced that he had been robbed by a legionnaire was a trivial matter.

In this, at least, my employer was fortunate enough to have an eminently qualified subordinate to whom he could delegate the job of identifying the robber. Sushi's computer skills were as good as any in the company. But it was his newly acquired status as a Yakuza overlord that gave him access to the information on which to proceed.

The perhaps not entirely inadvertent result of taking on this responsibility was the transformation of Sushi into a rather good facsimile of a valuable member of the company. While my employer saw this as a desirable alteration, that opinion was not necessarily universally shared.

* * *

"Yo, Soosh, you still workin'?" Do-Wop stood in the doorway of the hotel suite, obviously with several beers on board. Behind him were Super-Gnat and Tusk-anini. "You know what time it is, man?"

"I thought the one staying home was supposed to ask that question," said Sushi, looking up from the computer screen. "It's two in the morning, just in case your chronometer's broken. And yeah, I'm still working. Did you guys shut down the bar again?"

"Hey, somebody's gotta do it," said Do-Wop. He sauntered into the room, fairly steady on his feet, and slouched into an easy chair. Tusk-anini and Super-Gnat followed him, taking seats on the couch. "Everybody's worried about you, man," he added. "You workin' that hard, you gonna give yourself headaches or somethin'."

"I already have headaches, Do-Wop," said Sushi, turning his chair around to face his partner. "But this is a different kind—the kind I can get rid of by finishing up this job. And the best part is, when the job's done, I can go back to hanging out with the guys."

"You been saying that for weeks now," accused Do-Wop. "After a while, it sounds like nothin' more than an excuse." He sat up in the seat and pointed a finger at Sushi. "I told you this before, and I'll tell you again. You're startin' to act like an officer, man."

"Hey, cut the squabbling," said Super-Gnat. "We didn't come by to watch you guys fight." She reached down into her bag and pulled out a bottle of Atlantis Amber, beads of condensation on its surface. "Here, Sushi, we thought you'd like a cool one to wet your throat after working all night."

"She mean wet *inside* of throat," explained Tusk-anini helpfully.

"I'd never have guessed," said Sushi, smiling. He took the beer and opened it. "Thanks, Gnat," he said, raising the bottle in a salute and taking a sip.

"No prob, Sushi," she said with a smile. "We did miss you, y'know. We got talking about where we're going next, and there were some pretty weird ideas going around—stuff that makes Chocolate Harry's shtick about the renegade robots look fairly logical."

"Well, some people are buying that line," said Sushi with a wry grin. "Either that, or there's an incredible bargain on purple camouflage somewhere in town."

"I not believing renegade robots," said Tusk-anini. "Chocolate Harry must make a mistake."

"If it's a mistake, it's a damn lucky one for the sarge's bank balance," said Do-Wop. "Wonder where he found all that purple stuff anyhow?"

"Some surplus catalog is my bet," said Super-Gnat. "But here's my question, Sushi. You've been doing this job for the captain. Do-Wop says he was here talking to you this afternoon. So, naturally, we sort of wondered—any chance he dropped any hints where we're going?"

Sushi thought for a moment, tapping his fingers on the cool glass. "I'm not sure," he said. "But Chocolate Harry let something slip in between his pitches for robot-proof camouflage. The captain's bought a special modular base camp—MBC—that he's going to have us practice setting up. What I think that means is, there aren't any hotels where we're going. That makes me think we're going to a world without a large human population. Maybe even none at all."

"No hotels?" exclaimed Do-Wop. "Does that mean no bars? That sucks, man!"

Tusk-anini sat up straight, which made him nearly as tall as Sushi would have been standing. "Maybe we go to my home world," he said. "That would be good. Not such bright sun, good food ..."

"Don't let Escrima hear you say that," said Super-Gnat with a chuckle. Then she added, "It'd be interesting to see your world, though. Anybody who wants to stay in hotels his whole life doesn't have any business joining the Legion." She shot a sharp glance in Do-Wop's direction.

"Look who's talking," said Do-Wop. "You ask me, ain't nobody here had a whole lotta business joinin' the Legion."

"I join Legion for business," said Tusk-anini. "I join to learn about humans, so I can teach other Voltons about you people."

"Have you learned anything?" asked Sushi. "I sometimes wonder whether that Leftenant Qual wasn't right in his report on us, that we're the most dangerous race in the Galaxy because we're so unpredictable ..." He stopped and put his hand to his chin. "Say ... you don't think we might be going to the Zenobians' home world, do you?"

"Zenobia?" Super-Gnat whistled. "That'd be something, wouldn't it? As far as I know, we'd be the first humans to see their world. I wonder what it's like."

"Hot, I guess," said Sushi. "And swampy. They think our worlds are cold and dry."

"Dry's the word," said Do-Wop glumly. "Qual never took a drink of liquor the whole time he was with the company. I knew it, a place without bars. I'm gonna purely hate this."

"Hey, we don't even know if it's true yet," said Super-Gnat. "It's just a guess so far."

"Besides, Chocolate Harry'll make sure there's something to drink," said Sushi. "He's not gonna miss the chance to sell the whole company its daily hooch. Say, maybe we should lay in a supply, see if we can make a little profit on our own."

"All the other times we've moved, we've had pretty tight limits on personal supplies," said Super-Gnat. "It'd be hard to take along enough to compete with Harry. He can bring in anything he wants, as long as he can claim it's for the company."

"It ain't fair," said Do-Wop. "The damn sergeants and officers get all the edge."

"Now you know why I've been acting like an officer," said Sushi. "Get the captain owing you a couple of favors, and you just might be able to turn them to your advantage." He knocked back his beer and stood up to take the bottle to the recycler. Then he stopped and grinned. "If I play my cards right, it might even be worth missing a night or two in the bar."

Do-Wop's mouth fell wide open. He made a couple of tentative efforts to say something, but then, stunned with the enormity of Sushi's statement, he simply shook his head in incomprehension. In his universe, there was no conceivable favor a captain could dispense that would make up for a lost night in the bar.

Sushi didn't stop grinning. But privately, despite all his instincts and training, he found himself wondering whether, on this particular topic, Do-Wop might not be right after all.

CHAPTER SIX

Journal #523

S et a thief to catch a thief" is, in the abstract, excellent advice. After all, who knows the tricks of the trade better than an experienced practitioner? Thus it is that the galaxy's most successful police forces recruit their members from the very class of society that produces the criminals they combat. But when an entire society, as on the space station Lorelei, is oriented toward quasi-criminal activity, this formula does not necessarily ensure success. In fact, it may mean only that the laziest and least intelligent members of the criminal classes end up as police.

* * *

It wasn't the most elegant space liner, and it certainly wasn't the fastest, but the *Star*Runner* was leaving Lorelei *now*, and that was what mattered. Lola and Ernie stood in the boarding line, doing their best not to look over their shoulders or otherwise attract the attention of anyone who might have the authority to ask what was in the large trunk Ernie had on the luggage cart beside him. If it came to that, the two kidnappers had agreed to abandon the trunk and do their best to elude capture by the station's security forces. Lola hoped they could call in enough favors from their underworld contacts to get them smuggled off the station somehow. If not, well, they'd deal with that when they had to.

A lot depended on whether or not the Fat Chance had put out a bulletin on the missing robot. Lola was betting that the casino's instincts would be to keep the theft secret. After all, if the local criminals knew the casino's owner had left a robot to look after his property, there'd be nothing to deter a serious takeover attempt. As long as they'd believed the most charismatic officer in the Space Legion was there to guard the place, they'd kept their distance. But if it became general knowledge that the Fat Chance was a paper tiger …

Lola hadn't immediately grasped the implications of that particular piece of information. Now she was beginning to see that it might, in and of itself, be worth more than the robot. The question was, how was she going to take advantage of her knowledge without sticking her own head into a noose? The obvious approach was to let the Fat Chance know that *she* knew, and milk it for as much as it was worth. Not just for returning the robot—although that'd be worth a fair amount—but for her silence about the robot and what it represented. And, of course, there were potential customers for the information that the Fat Chance was a hollow shell—although the window of opportunity to make capital on that was narrow.

The boarding line edged forward, and she snapped back to reality. None of those plans would much matter if they were intercepted before the liner kicked into FTL and they were out of the local authorities' reach. Then she'd have the luxury of long-range planning. For now, she had to be ready to cut her losses and run for her life at a moment's notice.

"Destination?"

Lola started, realizing that in spite of her determination to be alert, she'd been lost in her thoughts. The woman asking the question was short, with shoulder-length brown hair and a neat Lorelei Station Administration uniform with a name tag reading Gillman. She had her hand held out, presumably for the ticket.

"Kerr's Trio," said Lola, handing over the coded plastic card that served as her ticket, passport, and luggage check all in one.

The Kerr Trio was a system of three Earthlike planets in close orbits around a midsized G star, well developed and populous. A high proportion of Lorelei Station's customers hailed from there, since the journey was comparatively short and inexpensive, as such things go. Lola had chosen the destination for no other reason than its being the first stopover on the first ship headed out. There, she hoped, they could cover their tracks and choose a final destination more to their liking.

The woman behind the counter slid the card into a reader and glanced at the readout. "Anything to declare?" she asked in a bored voice.

"No," said Lola. "A few gifts for my family." The question, she knew, was routine and perfunctory. A few planets monitored the departure of indigenous artifacts, but on a station like Lorelei, where the entire economic base was gambling and tourism, the only things likely to be leaving were souvenirs. The occasional visitor might get lucky and leave with more money than he'd come with, but it didn't happen often enough to be any threat to the station's solvency.

"OK, you're in stateroom twenty-three A, on deck three," said the woman, gesturing vaguely with her left hand. "Turn right at the head of the stairs, and there'll be a steward there to show you the way. Need any help with the luggage?"

"We've got one big case we could use a hand with," said Lola, pointing to the trunk Ernie had been wheeling along.

"Wait over there, and a spacecap will be along to help," said the woman. "Have a nice voyage. Next?"

"What the hell are you doing?" whispered Ernie as he took a position next to her. "This guy gets a notion we're up to anything funny, and we'll be up to our ass in trouble."

"Relax," she said. "This is the right way to do it, believe me." She was right, she knew. Now the luggage handlers would remember them as one more pair of passengers with a heavy bag, one more tip, not as some pinchpennies who insisted on wrestling their own bag through tight passageways. A few more minutes, and she could almost relax.

Robert Asprin and Peter J. Heck

* * *

Brandy watched the legionnaires of Omega Company put the final pieces of the modular base camp back into its trailer. The exercise had gone remarkably well, she thought. At least, in a prepared space, with no worries about possible hostile action and no weather to complicate things, the legionnaires had been able to erect the MBC in the planned-on time. Nobody had gotten hurt, nothing was damaged, and the equipment appeared to be as advertised. She was sure there was something important they'd overlooked, but at the moment she couldn't put her finger on it.

"Piece of cake, hey, Top?" said a deep voice to her right. She looked to see Chocolate Harry standing there, wearing a purple camouflage cap and vest over his regulation black uniform. Still promoting his "robot-proof" line of supplementary equipment.

"You bet," she said, nodding. "If it goes anywhere near this well when we have to do it for real, I'll be thrilled. I ought to find some wood to knock on so I don't jinx us."

"One thing about the cap'n, he gets the best stuff you can buy," said the supply sergeant appreciatively.

"Yeah, I remember when we used to have to sleep in tents when we were out in the field," said Brandy. "Leaky, cold tents, cold ground under you, too. Had to do that again, I'd hand the captain my retirement papers."

"You wouldn't," said Harry. "Neither would I—not as long as the cap'n's running the company. If he put us in tents, we'd know it was because tents was the only way to go, and they'd be the best damn tents anybody could buy. I swear, that man's likely to make *me* re-up, and I'd have told you you was crazy if you'd told me that a year ago."

"Ah, you'd re-up just so you could cheat the troops some more," said Brandy. "How much are you making from that purple junk you're selling, anyway? Where'd you get the idea we're going to fight robots?"

"It just so happens I got a deal on the robot camo," said Harry indignantly. "I'm passin' along the savin's to the troops. They'd never get the stuff as cheap anywhere else."

82

"Sure, and your mother's a virgin," said Brandy, punching him in the shoulder. "We're about as likely to see combat against robots as we are to invade a candy factory. Nah—we're *more* likely to invade a candy factory."

"Hey, it could happen," said Harry, looking sheepish. "The Legion way is, you gotta have the troops ready for anything."

"Sure, but some things are a lot more likely than others," said Brandy. "You're trying to make the troops think you've got inside information, and you don't know any more than they do. Well, since you knew this equipment was coming, you must have figured out we're going someplace where the captain can't just move us into a hotel. But it's a long way from that to these renegade robots you're kicking up such a scare about."

"Safety first, that's my motto," said Harry. "Nobody's gotta buy the stuff if they don't want to. But believe you me, when we get to where the robots are shooting at us, you'll be mighty sorry if you ain't got something purple to put on."

"Right," said Brandy, scoffing. Then her expression turned serious, and she said, "And if we end up anywhere else, everybody wearing that stuff will stick out like a cactus in a snowbank. I don't mind you grabbing an extra buck where you can, Harry. And the captain sure doesn't mind it. But if any of my people get hurt because you sold them something that put them in danger they wouldn't have been in without it, you're gonna answer to me. You got that?"

"Sure, Brandy, sure, I got it," said Chocolate Harry. "Don't you worry, won't nobody get hurt. And if we do have to fight those robots, everybody will be a lot safer."

"Fine," said Brandy. "Just remember. If this camouflage is bullshit, you won't be the first one that gets hurt. But I can guarantee you'll be the second."

Chocolate Harry put his index finger in the middle of his chest. "Brandy," he said, "a man that rode with the Outlaws ain't scared of much the Legion can throw at him."

Brandy stepped forward and grabbed the collar of his uniform and lifted. Big as he was, Harry found his heels coming off the ground. "Maybe you should be scared of what I can throw at you.

Or of what I can throw you *at*," she growled. She let go of his collar, and Harry fell back onto his heels, staggering a step.

"Uh, check, Brandy," he said. But she had already turned around and was stalking away from him. Harry reached into his hip pocket, pulled out a handkerchief to wipe the sweat off his brow. He swiped it across his face, then took a look at it. It was camouflage purple. "Awww, *shit!*" he said, and stuffed it back in his pocket.

* * *

Phule was working up a good sweat on the rowing machine, getting into a rhythm that was comfortable without being too easy, putting his back into the effort. He'd been neglecting his workouts for too long, and it felt good to get into the routine again. When his communicator buzzed, he muttered a single annoyed monosyllable, then put down the oars and lifted his left wrist to mouth level. "What's up, Mother?"

"Good news, sweetie," came the saucy voice. "Sushi says he's identified the man who robbed that restaurant."

"Great news, for sure," said Phule. Then, after a pause, "Uh, it's not one of us, is it?"

"Well, it's not me, and I'm pretty sure it's not you," said Mother. "Who else did you have in mind, lover boy?"

"What I'd really love is for it to be a civilian," said Phule. "But it looks as if I'm going to have to talk to Sushi to get a straight answer. Put me through to him, will you?"

"Why, I can't believe you'd insult me that way," said Mother, doing a passable imitation of wounded innocence. "I give you straight answers all the time, when you ask the right questions. It's not my fault when you ask a wrong one. But have it your way, sugar pie." Her voice cut off and Phule heard an electronic signal: Sushi's communicator signal ringing.

"Hey, Captain, I've spotted our man," said Sushi, after a moment.

"Good news," said Phule. "I was beginning to worry we'd have to hand the case over to the local cops and leave the planet without solving it. Is it a civilian you've identified?" After Mother's semiserious reprimand, he'd unconsciously phrased his question in a more precise form.

"Yeah," said Sushi. "Definitely not Legion."

"Well, that's a relief," said Phule. "Have you told the police yet?"

"Nope. I didn't know whether you'd rather let them make the pinch or do it ourselves. Your call, Captain. If you just want to tell the cops, I can handle it and let you get back to work."

Phule shook his head. Then, remembering that Sushi couldn't see him, he said, "I told the Landoor police they couldn't arrest one of our men without my permission. I'll extend their civilians the same courtesy. We'll offer any assistance they'd like and let them decide. Why don't you zip me the data, and I'll pass it on to Landoor authorities."

"You got it, Captain," said Sushi, and he broke off the connection. Phule looked down at the oars he'd let drop and thought for a moment about picking them back up and rowing some more. But he'd broken his rhythm, and he might as well finish this business. He stood up, stretched his arms, and headed for the showers.

Journal #525

The Landooran police were at first reluctant to accept at face value my employer's information that the robber had been identified. Despite his general display of cooperativeness, they retained a degree of suspicion about the motives of the commander of an occupying force. Having intended to reveal the suspect's identity and then gracefully bow out of the police investigation, my employer found himself instead working to show the police how to interpret the evidence and then lending them assistance for the actual arrest. While he could little afford to spare the time or personnel at this critical juncture, the alternative seemed worse to him.

Now the question became how to assist without seeming to take control of the entire operation. It began to become apparent to my employer, as perhaps it should have some time earlier, that the civil authorities on Landoor were not necessarily the most efficient in the Galaxy at their assigned roles.

* * *

"Tell me again how you know this guy's the one," said Patrolman Dunstable. He was a big, beefy veteran cop, and he looked at Phule and Sushi with the weary air of having heard every possible story at least twice and not having believed a word. At the moment, they were sitting in a police hovervan disguised as an antigrav installer's truck outside the suspect's apartment building, waiting for him to come home from his job. Another team waited inside the building's lobby.

"Well, you gave us copies of the surveillance vids of the restaurant robbery," said Sushi.

"Right," said the cop patronizingly. "And if you looked at 'em, you know they're worth just about nothin'. Those things are so out of focus and jerky that you wouldn't recognize your own wife half the time."

"Right," said Phule. "But in the Legion, we've got some pretty good equipment for enhancing that kind of raw material. And Sushi's our best computer man—"

"Sure, and you think that's gonna nail the perp," said Dunstable, shaking his head as if Phule had told him he thought the robbery had been committed by little green elves. "I'll tell you, the better computer enhancement gets, the less I trust it. The operator can make it look like anything he wants by the time he's done, and ain't nobody in the world can tell you how he got from where he started to where he ended up."

"Give me a little more credit than that," said Sushi. "We aren't just clearing up the picture; all that does is show us the person's appearance, which a good disguise or plastic surgery is going to change anyway. With this equipment, I can pick out subtle patterns of movement and posture that are unique to the person, things even a trained actor can't disguise."

"There's another point, too," said Phule. "Sushi has certain contacts that—well, maybe I'd better not say too much about *them*. But they gave us a much wider sample of suspects than you'd come up with. As our chaplain told you, there are plenty of Landoorans that fit the description of the robber. But the man we're after today doesn't just fit the description, he has the right walk and everything else."

"He'd better have the right fingerprints and DNA profile, too," said the cop. "Arrestin' a citizen for something we can't prove can get us in a lot of trouble."

"Gee, you didn't seem to worry about that when you thought the robber was a legionnaire," said Sushi.

The cop glared at Sushi, but before he could say anything, Phule hissed, "Here he comes!"

They turned to look out the windshield along the street. Sure enough, here came a black-garbed figure, whose dark pompadour and long sideburns were visible even at a distance, rounding the corner just behind a young woman pushing a baby carriage. Dunstable pressed a communicator button to alert the indoor team, then turned to Phule and said, "That looks like the perp, all right. But like you said, there's dozens of guys look like that. How do we know this is the one who robbed Takamine's joint?"

"This has got to be him," said Sushi. "He's the only member of the Church of the King who lives in this part of town. It'd be way too much of a coincidence for another one to show up here right when he's due home from work."

"You been a cop as long as I have, you seen lots of coincidences," said Dunstable.

"Yeah, and I bet you arrest 'em anyway," said Sushi. Then he said in a lower voice, as the suspect came closer, "Are you sure he can't see us?"

"Not unless he's got X-ray eyes," said the cop. "OK, he turns up the walk, we get out and cut off his escape, just in case he spots the inside team and spooks."

The suspect came closer, strolling unconcernedly behind the baby carriage, and his features became clearer. Phule found himself thinking that, now that he had a reason to distinguish between dozens of King look-alikes, how easy it was to spot differences. This one, for example, was obviously of Asian ancestry, a fact the alteration of his features could not conceal. Phule was beginning to understand how computer image analysis could single out this one man from a crowd of faces that, to the casual eye, looked exactly the same.

Of course, once they caught him, they'd still have to convince a local jury that the evidence was as damning as Sushi claimed it was. If the suspect's lawyer got his trial delayed until the company was off Landoor and Sushi's expert testimony unavailable, he might win an acquittal. Even if Sushi did take the stand, he might get an acquittal. Phule wasn't sure he himself understood all the wrinkles in the case, and it had been his idea.

The suspect cut ahead of the stroller and turned toward the building, and Dunstable grinned wickedly. "OK, let's get this creep," he said and threw open the hovervan's door, ready to close the trap behind their quarry.

Unfortunately, exactly at that moment, the young woman with the baby carriage gave out a monumental sneeze. The suspect turned around just in time to see Dunstable leap out onto the sidewalk with Phule and Sushi behind him. A glance toward the building showed him several uniformed policemen emerging from the doors. At that, the suspect dropped his lunchbox and began to sprint across the flower beds. That was enough to convince Phule. "Stun him, Sushi," he shouted, and dropped to one knee to allow a clear shot.

But Officer Dunstable didn't know about the stun ray, and neither did the woman with the baby carriage. Or perhaps the fleeing suspect deliberately used them as shields. In any case, both were in the direct line of fire. Sushi raised his stun gun, then shook his head. With others in the line of fire, he wasn't going to risk it.

Meanwhile, the woman and her carriage were directly in Dunstable's path. He came to a halt just short of running them over. The woman let out a shriek and stopped. But when Dunstable made as if to go around them to the left, the woman took a step back and pulled the carriage toward her, blocking him again. This time, he stopped so abruptly his feet tangled under him, and down he went in a heap, just managing to miss the carriage. He stumbled to his feet, but by then the suspect had disappeared around the corner.

The other cops saw the suspect running too. A group of them cut across the garden to intercept him. But before they got more than a few steps, they found themselves at a thick hedge. A young policeman with a square jaw and muscles like an athlete's tried to force his way through. He immediately got stuck on the inch-long thorns that had kept the others from trying. This left him squealing and leaving behind small bits of his uniform and person as his partners tried to haul him out, joining him in occasional indecorous exclamations as the thorns caught them, too. Meanwhile, the suspect could have walked away.

"The robber's escaped," said Phule, smacking his hand into his fist. "Now we'll never be able to clear our people of suspicion."

"Oh, I don't know," said Dunstable, returning. "I think you've got a good case now. The guy took off the moment he saw us, and that's proof he's guilty of something."

"Yes, but maybe it's no more than unpaid parking fines," said Phule dejectedly. "I want my company cleared of all suspicion, and as long as this fellow's running free, someone can still say we left the planet under a shadow."

"Hold on, Captain, my backup plan might still work," said Sushi, looking in the direction in which the fugitive had disappeared.

"Backup plan?" Phule turned and looked accusingly at Sushi. "You didn't mention a backup plan!"

Sushi answered with a sheepish expression, "That's because if we didn't need it, nobody needed to know about it. Especially not the cops."

Phule stiffened. "It's not your place to decide what I need to know, Sushi. I'm your superior officer."

"And I'm the head of an interplanetary, uh, organization," said Sushi. "Which on behalf of our restaurant owner, Mr. Takamine, I decided to call in a favor from. We'll see if it works."

"The Ya—" Phule began.

"Ya, ya," Sushi cut him off with a finger to the lips. "No need to mention names here," he said, looking at Officer Dunstable.

"What the heck you talkin' about?" said the policeman, but then a shout came from the cops extricating their brother officer from the thorn hedge, and he turned to look. "I'll be damned, he's coming back!"

Sure enough, the suspect was walking slowly back toward them, a resigned look on his face. His body language radiated utter defeat. A short distance behind him—almost as if by accident—a stout, middle-aged Japanese man walked with a small, nervous dog on a leash.

"See? I told you that business venture of mine would come in handy one of these days," said Sushi. He turned to Dunstable. "I don't think you'll have any more trouble with him," he said. Sure enough, even as he spoke, one cop took the suspect in hand, and he surrendered without the least sign of resistance. The middle-aged man walked on, speaking softly to his little dog, and nodded politely to the policemen as he passed.

Only someone who was looking for them might have noticed the elaborate tattoos that identified the man as a member of the Yakuza.

Journal #526

With the capture of the robber, the company's last business on Landoor was effectively over. My employer now concentrated his efforts on the transfer to our new base. And the troops' curiosity was to some degree assuaged when their captain finally received permission from State to reveal the Company's destination.

Of course, that just started speculation in a new direction.

* * *

Tusk-anini squinted in the bright sunlight reflecting off the Landoor spaceport's tarmac, then reached into his uniform pocket and put on his dark sunglasses. Over his warthoglike snout, the effect was comical, but the Omega Mob had gotten used to it, just as they'd gotten used to the fact that the swinish-looking Volton was one of their most intelligent comrades. "Gnat, why Zenobians ask for military advisors?" the Volton asked. "They look like good fighters to me."

Super-Gnat shifted her duffel bag off her left shoulder onto the ground and looked up at her partner. "I've been wondering about that myself," she said. "If Flight Leftenant Qual is a fair sample of what they've got, I'd hate to see the kind of trouble that makes them ask for outside help."

"Hate it or love it, we getting to see it soon," said Tusk-anini glumly. "Why else they want us go there?"

"To show them we are the best," said Spartacus, one of the Synthian legionnaires. His duffel bag was riding behind him on his glide-board. "To show them how all races can work in harmony to defeat the enemies of the people."

"Yeah, but who are the enemies of the people?" said Super-Gnat. "It's gotta be somebody pretty fierce to make the Zenobians call for help."

Tusk-anini grunted. "And whoever, why they our enemies? They no hurt Tusk-anini. Why we need to go fight them?"

"Nobody's said we're going to fight anybody," said Brandy, dropping her own duffel bag with the others in the staging area. "We're advisors, remember? We aren't going to get in any fighting unless somebody attacks *us*. Besides, nobody's said that the Zenobians are being attacked, either."

"Whatever you say, Brandy," said Super-Gnat, but her expression was skeptical.

"That's right, whatever the sarge says," agreed Rev with his usual crooked smile. "We're all just soldiers here, followin' orders and waitin' for our big chance."

"We're legionnaires, not soldiers," said Brandy, frowning.

"Sure, Sarge," said Rev with a little grin that made it clear that *he* didn't think the difference was important. A couple of legionnaires—ones who'd had their face reshaped in the image of the King—chuckled.

Brandy frowned again but didn't push the issue. She still didn't entirely appreciate the chaplain's influence on her troops, especially not when he said things that cast him as the troops' friend and her as something else. There were times when a top sergeant needed to motivate her troops by intimidation and other times she needed to be a confessor and big sister to them. Rev was doing his best to co-opt the latter function. It occurred to Brandy that part of the chaplain's job might be to make things harder for sergeants. That didn't mean sergeants had to like it.

"I hear the lizards are trying to overthrow their emperor, and the government wants us to help 'em beat the rebels," said Double-X, who'd been hovering around the fringes of the group. "So it's lizard against lizard, which is why they're having so much trouble."

"That'd make sense," said Spartacus. "But we should be joining on the side of the people, not of the tyrants."

"The Alliance wouldn't send us to take sides in a civil war," said Super-Gnat. "That's asking for trouble."

"Hey, this planet right here was in the middle of a civil war when we came in, right?" said Double-X. "If the captain hadn't got both sides interested in something other than fighting—"

"Not the same thing," said Brandy. "The war was over when we got here, and Landoor was already part of the Alliance. The lizards just signed on. I can't see how the government would let us be used that way."

"I know what it is," said Tusk-anini. "Legion headquarters don't like Captain Jester. They try get him in trouble all the time. Maybe they trying to send us someplace where there more trouble than we can handle."

"That's enough of that," said Brandy sternly. "We're Legion. The brass aren't going to put us in any situation we can't handle. Don't go asking for trouble, Tusk."

"I never ask trouble, Sarge," said Tusk-anini. "I get plenty without asking." But he didn't say anything else.

Brandy was just as glad. They'd have enough to worry about just going onto a brand-new planet—new to the Legion, anyway. It didn't help to have the troops thinking the brass were trying to walk them out on a limb and saw it off. Even if, as Brandy suspected privately, Tusk-anini was damn likely right.

Then, somewhere in the distance, a band struck up a lively march. Its sound came closer, and the waiting legionnaires saw flags and the glint of sunlight on polished brass and chrome. "All right, guys, let's see you form up nice and pretty for the departure ceremony," said Brandy. "You aren't gonna get this too many times, so we might as well enjoy it."

Besides, she thought to herself, *they're always glad to see the troops leave. It's a whole different story when we show up someplace for the first time.* Not even Captain Jester had managed to change that eternal verity of Legion life.

CHAPTER SEVEN

Journal #528

For reasons familiar to those who have worked in any sort of bureaucracy, my employer's success in achieving his goals was not matched by an equal rise in his esteem with his superiors. Or, to put it directly, General Blitzkrieg's enmity was a constant.

But the company's new assignment had been initiated by State, and the foreign power in question had specifically requested Omega Company to serve as advisors in their current crisis. So the general had little choice but to acquiesce in the decisions made by those in positions of greater power.

But while someone who has no choice about a matter is often well advised to make the best of things as they are, General Blitzkrieg was of a different school. Given lemons, he was not only reluctant to make lemonade; he made the most concerted effort I have ever seen to convert the lemons into rotten apples.

* * *

Major Sparrowhawk cast a speculative eye on the young officer standing in front of her desk. Major Botchup, his name tag said. *Young* was the definitive word for him; despite his having achieved the same rank she had reached after eleven hard years of

Legion service, he couldn't have been much over twenty years old, Standard. *Rich parents bought him a commission*, she thought sourly. It was the normal way such things happened in the money-starved Space Legion.

"General Blitzkrieg will see you in just a moment," she said, doing her best to cover up her almost instant dislike for this pipsqueak. There was something in his face and in his bearing that would have made him annoying even if he'd been an enlisted legionnaire or a civilian.

And above all in his voice, she was reminded as he answered her, "Thank you, Major." He managed somehow, in three superficially harmless words, to convey the strong impression that, despite their equality in rank and her status as aide-de-camp to a Legion general, he considered her his inferior. Well, as long as he could do the job the general had for him, it wasn't her job to find fault with him. Still, she felt like letting him sit in the outer office for an hour or so, cooling his heels, instead of showing him in when the general emerged from the restroom.

She made no effort to strike up a conversation with Botchup. What would they talk about, his hair stylist? Instead, she turned back to her computer and the speech the general had given her "to proofread," which meant rewriting it nearly from scratch to keep him from appearing even more of an ass than he was. Given the necessity of keeping most of his opinions intact (although she did what she could to disguise the most fatuous ones), this was no mean feat. For a moment, she wondered whether talking with Major Botchup might not, after all, be preferable to salvaging the speech, but then the general stuck his head out the door and said, "Welcome, Major! Come on inside," and the moment was gone. The major swept into the inner office, the door closed, and she returned to unsplitting the general's infinitives and unmixing his metaphors, a job comparable to unscrambling eggs.

She was trying to figure out whether Blitzkrieg meant anything in particular by "Every legionnaire must be ready to confront the vissicitous priorities that may have been left on his back burner for the time being but always remembering that the hand of fate has a way of stepping in without preamble or precedent." She had just about decided to leave it the way it was and hope somebody in the audience asked him to explain it, when he signaled her. "Major, I thought I asked you to give me the personnel files for Omega Company," he said over the intercom.

In fact, she had given them to him when he'd first asked for them. She suspected they were somewhere in the mess atop his desk, in which he claimed to be able to lay his hands on anything but almost invariably couldn't. "Oh, I have them right here, sir," she said innocently and picked up the duplicate set she'd made. "I'll bring them right in."

She found the general standing with his hands behind his back, looking out the office window, while Major Botchup sat in a chair in front of the desk, sending a reproachful stare at Sparrowhawk. *Little do you know, sonny*, she thought. "Here are the files you wanted, sir," she said, ignoring Botchup and placing the printouts on the general's desk. The general always wanted printouts; she suspected that was because he hadn't learned how to open electronic files.

"Ah, at last," said the general. He walked over and picked up the folders and said, "Now, Major, here's everything you need to know about this outfit. I don't mind saying that they need a good man to put the company to rights. The thing is, you're going into a possible combat situation, and I'll uphold whatever measures you judge necessary. We can't have legionnaires exposed to danger because of incompetent officers. When I first sent Jester in, I thought he might be up to the job, but he proved me wrong almost at once. No point dwelling on it, of course."

"Of course," said Botchup smugly. "In a case like this, it's best to clear the screen and start from scratch. Make sure they know what you expect, and then hold them to the letter of the law. I suspect I'll have to make examples of a few of them before the rest realize the party's over. But I can promise the results will be worth it." After a beat, he added a very perfunctory "Sir."

Blitzkrieg didn't notice the perceptible pause. "Good man, Major, that's the spirit I'm looking for. Now, I want you to hold Jester to the same standard as the rest of them. I'll warn you, the fellow's spent so much time currying favor with the troops that they may resent you coming in, but that shouldn't hinder a good officer like you."

"I have a better regard for my position than to cotton to the dregs of the Legion," said Botchup with a slightly raised eyebrow. "If you'll pardon my saying so, of course."

"No, no, Major, never any harm in telling the truth," said Blitzkrieg. His grimace was full of malice. *Heaven help Phule and his men when this little snot gets hold of them*, thought Sparrowhawk. Then, after a moment's reflection, she amended the sentiment: *Heaven help the Legion if this little snot actually succeeds.*

* * *

It was after midnight, Galactic Standard Time, and the space liner's passageways were empty, the lights dimmed to conserve energy. Except for a few scurrying maintenance droids, the ship was quiet; even the crew member nominally on watch had dozed off, relying on the ship's automatic systems to warn him of anything requiring his attention. He really wasn't needed. Odds were, any emergency the automatics couldn't handle would kill the ship no matter what the man on watch did. The starship line didn't tell its passengers that, but the experienced travelers had long since figured it out. It didn't stop very many people from traveling.

So there was nobody awake to see the hatchway to Ernie and Lola's stateroom slide open and the custom-designed Andromatic robot they'd stolen from the Fat Chance Casino step quietly into the passageway. It looked both ways, determining its location within the ship—its memory had diagrams of all standard starship models stored—and headed aft.

The robot's incredibly realistic external appearance notwithstanding, its programming was, at core, very simple. While its appearance had to deceive not just casual observers but reasonably close acquaintances of the person it was designed to mimic, its internal list of tasks was short and basic. It could carry on a simple conversation long enough to give the impression of independent thought. It could notice who was listening so as not to repeat itself too obviously when mingling with a crowd. It could respond appropriately to a fairly wide range of questions or to situations requiring action.

As long as it made every effort to follow orders and to protect human beings, it could act to protect itself and to preserve its owner's investment in it, a sum that even a multimillionaire might not consider small change. And so, being stolen had called its self-preservation program into operation. Its Asimov circuits had prevented it from making its escape while the humans who had stolen it were still awake—if they tried to recapture it, it would be forced to choose between saving itself and harming them. Best to avoid that conflict. But now the two humans had fallen into an exhausted sleep. It was a matter of moments to escape the primitive restraints they had attached to it and leave the cabin. Now its primary purpose was to find a way to return to its owner.

The lifeboat bay was a rarely used area of the ship. Regulations required a lifeboat drill within twenty-four hours of departure from any port where passengers had come aboard, but on most ships this was a formality, carried out with the aid of realistic holos. A passenger who was so inclined could follow the drill from the comfort of his cabin or the first-class lounge. But most passengers simply ignored it. As a result, the robot found the lifeboat bay deserted.

A human wanting to commandeer a lifeboat would have had a hard time overcoming the electronic safeguards built into the system. For an Andromatic robot, the process was simplicity itself. Overriding outdated civilian security hardware aboard the ship was child's play for the milspec programming Phule had ordered installed in his robot double. The first thing the crewman on watch knew of the escape was when an alarm buzzer woke him. By then, the lifeboat was clear of the ship, accelerating away. The crewman stared at the blinking dot on his radar screen and cursed.

Once free, it would automatically seek out the nearest human-habitable planet and make a soft landing there. The lifeboat had only rudimentary controls on board, for dodging debris in the vicinity of a damaged mother ship. There was no way to take control of it remotely. The only way to prevent the escape would have been to send another, faster lifeboat, equipped with grappling gear—something only a military vessel would carry.

The crewman looked at his screen again. The skipper would have his hide for this; lifeboats were expensive, and he might have been able to prevent its loss if he'd been alert. He hadn't been, and it was probably going to cost him his job. But he was already in all the trouble he could get into, and there was really nothing more he could do about it. Having come to that conclusion, he yawned. The skipper would learn what had happened in the morning, and that would be time enough to face the consequences. He yawned again and settled down to go back to sleep.

On the screen, the blinking light moved slowly away from the ship, seeking a planet to land on.

Journal #533

To call Zenobia a swamp world is, of course, a gross oversimplification. As with any world large enough to support highly evolved life-forms, it presents a rich variety of habitats, from warm, tropical bays to frozen tundra, from mountain meadows to salt marshes, from rain forest to stony desert. Not to forget, of course, that as a planet that has given birth to an advanced technological civilization, it has by now become, to a great extent, an urban landscape. The capital city boasts as much square footage of glass, concrete, and polished metal as any city of old Earth.

But the Zenobians themselves evolved from swamp and jungle dwellers, and (not surprisingly) they retain the habits and preferences of their remote ancestors. Landscape designers work overtime to create the illusion of deep jungle on the grounds of popular resorts, and some of the most affluent suburbs of the great cities look, from the air, much like primitive swamps. Where a human civil engineer would be looking for ways to drain a swamp to get some buildable land, a Zenobian looks for ways to drown a desert.

So, despite the popular image of the Zenobians as swamp dwellers, it came as no surprise to my employer when the Zenobian government requested that he set up his base in a semiarid highland some distance from the capital city. They were no more likely to ask him to set down in swampland than a

Terran government would ask off-world visitors to locate in the middle of a golf course or football stadium. The fact that it was comparatively comfortable to us had nothing to do with it.

What mattered to the locals was that it was, from their point of view, a completely worthless piece of property. And of course my employer had no intention of letting them know that it had any attraction whatsoever to him.

Of such conflicting values are bargains created.

* * *

The black ship settled onto its landing skids, surrounded by a cloud of dust from the dry land underneath. After an interval, the dust settled and the rear hatch swung down. A moment later, a party of armored legionnaires were out onto the ground, taking up strategic positions. Above them, a bubble turret popped up from the lander's roof, with energy weapons poised to fire on anything that threatened the landing.

When the advance scouts were in position, they began digging in. So far, nothing unexpected had happened. Lieutenant Armstrong, who led the initial party, spoke into his wrist comm unit. "All elements in place," he said. "No sign of resistance; no hostiles in view. Perimeter secure, in my opinion."

"Reading loud and clear," came Mother's teasing voice. "Electronics report no power equipment except ours in use within five kilometers. And there's no sign of any large life-forms within the same radius. So it looks as if you're all safe for now, cutie pie."

"Good," said Armstrong crisply. "Get the next wave out, then. The sooner we get some shelter set up, the happier I'll be. This place is *hot*."

"Aww, don't you fret, now, Armie," said Mother. "We'll send somebody out with a nice cool drinkie for you. Just keep your pants on." She broke the connection.

Almost immediately, the second echelon, led by Chocolate Harry on his "hawg," began to roll down the shuttle's ramp. Where the first wave had been equipped to deal with possible enemy action, this group's mission was to get secure shelter set up in the shortest possible time. For the first time since Phule had taken command, the company wouldn't be quartered in a first-class hotel; the Zenobians' buildings were scaled for their own race, far too small for comfortable use by humans.

Chocolate Harry's team steered a large trailer carefully down the ramp and across the landing area until it was well clear of the shuttle—nobody wanted to spend time setting it up if it was going to be knocked off its moorings by the departing lander. Harry scowled at the site the remote sensors had selected for setting up the structure, pacing its length and width, looking at the ground for any sign that the electronics had been wrong. At last, satisfied that everything was up to spec, he nodded. "OK, let's get this muvva set up," he said. "You ready, Double-X?"

"Yeah, Sarge," said the legionnaire from a perch high atop the MBC. "All systems nominal; ready to assemble on your signal."

"All right, you heard him," shouted Harry to his team. "Take your positions and be ready to assemble."

The legionnaires scurried to their assigned positions while Double-X went down a last-minute checklist, reading his instruments to be sure the MBC was level, the mechanicals powered up, the structure solid after being loaded on a shuttle, flown several dozen light-years, and unloaded on an unfamiliar planet.

"All settings nominal," Double-X finally shouted, looking up from the instruments. "Ready to deploy shelter."

"OK, look alive, people," said Harry. "You've all done this before, so it should be a piece of cake. If anybody screws up, your ass is *mine*." He paused and looked around at the circle of legionnaires. Satisfied that everyone really was in position and ready to do his job, he shouted, "OK, Double-X, let 'er rip."

"Aye, aye, Sarge," said Double-X, and he pulled the starting lever. Harry held his breath. They'd practiced this operation back on Landoor, but back there, if the MBC didn't work right, they could just go back to the Landoor Plaza Hotel and try it again the next day. Here, if it didn't work, they'd be living on the shuttle— or out in the open, once the shuttle left—until they got it fixed. They had no experience sleeping in the open on this world, but if the conditions now were any indication, it was likely to be uncomfortable. Chocolate Harry *really* didn't want to have to explain to the captain why the shelter wasn't ready—not when he knew how much the captain had paid for this full-featured deluxe housing module.

But there weren't any obvious problems yet. The MBC had quietly begun to unfold along previously invisible joints in its surface, doubling, redoubling, and again redoubling the size of its footprint. Somewhere near the center, a pipe was augering its way down into the ground, anchoring the structure firmly. At the same time, it was seeking out the water that instruments had located somewhere below the surface. Combining the water with common elements from the soil and air, the MBC would synthesize many of its major structural elements within the next hour—assuming the water was where the instruments said it was.

With the structure's main skeleton now laid down, the rest of Harry's crew leapt into action, moving swiftly along the outflung structural members to throw switches, open valves, and check readouts. The unit sent additional anchors into the soil, and once they'd gotten a grip, began to erect uprights to support the walls and ceilings. Subunits of the main engine began to click online, and electrical outlets, comm connections, ventilation ducts, and plumbing fixtures began to unfold in place. Crew members marked them on their charts; later crews would verify that everything worked properly.

Reaching the center of the structure, Harry stopped and turned in a full circle, admiring the rapid progress of the job. The rest of the company had begun to come out of the shuttle, too, unloading equipment and supplies, setting up additional structures, and in general preparing the area for an extended stay on Zenobia. He smiled, but only for a moment. Then his eyes opened wide, and he shouted, "Yo, what the hell you think you're doin'? Let go of that thing! You wanna tear down the whole wall? *Let go of it!*" He began to move his considerable bulk in the direction of the impending disaster, cursing under his breath. Omega Company might have brushed up its image, but deep down, it still had the capability for instant catastrophe.

It made for interesting times, even when things seemed to be going right.

* * *

At last, darkness was falling on Zenobia, and Lieutenant Rembrandt scanned the Legion encampment with a satisfied expression. There had been screwups—with this outfit, there were *always* screwups—but on the whole, the MBC had gone up without a hitch and with a minimum of damage to the troops erecting it. A few sprains and minor cuts, not to forget a few frayed tempers, was a small price to pay for what they'd accomplished today. The captain's investment in the new equipment had more than repaid itself, she thought.

By dinnertime, the troops had sat down together in the new mess hall to a hot meal. Of course, Sergeant Escrima had complained vociferously about the primitive facilities he had to work with and the shortage of fresh ingredients—that last would be remedied as soon as they could find local sources of supply—but Rembrandt thought the food was every bit as tasty as what the cooks had turned out in a state-of-the-art hotel kitchen. And if anyone else had noticed a decline in quality, she hadn't heard them say so. That was probably just as well, given the mess sergeant's hair-trigger temper and homicidal fury.

The other camp buildings had gone up quickly too, and there was a second well already drilled in the center of the compound. Chocolate Harry had put up a supply depot as soon as the living quarters were done, and all the company's motorized equipment and electronics were now safely under cover. The company had only a general idea what kind of weather this planet offered, but unless a tornado sprang up out of nowhere, the equipment could probably survive it.

Meanwhile, the troops had established a secure perimeter and systematically begun to extend their control into the countryside beyond it. Electronic surveillance equipment had been put in place, and they were ready to tap into the natives' military intelligence satellite network as soon as the captain had gotten passwords from the government. Rembrandt hoped those would come through soon; they were secure against anything local, but to do the job they had been sent for, the company needed to know what was brewing beyond their line of sight or on the planet's other continents.

What worried Rembrandt was the natives' silence about the exact nature of the threat they were facing. That made no sense. You didn't take your skimmer to a mechanic and then refuse to tell him what was wrong—not if you wanted the problem solved, you didn't. But the little lizards hadn't said word one about who or what they'd called the Omega Mob here to advise them how to fight. If they continued to keep their mouths shut, it could mean big trouble.

With any luck, they'd have the answer before much longer. The captain had landed directly in the Zenobian capital to meet representatives of the local government for a full briefing on their mission here. He wasn't likely to be satisfied until he'd found out exactly what mysterious mission the Zenobians had requested Omega Company for.

She hoped they wouldn't find out the hard way, before the captain got back.

* * *

Chief Potentary Korg grinned. It was not a spectacle calculated to put Phule at his ease. The xenosemanticists who'd briefed him back in the Alliance swore up and down that the expression meant exactly the same in the Zenobians as it did in humans. That didn't make it any more reassuring, given Korg's full complement of razor-sharp teeth. The oversized sunglasses the Zenobian wore did nothing to improve the image.

"It is great privilege at last to meet you, Captain Clown," said Korg. "Flight Leftenant Qual has been enthusiastic in detailing your species' peculiar adaptations for warfare, and it is very much our pleasure to see that you have accepted our invitation to advise us on defending ourselves against the invaders."

"I am honored to have been invited," said Phule, who along with Beeker had attended a welcoming ceremony in the Zenobian capital while his company set up their camp out in the boonies. They were sitting in a reviewing stand of sorts, constructed of some local vegetable material that, without quite being wood, had a similar degree of rigidity and ease of assembly into useful structures. Before them was arrayed a large assembly of Zenobian military in the uniforms of various service branches. They were distinguished primarily by their berets: red for the Mudrovers, blue for the Swamplurkers, green for the Paratreetoppers, and so on. And all of them wore sunglasses.

"I can assure you that the Alliance will do everything possible to assist your people in meeting the threat you are facing," Phule added. "But perhaps we should talk about the exact nature of this threat."

"But undeniably!" boomed Korg's translator. "As soon as we have done with the display of our disputatious spirit and thorough preparedness, all shall be revealed to you!"

The display was long and instructive. Having seen Flight Leftenant Qual in action, Phule already knew how agile the Zenobians could be; now he saw that Qual was merely a somewhat above average specimen of his race. Many of the troops in the review were larger, faster, stronger, and far more agile than the flight leftenant. Several of their weapons (such as the stun ray, the design of which Phule had acquired for his father's munitions company) were more advanced than those of the Alliance races. Korg's grin seemed to have grown wider with each contingent of troops or display of equipment that passed the reviewing stand. And Phule was quite certain that not everything was being shown to him. After all, the alliance was only a few months old and had barely been tested. Any sensible race would have a few hole cards it wouldn't be showing a newly acquired ally. He was just as glad he had gotten off on the right foot with them.

Finally, the demonstration concluded with a convincing demonstration of unarmed combat—a somewhat paradoxical concept when applied to a race naturally equipped with a saurian predator's teeth and claws. Korg turned to Phule and said, "Now, Captain, let us retire for refreshment and some candid conversation."

"I look forward to both," said Phule, and he and Beeker followed the Zenobian leader into a nearby building. To one side, a buffet was laid out with a variety of foods.

* * *

In deference to the humans' dietary prejudices, the spread included several cooked dishes, as well as a selection of vegetables (many no doubt imported for the occasion). And whoever had been involved in the planning had thoughtfully laid in a full Terran bar. After filling their plates and glasses, Phule and Beeker joined Chief Potentary Korg and his adjutant at a table. Korg played host to perfection, making certain that both Phule and Beeker got everything they wanted.

"That was a very impressive display," said Phule politely. If anything, it was an understatement. The Zenobians would be a formidable opponent for any race that went to war with them. Except that their request for Phule's company as military advisors seemed to indicate that they'd encountered something they couldn't handle. *Exactly what was it they couldn't handle?* Phule wondered. *And what made them think that Omega Company could handle it?* It was very puzzling.

"Thank you, Captain," said Korg, flashing his saurian grin once more. At least he'd removed the sunglasses now that they were indoors. "It would please me, sometime, to see a similar demonstration of the Alliance's capabilities. But in due time, all in due time. Meanwhile, as you can undoubtedly guess, we have invited your company here for a very good reason."

Aha, here it comes, thought Phule. "I find it hard to imagine an adversary that your forces wouldn't be able to deal with on their own," he said.

"Nevertheless, we have encountered one," said Korg. "They are here on the planet even as we speak. And yet I tell you in all candidacy, we have been unable to make even the slightest maneuvers against them."

"That's very surprising, sir," said Phule. "What can you tell us about these invaders? The more intelligence you can give me, the better we can determine how to assist you."

"What we have, you shall have," said Korg. "All our intercepts of their communications shall be given to you. But to initiate you into the situation, behold! Here, in the shell of an armored land beast, is what we know." He waved his foreclaw, and an assistant turned on a view screen.

An aerial view of the Zenobian capital appeared, recognizable despite an odd distortion. "This is an intercepted high-frequency signal from an alien surveillance device," said Korg. "Without going into details, I will tell you that this and several other devices have been systematically monitoring our major population centers and military installations."

"I see," said Phule. "Have you eliminated the possibility that these signals are from some internal agency—monitoring the traffic or weather, for example?"

"This occurred to us, but it seemed very unlikely, even at first," said Korg. "To begin with, the frequency employed is not one used by any of our normal communications equipment. In fact, the signals were first discovered quite by accident. Only when it was discovered that the source was mobile did we know they were artificially generated."

"A mobile source," said Phule, nodding. "Some sort of surveillance drone, then. Have you been able to intercept one of the drones?"

"No," said Korg. He reached one of his foreclaws up to pick a small piece of meat from between two teeth. "To be absolutely veracious, other than by their signals, we have had no success whatever in detecting these drones. It is as if they are invisible."

"Invisible!" said Beeker, leaning forward. "That would seem to defy the laws of physics, would it not, sir?"

"It would seem so," said Phule. "Possibly it has something to do with your equipment, though. Our two races use different frequencies, and not all the Alliance races use the same frequencies for their internal communications, either. Once our base is properly set up, we'll see whether these signals register on our own equipment. Have you been able to trace where the drones come from?"

Korg grinned again. "We have made every effort to do so, and in fact we have identified several locations from which they might originate. Unfortunately, we can identify nothing at those locations which we can recognize as of intelligent design."

"Very interesting," said Phule. "You'd think the beings who made these devices would have a base, even if it was camouflaged. Have you sent ground troops in to investigate the areas where they originate?"

"We have done so, and found nothing," said Korg. "It is a puzzle, I must confess. But of one thing there is no question: We cannot allow them to usurp our territory unchallenged."

"Why, sir, have they done you any harm?" asked Beeker.

"None directly," admitted Korg. "Their signals have created undue noise in our communications, and we fear they can receive our messages. This is why we waited to inform you snout-to-snout of what we are facing."

"And what is your greatest concern, in a nutshell?" asked Phule.

"It is mostly our worry as to their capabilities and intentions," said Korg. "No wise race allows a strange beast to sit on the edge of its nest unexamined."

"Well, we'll see what we can do for you," said Phule. Then he added with all the confidence he could muster, "We've got the most sophisticated equipment in the Alliance, and some people who can make it do tricks even the designers never thought of. We'll get to the bottom of it, don't you worry."

"Flight Leftenant Qual's reports have given me great faith in you, Captain," said Korg, grinning again. "I am sure you will come up with a solution."

Phule wished he was anywhere near as confident as Korg seemed to be.

Chapter Eight

The curious thing about the Zenobian Empire was that it largely overlapped Alliance territory. The Zenobians had even settled colonies on planets in several systems the Alliance thought of as its own. But the lizardlike aliens preferred an environment that most of the Alliance races found oppressively hot and therefore tended to settle planets closer to the primaries than those settled by other sophonts. Since space travel was normally conducted at light speed, and the two races used entirely different frequencies for communication, there had been no direct contact between the races until one of their ships made an emergency landing on Haskin's Planet and was discovered by members of my employer's company.

Now that the Zenobians had declared their intention of working with the predominantly human Alliance, the two species were amazed to learn just how many systems they had inhabited in common without at all interacting, like fish in the depths of a mountain lake and gorgeous flowers on the bank.

One of the biggest surprises was the location of the Zenobians' home planet.

* * *

The knock on the stateroom door was expected. With a sigh, Lola stood up and went to open it. Out in the corridor stood a dark-haired man in ship's uniform, carrying an electronic notebook. He showed an ID card and said, "Good day, ma'am. I'm investigating an incident overnight. Would you mind answering a few questions?"

"Why, of course not," said Lola, looking at the card. "Master-at-arms—that sounds exciting. Was the ship attacked?"

"I could do without that kind of excitement, ma'am," said the officer with a low chuckle. "Master-at-arms is just an old-fashioned title for a ship's security officer. On a ship like this, that's a part-time job. I earn my keep by being purser, and second engineer in a real pinch."

"Well, I don't know whether to be disappointed or not," said Lola with a flippant gesture. "Space travel is so ... *unromantic*. I've had more excitement on a hoverbus. What kind of incident are you investigating, Mr. ... uh, Mr. Hernandez?"

"One of the lifeboats left the ship, and about the only way that could have happened was if there was a person on board. So we're checking to see if anyone's missing. I have this cabin listed as a double. You're Miss Miller, I presume—sharing with a Mr. Reeves?"

"That's right," said Lola. She took a seat on the love seat to one side of the small stateroom and crossed her legs. "Ernie's gone to the lounge for a drink. I expect he'll be back to change for dinner, say in an hour or so. Did you need to see him now?"

"Not really, ma'am," said Hernandez, "Right now, we're getting a quick count of passengers so we can determine who's missing. Then we'll know who took the lifeboat."

"What will you do when you learn that?" asked Lola, leaning forward and toying with a strand of hair. This officer might be an interesting person to get to know better, she thought. After all, the ship's purser might have access to a fair amount of money.

"I expect we'll try to attach the hijacker's assets," said the officer. "One of these lifeboats costs as much as a small intra-system space yacht. If you've ever priced those, you know it's no joke. Even if we recover it in one piece, it'll cost us a fair amount to get it back into service."

"I can imagine," she said. "I wonder why anyone would take it. Where would this hijacker be planning to go?"

"His plans don't matter much, ma'am," said Hernandez. "Once the boat's launched, it's programmed to find the nearest planet that humans could survive on, and land there. There's no manual override at all. After all, the designers have to assume that it'll be carrying passengers with no astrogational skills. Trying to land other than by automatics would be sheer suicide."

"The nearest planet," mused Lola. "Where would that be, now?"

"When the boat deployed, we were still within the system where Lorelei station's located, ma'am," said the officer. "There's one marginally habitable planet, listed on our charts as HR-63. A hot one, but breathable air and a solid surface. Our fellow will be landing there, probably in two or three weeks' time, and the boat has sufficient supplies to keep one person alive for a couple of years. I doubt he'll need them for long, though. We've recently learned that the planet is inhabited, and the indigenes have joined the Alliance. We'll have to go through State, but maybe they can get them to take him into custody until he can be sent back to face charges."

"Oh, that would be good," said Lola, trying to sound enthusiastic about it. This was bad news. It meant that she and Ernie would have to take evasive measures after all. She'd been hoping the boat and the robot would simply disappear into empty space, leaving no clues who had stolen it. On the other hand, it might take a while for the indigenes to turn over the robot, which would give her and Ernie plenty of time to disappear on their own. "What's this new race I haven't heard about?" she asked, fluttering her eyelids. If she was going to get this purser to pay attention to her, she had to keep him talking.

"A bunch of miniature dinosaurs," said Hernandez with a quirky grin. "They call themselves Zenobians."

*   *   *

"Invisible alien drones, huh? That's one I ain't heard before," said Do-Wop.

"There's got to be an explanation for it," said Sushi. "Invisibility doesn't work, except in specially rigged circumstances. It's easy to make something hard to find from a certain angle or direction—say, for a magician working on holovision or on a stage. But even when it's invisible from the audience, somebody watching from backstage or the wings would usually be able to see how it's done."

"I'll take your word for it," said Phule, who'd called his new base as soon as the conference with Korg was over. "The point is, you two are the champion tricksters in the company, and that means you're the best I'm likely to get. If there's any way to make something invisible, you'll either know it or figure it out. So that's your job. Figure out how these drones are staying invisible. I'll bring you the Zenobians' intercepts of the alien signals. Anything you need in the way of equipment, it's yours. I want results as soon as you can get 'em."

"Sure, Captain, you got it," said Do-Wop. He rubbed his hands together and said, "Me and Soosh can't figure it out, it can't be done."

"We'll get an equipment list to Chocolate Harry as soon as we've checked out the data," said Sushi. "Any chance of a look at the Zenobians' equipment? I could tell a lot more if I knew what its capabilities are."

"I think we can manage that," said Phule. "Korg says he's ordered his military people to cooperate with us, although I doubt they'll show us any really secret stuff. Anything else?"

"Sure, some dancing girls and a keg of beer, while you're at it," said Do-Wop. "Can't expect us to come up with brainstorms without the necessities."

Phule smiled. "I'll remind you that we're a bit off the usual supply routes for dancing girls; they may take a while to deliver. You can requisition beer through the usual channels."

"Man, that's just not the Omega Mob way," griped Do-Wop. "This outfit does everything first class, don't ya know?"

"I'm glad to hear you say that," said Phule, laughing. "If you'll think back a moment, you just might recall that I'm the one who invented the Omega Mob way. Or have you mercifully blanked the swamps of Haskin's Planet out of your memory?"

Without batting an eye, Do-Wop pointed out the window to the desolate Zenobian landscape: scraggly brush, sunbaked rocks, arid streambeds, low hills in the distance. He turned back to the communicator pickup and said, "You're telling me this joint is some kind of improvement, Cap?"

"Sure," said Phule, deadpan. "Think about it. Back on Haskin's, you were either up to your boot tops in swamp or sitting in a run-down camp waiting to go back to the swamp. Here, you've got the latest state-of-the-art field encampment, and the Zenobians probably won't let you anywhere near the swamps."

"It's still way too much like bein' in the Legion for my blood," said Do-Wop. "But I guess I don't have any selection as far as that."

"Of course not," said Phule, leaning closer to the pickup on his end. "You two draw up the list of equipment you'll need, and get it to Harry ASAP. I want you to drop everything else for this project, understand?"

"You got it, Cap'n," said Do-Wop, suddenly enthusiastic. He nudged Sushi, then (just to be on the safe side) asked Phule, "This means no regular duty of any kind, right?"

"Consider this your regular duty for now, and give it your full attention," said Phule. "I'll expect a preliminary report to be on my desk as soon as I return to camp—the day after tomorrow, if things go according to schedule. Anything else? Good, then go to work." He cut the connection.

The two partners looked at each other. "Well, you heard the captain," said Sushi. "Let's get to work on this job before he decides to give it to somebody else and puts us back to doing real work."

"Man, I was really hoping for the dancing girls," said Do-Wop, pretending to sulk.

"Keep that up and you'll have Sergeant Brandy doing the not-so-soft-shoe on your behind," said Sushi. He punched his partner playfully in the shoulder and said, "Grab your comp-u-note and start listing stuff we can use."

"OK, then, first thing we gotta have is the beer," said Do-Wop. "Gimme enough of that, and I can think of almost anything."

"That's what I'm afraid of," said Sushi with a very convincing shudder. The shudder might even have been real.

* * *

"Sarge, we got a bone to pick with you."

Chocolate Harry looked up. He'd been sitting at his makeshift desk, reading *Biker's Dream* magazine. There stood half a dozen legionnaires with grim expressions on their faces. Only a veteran could have spotted (as Harry did) the edge of worry behind their determined front.

"Sure, dudes, what's up?" Harry shifted his bulk on the reinforced camp stool he occupied. Without making any particular deal out of it, he picked up a bayonet and began cleaning his fingernails with the finely honed point. Behind him was the prefabricated shed that was the company's supply depot here on Zenobia.

"Well, it's like this," said Street, who seemed to be the leader of this delegation. "You told everybody we were goin' to be fightin' them renegade robots, off on some asteroid—"

"Well, bro, that was the scuttlebutt at the time," said C.H. "You stay around the Legion long enough, you hear all kinds of stuff, and after a while you get a feel for what you can believe and what you can't."

Street's face took on a puzzled expression. "Man, it was *you* done told us that."

Chocolate Harry didn't look up from his fingernail cleaning. "Was it, now? You sure 'bout that, Street?"

Street turned to his companions for support, and when he saw them nodding their heads, he turned back to the supply sergeant and said, "Yeah, it was you, all right. You kep' tellin' us 'bout that asteroid full of renegade robots and how we was gonna need this here robot camo to keep 'em from zappin' us. Ain't that right?"

"What if it is?" asked Harry casually.

"Well, looks to me like this ain't no freakin' asteroid," said Street, sweeping his arm around the horizon in a grand circle. "So we done been skanked, is what I think."

Chocolate Harry's broad face took on an expression of profound sympathy. "Skanked? What makes you think that, Street?" He looked around at the others. "I'm surprised at you. Double-X, what're you doin' here? Brick, Slayer, you too? And Spartacus—you and me have always been tight."

"Sarge, you told us we needed that robot camo, and we paid you a pretty stiff price for it," said Double-X, trying to regain control of the encounter. Like the other legionnaires in the group, he wore several garments made of the purple-splotched fabric Chocolate Harry had represented as robot-proof. "But they sent us to this here world, not that asteroid."

"Now, you all must have misunderstood me," said Harry. "I never said we were gonna get sent to that asteroid, did I? I said that's where the robots was from, that's all. Now, here we are on a planet with an unknown enemy. Who's to say it ain't the renegade robots, huh? How you know it ain't, Street?"

"Hmmm …" Street scratched his head. "Well, you got me there, Sarge." He looked around at his companions again, fishing for support.

Chocolate Harry didn't give the moment of silence a chance to linger. "Now, the thing about a robot is, it's a machine," he said. "You can't fight a robot like you would a regular organic sophont. These Zenobian stun rays, they ain't worth a nickel 'gainst a bot, no way."

"I can see that could be a problem," said Brick, nodding. She'd experienced the stun ray firsthand and was among the company's best long-range experts with it. Then she furrowed her brow and said, "But it's only a problem if the robots show up here. How do we know they're going to show up, Sarge?"

"Well, that's where an old legionnaire like me can just feel a few things in his bones," said Chocolate Harry, leaning back and slipping the bayonet back into its sheath. "These Zenobians, they've had the stun ray longer than anybody, right?"

"Yeah, I guess so," said Brick. The others nodded, too. It seemed a logical conclusion.

Chocolate Harry spread the fingers of his left hand and began to count off his points as he made them. "So, they call us here. That's gotta mean they found an enemy they can't handle, right?"

"Yeah, that must be what it mean," said Street, a frown of concentration on his face.

"So what kinda enemy can't they handle with the stun ray?" said Harry, looking at the faces of his audience. "Gotta be robots!" He slapped his hand on his thigh with a loud smack.

"Sarge's makin' sense," said Double-X, almost against his will.

"Damn straight I'm makin' sense," said Chocolate Harry, seizing his advantage. "They've brought us in here because they have a robot invasion. It's as plain as the nose on Tusk-anini's face. The stun ray's worthless, and it's the Legion that's gotta pick up the pieces. And you know who that means."

He stared around at the ring of now-worried faces, hanging on his every word. "If I was you, I'd be makin' sure I had plenty of robot camo, and I'd be practicin' my conventional weapons. 'Cause when the hammer comes down, you're the ones gotta stop it. Got it?"

"Sure do, Harry, sure do," said Street. "Thanks for the tip-off." He began backing slowly away, and the others followed suit.

"If you need any more camo, you know where to get it," said Harry, managing somehow to keep a straight face. Nobody took him up on the offer. But he knew they would. All he had to do was wait for his new story to spread. He picked up the biker magazine and began searching for the article he'd been reading.

Journal #540

At the same time as my employer and I were visiting the Zenobian commanders, they had sent a delegation to our camp. Appropriately, it was headed by the Zenobian most familiar with our race and with Omega Company. It did not escape my observation that this state of affairs deprived my employer of his most likely ally in dealing with the aliens. And while my employer claimed to see nothing suspicious in this circumstance, the phrase "exchange of hostages" inevitably came to mind.

* * *

"Lieutenant Strong-Arm, it is a pleasure for me to welcome you to Zenobia!" The translator-altered voice startled Lieutenant Armstrong, but he recognized it even before he'd finished turning around to face the speaker.

"Flight Leftenant Qual!" Armstrong allowed himself a broad smile. The little Zenobian had been a military observer with Omega Company, both on Lorelei Station and on Landoor, and after an initial period of distrust, he had become a favorite with the company's officers and enlisted legionnaires. Now, here he was, stepping out of a hovercar of what must be the local design. Two uniformed companions followed him through the doorway. "Welcome to our camp," said Armstrong.

"This is a very fine station, Lieutenant." Flight Leftenant Qual made a sweeping gesture, indicating the entire Omega Company encampment, nodding vigorously. "The resourcefulness of you humans impresses. I am here to provide briefing as to your mission at the same time as Captain Clown receives it from my superiors."

"Very good," said Armstrong, who had already been informed of Qual's imminent arrival. "Would you like me to show you the camp, or do you need to get to work?"

"I will instruct my subordinates to set up our shelter," said Qual, indicating a large bundle the other two Zenobians were unloading from the Zenobian hover vehicle, which had landed just outside Omega Company's perimeter. He turned and gave instructions to his soldiers, who replied in his own language. After a bit, Qual nodded and turned to Armstrong again. "All is preparing. We locate adjacent to our machine, so that attaching to it, we do not depend on your power supply. Now, the time is to provide briefing."

"OK, Rembrandt's in command while the captain's away, so she'll need to hear this," said Armstrong. "She may want to bring in the sergeants, too. Let's go to headquarters and find out." He led the way to the MBC, with Qual waving to various legionnaires who recognized their old friend.

At headquarters, Rembrandt, Armstrong, and Brandy were waiting: Phule's major subordinates. Sushi and Do-Wop, who'd been assigned to investigate the invaders' invisibility, had also come to the briefing.

After a quick round of greetings, Qual came directly to his point. "What I am here for is to find what you need in the way of intelligence to carry out your mission against the Hidden Ones," he said.

"Hidden Ones?" Sushi's eyebrows went up a notch. "Oh, I get it—you're talking about the invaders. The captain's told us a little about the problem. We're working on it, although we haven't had time to get much beyond the basics. What I'd really like to figure out is how these aliens have avoided detection."

"Yes, manifest accordance," said Qual. "There is a great military secret there, I am sure, and one that both our forces would doubtless wish to have access to."

"That's right," said Rembrandt. "Do you have any leads yet, Sushi?"

"It's a stumper," admitted Sushi. "But as far as theory goes, I can't see any easy explanation that fits in with accepted science. You shouldn't be able to change the molecules of a living body so that light can pass through them unaffected—not and keep the body alive."

"Maybe the theory's wrong," said Armstrong, fiddling with a pencil. He was always impatient with abstractions.

"Could be," said Sushi, shrugging. "But molecular structure's just one problem. Invisibility flies in the face of half a dozen principles. With all those impossibilities piled on top of one another, maybe the original premise is wrong somehow."

"Oho, Sushi, I see how you are intending," said Qual. He opened and closed his mouth, with a very impressive display of fangs. "Nonetheless, I can tell you, we have left nothing to chance. The coordinates of the Hidden Ones' transmissions were most carefully plotted, and the arrival of our forces was kept masked until the ultimate moment. The site was investigated with thoroughness, and nothing was learned. I can speak with certainty, for I was among the investigators."

"Well, I'd trust you to spot anything that was there to be spotted," said Rembrandt. "I can see what Sushi's getting at too, but I think we've got to assume the Zenobians know what they're talking about."

"I'll take Qual's word for the observations," said Sushi. "What I question is the Zenobians' conclusion. The Alliance uses a lot of camouflage and stealth technology. What's to say that these invaders don't have even more advanced stealth technology than our forces?"

"Well, that's precisely what we're assuming," said Rembrandt. "But the Zenobians detected the Hidden Ones' signals very easily once they found the frequency. That argues that their technology isn't particularly advanced. Why, any properly stealthed signal is practically indistinguishable from normal background radiation."

"So it is," said Qual. "Our inability to locate these Hidden Ones is strong evidence that in one respect, at least, they are more advanced than either of us. It is not a good idea to underestimate them."

"That's what I'm worried about, yes," said Armstrong. "It's never a good idea to underestimate somebody who might be invading you."

"Captain Clown can tell you that we are estimating the Hidden Ones as a big difficulty," said Qual. "It is clear from their transmissions that they are already on our planet, scouting for suitable sites to establish settlements. But they make no attempt to contact us, do not reply to our signals on their own wavelengths. We must by default conclude that their intentions are hostile."

"Yeah, I'm afraid that's the obvious conclusion," said Rembrandt. "The question that raises is, what are we going to do about it?" She looked around the room, but nobody seemed to have an answer.

* * *

"Do you really intend to give that pair of scamps *carte blanche* to investigate this problem, sir?" Beeker's disapproval was plain on his face.

"Sure, why not?" Phule looked puzzled. "I'm sure the Zenobians have their experts working on all the conventional ways to solve the problem. We might as well put our money on the unconventional approach. Sushi's as good on the computer as anybody in the company, and Do-Wop's got the equivalent of a master's degree in low cunning. Maybe they'll crack it—and if they don't, this'll keep them out of trouble for a while."

"You assume that the aliens' apparent invisibility is the result of some kind of trickery," said the butler. "What if it is inherent in their very nature?"

"Natural camouflage of some sort?" Phule rubbed his chin. "I suppose it's possible. There are plenty of species that can blend into the landscape almost undetectably. Although here, we're talking about electronic surveillance, which is a lot harder to fool than the bare eyeball. Besides, you'd think that a species from another planet would be evolved to match the landscape of its own home world, not one they've invaded."

Beeker steepled his fingertips. "That argument overlooks how similar the environments of life-bearing planets are, sir. The minerals that make up the soil are very much the same here as on the other worlds we've been on, although they differ in their proportions. A desert creature from Earth—or from a dozen other worlds—would blend in very well with the dry country we flew over on the way here, I think. I suspect that their swamp creatures will turn out to mimic the color of the local mud."

"Parallel evolution," said Phule, nodding. "Sure, the scientists have found plenty of examples of that. But at the same time, there are always unique qualities to a planet's style of life. Tusk-anini's face may look like a warthog, but he's got opposable thumbs and upright posture—"

"Which I must point out, sir, are parallel to features found in other Earth creatures," said Beeker, unperturbed.

Phule raised his hand, forefinger in the air. "The Synthians—"

"Yes, sir," said Beeker, cutting him off. "I am certain we could trade examples and counterexamples all day. That would not prove or disprove my point, which is simply that life adapted to one planet is not automatically out of place on another. Look how many worlds we humans have successfully colonized. My original point, sir, is that Sushi and Do-Wop ought to be reminded to look for solutions that do not depend on advanced stealth technology."

"I'll trust Do-Wop to check out the low-tech end," said Phule. "The lower it is, the more likely he is to think of it—"

"Undeniably," said Beeker. His face remained placid.

After a moment, Phule frowned. "All right, Beek, I know that act," he said, pointing a finger at his butler. "You think I'm doing something stupid, but you don't think it's your place to call me out on it. So you'll let me fall all over myself doing it, and then pick me up with a smug I-told-you-so expression. Or you'll pull strings behind my back to make me do what you think I ought to be doing, without knowing it was your idea. Am I right or wrong?"

"I would not put it in quite those terms, sir."

"I don't care what terms you want to put it in," said Phule. "We're in a different situation; this is a military operation, and more than just saving face could be at issue. If it's something I need to know, I need to know it before we get into real trouble. So cough it up, Beek."

Beeker drew himself up straight. "Sir, as I have told you more than once, I have no special expertise—nor special interest, either—in military affairs."

"I don't think that's relevant," said Phule sharply. "Come on, now. There's something you're holding back, and I want to know it."

Beeker put his hands behind his back and said, "Very well, sir. Is there someplace we can speak in complete privacy?"

"What's wrong with here?" said Phule, looking around at the apartment the Zenobians had given him for his use during his stay in their capital. Then a light came into his face, and he said, "Aha, I see what you're getting at. Sure, I think we can find someplace. Let's take a walk."

Phule and Beeker walked out the door—ducking their heads, since it had been built for a race just over half normal human height—and headed down the hallway toward the street exit. A Zenobian in uniform—a Mudrover, to judge by its color—was on guard in the hallway. The alien rose to its feet and made a hissing sound; Phule had donned a translator for the purpose, and almost as the Zenobian spoke, he heard a mechanical voice in his ear: "Greetings, Captain! May I be of service?"

"Thank you, no," said Phule. "My butler and I have decided to get some exercise before our meal. We will walk around on your streets for a while and return here shortly."

"It may not be safe," protested the Zenobian. "I must accompany you, to see that you encounter nothing perilous."

"You are welcome to join us," said Phule solemnly. He looked at Beeker, raising an eyebrow.

Beeker shrugged. "I suppose this simply confirms what I had suspected. However, there may be a way around the problem."

"To begin with, I'll turn off my translator," said Phule, reaching down to his belt and touching the switch. "Then they'll have to record and replay our conversation through a translator to get any idea of what we're talking about."

"I believe we can expect them to do exactly that," said Beeker. "However, I think there may be a way to complicate their task." A little smile came to the corners of his mouth, and he said, "Ow-hay ell-way o-day anslators-tray andle-hay ig-pay atin-lay?"

Journal #542

Conveying my concerns to my employer was a simple matter once we hit upon a proper method for clandestine communication, which, if I properly read the expression on the face of our Zenobian chaperon, the mechanical translator rendered as pure gibberish. The Zenobians would undoubtedly find ways to penetrate the subterfuge, but it would probably take them long enough that my employer and I had a short period, at least, during which we could communicate privately.

And, while my employer did not entirely agree with my assessment of the situation, he did agree that Sushi and Do-Wop needed to take my questions into consideration. For the moment, unless we got strong evidence that something more than we had so far seen was taking place on Zenobia, that would have to suffice.

However, I had the strong premonition that only with our return to Omega Company would we begin to see the full scope of the problem facing Zenobia and of our role in solving it.

As it happened, I was almost right.

* * *

Mahatma had just finished tightening down a few final bolts in the MBC's windscreen. Stopping to take a breather and glance at the surrounding territory, he noticed a bright object in the sky. From its motion, there was only one thing it could be. He set the wrench he'd been using carefully into its proper niche in the toolbox—Mahatma was very solicitous to treat his tools with proper respect, an attitude he only rarely extended to his military superiors—and hurried off to find someone to tell.

He found Chocolate Harry by the off-ramp of the landing shuttle, taking inventory of supplies. "Sergeant," said Mahatma, "There is a ship about to land nearby."

"A ship, huh?" Chocolate Harry looked at Mahatma, then followed the pointing finger to the bright object in the sky, now obviously lower and moving in a way that left its artificial nature unmistakable. "Yeah," he agreed. "That's a ship, or I'm full of it." He pointed to the communicator on Mahatma's wrist. "How come you didn't just use that thing, tell Mother to pass the word along?"

"It seemed important to get a corroborative witness," said Mahatma. "When I approach Sergeant Brandy, she takes on a skeptical expression. While it is good that she is learning to question appearances, it is perhaps better in this case for the company to act in response to the appearance and question its meaning later."

"Sure," said Chocolate Harry, although by his expression he was anything but. Nonetheless, he lifted his own wrist and activated the communicator. "Mother, we got a visual sighting of unknown ship approaching from the east, looks like it's gonna land near the camp. Get word to the officers pronto. ETA, maybe five minutes. Can't tell whether they're on our side or not, but I think we better be ready for anything."

"Got it, oh Large Sarge," said Mother. There was just a hint of a crackle around the edge of her voice—some kind of local interference, no doubt. "Is there anything out there big enough for you to hide under if they start shooting?"

"You talkin' to the man with *all* the guns," said Harry, but Mother had already cut the connection, presumably to alert the officers. He squinted at the sky again, trying to make out any identifying characteristics of the approaching ship. "Can't see squat in this light," he grumbled.

"What should we be doing, Sarge?" said Mahatma.

"What *you* should be doin' is the last thing you were told to do, until somebody tells you to do somethin' else," said Chocolate Harry.

"That is why I was asking you that question," said Mahatma, "but you have only answered half of it."

Chocolate Harry turned and frowned at him. The massive black sergeant's frown was rumored to have the power to dent heavy armor at short range, but Mahatma stood his ground, a beatific smile in place. After a moment, Harry shrugged. "Hell, I guess the same applies to me as to you. Until somebody tells me to do somethin' else, I got supplies to inventory. As for you—"

Whatever he was about to say was drowned out by the alarms on both their wrist communicators buzzing at once. "General alert!" came Mother's voice. "Unidentified intruder approaching base. All personnel report to battle stations. Repeat, all personnel to battle stations. This is not a drill."

"O-*kay*, you heard the lady," said Chocolate Harry. "Let's get it *on!*" He dropped his clipboard next to the pallet of battery packs he'd been checking in and headed off at a surprisingly quick pace, considering his bulk.

"That is a curious expression," said Mahatma, but the supply sergeant was already out of earshot. Deprived of an audience, Mahatma turned and headed toward his assigned position. There would be someone—probably Brandy—there to answer his questions, he knew.

And maybe, at last, he'd find out whether all the training he'd been questioning since his first day in the Legion made some kind of sense after all.

* * *

That was a lot faster than I'd have expected, thought Brandy, impressed in spite of herself. The months of drill seemed to have paid off, even when the company found itself in a completely new situation where the assignments and stations weren't already second nature, the way they ought to be in a real emergency.

Brandy smiled as she checked the disposition of her troops. Oh, there'd been enough screwups—everybody knew there'd be screwups. There was always going to be somebody in the latrine or the shower or otherwise less than prepared to have the whistle blow *right now*. Brick and Street were going to have people making wisecracks about their simultaneous arrival at their stations, both more than half out of uniform, for weeks to come. And Super-Gnat had taken a pratfall that might have been grounds for medical evacuation if Tusk-anini hadn't nudged her just enough for her head to miss a heavy structural beam. But everybody was in place, more or less ready for action, and now all they had to do was wait and see if there was going to be any action. Easier said than done.

The unidentified ship was definitely on course to land at their encampment; nobody doubted that now. Mother had been trying to hail it for several minutes, but the local interference was noticeably stronger. Maybe their signals had gotten through, and maybe not. Transponder signals indicated that the intruder was an Alliance transport of a standard model, although a clever enemy could fake that very easily. The best policy was to be ready for trouble. Brandy just hoped they were ready for the right kind of trouble. As to whether they could handle it—well, that was what they were paying her for, wasn't it?

The ship swooped lower, losing speed now. Brandy knew there would be weapons trained on it, in case of hostile action on its part; but if the transponder readings were correct, this model

Robert Asprin and Peter J. Heck

wasn't likely to be armed—or armored, either. That didn't rule out jury-rigged weaponry or a faked signal. She lifted her wrist and spoke into the communicator. "Any word from that ship, Mother?"

"Nothing, Brandy," said Comm Central. "Either there's too much interference, or they're up to no good."

Another voice crackled out of the loudspeaker: Lieutenant Rembrandt, acting as CO in Captain Jester's absence. "Brandy, are your people in position?"

"Yes, ma'am," said Brandy. "All present and accounted for. Say the word, and we can blow that ship to atoms."

"I hope I don't have to say *that* word," said Rembrandt. Her voice was calm, but Brandy thought she detected an edge to it. There had to be some emotion at the prospect of facing combat after all their time in the Legion. Every legionnaire expected this moment, trained for it, knew it could come at any time. It was still an unsettling feeling, standing in a defensive perimeter, waiting to see if the hammer was about to fall.

"Ship's landing," said somebody in the defensive line ahead of Brandy. Sure enough, it had lost more speed and was descending steadily, under power but committed to a touchdown. Now was the point at which it could most easily be destroyed. Once it was down, almost anything could happen. Brandy wished it would identify itself. Failing that, all she could do was wait for word from Rembrandt—or outright hostile action by the ship. If it came to that, it might be too late to do anything useful. She clenched her jaw. The ship continued its descent.

"Still no response from the ship," came Rembrandt's voice from the wrist communicator. "Maybe their equipment's just on the blink, or maybe it means something. We aren't going to take any chances, Brandy. Anything that looks like an attack, don't wait for word from me to defend yourselves. Got it?"

"Yes, *ma'am*," said Brandy. She turned and shouted to her squad, "All right, you bleepers. Get a bead on the exits from that ship the second it touches down, and be ready to take out anything you see moving. Nobody fires until I give the word, but everybody better have a target when I do give it."

"Sergeant?" said Mahatma's voice, not far away. "I have a question."

"This isn't the time for questions," roared Brandy. "Get in your position and pick a target. And be ready for my signal. Do it now!"

The nervous tension along the line went up perceptibly. Out in the open, less than half a kilometer away, the ship was settling down, kicking up a cloud of dust. Brandy growled. The dust would make it harder to see what was going on. She hoped there wasn't anybody aboard that ship planning to take advantage of that momentary cover. "Hold steady," she muttered into her communicator. The ship was definitely on the ground now.

Through the cloud of dust she could make out a hatchway beginning to open. She lifted her stereoculars to her eyes, trying to make out more detail. This hatchway could be a decoy, with the main force unloading on the far side of the ship. Was there movement inside the ship? She fiddled with the resolution, trying to cut through the dust. Something was coming out the hatchway, down the ramp that had deployed beneath it. Something dark, and man-sized. "Brick, Slayer, Mahatma, take a bead on that hatchway," she ordered—those were the squad's best marksmen. "The rest of you, keep an eye out for anything coming from behind the ship."

The figure exiting the ship was now all the way on the ground and moving steadily toward the Legion camp. Another figure, also clad in black, emerged from the hatchway behind it. "Keep a steady bead, but hold your fire," said Brandy.

Now the dust had settled enough for her to make out the figures more clearly. "What the hell?" she said. "Hold your fire, people; those are Legion uniforms." What Legion officer—she had no doubt these were officers, to justify a special ship to bring them here—would be coming here? She waited as the two men came closer. Steadily they marched toward the camp, the smaller figure behind carrying a couple of briefcases and a computer bag. Behind them, a robot baggage handling cart was emerging from the open hatchway, piled high with luggage.

Straight ahead came the two Legion officers. At last, perhaps a dozen paces from the perimeter, the lead figure stopped and looked at the startled Omega Company defenders. "Well, it *looks* like a Legion base," said a high-pitched, whining voice. After a suspenseful pause, it added, with a definite snarl, "Enough to fool a civilian, maybe," and started forward again.

Brandy still didn't know who she was looking at, but she stood up and said, "Halt and identify yourself."

The lead figure didn't even slow down. Instead, it said, "Major Botchup, Commanding Officer, Omega Company, Space Legion." It kept on coming.

"Commanding officer?" Brandy's jaw fell. "Sir, the CO of Omega Company is Captain Jester."

"*Was* Captain Jester," said Major Botchup. He was now close enough that Brandy could make out his sneering face. He was surprisingly young, she thought. He looked up and down the line and made a sour face. "You clowns have had your little picnic long enough. I'm your new CO, by orders of General Blitzkrieg, and things are by God about to change around here!"

CHAPTER NINE

Journal #545

Modern communications are a wonderful thing. They allow persons to wait endless hours for the download of information that the possession of a few choice reference books would put at their fingertips. They make it possible for salesmen and bill collectors to harass their customers during the dinner hour or at other inconvenient times without the least risk of a poke in the snoot. They allow the young of both sexes to carry on endless conversations, if the term may be applied to a verbal exchange almost entirely devoid of actual content. All these are good things, especially if one is a stockholder in the communications cartels that provide these dubious services. Others will no doubt consider them in a less positive light.

Curiously, the petty annoyances of a civilized world are often precisely those things one most fervently desires when one is roughing it in the wilds of Zenobia, and they fail to function in the accustomed manner.

*　*　*

Word of Major Botchup's arrival spread like wildfire through Omega Company. The new commanding officer had commandeered the office set aside for Phule, then summoned

Lieutenants Armstrong and Rembrandt for a closed-door executive conference with him and his adjutant, Second Lieutenant Snipe. This left Brandy with the unpleasant task of trying to inform Captain Jester of Legion headquarters' latest stratagem to counteract the innovations he'd instituted with Omega Company.

As usual, Comm Central had already heard the news. After all, Mother's job was to monitor all communications and make sure that information got passed to those who needed it most. So when Brandy came into the equipment-crowded room, Mother had already taken it upon her own initiative to contact the absent captain. Tusk-anini was standing behind the desk, looking over Mother's shoulder with an unusually deep frown as Brandy swept through the door.

"I can see you two are on the ball," said Brandy, coming to a halt by the main comm desk. "Have you talked to the captain? How's he taking the news?"

"wblftgrwmmmtfts," whispered Mother, shrinking down behind her equipment as she was suddenly confronted with an actual person instead of a disembodied comm signal.

"Oh, damn, I forgot," said Brandy. "Sorry, Mother, but this is priority one. Tusk, can you fill me in? What's the story?"

"Is no story," said the Volton. "Noise and more noise is all we receive. Some bad storm in desert, we think. Mother sends messages, but no way to tell if captain getting them." As if to confirm his words, a rattle of static emerged from the speakers.

"Oh, great," said Brandy. After a moment's thought, she asked. "How about calling on the Zenobian military frequencies? They ought to be reliable, if anything on this planet is. Maybe you can get in touch with them and ask if they'll relay a message."

"Is good idea. Mother already trying it, too," said Tusk-anini. "Having nothing for luck, is what happens."

"Well, if that's the deal, that's the deal," said Brandy. She stalked over to a nearby chair and took a seat. "I can probably hang out here until the major decides he wants me for something, which if I'm lucky won't be until sometime tomorrow. Keep trying, OK, Mother? And let me know if you get even a momentary connection. The captain may not be able to do anything about this bird coming in over his head, but he at least deserves a chance to walk in with some advance notice."

"brglyfrtz," agreed Mother, and she went back to work adjusting dials and speaking the occasional test phrase into her microphone. The static fluctuated constantly, but there was never more than the bare hint of a coherent signal. The legionnaires' faces got longer and longer, but they kept trying.

Finally, after several hours, Major Botchup called Brandy to order an inspection of all troops first thing next morning. She acknowledged the order, then turned to Mother and Tusk-anini and said, "Well, that's that. I need to get some sleep, or I won't be worth a bucket of sand in the morning. Keep trying, and call me to patch me in if you hear anything at all from the captain, OK?"

"tbwfplt," said Mother.

Tusk-anini added, "You don't worry, Brandy, we tell you right away. Go rest, now."

Much to her surprise, Brandy fell asleep the minute her head hit the pillow, to be awakened at last by her morning alarm. She leapt out of bed, ready to greet the day—until she remembered what she had to look forward to, and kicked the leg of her bed so hard that it slid half a meter across the floor. If Omega Company had ever had a habit of turning out for inspection at six in the morning, it long since had broken that habit. Phule's interest in that particular military custom had never been strong, and most of his subordinate officers and NCOs had followed his lead. Lieutenant Armstrong, Moustache, and a few others maintained a spit-and-polish personal appearance and a strong concern for military discipline and Legion tradition. But they were the minority and knew better than to try to impose their preferences on the rest of the company.

Major Botchup, on the other hand, had made it quite clear that this was one area in which he fully intended to change the Omega Mob's image, and without delay. The major was personally rooting out every loose button, unkempt head, and slouching shoulder in the company, with the expression of a backyard gardener discovering vermin. And he was handing out reprimands at a record pace, spiked with blistering sarcasm. Next to him stood his adjutant, Second Lieutenant Snipe, smirking as he jotted down every demerit.

The newest recruits seemed to be particular targets of the major's wrath. He stood in front of Roadkill for a good twenty minutes. "That's not a military haircut," he began. "You'll report to the company barber immediately following inspection, and to my office as soon as he's done, so I can determine whether you're still in breach of regulations!"

"Uh, Major—" Roadkill began.

"No back talk, legionnaire!" the major barked. "Perhaps that's an unwarranted compliment—I don't see anything that looks like a legionnaire here—you or anyone else in this formation. What's that hanging from your ear?"

"It's my club ring, Major," said Roadkill. "Back on Argus—"

"A club ring is no part of your uniform," said Botchup. He reached up as if to snatch it off the ear. Lieutenant Snipe snickered.

Roadkill got his hand to the earring first and managed to remove it quickly without damage. "I'll leave it off," he said with a grin he meant to be conciliatory.

"You'll leave it off, *what?*" roared Botchup.

"Off my ear," said Roadkill. "That's where it was, wasn't it?"

"Off my ear, *sir*. And wipe that smirk off your face!" Botchup shouted. "Hasn't anyone taught you how to address a superior officer?"

"Sure, but they didn't bust balls about it," said Roadkill. He looked at Botchup as if deciding whether he could take him in a fight. "At least not until you—"

"You better forget anything you learned before I got here," said Botchup. "I'm the commanding officer, and you're going to do things my way—starting *now*. Is that clear?"

"Yeah, I hear what you're asking for, Major," said Roadkill with a most unmilitary shrug. "They've been asking for ice cream in Hell for some time now, too. Doesn't mean they're getting any—"

"Sergeant, this man is confined to base for ten days," said the major, turning to Brandy.

"Yes, sir," said Brandy. She refrained from pointing out that there was no place outside the company perimeter worth visiting.

After nearly an hour of nonstop nitpicking and brow-beating, Major Botchup finally stomped away from the troops and mounted a reviewing stand he'd ordered built the evening before. Chocolate Harry's supply squad had worked into the wee hours getting it ready.

He stood and glared at the troops for a minute. Finally, he barked, "There's an enemy out there, and we're going to go hunting for him." For the moment, the legionnaires, standing in formation, made no response. Botchup didn't expect any. He'd made it amply clear by now that the only response he wanted from them was unthinking obedience. Perhaps he might have gotten that from most other Legion companies, but this was Omega Mob. Its members might not do much thinking, but they were *not* in the habit of obedience.

Lieutenants Rembrandt and Armstrong, standing beside the major, looked out at the formation. It would have been impossible to tell, by looking at Armstrong's face, what he thought of his new commanding officer. Then again, his face did not reveal a great deal of emotion in any circumstance. Rembrandt's expression, in contrast, was one of ill-concealed dismay. Botchup's failure to notice this might have been no more than youthful arrogance; in any case, it was ample proof that General Blitzkrieg had chosen the perfect anti-Phule to undo his predecessor's work.

"For a change, this company is going to do things the Legion way," Botchup continued. "You people have been coddled and pampered, living like a bunch of playboys. Well, there's no room for that in the Legion."

"Where *is* there room for it?" came a voice from the back of the formation. "We wanna go there!"

"Who said that?" snapped Botchup. There was no answer.

"*Who said that?*" Botchup leaned forward on the podium, a snarl on his lips. When nobody responded, he continued, "First Sergeant, I want the legionnaire who said that brought forward to be disciplined." Lieutenant Snipe pulled out his notebook again and stood poised to enter the offender's name.

"Begging the major's pardon, but I haven't the faintest idea who said it," said Brandy.

Botchup was incredulous. "You don't know the voices of your own troops, Sergeant?"

"Not all of them, sir," said Brandy. "We have new recruits in the company."

"A good while since, if I recall," said Botchup, frowning. He shook a finger at the sergeant. "You should know them by now."

"Yes, sir," said Brandy, spitting out the words as if they were burning her tongue. Her face was as expressionless as Armstrong's, but even a new recruit would have spotted her blazing eyes, and—if he valued his hide—proceeded to make himself scarce. Very scarce.

An experienced officer ought to have spotted the eyes, too. But if Major Botchup was aware of Brandy's eyes—or of what they might suggest—he gave no sign of it. Instead, he said, "If you can't find the individual who spoke out, I'm going to order the entire company punished. A breach of discipline reflects on everyone, after all."

"Yes, sir," said Brandy, clenching her jaw. "What punishment does the major wish to impose?"

"Extra guard duty," said Botchup. Snipe duly noted it in his little book. "Make it nighttime guard duty—and they'd better all stay awake, Sergeant. I've been known to make surprise inspections to make sure the troops are on their toes. If I catch someone asleep—well, this *is* a war zone, Sergeant. You know what that means."

"Yes, sir," said Brandy, coming to rigid attention and snapping off a brittle salute. "Understood entirely, sir."

"Now, if the individual responsible wants to confess, he can save his comrades the punishment ..." said Botchup, with an unpleasant smile.

"I did it, sir!" A voice came from the ranks—perhaps the same voice, perhaps not. Brandy and the major turned to see Mahatma stepping forward.

"Ah, so, you're at least loyal to your comrades, if a bit stupid," said Botchup. "You're going to the stockade, boy—for ten days."

"Yes, Major," said Mahatma with his usual smile. "I didn't know we had a stockade yet. Am I going to have one built for me?"

"That kind of impertinence will get you an extra ten days, legionnaire!" Botchup barked. Behind him, Snipe scowled.

"He's full of crap, Major," said another voice. "I'm the one you're after."

"Who said that?" Botchup whirled to look at the other legionnaires standing in formation.

Six legionnaires stepped forward. "We did, sir," they chorused.

"No, it was me," came a synthesized voice, and a Synthian slid forward on a glide-board. "Put *me* in the stockade, Major!"

Botchup turned to Brandy. "How do you explain this rank insubordination, Sergeant?"

Brandy favored him with a cool stare. "I don't, Major. Never had any problem with it before. They usually look for ways to stay *out* of the stockade."

"I believe that, at least," said Botchup, frowning at the legionnaires who had stepped forward. Then, as if he was worried that the entire formation would step forward if he keep watching, he turned his back and pointed a finger at Brandy.

"I'm going to leave you to sort this mess out, Sergeant," he said. "I don't care how you do it, as long as the legionnaire responsible is properly disciplined. I'll expect a report. And the entire company is confined to the post until further notice!"

"Yes, sir!" said Brandy stiffly, but the major had already whirled around and stalked off, with Lieutenant Snipe close behind.

Somehow, all the legionnaires managed to keep serious expressions on their faces. Except for Brandy. She didn't have to try.

* * *

Chief Potentary Korg looked carefully at the list Phule had given him. Prepared in both Zenobian and Standard English, it represented an agreement for the Zenobians to supply the Legion company with certain essentials during its stay on the planet, as well as specifying the details of delivery. "Yes, this is all in order," said Korg. The wattles at his throat shook as his head nodded—a gesture the Zenobians and humans had in common. "I will see to it that the first deliveries arrive at your camp within two cycles of the primary."

"Excellent," said Phule. "This will give us greatly improved logistics. Being dependent on material brought in from off-world is never ideal. We're lucky that our two industrial bases are similar enough for us to exchange products."

"Yes, except for discrepancies of measurement," said Korg. "Your units have mystified our engineers. Why in Gazma's name do meters and kilograms multiply by tens, and seconds by sixties?"

"Ancient Earth history," said Phule with a shrug. "I'm a soldier, not an engineer. I just have to use the stuff, not make sense of it."

"I foresee difficulties when trade between our worlds extends beyond raw materials," said Korg, ambling over to stare out a window at the busy Zenobian capital city. "I assure you, our factories will not be happy if they must retool to match Alliance standards."

"That won't be as big a problem as you think," said Phule. "We're already dealing with four advanced races, each with its own standards—and nobody wanted to change, believe me. Most of the worlds still use their own standards for internal markets. But when you become a major player in inter-world trade, you'll find that the profits are significant enough to make retooling worthwhile. My father's done it plenty of times in his munitions business. Just for one example, you'll find that his copy of your stun ray is part-for-part interchangeable with your original."

Korg turned and looked at Phule with what appeared to be a puzzled expression. "Why would he do that? Would it not be easier to capture the market for himself if he made the copy to his own standard?"

"Maybe, but this way, your forces can become customers. He's willing to bet he can match your quality—or top it. And having more than one source of standard replacement parts is a selling point. His customers are less likely to get hit with shortages. To take the obvious case, it's a lot easier and cheaper for Omega Company to buy spare parts from you than to bring them in from off-planet. And if you send forces off-planet, odds are they'll do business with Phule-Proof."

"Very interesting," said Korg, clapping his hands together. "This opens up possibilities I had not foreseen. Our economists will want to scrutinize this theory. Perhaps I will call you back to address a group of them, when you have settled your company in place."

"I'm not an economic theorist, but I'd be glad to share a few ideas with your people," said Phule. "But your mentioning my company reminds me. I do have work to do at the camp, and it's past time I got down to it. Thank you for your hospitality, and I hope we can help you solve the problems you called us in about. I've got a couple of my best people working on possible answers, and we'll let you know as soon as we have anything to report."

"Very good," said Korg. "Your vehicle has been fueled, and you should find all in readiness. I look forward to working with you and your people, Captain Clown."

"The pleasure will be mutual, I'm sure," said Phule. He snapped off a salute and gathered up his papers for the trip to camp. He was especially anxious to see how the new equipment was working in his absence—as well as how the company had handled its responsibilities under Rembrandt and Armstrong. He'd been delegating more and more responsibility to them, and they'd responded by growing into the expanded roles he'd given them. If this kept up, the company would be able to survive the worst assaults of its enemies, who, he increasingly suspected, were thicker in Legion Headquarters than here on Zenobia or anywhere else.

* * *

Major Botchup had ordered Lieutenant Armstrong to show his adjutant, Lieutenant Snipe, the camp, an assignment that Snipe took as license to treat Armstrong as his personal lackey.

Armstrong was already silently fuming even before the pair arrived at Comm Central. He ushered Snipe through the door and said in a low voice, "This is the base's real nerve center. With our wrist communicators, every legionnaire in the company can reach anyone else on a moment's notice."

"That sounds like a security risk," said Snipe. "What if the enlisted men listen in on the officers' communications?"

"Not a problem," said Armstrong. "We have private circuits for the officers when we need to talk among ourselves."

"As long as nobody's eavesdropping," said Snipe, tapping his finger on the top of a counter. "The major will want to take a good, close look at that system. We aren't in friendly territory here. The enemy could know every move you're planning before your own men do."

"Oh, I doubt that," said Armstrong. "The captain's brought in all the best new equipment. It's got security features well above milspec."

"Security features that anybody else with enough money can buy. Or buy the equipment to bug everything you say," sniffed Snipe, clearly unimpressed.

While they'd been talking, Mother had been sinking lower and lower behind her equipment console. Finally, when Snipe turned and pointed at her and snapped, "Who's that?" she gave a little cry and sank entirely out of sight.

Snipe turned to Armstrong and said, "Who is that person? Doesn't she know the proper way to act when an officer enters the room?"

"Pgfkr," said Mother, almost inaudibly, from behind the desk.

"Speak up!" said Snipe. "If you're going to address an officer, do so in a proper military manner! What is your name and serial number, legionnaire?"

"Gmafngbrkshl," said Mother, even more inaudibly. Suddenly she leapt up and bolted from the room.

"What the hell was that?" said Snipe, staring at the departing legionnaire.

"Uh, Mr. Snipe, the comm engineer is rather sensitive," said Armstrong, leaping to Mother's defense. "She really isn't at her best in a face-to-face situation with superior officers—"

"Well, it's time she got over that quirk. If she won't talk to her officers, she should be replaced with somebody competent," barked Snipe. "Whose idea was it to put her in such a critical position?"

"Captain Jester's, of course," said Armstrong, uncomfortably aware that Snipe was likely to take it as evidence in the case the new regime was obviously building against the captain. "You see, she's really completely different on the air—"

"No reason to coddle her neurosis," said Snipe, looking around. His eye focused on a doorway at the end of the counter where they were standing. "Ah, there's someplace I want to see. I hope this is more in keeping with the Legion tradition than the rest of the base."

"That's the officers' lounge," said Armstrong.

"Yes, of course," said Snipe. "That's why I wanted to see it. Or did you forget that I am also an officer?"

"Lieutenant, you hardly give me a chance to forget it," said Armstrong, attempting a rare ironic sally.

Snipe ignored him and made a beeline for the lounge. But he stopped at the door with an astonished expression on his face. There on the couch sat Tusk-anini, seven feet tall with the face of a giant warthog and a thick book in his hands, taking up half the room. "What on earth are you doing here?" said Snipe after gaining his composure.

"Am reading *Seven Types of Ambiguity*," said Tusk-anini, peering truculently at Snipe. "Your planet people never read twentieth-century Earth books?"

"Is this … *sophont* an officer?" Snipe turned to Armstrong and asked, quite unnecessarily.

"No," said Armstrong. "We let Tusk-anini come in here to read when he's not helping Mother. He's the only one who uses the place much, late at night."

"A very bad precedent," said Snipe, peering at the Volton.

Tusk-anini peered back at him. "What you got against new critics?" he growled. "You deconstructionist?"

"I am an officer," sputtered Snipe. "And you are *not*."

"Noticing that already," said Tusk-anini, closing the book but keeping his place with a large foredigit. He stood up, looming over the two lieutenants. "You making a point, or you just like a lot talking?"

"This is insubordination!" said Snipe, turning to Armstrong. "And he's threatening an officer as well! I want this legionnaire arrested!"

Armstrong blinked. "Tusk-anini? Threatening you? That's preposterous, Mr. Snipe. Why, he wouldn't harm a fly—"

"Would too," said Tusk-anini pedantically. "But only if fly biting me."

"I want this legionnaire confined to quarters!" howled Snipe.

"Lieutenant, you're overreacting," said Armstrong. "I'm as much a rulebook man as anybody, but you have to make allowances. Tusk-anini's been an asset to the company, and his reading doesn't lower our effectiveness in any way."

"I see, *Lieutenant*," said Second Lieutenant Snipe. "Well, if that's the way the wind blows, I'll just take the matter up with Major Botchup. And if he sees things my way, I suspect you'll have something to answer for as well."

"Mr. Snipe, I'll take my chances," said Armstrong. "Would you like to finish inspecting the base before you report to the major?"

"Very well," snapped the other lieutenant. He stomped out the door, and a keen nose would have detected smoke coming from his ears.

Armstrong turned to Tusk-anini and shrugged. "Things are going to be tricky until the captain gets back," he said quietly. "Until then, I suggest you lay low."

The Volton nodded but said nothing, and Armstrong hurried to catch up with Lieutenant Snipe. He managed to avoid any overt confrontations for the rest of the inspection tour, but he knew very well that Snipe would concoct some pretext to find fault.

* * *

Chocolate Harry flipped through the pages of his latest issue of *Biker's Dream*. Somewhere, he'd seen an ad for a new modification package that sounded like just what he needed to get that extra millimeter of performance out of his hawg. Thanks to the traffic in anti-robot camouflage, he'd accumulated a nice bit of spare change for just such a purpose. The ad had been somewhere in the back of the mag …

He was still searching when a voice broke through his concentration. "Yo, Sarge, I gotta have a couple of reels of sixteen-gauge copper wire!"

With a sigh, Chocolate Harry set down the magazine. "Couple of *reels*? What for you need all that copper, Do-Wop?" He didn't bother shifting his feet from off the desktop.

"Captain's orders, C.H.," said Do-Wop, leaning over the supply sergeant's desk. "Me and Soosh gotta find the Hidden Ones, special assignment, top priority. Just ask the captain, you don't believe me—"

Chocolate Harry held up a hand for silence. "I know all about the special assignment, dude; that ain't what I asked you. What for you need that much copper? That's damn near a year's supply for the whole company, and we aren't exactly where I can resupply all that easy. If there's somethin' else you can substitute, I—"

"Nah, Soosh says it's gotta be copper, Sarge," said Do-Wop, a distinct whine in his voice. "You don't wanna mess up this special assignment Captain Jester gave us, do ya? He'll be really mad if it don't get finished because you wouldn't give us the stuff we needed."

"Ain't nobody said I wouldn't give it to you," said C.H. He swung his feet off the desk and sat up straight in the chair. "But you do have to give me all the right paperwork, cap'n's orders or not. Now, for starters, where's your Form SL-951-C-4? Can't give out strategic supplies without that one, in triplicate."

"Man, nobody told us we needed no forms," said Do-Wop, a look of dismay on his face. "Can you give me the wire and the forms, and I'll bring 'em back later?"

Chocolate Harry shook his head gravely. "Not unless I want to get in a heap of trouble myself. This new major's a stickler for routine. Forms first, then your copper. That's definitely strategic supplies. Unless maybe you're gonna use it for some nondesignated strategic purpose, in which case maybe I can dispense with the SL-951-C-4. But I gotta know up front."

"Uh, yeah, non-designated strategic purpose, that's the ticket," said Do-Wop, grinning. "Got yer strategic purpose right here. Soosh tells me, he's gonna set up a biomass detector to search for the Hidden Ones the lizards have been trying so hard to catch, which they ain't seen hide nor hair of 'em except their comm signals."

"Biomass detector?" The supply sergeant frowned. "With two whole reels of copper wire, you oughta be able to track a stray geefle bug halfway across the galaxy. What do you clowns think you're looking for?"

"All we know is it's too hard to find by bare eyeball," said Do-Wop. "That's why Soosh decided to rig something special. He dug out the designs from some old program, and he's doin' some custom mods ..."

Chocolate Harry rubbed his bearded chin, speculating. "Man, I know you're just followin' the captain's orders, but maybe you should look around a minute before you get in over your head. Have you dudes ever thought that maybe the reason the Zenobians can't find no enemy is that the enemy ain't alive?"

Do-Wop frowned. "Ain't alive? You mean we're looking for spooks?"

"Nah, nothin' like that," said Chocolate Harry. "I'm thinkin' robots."

Do-Wop laughed. "Robots! You trying to run that crazy scam on me? Half the company must be wearin' that purple junk you're sellin'."

Chocolate Harry's face turned solemn. "Do-Wop, it pains me to have you question my good intentions. This here robot camo is guaranteed effective. Ain't a robot in the Alliance can spot you, if you're wearin' it. If one of those renegade robots gets you in its sights, and you ain't camouflaged—"

"Aww, save the scare stories for the rookies, Sarge," said Do-Wop with a wave of his hand. "Now, are you gonna make me fill out twenty pages of papers, or can I get that copper Soosh wants?

Or do we have to call the captain and tell him you won't let us have it?"

"All right, all right," said Chocolate Harry. He thought a moment about making Do-Wop go to the major to get the papers signed, but on second thought decided there was no percentage in calling the new CO's attention to Supply just yet. That round of trouble could wait indefinitely, as far as he was concerned. He shrugged and said, "I'm just tryin' to make sure my buddies' behinds are covered, is all. Go on around back and tell Double-X what you need. If he gives you any hassle, tell him it's cool with me, OK?"

"OK, Harry. I knew you'd see it my way," said Do-Wop, grinning. "I'll tell Soosh about that robot theory, and maybe we'll add metal and plastic detectors to what we're setting up. Thanks!"

"Think nothin' of it," said Chocolate Harry. He picked up his copy of *Biker's Dream* and began looking for the ad again. Maybe this time he could find it without being interrupted for company business.

* * *

Phule had booted up his Port-a-Brain and settled back to look over his investments—there were a couple of items in his portfolio that hadn't been performing well, and he thought it might be time to divest them—when the hoverjeep's engine alarm began to beep. "What does that mean, Beeker?" he said, looking up from the screen. They'd put the vehicle on automatic for the trip back to base, expecting no traffic or weather problems. Now, halfway home, something was going wrong.

"We seem to be approaching a magnetic anomaly, sir," said Beeker, who was sitting in the front seat near the instrument panel. He peered at the readout and said, "Power seems to be dropping abruptly."

"That's not good," said Phule. "Let's find someplace to set down before power runs out entirely. If worse comes to worst, we'll call base and have somebody take a run out and pick us up."

"Yes, sir," said Beeker. "There's a clear area just ahead. I'll put us down there." He slid into the driver's seat and flipped the control switch over to manual. After a moment, he said, "The controls aren't responding, sir. Shall I activate the emergency signal?"

Phule nodded and took up an extra notch in his safety belt. "Yes, and I'll try to raise the base on the comm." He touched the *On* button on his wrist communicator and lifted it closer to his mouth. "Mother, come in. This is Jester with a priority call. Mother, come in." The communicator emitted a loud burst of white noise but nothing resembling a coherent signal. "Mayday. Mayday. Mother, can you hear me?"

Beeker turned around to look at him. "Sir, if I may make a suggestion, perhaps you should continue to transmit, on the chance that she can hear you but cannot reply. Tell them our position, and perhaps they can send someone to aid us. I will attempt to regain control of the vehicle."

"Good plan," said Phule. "If you can just get the thing stopped, at least we won't have to worry about hitting anything."

"That is what I have been attempting, sir," said Beeker. He returned his attention to the controls. After a few moments, he said, "We are veering off course, sir. The vehicle appears to be under external control. Should we abandon it?"

Phule looked at the boulder-strewn ground passing beneath the jeep and shook his head. "We're still moving too fast," he said. "I think we're better off riding it out—unless something happens to make staying aboard worse than jumping. If we do get stranded out here, we'll probably need the jeep's emergency kit."

"Yes, sir," said Beeker, reaching up to hold his hat. "The power readout's still dropping, sir. I don't think we've slowed down, though."

If anything, it felt as if they'd picked up speed. The jeep was headed almost at right angles to its original course now, and none of Beeker's efforts made any apparent difference. In the usual course of things, if power failed, the grav units would've lowered the hoverjeep gently to the ground—but at this speed, there would have been nothing gentle about it. The only thing to do was hold on and hope the crash protection was up to its job if they hit anything too solid.

As the jeep sped onward, Phule kept sending his Mayday message while Beeker kept a lookout for any sign of imminent collision or other danger. But neither the jeep's built-in comm unit nor Phule's wrist communicator showed any sign that it was in contact with the base. Phule was still trying to give Mother (who might or might not have been able to hear him) his best guess of where they were and what was happening, when the jeep suddenly lost speed and came slowly to the ground.

CHAPTER TEN

Journal #550

Second Lieutenant Snipe was almost instantly dubbed "Lieutenant Sneak" by the Omega Mob. He was, if possible, more cordially hated by most of the enlisted legionnaires than even his superior, Major Botchup. And while the two other lieutenants were more or less forced to tolerate him, they were unable to find even the smallest ground for camaraderie with him.

This no doubt derived in large part from their having seen the transformation of Omega Company, under my employer's guidance, from the least desirable billet in the Legion into a place where one might build a career. Botchup and Snipe had not been part of that transformation; instead, they were seen (quite accurately) as being sent to tear down everything that Captain Jester had built.

Neither the callow major nor his smirking subaltern—and certainly none of the brass who had sent them on their mission—quite understood that before they could persuade the newly liberated genie to return to its bottle, they would have to reconstruct the original bottle, which had long since been broken into a million fragments.

* * *

"Well, Snipe, what do you think of this outfit?" said Major Botchup. He was firmly established in Phule's office, which was specially set up as a command center in the event of military action. A thick stack of Omega Company personnel dossiers was on his desk, and the screen of the major's computer was already filled with his notes.

Snipe twisted his mouth. "A very poor excuse for a combat unit, sir," he said. "It's even worse than I expected. There's no sign of proper discipline, not even among the officers. Half the personnel is totally unsuited for the jobs they're doing. Believe it or not, the woman running communications can barely speak a coherent sentence. I suspect we'll want a psychological evaluation there, sir. The supply sergeant is grossly out of shape and sits around reading hovercycle magazines. The enlisted personnel have no respect at all; there's a Volton who insulted me directly and tried to browbeat me when I called him on it."

"We can't allow that," said Botchup. "Give me a written report with the details, and I'll take care of it. Just looking at these files, I can see that Jester has let them run amok." He shook his head. "They're lucky they've never had to deal with any real threats."

"Yes, sir," said Snipe. "It's a good thing General Blitzkrieg assigned you to set them right, sir. Captain Jester has let the company go completely to seed."

"I've been going over Jester's file in particular," said Botchup. He pointed toward a shipping box sitting on a chair by the door. The box was marked Captain Jester: Personal. It had been brought from Phule's office in the company's Landoor headquarters. Now that the CO's office belonged to Botchup, these personal effects would normally be removed to Phule's quarters, but the sealing tape was cut and the top lay open. "No warm laser crystals yet, but with all you've told me, it's just a matter of time before I find something big enough to have him booted out of the Legion entirely."

"None too soon, sir, to judge from what I've seen," said Snipe, nodding vigorously. "I suspect their combat readiness is as pathetic as everything else Jester's had a hand in. It's appalling that Omega Company was given a mission as crucial as this one."

"Chalk that up to Jester's being in bed with the politicos," said Botchup. "He pulled the wool over some ambassador's eyes and talked him into backing this company for Zenobia. I'm surprised he wanted it. Really—you'd think he'd have been happier with a soft billet like Landoor."

"Sir, perhaps Jester's angling for a political career after he leaves the Legion," said Snipe. "There's nothing quite like leading a unit in battle to convince the voters you're leadership material. They never ask how many casualties your unit took."

"That's the way of it," said Botchup. "The dilettantes get all the credit, while the real legionnaires do the dirty work. Well, this time, the real legionnaires are going to take back command of the company before the dilettantes know what hit 'em. And if I have to put half the company in the stockade to turn it around, that's what I'll do."

"Starting with the captain, sir?" Snipe grinned maliciously.

"Starting with the captain," agreed Botchup. "As soon as he gets back from his little junket to the native capital, he's going to have a lot of explaining to do."

"Very good, sir," said Snipe. After a moment's thought, he asked, "Should we order him back to base, sir? I'd think the sooner you can make him an example, the sooner this company will toe the line."

"No, I want time to build my case against him," said Botchup. "Besides, there's nothing he can do from a distance, and by the time he gets back, I'll have gone a long way toward establishing my own authority."

Snipe leaned forward and spoke in a quiet voice. "Should we take any steps to prevent the other officers from warning him, sir?"

"No," said Botchup with a nasty smile. "Let them yell their heads off, Snipe. If Jester realizes just what's in store for him, he may just cut and run. That's the usual way with his kind, and it'd suit me fine. Then I could get down to the business of turning this company around without any interference from him—or his cronies."

"Very good, sir," said Snipe. "I can see you're not going to be satisfied with half measures."

"Not at all," said Botchup. "Now, why don't you get started on your report. I want to know every single rotten spot in this particular apple, Snipe. You name the names, and I'll kick the asses."

"Yes, sir!" said Snipe with a salute that could have been molded in plastic and used as a model in the Legion Academy. He turned and strode out of the command center, grinning like a madman. It didn't matter at all to Snipe that he was planning to take the best company in the Legion and return it to the mediocrity from which it had arisen. His orders said to do it, and the last thing Snipe would ever do was question an order ... unless, of course, it was to his personal advantage to do so.

* * *

The Zenobian desert baked under its glowing primary, a hot, yellow G star. Until recently, humans had looked at the system and seen only worthless real estate: all the planets were in orbits either too close to or too far away from the primary for the system to be of interest. Except for one very useful space station, there was no Alliance presence here. Only when a Zenobian scout ship had made an emergency landing on Haskin's Planet, halfway across the galaxy, did the Alliance learn the real story of this unappealing world—unappealing to human beings, but not to the lizardlike race that called it home.

The Zenobians were swamp dwellers, evolved from quasi-saurian stock. In the manner of all intelligent races, they had transformed much of their world into the sort of environment they favored. But much still remained in a state of nature, inhabited only by untamed indigenous life-forms. A good third of its land surface was, in fact, arid, similar to this patch perhaps a hundred kilometers from the Alliance camp.

Neither the Zenobian astronomers nor human lookouts observed the fireball cross the sky. After all, there were dozens of such events on any given day, far too many to be of interest unless the objects causing them were large enough to damage a populated area. But this object was no threat, and so nobody even noticed when it rotated and fired braking rockets, or when, in the lower atmosphere, it popped a hatch and deployed a drogue parachute.

And when the escape capsule settled to the ground in a shallow depression that in the rainy season would briefly become a lake, only a few dull-witted desert creatures were there to see the main hatch spring open and a lone figure emerge.

This was just as well, since the figure that emerged looked ill-prepared for the environment it had arrived in. Dressed in a white dinner jacket and starched shirt, it looked as if it had come directly from a formal dance at some exclusive country club. Its highly polished shoes were obviously designed for a polished parquet floor or, at worst, a well-manicured lawn—hardly for a trek across untracked wilderness. Any man with a lick of sense would have been sobered by his first glimpse of the forbidding desert that stretched away from the escape capsule in all directions.

Of course, this was not a man but a custom-made Andromatic robot, designed and programmed to impersonate its owner, Willard Phule, in his role as owner/manager of the Fat Chance Casino on Lorelei. The Zenobian desert held no more fears for it than the hotel corridors from which it had been kidnapped. In fact, it had very few fears at all. In this detail, it was more like its human model than perhaps its builders realized.

After scanning the horizon in all directions, the robot Phule's delicate sensors detected a signal of human origin from a not-unreasonable distance. Without a glance at the considerable stock of survival gear with which its escape capsule had been supplied, the robot turned in the direction of the signal and began walking. There was an incongruous grin on its face.

The unimaginative desert creatures, having decided that the robot was neither a threat nor a potential meal, turned back to their business.

* * *

Double-X crossed his arms and stared at Brandy. "OK, Sarge, what's the story?" the legionnaire demanded. "Who's getting punished and how?"

Brandy stared back at him from behind the desk. In a lot of circumstances, she'd have bitten his head off for the impertinence. But this wasn't a lot of circumstances; the major's heavy-handed discipline had made her as angry as any of her troops. "The story is, the major's sticking to his guns. Which means punishment for the whole company."

Double-X's face turned red, and he angrily blurted out, "Yo, Sarge, you saw what the major did to Roadkill. I'm here to tell you, everybody in the company says that stinks."

"Tell me about it," she said wearily. "While we're telling each other about things, the major's pissed about discipline—like you guys talking back when I say something. He hears you interrupting me or griping about his orders, he's likely to bust humps a good bit more. Not that I can't handle it—or even worse—but a word to the wise, Double-X, a word to the wise."

Double-X looked around as if to check for eavesdroppers before answering. Then he put his hands on the desktop, leaned forward, and lowered his voice. "Man, that stinks even worse," he said.

"A brilliant deduction," said Brandy, slapping her hand on her desktop. "Just what do you suggest doing about the problem?"

Double-X fidgeted, his face screwed up in a frown. "I dunno, Sarge," he admitted at last. "If the cap'n was here, I bet he'd have some way to get us out from under this mess."

"I wish he was here, myself," said Brandy. "I don't think he'd be any happier than the rest of us with what's going down, but I know he'd have some ideas for fixing it." She paused and lowered her voice. "But don't get your hopes too high, Double-X. Botchup is the latest dirty trick from Headquarters, and he's got the full authority of the top brass backing him. I'm afraid not even the captain's going to be able to flick him aside all that easily."

Double-X shrugged. "All I know is, the captain's took 'em on and won before. If anybody can do it again, he's the man."

"Well, then you better hope he gets back soon," said Brandy. She paused a moment, then said, "You got anything else to gripe about, or are you going to hang out here until the major notices and puts you down for extra punishment?"

"Man, I don't need no part of that," said Double-X. "Catch you later, Sarge."

"Yeah, see you on punishment duty," said Brandy. She didn't laugh, and neither did Double-X.

* * *

"Where are we?" asked Phule. He had opened the jeep's canopy and was standing up, scanning the horizon for signs of ... He realized he wasn't sure what he was scanning for, but at the moment there was nothing noteworthy in sight, unless the boulders and scrubby vegetation concealed secrets beyond his guessing.

Beeker looked up from the map he had taken out. "Very approximately, sir, we are midway between the Zenobians' capital and our own base. We have strayed some distance off our original course, however, and I cannot locate us exactly. Our instruments are not providing meaningful information at the moment."

"Yeah, I got that impression," said Phule. He sat down in the seat and looked over Beeker's shoulder. "Does the map show any landmarks in this general area?"

"Nothing, really," said the butler. "But this is an ordnance survey map provided by our hosts. They could conceivably have omitted items they preferred not to let us know about."

"That'd be a lot of trouble to confuse an ally," said Phule, although even as he said it, he remembered being ordered to provide similarly doctored information to Leftenant Qual when the Zenobian had been an observer with Omega Company. He shrugged. "Anyway, there's nothing obviously military in eyeball range. Unless they've got it pretty well camouflaged, that is." He paused. "Hmmm ... we *are* trying to locate an invader that appears to have unusually effective camouflage ..."

"You don't think the Hidden Ones brought us down here, do you?" Beeker laughed. "What reason could they have for that? Although I don't pretend to comprehend the psychology of an alien species; quite frankly, the human race gives me enough trouble." He accompanied this remark with a meaningful nod in Phule's direction.

Phule ignored the nod—or perhaps he simply missed it. "There's not much research on the psychology of interstellar warfare," he said seriously. "There haven't been a whole lot of examples to study, partly because it's usually not cost-effective. But any race that gets cheap FTL has at least the capability to wage interstellar war. That's why there's a Legion—so that if some rogue species tries to attack another race's world, we can stop it."

"In theory," said Beeker, peering nervously at the landscape beyond the hoverjeep. "Still, someone appears to have invaded this world. Unless the Zenobians are deceiving us for some reason."

"I've considered that," said Phule. "Even the ambassador had some suspicions on that score. Don't worry, old man, I'm keeping an open mind about it. On balance, I think they're telling the truth about the invasion. There are still some questions I haven't gotten good answers to ..."

"Sir ..." said Beeker, tentatively.

Phule ignored him. "The ambassador was worried they might be trying to get a fully equipped Alliance military unit on-planet so they could knock us out quickly and gain access to our equipment. But that assumes that our equipment is superior enough to theirs that they'd risk an interplanetary incident to get some, then expect to be able to replicate it before the Alliance could respond. I can't see that."

"Sir!" said Beeker, touching his employer's elbow.

"Not that it wouldn't be a good idea to develop some defense to the stun ray," Phule continued. "I'll bet you *they* have one, even though they haven't mentioned it to us. You don't deploy a weapon that powerful without ... What is it, Beeker?" The butler was now tugging on Phule's sleeve.

The butler pointed abruptly to the left. "Sir, that boulder over there just moved." Phule turned abruptly.

"What boulder?" he said, reaching for his sidearm. But it was too late.

* * *

"Don't like Major Botchup," said Tusk-anini with characteristic bluntness.

"Well, that puts you with the majority," said Super-Gnat, sitting at the far end of the mess hall table. "He's about as popular as the itch."

"Itch not popular," said Tusk-anini, squinting at his partner.

"Sure it is," said Do-Wop, scratching his left armpit. "Everybody's got it, ain't they? If it was a vid show, it'd be numero one-o."

"Having it doesn't mean you like it," said Super-Gnat. She took a spoonful of soup and continued, "Besides, Do-Wop, you shouldn't confuse Tusk. It just makes him ask more questions."

"There's nothing wrong with asking questions," said Mahatma, setting down his tray at a vacant spot at the table. "It's the best way for people to learn things. I have to keep telling Sergeant Brandy that."

"The NCOs aren't sure your main reason for asking questions is to learn something," said Super-Gnat with a frown. "Then again, maybe you've got a better reason."

Mahatma shrugged. "I didn't say that the one asking the question was the only one to learn things, did I?"

"Well, I wish you'd go ask Major Botchup some questions, then," said Do-Wop. "That sucker's got a *lot* to learn, and I hope he learns it fast."

"I hope he learns it without getting anybody hurt," said Super-Gnat. "That kind of ignorance is dangerous—and not just to the ignoramus, if you know what I mean."

"Who you callin' ignoramus?" said a booming voice. They jumped and looked up to see Chocolate Harry, balancing a mess tray and grinning at them. After they relaxed, he said, "Mind if a sergeant sets his tray down?"

"What we gonna say if we do mind?" said Do-Wop. "Hey!" he added as Super-Gnat elbowed him in the ribs.

"Sure, C.H., join the party," said Gnat, acting as if nothing particular had happened. Do-Wop glared at her for a moment, but he knew better than to say any more.

Chocolate Harry slid his tray onto the table and settled into a chair. He took a sip of his coffee and smacked his lips. "Man, Escrima is a genius," he said. "Dude can cook as good a meal in the middle of no place as in the best hotel you ever saw." He paused and thought a moment, then added, "Course, on this planet, maybe we're *in* the best hotel there is."

"Well, I'm not griping about the food," said Super-Gnat.

"Right," said Chocolate Harry. "So what *are* you gripin' about?"

There was an uncomfortable silence as the group around the table glanced at one another. Even Mahatma, who was usually eager to make his opinion known, seemed reticent. At last, Tusk-anini broke the silence. "New major making everything worse," he said with characteristic directness.

"Everything?" said the supply sergeant, raising an eyebrow. "Hell, the food ain't any worse. What else?"

When Do-Wop muttered something foul sounding, Harry turned to him and said, "Yo, Do-Wop, either tell me what you wanna say or keep it buttoned. I can't fix somethin' I can't hear about."

"Maybe you can't fix this, neither, so why tell you?" said Do-Wop. Harry just stared at him. After an uncomfortable couple of moments, Do-Wop shrugged. "OK, man, it's just all the chicken shit. *You're outta uniform, you gotta shave, you gotta salute your officers, you gotta get up at O-five-hundred hours, you gotta say 'sir' when you talk to me, yada yada yada, blah blah blah.* We were doin' fine without that crap, so what's the major gotta bring it in for?"

"He does not respond to questions," added Mahatma.

"He says he going to break up partners," said Tusk-anini, glowering as only he could. His huge hand rested on Super-Gnat's shoulder.

"That's his rights, you know," said Chocolate Harry reasonably. "Most other Legion units, they ain't got partners."

"We Omega Mob, not other Legion," said Tusk-anini. "Omega Mob better than other Legion. Don't care about other units. Major take good company, make it bad again. Don't like that."

Chocolate Harry looked at Tusk-anini, then at the other faces all turned toward him, awaiting his answer. "Yeah," he said at last,

"I hear ya. Now, bein' a sergeant, there ain't much I can say against the major. But maybe there's a few things people could do. You didn't hear it from me, but think about this ..."

The supply sergeant spoke briefly and quietly. By the time he was done, his little circle of listeners was nodding in approval. "Yeah," said Super-Gnat. "I think you've got an idea or two there, Sarge. I'll pass word along to a couple of people, and we'll see what happens."

"You're on your own. You know that," cautioned Chocolate Harry. "Remember, you never heard anything from me."

Super-Gnat grinned. "Heard from you? I haven't heard anything from you except that spiel about renegade robots, and we all know better than to believe that stuff."

* * *

Perimeter guard duty was assigned on a rotating basis. Tonight, Garbo and Brick had drawn the first nighttime watch. They'd come on board at the same time, new recruits assigned to the Omega Mob at Lorelei. Noticing that both of them were standoffish in the company of their own kind, Phule decided to try the two of them as a team. Surprisingly, after a brief period of awkwardness, the two loners—one Gambolt, one human—had forged some sort of bond and were now almost inseparable, off duty as well as on.

Lieutenant Armstrong met them at their post and checked their equipment. "Most of this is standard Legion issue," he said. "Brandy should've shown you how it works. Have you had a chance to check out the new night goggles, though?"

"Yeah, they're super triff," said Brick, who'd picked up a fair share of Landooran slang during their stay on that planet. "I don't think Garbo likes 'em, though."

"Really?" said Armstrong. "Why not?"

"They hurt my eyes. All the colors are wrong," said the Gambolt, speaking through the translator. "Besides, they don't show me anything I can't already see."

"Ah, that's right," said Armstrong, snapping his fingers. "Our Terran cats can see in the dark. Stands to reason that you Gambolts can, too."

"She sees as much without 'em as I can with 'em," said Brick, her voice showing pride at her partner's abilities. "And she's right about the colors—they *are* weird, but I can see so much more, I don't mind."

"Well, you're not likely to see much tonight," said Armstrong. "We've swept the area for a kilometer in all directions, and there's nothing bigger than a floon out there—and none of it is dangerous to something human-sized. So stay alert, but don't get trigger-happy."

"Yes, sir," said Brick. "What if something unexpected shows up?"

"As long as it doesn't attack, let it be," said the lieutenant. "We've got a perimeter fence set to give a little warning zap to any local vermin that try to cross it. Anything that keeps coming in spite of the zap, don't be heroes. Hit it with the stunners, then call Mother, and she'll get you backup pronto. Got it?"

"Yes, sir," said Garbo. "Stun and call in. Will do, sir."

"Carry on, then," said Armstrong, and he strode back to the MBC.

After the lieutenant was out of earshot, Brick peered out into the brush and said, "This place gives me the freddies, Garbo. I've never been anyplace where it gets so dark at night."

"You grow up in the city, no?" the Gambolt asked.

"Yeah, sure did," said Brick. "Plenty of light, plenty of people. This place is just too … *empty* for me."

"City's scarier, if you ask me," said Garbo. The two sentries began walking slowly along the perimeter, keeping their gaze turned out into the dark around the camp. "You get too many beings in one place, some of them are going to be bad ones. Out here, just a few animals to worry about, and mostly they mind their own business."

"Just a few animals?" Brick stared out into the darkness. "Maybe. But if there's just animals, why's the major got us out on guard duty? There's got to be something else out there—maybe those Hidden Ones the Zenobians are talking about."

"If you ask me, I think the Hidden Ones will stay hidden," said Garbo, scoffing. "They have no reason to bother us—"

There was a loud crack from somewhere in the dark outside the perimeter. "Ssst! What's that?" Brick hissed suddenly. She turned and pointed into the darkness, crouching to present a smaller target.

"Something moving," said Garbo, ducking down beside her partner. "Something big. Wind's the wrong way to pick up scent."

"There's not supposed to *be* anything big out there," said Brick, her voice a whisper. "What do we do?"

"Remember orders," murmured Garbo. "First wait and see. It might not come any closer. If it does, we use stunners and call for backup."

"Stunners, right," said Brick nervously. She clicked off the safety on her stunner and peered over its sights toward where the sounds had come from. Not for the first time, she wished she had the Gambolt's hypersensitive ears and nose. Even with the night vision goggles, it was hard to make out anything beyond the edge of the camp. The landscape appeared in false colors, according to temperature; in Earth-like ecologies, that meant that large life-forms generally stood out in bright contrast to the cooler background. But here, with only a few warm-blooded native life-forms, the colors were uniformly muted. And despite the noise they'd heard, nothing seemed to be moving.

Then, slowly, from a small arroyo a short distance away, a large form loomed up and began advancing toward them. In the night goggles, it stood out as a bright, throbbing presence, big as a man, moving directly toward the waiting sentries. "Gemini!" said Brick, and without waiting, she raised her weapon toward it.

"Hold it; that's a person," said Garbo, but she was too late: Brick had already depressed the firing stud.

In the night goggles, the stun ray appeared as a narrow cone of blue green light expanding toward the target. The cone enveloped the approaching figure, which was suddenly surrounded by a haze of reflection, and Brick lowered the muzzle of her weapon, waiting for the target to fall.

Except this time, nothing happened.

The figure continued to advance on them. "Stop or I'll shoot," shouted Brick, now thoroughly befuddled by her stunner's failure. "Put your hands up!" She aimed the stunner toward its head even while she wondered what she was supposed to do now that the weapon wasn't working. It *must* be broken; she'd seen it hit the target, no question at all. But if it wasn't working, what was she going to do if the intruder attacked? Then it came to a stop, facing them, and raised its hands.

"Identify yourself!" she shouted. Behind her, Garbo was calling Mother, asking for backup.

"No reason to shoot," came an eerily familiar voice. "I'm not armed. Can I come closer?"

"The captain!" Brick said, standing up to look more closely. It was impossible to make out facial features at this distance, especially with the odd color substitutions she saw in the night goggles; but the voice was undeniably Captain Jester's.

Garbo turned to look. "It can't be," the Gambolt said; then, after a long stare into the darkness, she whispered, "Let's play it safe. Keep him covered till the backup gets here. We'll let somebody else decide." She raised her voice. "Stay right there; we've got you covered. Don't move, and we won't hurt you."

"I won't move," came Phule's voice, sounding far more cheerful and reasonable than someone stopped at gunpoint by his own troops ought to sound. "I hope your backup comes before too long, though. It's no fun waiting in the dark."

"It'll be here," said Brick, trying to sound tougher than she felt. "You just stay put till then."

The captain's voice chuckled. "I'm not going anywhere," it said. "Not yet."

Brick barely had time to start wondering about that before the backup arrived, and she and Garbo were off the hook.

CHAPTER ELEVEN

Journal #560

T he *Andromatic robot duplicate of my employer was programmed to impersonate him in his role as casino owner. It had seemed sufficient to give it only a perfunctory knowledge of military protocol. After all, the "troops" at the Fat Chance Casino were in fact actors, most of them without actual military experience. On the off chance that the casino might play host to a current or former Legion officer, the robot was programmed to sidestep any talk of military matters in favor of more general topics. To date, nobody had noticed the impersonation.*

It was only when the robot walked into a Legion camp, where its real-life counterpart was a key figure, that these omissions became critical. And, of course, the one person who could have set things straight was a considerable distance away.

* * *

Phule came awake to find himself in a tentlike structure, except that the walls and roof seemed to be made of something other than cloth. There was a dull ache at the base of his skull, as if he'd been drinking at the kind of place the enlisted Legion frequented. "Where am I?" he asked, aware even as he said the words that he was acting out the oldest cliché in the books.

"Sir, we seem to have been taken prisoner by the Hidden Ones," said Beeker's voice, close to his right ear. "They apparently used something much like the Zenobian stun ray to subdue us."

"Have you seen them?" Phule sat up and reached out to touch the walls of their current lodging. The material was soft and smooth but had very little give to it. There was no sign of any opening to the outside, although the air seemed reasonably fresh.

"Not a glimpse of them," said Beeker. "But I haven't been conscious much longer than you, sir. Perhaps they'll make their appearance now that we're both awake."

"I hope they're *going* to make an appearance," said Phule, experimentally poking another portion of the walls. "I can't see any way out of here."

"One would assume we've been kept alive deliberately, sir," said Beeker. "Had our captors intended our demise, I doubt we would have awakened at all."

Phule grimaced. "That assumes a lot. If we've been captured by aliens of an unknown race, we can't take anything for granted. Remember, the Zenobians like their meat freshly killed …"

"I should certainly hope we aren't being saved for *that* purpose, sir," said Beeker, his face as unperturbed as ever, although Phule thought he noticed an unusual degree of stress in the butler's voice.

"I'll settle for not being starved to death," said Phule. "Whoever's captured us doesn't necessarily know what we like to eat—or how often. We could be in a real pickle."

"Sir, I should consider our present situation to be a 'real pickle,' as far as I understand the term," said Beeker. "It is not too early to begin thinking of escape."

"Yeah, we've got to look into that," said Phule. "But we're not going to rush into it. We've got a golden opportunity to find out who these Hidden Ones are—or whatever they call themselves. It's a good thing we have a couple of translators in the jeep; at least, when they do show up, we'll be able to communicate with them."

"A very debatable assumption, sir," said Beeker. "Why, I find some of your legionnaires all but incomprehensible, despite our nominal possession of a common tongue. But above and beyond that question, we cannot take it for granted that our captors will allow us to retrieve our equipment from the hovercar."

"Hmmm ... that *would* complicate things," said Phule. "How are you at sign language?"

"Quite competent within a very narrow range, sir," said Beeker. "I am certain that I can communicate hostility and frustration with no risk of misunderstanding. More complex matters might exceed my abilities."

Phule nodded. "Well, I might not be able to do much better. But between the two of us, we'll have to figure out how to convince them to let us get hold of those translators. Once I can actually talk to them—"

"Sir!" said Beeker, in an urgent whisper. "Something's happening."

"Where?" said Phule. Beeker's pointing finger gave him the answer. One end of the enclosure was turning darker and becoming porous, as if it were made of some fibrous substance. Together, they backed off and stood watching. Whatever was going to happen to them, it was evidently happening now.

* * *

"What were you doing in the desert out there?" said Lieutenant Armstrong. He and Phule were huddled together in the comm center, just out of sight of Mother. Cool drinks had been brought out, and both were slaking their thirst—though the captain was taking only small sips. Satisfied that the captain was displaying no evidence of physical distress, Armstrong began a rapid-fire series of questions. "Did something happen to your hovercar? Are you hurt? And where's Beeker?"

"Slow down, Lieutenant, slow down," said the captain with an easy smile. "That's a lot of questions to throw at a fellow all at once. But no, I'm not hurt, just a little dusted up is all. I'll be fine after a shower and a change of outfit—and a cool drink. As for Beeker, the old rascal's off-station, taking care of some business for me. He'll be back as soon as he's got it all wrapped up."

"Well, I'm glad you're not hurt, Captain," said Armstrong, somewhat reassured. "How did the negotiations with the Zenobians go? We're starting to wonder if—"

"Don't worry, old fellow. Everything's under control," said Phule, still smiling. "Now's when you should be relaxing, letting yourself enjoy things. There'll never be a better chance."

"Do you really think so, sir?" said Armstrong, surprised. "I know you think I'm a bit inflexible sometimes, but with a new CO on board, this hardly seems the time to slack off—"

"No time better, Lieutenant," said Phule. "Here we are jawing at each other, when you could be out winning yourself a fortune. And I need to get that shower."

"A fortune?" Armstrong frowned. "Well, perhaps I haven't paid as much attention to my investments ... not that this seems quite the proper time for that ... besides, we need to get you ready to meet the new CO as soon as possible."

But even as he spoke, Phule clapped him on the back and winked at him. Then the captain turned and headed back toward the center of the camp, leaving Armstrong to puzzle over what he'd meant. Since Armstrong had been trying, without notable success, to figure out his captain ever since Phule had first arrived at Omega Company, Phule's words set off no alarm bells in his head.

The fact that they didn't goes a long way to explain why, after three years in the Legion, Armstrong had risen to no higher rank than Lieutenant.

* * *

"We've got some kind of signal," said Sushi. His gaze was fixed on the primitive instrument sitting atop the makeshift desk in the room he shared with Do-Wop.

"Y'know, that's about the tenth time you've said that," said Do-Wop, looking up from the handheld action game he was playing. "Last about nine times, what you got when it was all over was nothin'. Flat-out, I mean, *nothin'*. And that's just with *this* gizmo—what is it, the third different one you've built?"

"I really appreciate the support," said Sushi, his gaze still on the readouts. His hand moved a potentiometer a tiny notch higher, and one of the readouts registered an increase in the signal. "It's times like this, when a man starts to think he's completely on the wrong track, that positive input from coworkers is so important."

"Huh?" said Do-Wop.

Now Sushi looked up at his partner. "What I'm saying is, you're part of this project too. And this isn't just some wild banth chase; we're here to help the Zenobians find those invisible aliens. The captain gave us this job, and until he tells us to quit, we're going to keep working on it. Even if there are a few false starts."

Do-Wop scratched his head. "What about the new major? He's pretty much thrown the captain's ideas out the window."

"What he doesn't know won't hurt him," said Sushi. "He hasn't told us to quit, and until he does, we don't worry about what he thinks. In fact, since what we're doing is a direct part of our mission, maybe the major will let us keep doing it even though he didn't think it up himself. I hope so, anyhow, because I think there's more to be found out there than just those aliens."

"Yeah? Such as?"

"Beeker," said Sushi. "The captain's back, but he hasn't said much about Beeker, and that's suspicious, in my book. Maybe he's putting on an act, trying to make the major underestimate him. Maybe when he's ready, he's going to spring a surprise. He'll solve the Zenobian mystery all by himself and make the major look like a nineteenth wheel. That'll show the brass that we didn't need a new CO after all, and they'll give the company back to him."

"The Legion don't work like that," said Do-Wop dubiously.

"No, but the captain does," said Sushi. "And if you ask me to bet on whether the captain can outsmart the Legion, I'd put my money on him every single time."

"I still don't get it," said Do-Wop. "If the captain's playing some kinda game, what's Beeker gonna do out there in the brush?"

"I think the captain and Beeker found the aliens," said Sushi. "And at just about the same time, they found out the brass had sent the major to take over the company. I bet the captain got the news and decided to come back on his own. He left Beeker behind to negotiate with the aliens—in fact, I bet the signal we're picking up has something to do with that—it's sure not anything on our usual frequencies."

"Yeah, well, maybe you're right," admitted Do-Wop. He bent over and looked over Sushi's shoulder at the readout, then said, "But what if this signal's as bogus as the others? You can't get anywhere if all you've got is phony signals that disappear right after you discover 'em."

"I spent last night putting in a refinement to the system," said Sushi. "Last night, when you were sleeping like a log. Now, with any luck, I can get a fix on these signals before they fade out. In fact ..." He reached out and pushed a button on the console. A light started blinking.

"What's that?" said Do-Wop.

"You should've paid more attention when we were setting this thing up," said Sushi. "It's a recording disc, and with the information we'll have saved on it, we can pinpoint the origin of this signal, even if it fades out."

"Oh yeah? Where's it from?"

Sushi looked at his readouts. "I have to do the math to be sure, but at a guess, I'd say just about halfway between here and the Zenobian capital city. Right on the captain's course."

* * *

The opening in the wall had revealed only two dishes containing food and two cups of water. The food was warm, if a bit bland. One dish could have been passed off as mashed potatoes with a dash of cinnamon, and another was a sort of meat that tasted remarkably like ... baked chicken. The water was cool and fresh. At least their captors did not intend to starve them.

The question remained: What kinds of creatures had taken them prisoner, and why? The evidence remained scanty; even the dishes were of unexceptional design, made of a ceramic material that could have been produced on any of a hundred worlds. And they had still seen nothing of the creatures who made them.

"It's amazing that the Hidden Ones have managed to avoid detection by the Zenobians," said Phule. "Why, they must have been right under their noses—"

"Not necessarily, sir," said Beeker. "If you remember, the Zenobians avoid the dryer areas of the planet. They're no more familiar with them than humans are with the polar regions of our own worlds. We've sent out a few exploring parties, but we can hardly claim to know them intimately. An alien race adapted to arctic conditions that landed near the South Pole of Landoor or Haskin's Planet could escape notice for many years. In fact, on many worlds, there are reports from sparsely inhabited areas of large animals that have not yet been seen by scientists."

"Large animals are one thing," said Phule. "An invasion by a space-going race is something else entirely."

"In theory, sir, I agree," said Beeker. "But if the aliens were not aggressive, there might be a considerable interval before they interacted. Especially if the invaders find the swampy areas of this world as unattractive as the natives do the deserts, there is no reason they would have come into contact before now."

Phule grimaced. "They're welcome to the swamps and deserts both," he said, fanning himself with his hat. "Anyhow, we know for a fact they're here, just not what they look like. Now, if we can get them to return us to the hoverjeep, we can use the translator instead of trying to communicate by gestures and guesses. Any ideas how we can do that?"

Beeker leaned his chin on the back of his right hand. "We appear to need the translator to communicate, yet we cannot communicate to our captors that we require it. This is the sort of circular logic puzzle that one might find diverting if one were to read about it in a story."

"Maybe you like that kind of puzzle, but it's driving me crazy," said Phule. "If you find it so diverting, you're welcome to solve it yourself."

"Alas, sir, I have already devoted considerable thought to it," said Beeker imperturbably. "As yet, I have not obtained a satisfactory result. I continue to ponder the question."

"Ponder faster, Beek," said Phule. "Getting out of this cell may depend on it. Not to mention getting something better to eat …" He pointed at the remains of their meal.

Beeker shrugged. "I find it as bland as you do, sir. But for all we know, from our captors' point of view, this may be the equivalent of five-star cuisine."

"Nobody gives prisoners five-star cuisine," said Phule. "Not even the condemned man's last meal." He stopped and looked at his butler with sudden apprehension. "I wish I hadn't thought of that."

"One would not expect an alien race to be cognizant of that tradition," said Beeker. "We need not fear on that account, sir. Nor, I think, do we need to fear that they are fattening us for the slaughter."

"Beeker, you can't imagine what a relief it is to hear that," said Phule. "My whole outlook on life just brightened, you know? Why, I can almost reconcile myself to spending the rest of my days locked up in this … whatever it is."

"You really shouldn't attempt sarcasm unless you have a proper sense of how to deploy it, sir," said Beeker. "Sarcasm ought to come from a position of assured superiority. It undermines the entire effect to end a sentence with a phrase that so openly admits one's ignorance as 'whatever it is.'"

Phule stared at the butler a moment, then sat down in a corner of the enclosure. "The ironic thing is, I've just figured out what this place is, five seconds too late to get any use out of it."

"Really, sir?" Beeker's eyebrow went up a notch. "What, pray tell, would you call this place, then?"

"A torture chamber. What else would you call a place you have to share with somebody who corrects every remark you make?"

"Perhaps you are right, sir," said Beeker. "I hadn't seen it in quite that light. And after all, it does work both ways."

Phule looked up. "Both ways? What do you mean?"

"What else would you call a place where your only companion is constantly making remarks that cry out for correction?"

* * *

"Where is Captain Jester?" demanded Major Botchup. His tone suggested that anyone who couldn't answer was in trouble. "Mr. Snipe tells me the fellow's come sneaking back. Why hasn't he reported to me?"

"Yes, sir, the captain has returned," said Armstrong. "His hoverjeep malfunctioned out in the desert, and he walked into camp—"

The new officer grunted. "Malfunctioned, hey? Sounds as if somebody's slacking off in your motor pool, Lieutenant." It was clear he considered it Armstrong's fault.

"Oh, no, sir," said Armstrong, beginning to sweat. "Our motor pool is up to Legion standards—"

"We'll see about *that*," said the major. "When the CO's personal jeep breaks down in the boonies, what kind of attention are the other vehicles getting, I wonder? Omega Company's not drawing soft barracks duty anymore, Lieutenant. This planet's at war, you know."

"Not exactly a war, is it, sir?" said Armstrong meekly. "We were asked in to help the locals find out—"

"Not a war?" the major stopped and turned on his heel to face Armstrong. "That's naive of you, Lieutenant, wouldn't you say? These lizards bent over backward to get into the Alliance, and the ink was barely dry on the treaty when they asked for this outfit— which they seem to think is some sort of elite company, God help 'em—to come in as military advisers. What other than a war could be so urgent, hey?"

"Preventing one might be, Major," said a new voice, calm and genial. "That'd be at the top of my list of priorities, anyway."

Major Botchup whirled. "Captain Jester!" he said. He drew himself up to military posture and said, "I'm surprised it's taken you so long to report, Captain. As you must have heard, I have been assigned by Legion Headquarters to take over command of this company. Frankly, I don't like what I've seen so far."

His glower made it obvious that he included Phule in this assessment. The captain was wearing a white dinner jacket with a plaid bow tie and matching cummerbund—appropriate attire for greeting customers at the Fat Chance Casino, but a bit out of place in the field. And he was carrying a martini glass in his left hand. The major's eyes settled on it in an instant and radiated disapproval.

Surprisingly, Phule showed no reaction to the criticism implicit in the major's voice. He reached out his right to shake hands with the officer. "Armstrong, see if the major wants something to drink," he said, then grinned and added, "it's on the house."

The major stiffened. He looked down his nose at Phule and said, "Captain, I had heard appalling stories about this command, but I thought they had to be exaggerated. I'll grant you, Legion tradition allows a certain degree of liberty. But our officers are supposed to be gentlemen, and that implies a degree of discretion. Here you are, in a combat zone, out of uniform and—not to put too fine a point on it—soused before noon! I can see the general was right to relieve you of command. You will return to your quarters at once and make yourself presentable. Then report to me to be assigned your new duties. I'm sure we can find something you can do without screwing it up. If not, I may have to send you back to headquarters as unfit for duty!"

Phule grinned inanely. "Now, Major, let down your hair and relax a while. This is a place to forget your troubles."

The major turned to Armstrong and barked, "Lieutenant, put this man under house arrest! And make sure he doesn't drink any more until he's in shape to understand the trouble he's in!"

"Yes, sir!" said Armstrong, saluting. His expression was troubled, but he took Phule's elbow and said as gently as possible, "Captain, it's time for you to get some rest. Let me help you to your quarters."

"The cashier will give you quarters," said Phule, grinning like an idiot. "But I'll give you a tip—the dollar slots give better odds. Why not go for the gold?"

"Get him out of my sight!" bellowed the major. Visibly disturbed, Armstrong somehow managed to lead Phule away, and the major turned and stomped off toward the command center. It was time to determine just what was needed to get this company into shape and to bring it unequivocally under his own control. Grim-faced, he marched through the entrance to the MBC. There was work to do.

* * *

It was the second day since Phule had returned to the company and had been relieved of command by Major Botchup. A group of legionnaires stood outside the MBC; breakfast was over, and there was a little time still to shoot the breeze before they had to report to morning duty. Being Omega Mob, they were not about to let a chance to do nothing in particular escape them.

As they milled about, forming into groups for talk and banter, the entrance to the MBC opened and Captain Jester emerged, carrying an attaché case. He went over to a table in the shade of a canvas awning and sat down.

It had become obvious even to the major that a certain amount of routine administrative work that needed to be done could most easily be performed by the captain, who after all knew the company's personnel and history. So the confinement to quarters was modified to allow him to do routine paperwork. With the major having taken over the commanding officer's office, the captain was allowed to work wherever he could find space. And, as it happened, there was plenty of space in the open air. He opened the case and began to leaf through its contents, not paying any attention to the group of legionnaires a few meters away.

After a minute or so, Brick noticed him sitting there. She nudged one of her companions and said, "Be back in a minute. I'm going to go ask the captain about those renegade robots Chocolate Harry says we might have to fight. He'll give us the straight story."

"Sure, let me know what you find out," said the other legionnaire. Phule had always been open to questions and suggestions from the troops.

"Captain? I'm sorry to interrupt ..." Brick hovered near the camp stool where Phule sat, a stack of printouts on the table in front of him.

Phule looked up with a quizzical expression. "Yes, who is it?" he said.

"Oh, I'm Brick, Captain," she said. "I'm new with the company, so I guess you don't know me yet ..."

"Oh yes, of course," said Phule, flashing a fixed smile even as his head swiveled from side to side, as if trying to locate the source of Brick's voice. "What's the problem, uh, Brick? You don't have to hide—come on out where I can see you!"

"Excuse me, sir?" said Brick, puzzled. She was right in front of the captain, so he must be playing some kind of joke. Either that, or his ordeal in the desert had taken far more out of him than anyone had at first thought. Come to think of it, his behavior had reportedly been a bit strange ever since he had arrived back at the Legion camp. After a moment, she decided she was better off just asking her question. "It's like this, sir. There's a rumor we might be facing renegade robots here. As you can imagine, all of us want to know the straight dope on that, as far as you can give it. We understand the need for security—"

"Renegade robots?" Phule scoffed, even while his eyes kept flicking this way and that. "Now, I can tell you with pretty solid authority there's no such thing. Robots are fine machines, Brick, made to exacting specifications, incapable of error. Except human error—you'll get that every now and then, of course. You can trust robots, Brick. Anybody who tells you otherwise is dead wrong—dead wrong, I tell you. Take my word for it. I ought to know!"

"Yes, sir," said Brick, somewhat surprised at Phule's sudden vehemence on the subject. "Then you don't think we're likely to see any combat against them?"

"Combat? Don't be ridiculous," said Phule. "That's off the charts, Brick, completely off the charts." He paused a moment, then said, "What's going on, anyway? Are you hiding from me?"

"Hiding?" Brick took off her purple robot camouflage cap and said, "No, sir, I'm not hiding. Maybe you need a cool drink of water, sir. The desert heat may be affecting you—"

"Oh, there you are!" said the captain, suddenly looking her straight in the face. "Well, the heat isn't really that bad, but it's a good idea to take sensible precautions, isn't it? Well, if you don't have any other questions, I have these reports to go through ..."

"Yes, sir!" said Brick, replacing her cap and saluting. She turned and went back to her comrades, shaking her head.

"So, what's the word?" asked Roadkill. "We gonna fight the robots or not?"

"Captain says no," said Brick. "Problem is, I'm not sure just how far to trust his word, Roadie. I think the desert heat has cooked his brain. He was acting as if he couldn't even see me."

"Wow, that's a shame," said Roadkill, turning a sympathetic glance toward the captain, who was riffling through papers. "Let's hope he gets back to his old self. We sure need him to set things right. Maybe he could even figure out how to get the major off our backs."

Before Brick could reply, Brandy strode up to the group and barked, "Okay, okay, don't you birds have jobs to do? This is the Space Legion, in case you've forgotten it."

"Lord help me, Sarge, how could I forget it?" groaned Roadkill. He and the other legionnaires scattered to their morning assignments, and Brandy nodded. As long as the troops looked busy, the major had one less excuse to bust chops. She'd thought the days were long over when her main concern was keeping officers off her back.

Well, maybe the problem would be short-lived. She glanced over at Phule, who sat there grinning as he shuffled papers. Roadkill had been right about that; he was their best hope to figure out a way to reduce the major's influence. And until that happened, Omega Company was going to be a lot less fun than it had been, even for top sergeants.

*　*　*

A knock came at the door. Lieutenant Rembrandt looked up and smiled. "Chocolate Harry! Come in and sit down," she said. She put down the report she'd been reading. Before Major Botchup had arrived, she'd had the occasional report to read, usually something of importance to the company. Now she was drowned in reports, most of them irrelevant and unreadable. Any break from this routine was welcome. Any kind of break at all.

The supply sergeant nodded and took a seat opposite her. "Got a problem, Remmie," he said without prelude.

"I figured as much from the way you look," said Rembrandt. "What's up, C.H.? Don't tell me those bikers are after you again. We must be a dozen parsecs away from *them*."

"Nah, nothin' that simple," said Chocolate Harry. He pulled his chair closer to the desk and leaned forward. "I'm worried about the cap'n," he said in a lowered voice.

"We all are," said Rembrandt, also quietly. "He's let this new CO's being appointed over his head throw him for a loop. It can't be easy having your command taken away from you."

"Yeah," growled Harry. "That really stinks—not that it surprises me, knowin' the Legion like I do. This new major is pure chicken shit, the kind they only make at Legion Headquarters. He hasn't started messin' with my end of things so far, except for asking for a bunch of fool reports. If he never gets around to me, that'll be damn soon enough. But that ain't what I was worried about."

"You said it was the captain ..." Lieutenant Rembrandt paused and looked inquisitively at Chocolate Harry.

"That's right. He's actin' kinda flaky, Remmie."

"Flaky? How?"

Chocolate Harry rubbed his beard, considering his words. After a moment he said, "I dunno. He's acting like he's back at the Fat Chance. I mean, he's walking around wearin' that monkey suit, like he was gonna have dinner with the ambassador, and there's no ambassadors here that I can see. Looks mighty like a desert out there, in fact."

"Yes, that is unusual," Rembrandt admitted. "He's always told us to be proud of our uniform, and he's set an example by wearing it."

"Right, and he talks like we're at the casino too," said Harry. He paused again and said, "I think somethin's touched his brain, Remmie."

"The heat out in the desert could have done that," said Rembrandt. "The sentries who met him when he came in said he was already acting strangely, and Armstrong confirmed it. They fired the Zenobian stun ray at him before they knew who he was. Maybe that could've had an effect …"

"It could be the heat," said Chocolate Harry. "But I'll tell you what I think." He leaned closer and whispered, "It was right after he got back from that conference with the Zenobians, Remmie. And Beeker ain't come back yet. What do you want to bet they've got some game goin'?"

"What do you mean?" asked Rembrandt, surprised. She hadn't even considered that the planet's natives might have had something to do with the captain's strange behavior.

"I think they slipped somethin' into his food or maybe a drink, that's what I think," said the supply sergeant. "We're sittin' here with a camp full of state-of-the-art Alliance military equipment, and if they can get their claws on it, they'll have a real edge on us. That business about invisible aliens—that sure sounds like jive to me. I bet the lizards figured they'd dope up the captain and he'd just hand it over to 'em."

"That's a serious accusation," said Rembrandt. "We'd need something more to back it up before we took any action on it."

"That's why I'm talkin' to you, Remmie," said C.H. "Major Botchup, I don't know how he'd act. Except he'd try to do everything by the book, and that ain't gonna work. We gotta figure out what's really goin' on before we tell the major."

Rembrandt didn't answer right away; withholding something potentially so explosive from her commanding officer was asking for a court-martial. And like him or not, Botchup *was* her commanding officer now. On the other hand, he'd already decided there was something wrong with Captain Jester and taken the steps he considered appropriate. So there was no need to tell him that. All she'd be doing was refining the diagnosis. Until she knew for a fact that there was some external threat to Omega Company's security, she didn't need to get Botchup involved. But unless she was going to dismiss Chocolate Harry's suspicions out of hand, she needed to find out what was really going on, and she couldn't wait much longer.

"All right," she said. "Where do we start?"

"Damn good question," said Chocolate Harry, but he didn't volunteer an answer.

CHAPTER TWELVE

Journal #569

Being in command of Omega Company had greatly broadened my employer's horizons. For one thing, he had become familiar with members of several other intelligent races, from the sluglike Synthians to the feline Gambolts. He had even been so fortunate as to make the human race's first contact with the Zenobians, whom he subsequently helped bring into the Alliance. And he had been given ample opportunity to observe their differences from humanity, a species that was not by any means uniform in its culture or psychology.

But nothing had quite prepared him for the job of trying to understand a race that neither he nor anyone else had ever seen.

* * *

"Still no sign of them," said Phule. He had been pacing the small confines of their prison for the last hour. "When are they going to show themselves?"

"Perhaps they have, sir. Perhaps we're incapable of seeing or hearing them," suggested Beeker. The butler had scrunched into a corner and drawn up his legs to stay out from under the nervous captain's pacing.

"I still don't see how that could be," said Phule, stopping and turning to look at him. "The problem of invisibility has been pretty thoroughly investigated. Believe me, if there were some workable technique for it, every military unit in the galaxy would be using it. It only works in special circumstances, like on a magician's stage set."

"That is not an inapt comparison, sir," said Beeker. "Our captors may have set up almost any imaginable kind of equipment beyond these walls. Nor can we guess what substances they may have put into our air, our food, or our drinking water. One wonders what benefit they derive from the deception. It must cost them a fair amount of time and effort, if not actual money— assuming they use any such thing."

Phule paced around the cell a moment, then said, "You know, Beek, maybe that doesn't bother them. The biggest thing I learned from the Landoor mission was to stop worrying about money. That was the first time I've ever let the projected cost of something bother me, instead of just trusting my instincts to keep me in the black. And I didn't need to worry at all. With the people I had on the job, you among the most important, I ended up with more than I started out with."

Beeker frowned. "Yes, sir, but it was a very close thing …"

"And we came out the other side just fine," said Phule, waving the objection away. "The worrying didn't make a nickel's worth of difference in the long run. All it did was make me unhappy when I should've trusted my people to get the job done. Well, I can draw a conclusion as well as anybody else. I've got Sushi and Do-Wop on the job of investigating the Hidden Ones, and that means they'll eventually figure out what's happened to us. And once they know that, they'll find a way to get us loose. So why worry about it?"

Beeker clasped his hands together. "I am glad that you have stopped worrying about money, sir." He smiled. "If that is the case, and considering that you evidently value my suggestions, I think it is high time for us to discuss an increase in my salary."

"We can talk about that if we ever get out of this place," said Phule. "Not much you can do with money in here, is there?"

Beeker's face was stoical. "The accumulated interest from the date of the raise could be significant, sir."

"You do have a point there," admitted Phule. Then his eyes grew wide. "Wait a minute ... it's opening again."

They turned to see a portion of the wall again darkening and becoming porous, as it had when their captors had fed them. Were they going to see their captors at last? Or were they simply going to be fed again? The Hidden Ones did not necessarily have any notion of how frequently humans needed to eat, although the food they had provided before indicated familiarity with their nutritional requirements.

Phule stooped, trying to see if he could detect anything from a lower angle. But, as before, the opening stayed opaque, although apparently perfectly transparent to material substances. Through it, a round object about the size of a person's head came bouncing, making a jingling noise as it rolled across the enclosure and came to a stop at Beeker's feet. The butler bent to pick it up. "What in the world is this, sir?" he asked, holding it balanced on his palm.

Phule looked at the object, then said, "If I didn't know better, I'd say it was a gravball. Except they've put a bell inside it for some reason."

* * *

Rembrandt had taken advantage of an hour off duty to sketch the rugged terrain just beyond the Legion camp's perimeter. As always, she found that the challenge of turning blank paper into a recognizable picture of a specific landscape helped clear her mind of other matters—of which there were far too many at present—for a short time. But, as too often happened, other matters had come looking for her, and now she was going to have to deal with them.

"OK, Sushi, tell me what you've found," she said, wearily setting aside her sketchpad and pencil. "I won't even ask where you and Do-Wop have been hiding."

"I wouldn't tell you," said Sushi. "Major Botchup hasn't found out about us yet, but somehow, I don't think he'd authorize us to continue the search. And we have every intention of keeping it going. As Do-Wop says, 'If the major don't like it, he can shove it.'"

"Sounds just like what he'd say," said Rembrandt. "But maybe you should ask yourself, what if *I* don't like it?"

"Well, we'd have to take that pretty seriously," said Sushi. "But as far as I'm concerned, the person with the final say is Captain Jester. If he tells me to give it up, that's final. Anybody else, I reserve the right to disagree."

"And what has the captain said?"

Sushi paused, then admitted, "I haven't talked to him. But from what I hear, he's acting very strange. Maybe being lost in the desert threw him into a loop—I don't know. Anyhow, I think my best move is just to keep on with the job he gave me."

Rembrandt sighed. "Sushi, even in Omega Company you can't just ignore a superior officer's orders. I wish the major had never been sent to us, but that doesn't change the rules. He's still our commanding officer, no matter how you feel about it."

Sushi winked at her. "I'm not ignoring his orders, Lieutenant. He hasn't given me any yet."

"Because Do-Wop and you have been AWOL ever since the major stepped out of his lander," said Rembrandt. "In fact, I'm technically violating the Legion Code of Conduct myself for failing to report you two."

"We won't report you if you don't report us," said Sushi. "Now, why don't I tell you what I came here for, and get away before somebody else sees us and has to agonize over whether to report us both?"

"You know I wasn't going to report you," said Rembrandt. "But yes, if you've come out of hiding to tell me something, I'd better hear what it is. And then you'd better take off before somebody *does* see us together."

"Ah, you anticipate my plan," said Sushi, in a mock-villainous accent. He leaned forward and said, "Our new apparatus has picked up a signal from out in the desert; I'm pretty sure it's the aliens the Zenobians have been looking for."

Rembrandt sat up straighter. "A signal. I'll take it for granted you've eliminated other local sources. So, if you're right about what you've got, you and Do-Wop have just accomplished one of our main mission objectives all by yourselves." She stopped and looked him in the eye before continuing. "Why are you telling me, anyway, instead of taking it to the CO? He's the one who needs to know it. Hey, he might even give you a citation."

"Whoopee," said Sushi, twirling a finger in the air. "Seriously, Remmie, I don't think so. The major got sent here for just one reason: to undermine Captain Jester. And the captain's got Do-Wop and me working on just the kind of wildcat scheme the brass hats hate. The major would rather fail doing things the Legion way than succeed any other way, especially if it comes from the captain. The best that could happen if I told him what I've got is that he'd ignore me. No, the best that could happen would be that he'd go ahead and let me finish up and do his damnedest to steal credit for it. Then, at least, something would get done."

"What needs doing?" asked Rembrandt.

"What needs doing is tracing that signal and seeing where it comes from," said Sushi. "I think that when we do that, we'll find the captain's hovercar and Beeker, and maybe we'll learn what happened to the captain and how to fix it."

"That's worth doing," said Rembrandt, nodding. "Chocolate Harry already asked for a team to go find the hovercar, but the request is backed up in the paperwork on the major's desk. Meanwhile, everybody in the company knows the captain's not acting like himself, but he won't let the autodoc check him out, and the major's not interested in helping him. And most of the troops think the captain's getting away with something they wish they could do themselves, and they root for him when they think the major's not paying attention. Probably the only person with any chance to get him to take care of himself is Beeker."

"Right," said Sushi. "That's why we need to find Beeker and bring him back—if we can."

"I see," said Rembrandt. "So what do you want me to do?"

Sushi smiled and said, "Here's my plan ..."

* * *

Lieutenant Snipe squinted into the blazing sun. His brow was already covered with sweat, and he could tell that his uniform was going to be soaked if he spent more than a few minutes outside his air-conditioned office.

The Legion might have picked a somewhat more comfortable place to send him, he thought with some annoyance. If the brass had its mind so set on replacing Jester, why hadn't they come up with the plan while Omega Company was still at the luxury resort that had been its barracks before this assignment? The MBC was more comfortable than any standard barracks, but still ...

Well, if he'd missed one opportunity, it was all the more reason to seize the one that had come along. Major Botchup was Snipe's first-class ticket to favor with Legion Headquarters, and he'd be an idiot if he didn't make the most of it, scorching climate be damned. And the first step on the ladder he meant to climb was making himself as useful as possible to the major. That meant discovering as many ways as possible for the major to discredit—and, ultimately, to destroy—his predecessor in command. Luckily, that part of the job was turning out to be quite easy.

Snipe spotted a group of legionnaires busy at some task or another and strode over to inspect what they were up to. It was almost a given that there'd be something to find fault with, and he could add another item to the list of failures being chalked up against Captain Jester's record. He smirked. Chewing out these sorry specimens would almost make up for the despicable heat.

The legionnaires noticed the lieutenant's approach, for he heard a low voice mutter, "Yo, here come Sneak." Snipe frowned; his hearing was good enough to make out the words, but he couldn't be certain which legionnaire had said it. Well, no officer worth his salt would let his inability to spot the offender keep him from imposing proper discipline. It would be even more satisfying to make them all pay. For the moment, he'd pretend to ignore the insult.

"What are you men doing?" he snapped, balling his fists and putting them on his hips. The posture, intended to establish his authority, instead made him look faintly ridiculous. Even so, the group of legionnaires stopped whatever they'd been doing and turned to face him.

"We workin', Lieutenant," said one man. He was a lanky fellow whose name tag read Street, and his accent was so thick that Snipe had to think a moment before he realized what the man had said.

"Working?" Snipe stared at the group. "You'd better be working. This isn't a leisure club, you know."

"Man's a genius," muttered somebody just out of Snape's direct line of sight.

Snipe decided to ignore the sally, which after all might be interpreted as a compliment of sorts. "Exactly what sort of work are you doing?" he asked.

A young, round-faced legionnaire with old-fashioned eyeglasses answered him. "That is an excellent question, Lieutenant. Perhaps if we all inquire carefully, we will learn the answer."

"What do you mean by that,"—Snipe peered at the legionnaire's name tag—"Mahatma?" Snipe took a closer look. The name and face seemed familiar now. Wasn't this the legionnaire who'd been impertinent at inspection? "Are you saying that you people don't know what you're doing?"

"Does any of us really know what we are doing?" asked Mahatma, a faint smile on his face. "The simplest action has consequences no one can foresee."

"Deep, Mahatma, deep," murmured Street, nodding appreciatively and rubbing his hands together.

"This is the Legion," said Snipe, directing what he hoped was a steely gaze toward Mahatma. "It's your officers' job to think about consequences. Your job is to follow orders, and if you do, everything will be fine." He left it to the legionnaires' imagination to conjure up what would happen if they didn't.

Snipe had not reckoned on Mahatma's imagination, which was more than equal to the task. "Lieutenant Snipe, may I ask a question, sir?" Mahatma was holding up his hand like an eager schoolboy. It was almost impossible to ignore him.

"What is it, Mahatma?" asked Snipe. He frowned, vaguely aware that the confrontation was leading away from his original purpose. Well, he'd get it back on course quickly enough, once he'd dealt with this digression.

Mahatma asked, with a very serious expression, "Lieutenant Snipe, should we not know who is giving us an order so we can determine whether it is correct to follow it?"

Snipe favored Mahatma with a glare and said, "I don't see how that applies—"

"Oh, but it does very much apply, sir," said Mahatma, so polite it was impossible to find fault with him. "It is not always easy to tell one person from another, and what if one of those persons is an officer and another is not? If a person we do not know comes and says he is an officer, should we obey him, or should we learn what his authority is before following his orders?"

"Oh, no, you won't catch me on that one," said Snipe with a ferocious grimace. "The major was given command of this unit by Legion Headquarters. He showed his orders to Captain Jester."

"But Captain Jester was not here when the major came," Mahatma pointed out. "He did not show the captain his orders, and yet he assumed command immediately. How do we know his orders were legal?"

"Yeah, Mahatma's makin' sense," murmured the other legionnaires. "Deep, man, deep."

Snipe felt a slight tingling at the back of his neck. Were these men trying to work up a justification for mutiny? Should he try to talk them back into line or go inform the major and let him take whatever measures were necessary?

"Your other officers have accepted the major's authority," said Snipe, temporizing.

"I know they did, and that is why we have continued to obey orders," said Mahatma calmly. "But that was before the captain returned. Now, what if the captain tells us to do something? He is still an officer, is he not?"

"Captain Jester has been relieved of command," said Snipe, aware of a trickle of sweat on his forehead. "What is more, the major has placed him under arrest, pending investigation of his conduct in command. His authority is temporarily suspended."

"That is what we had heard," said Mahatma. "Does this mean we should not follow his orders?"

"You—" Snipe had opened his mouth to answer when he sensed another trap in Mahatma's question, and he bit off the answer. "That depends," he said, retrenching. "If his orders are legal, of course you should follow them. But if his orders go against the major's, you should not."

"Very good, sir; that is clear," said Mahatma, his smile even more beatific. "But one more question, please, Lieutenant Snipe. How do we know whether the captain's orders are legal until we know the major has approved them?"

"That's a good question," said Snipe. "I think, under the circumstances, that you should ignore Captain Jester's orders until you know that they have received the major's approval."

"Thank you, Lieutenant," said Mahatma. "I think I understand everything now."

"Good. As you were, then," said Snipe, and took advantage of the opportunity to make his getaway.

Later, he was to regret not having stayed around to see the consequences of his advice. But of course, having little experience with either the Omega Mob or Mahatma, he couldn't have been expected to foresee what they would make of it.

*　　*　　*

The Reverend Jordan Ayres blinked as he entered the lighted room and saw who was waiting for him. Armstrong and Rembrandt sat together on the couch, and Brandy was perched on its arm. "Have a seat, Rev," said Chocolate Harry, who'd called him to this clandestine meeting.

"Thanks, don't mind if I do," said the chaplain, pulling a straight-backed chair up to face the couch; Chocolate Harry perched his bulk precariously on the opposite arm of the couch from Brandy, making the two oversized sergeants bookends to the pair of lieutenants. Rev looked at the four faces staring back at him and said, "Must be somethin' important to bring all you together at once. Y'all gonna tell me what it is, or do I have to guess?"

"I think you already know what our main problem is," said Rembrandt, taking the lead as the senior officer present.

"The major," said Rev, and the four heads nodded in unison. Rev nodded, but after a pause, he shrugged and said, "Well, I can sure sympathize with that, but I don't know what anybody here can do about it. The Legion done sent him, and I reckon we gotta put up with him."

"Ordinarily, I'd agree with you, Rev," said Armstrong. "He's our properly appointed superior officer, and if he has different ideas from what we're used to, we can either shape up or ship out. Especially since his ideas are strictly by the books."

"That's jes' the way I see it, Lieutenant," said Rev solemnly. "When the King got called into the Army, he done what he was told like any other boy that went to be a soldier. No special favors for *him*. He even got his hair cut, and that wasn't no small sacrifice. If he could take it, I guess we can."

Rembrandt nodded. "That's a reasonable attitude to take," she said. "Our life would be easier if more legionnaires saw things that way. But, to tell you the truth, I don't know if it's what we need right now."

"Well, ma'am, I don't know whether I can accommodate you, then," said Rev. He stood up from his chair. "The King might have seemed like a rebel to some folks, but deep down inside, he was a great respecter of authority. Why, he even went to pay his respects to a man that—"

Brandy cut him off. "Sit back down, Rev. Let's get one thing straight. We don't need you to stir up the troops against the major. He's doing a pretty decent job of that all by himself. If they had any encouragement at all, they'd be doing everything they could to make *him* want to get transferred out. But the only man who could make them take that risk isn't saying anything, and until he does, they're afraid they'll hurt him more than they will themselves."

"You mean the captain," said Rev. He was still on his feet, but his hand rested on the back of the chair.

"That's right," said Brandy, fixing Rev with her gaze. "This whole company—officers, noncoms, right down to the newest rookies—would jump into a black hole for the captain. But as long as they're worried that they'd be hurting him, they won't take the first step. And the captain's acting pretty strange, in case you haven't noticed."

"Why, I reckon I have noticed, Brandy," said the chaplain. "He's been mighty distracted ever since he came back from the desert. Word has it the heat must have touched his mind. Have y'all found his butler yet?"

"No, Beeker's still missing," said Armstrong grimly. "We're working on something that might tell us what's happened to him, but I can't give you details. I'm afraid it's a long shot, though."

"A shame. He was a good feller, mighty good feller," said Rev, shaking his head. Then he sat down and looked at the four legionnaires. "But what do y'all want me to do, then?"

"We need you to go talk to the captain," said Rembrandt. "He's the one who asked for you to be sent to the company. We think maybe you have a chance to get through to him, even though he seems to have shut out the rest of us."

"Do you really think so?" the chaplain's expression took on a hint of soulful intensity.

"We do, Rev," said Rembrandt. "This is one area where you're the expert. We need you to help the captain. Once he's back in command of himself, then he can decide whether to try to recover command of his company. Until that happens, our hands are really tied. But we don't think that can happen without you."

"Without me?" Rev sat up straight, and his chest expanded. "Well, if it's a question of helpin' the man get back to his right sense of himself, you can count on me. I'll get right to it."

"Good, Rev, we appreciate it," said Rembrandt. "We knew you'd step up for us." She shook the chaplain's hand, and all the others shook his hand in turn. Then Rev turned and left the room, a man with a mission.

When he had left, Rembrandt turned to the other three and said, "All right, we've got Rev working on getting the captain back in shape. Now, what do we want him to do when we've got him back?"

There was a silence as they stared at one another, uncomfortable with the question Rembrandt had put on the table. Then, as if someone had thrown a switch, they all began talking at once.

It took them several sentences before they figured out they all wanted exactly the same thing.

* * *

The Reverend Jordan Ayres was not, on the whole, a man who placed great value on subtlety. He had found his answers to the problems of life, and they were big answers, flamboyant, in-your-face answers. And, in the manner of all true believers, he tried to make those answers work for everyone around him. For the most part, they did work, if only because the way people usually solved their problems was to do something, almost anything, besides sitting and brooding on them.

However, it seemed to the chaplain that whatever was ailing Captain Jester was going to require a more subtle approach than with the usual legionnaires who had come to him for counseling. Here was a man who was used to being in control, a man rich in power and possessions. A man whose clothes always fit perfectly, whose expression rarely showed doubt or frustration. A man, it occurred to him, much like the King. What worked to console a homesick Legion recruit might not be appropriate for the captain. An amazing percentage of life's little problems will shrivel up and blow away when one can wave a Dilithium Express card at them.

"Good mornin', Captain," said Rev, walking up to the bench where Phule sat riffling through a stack of Legion personnel forms.

"Why, good morning to you," said the captain, looking up with a bright smile. "It's great to see you again. Why don't you sit down for a minute and talk?"

"Don't mind if I do," said Rev, sliding onto the bench next to him. "Been a while since we had a good jaw session. Course, you've been away for a while, too. Must have been a mighty ... uh ... *interesting* journey you had there." Perhaps, thought Rev, talking about the journey would open the way for the captain to speak of his troubles.

"I suppose you could say so," said Phule with a shrug. "There's not much of a story to tell, though. I'm just as glad to be here at the end of it, if you want to know the truth."

"Yes, I suspect you are," said Rev. This wasn't going quite the way he'd planned; he shifted his tack, hoping to bring the captain out. "The terrible depredations you went through out in the desert might have took more out of you than you realized at first—"

"Oh, I wouldn't make a big thing of it," said Phule. "Now, I bet you've got some interesting stories of your own." He gestured toward Rev, as if inviting him to tell some of those stories.

Rev sighed. Maybe he was better falling back on his tried-and-true approach, despite the captain's difference from his usual converts. "The best story I know ain't about me, it's about a poor boy on old Earth," he began. "Didn't nobody pay him much mind when he was a little tad, 'cause his folks weren't rich or important. They was jes' plain folks, down on their luck—"

Phule held up a hand to break in. "Everybody has a streak of bad luck now and then. Best thing to do, if you ask me, is just keep plugging away and wait for it to change. Of course, you have to know the odds, and you can't take foolish risks. We want you to play with your head, not over it." He grinned as if he'd said something profound.

Rev frowned. "Why sure, Captain, jes' like you say," he said. He tried to steer the subject back to the point he was trying to make. "But this here boy I'm talkin' about, he had a fire burnin' inside him, sure 'nuff."

"That's good, really good," said Phule, nodding. "If you think he'd fit in with our operation here, that's the kind of person we're looking for. He could get in touch with personnel. Tell him to mention your name, and of course I'll make sure his application gets taken seriously—"

"Well, that's not really what I'm gettin' after, Captain," said Rev, scratching his head. Captain Jester didn't seem to really be listening to him, and that was unusual, in his experience. Every boss he'd ever worked for claimed that listening to his people was a main priority, and almost none of them really did it. The captain had always been one of those who listened, and better yet remembered what he'd heard, and—best of all—followed up. But now …

"I'm glad you were able to stop by for a while," the captain was saying. "I've gotten so busy I don't have much time to talk to my old friends these days. But of course, for you, the door is always open."

"Sure, Captain, but like I was saying—" Rev tried to get one last word in.

The captain cut him off. "I'm afraid I've neglected this pile of work as long as I can justify. So, as much as I've enjoyed it, I guess I'll have to drag myself away for now." He stood and extended a hand. "Be sure to drop in again, next time you're in the station."

"Uh, yes sir," said Rev, taking the hand and pumping it almost by reflex. "Uh, one more thing—"

The captain wasn't going to be swayed. "Why don't you just head on out and enjoy yourself while you're here? A chance to let your hair down and just be yourself is good for anybody. And one tip: Our dollar slots give the best odds on the station." He winked and then sat down to his papers with an air that made it clear the interview was over.

Rev walked away in a daze. Things were even worse than he'd feared. He made his way to Rembrandt, saying not a word. The lieutenant looked up from her desktop, an anxious expression on her face. "Well, Rev, how'd it go?"

Rev shook his head. "I hate to say it, ma'am, but it ain't good at all. Not one bit." He paused and turned his eyes to the ground, then looked back at her. "If you're expectin' help from the captain, I'm afraid you got a long wait 'fore it gets here."

* * *

Rev's report convinced Rembrandt that it was imperative to follow up on Sushi's plan to find out what had happened to Phule's hoverjeep—and to Beeker. With the plan jumped up to top priority, she began recruiting a search party.

Almost the entire company would have gone if she'd asked them. In the end, she chose six, with a particular eye to scouting skills and wilderness survival experience. Several legionnaires that her criteria kept off the team besieged her with complaints that their other skills more than compensated for these lacks. Remembering what had happened when she'd deferred to the troops in making up a similar "rescue party" on Landoor, Rembrandt stuck to her guns.

Flight Leftenant Qual was an obvious choice for the team. His local knowledge was orders of magnitude beyond anyone else's, of course, even when you remembered that he'd grown up in a swampy region rather than these semidesert conditions. Even then, she harbored some doubt whether the Zenobians were entirely trustworthy. After all, in one of his last messages, the captain had hinted that the local military was eavesdropping on him in between negotiating sessions. Also, considering how few members of his race were in camp, Qual's absence would be more easily noticed than that of any other possible participant. In the end, she decided that his local knowledge trumped all the objections.

Tempted as she was to include all three Gambolts, she reluctantly decided that she couldn't in good conscience leave the camp without any of the catlike aliens and their uncanny scouting abilities. So Dukes and Rube stayed behind, while Garbo—who, of the three, seemed best adjusted to working with humans—went with the team. So did Garbo's partner, Brick. Not just because the two were inseparable companions; as it turned out, Brick came from a backcountry region of her home world, an arid region known as Nueva Arrakis. She had the kind of instinctive knowledge of desert scouting that only comes to someone who'd spent their growing-up years in dry country.

Mahatma and Double-X had the skills she needed, while neither would be missed if they were away from base for a week or more. Except for the latter factor, Brandy and Escrima would have been her first choices for the assignment, but neither could just walk off without being missed. Well, she had the best team she could put together, and she'd have to trust it to do the job that had to be done.

She'd had the most difficulty deciding who was going to command the team. All three of the company's sergeants had wanted to do it, but none of them could just disappear from the base without being missed fairly quickly. Finally, Rembrandt took the bit in her teeth. "The major isn't any part of this mission, and the captain's not himself right now," she told them. "I'm next in rank, so it's my job to make the decisions."

That was before Sushi had stormed into her office, demanding to be put on the team. Her original instinct had been to leave him off the team, despite the fact that it was his idea to send the expedition out to begin with.

"Look, I can't bring you along," she told him. "You're a city boy. You'd slow us down way too much in the kind of country we'll be traveling in. Besides, we need you to monitor the alien signals so you can tell us about any changes in them. That means you have to stay behind and stay in touch via communicator."

Sushi wasn't budging. "Have you forgotten that the communicator's on the fritz?" he pointed out. "We can't pick up signals from more than a couple of miles beyond the perimeter, let alone where we're going to be. Now that I've figured out what frequency the aliens are using, I can monitor it with a handheld unit, which is what I've been working on the last couple of days. I've got it down to three kilos in weight, and it's no bigger than a shoe box."

After he showed her the new unit, Rembrandt was convinced, and she added him to the team. But this meant she'd have to cut somebody else to keep the team to a manageable size. That was going to be tricky; all the members had useful skills, although only Qual seemed really indispensable. Cutting either Garbo or Brick probably meant she'd have to drop the other, and she couldn't afford to lose both. So that left Mahatma and Double-X as the possible choices.

She agonized over it for a whole afternoon before a peremptory communicator message ordered the officers to the command center. Rushing to the meeting, she rounded a corner and nearly collided with Louie, who was speeding silently down the cross-corridor on his glide-board. The Synthian swerved just in time to avoid hitting Rembrandt; but in her abrupt stop, she wrenched her lower back. By the time she got to Botchup's office, it was starting to stiffen up. By the time the meeting was over, she couldn't stand. The autodoc scanned her, displayed a diagnosis of muscle spasm, and dispensed a bottle of pills that stopped the pain well enough for her to sit at a desk and work, but it was obvious she was in no shape to head a team into rough country.

That made Flight Leftenant Qual the de facto team leader. Now Rembrandt was glad she'd given in to Sushi's demands to be included; of all the remaining team members, he had the most leadership potential and the clearest sense of their mission. And, perhaps most importantly, he seemed to have the best idea what Qual was talking about; the translator's mangled renditions of the Zenobian language were sometimes more impenetrable than the Alliance tax code.

She hobbled out to see the team meet at the perimeter for their departure. They slipped out of camp after midnight, with only the light of the gibbous Zenobian moon to guide them. (According to the books, the local moon—Vono, the Zenobians called it—was a bit smaller than old Earth's famous Luna, but it was bright and impressive enough to these legionnaires, most of whom came from small-mooned or even moonless worlds).

Actually, the team could probably have made its move in broad daylight, since everybody in Omega Company except for Botchup and Snipe knew what was about to happen. Of course, if the major caught them and tried to make a big deal of it, they might have to break a few more regulations than they'd planned on breaking. Even the success of their decidedly non-regulation mission wouldn't necessarily excuse the violations if the major decided to get vindictive, which struck everybody as exactly how he'd play it. Just to avoid unnecessary complications, they'd decided to go at night.

After a final check of equipment and supplies, Qual led them off into the dark. With luck, they'd reach their destination without being detected by the aliens or missed by the major. Standing there watching them fade into the darkness, Rembrandt had a twinge of regret at not being able to join them. But another twinge from her back told her in no uncertain terms that she'd made the right decision. She turned and walked slowly back to her bunk, hoping all her other decisions had been right. She'd know the answer soon enough.

CHAPTER THIRTEEN

The Zenobian desert, like those on most other planets, was a far more diverse and fertile environment than most city-dwellers would have realized. Especially to the Zenobians, who were most at home in a swamplike setting, any large dry area seemed much like any other. But as the team set out to search for the source of the alien signals quickly saw, this was no simple unbroken expanse of dry sand. There was life aplenty here, some of it very lively and very dangerous to the unwary.

Flight Leftenant Qual knew some of it; city-bred though he was, he'd seen desert wildlife both during his military training and in zoos back home. By default, he was their native guide. But even he admitted that much of it was new to him. "If you espy anything you don't comprehend, make your path distant from it," he said cheerfully. The others nodded soberly and did as he said.

This policy was not easy to follow since (following the practice of desert experts everywhere) they planned to travel at night when the heat was least oppressive and when they were least likely to be picked out by anyone watching. Because the indigenous animals were themselves nocturnal in their habits, chance encounters were more frequent than the legionnaires would have liked. Every now and then something close by would make an unexpected noise, and one of the off-worlders was likely to jump. Sometimes Qual told them the names of the creatures: There was a loud-voiced, squatty thing he called a grambler, a little burrowing creature called a western flurn, and a furtive thing with eyes that shone brightly in their Legion-issue night vision goggles, which Qual's translator solemnly informed them was a spotted sloon.

Most of these were no trouble, but there was a lizardlike thing with half-inch-long teeth that could leap high off the ground to attack whatever had disturbed it. That little pest had them flinching at the least sign of motion in their pathway, with vigorous cursing in three languages and several dialects. The hopper-biter blended invisibly into the low brush. Even with the night vision goggles, it was hard to spot it in time to avoid a nasty bite. After a couple of near misses, the team took to detouring around any patch of vegetation—a tactic which, the farther they got into the desert, cost them more and more time.

Finally, confronted with a nearly unbroken patch of ankle-high brush to cross, Qual called a halt and turned to face the others in the party. "We are making too slow advancement," he said quietly. "Here is a technique that may expedite our forward gains." He loosened the sling on his stun ray and took the weapon in both hands.

"Oh, wow, I get it," said Brick. "We hose the area we want to walk through, and that knocks out the varmints so we can get past. Why didn't I think of that?"

"It is not a technique to employ constantly," said Qual. "With many stunners firing, there is danger of hitting one's teammates. If one is essaying a stealthy approach, it may alert the adversary if small animals in the path of approach begin to fall from their perches or drop from the air. And it is predestinated that a few of the stunned animals will be killed by falling or will be gobbled by others that recover more swiftly. And last, constant use dissipates the energy of the weapon, and it takes a certain time to recharge— a poor situation if one expects to encounter hostility."

"Which might or might not happen to us," said Sushi. He looked uncomfortable in his desert gear, but he'd kept up with the group fairly well. City-bred or not, he was in excellent physical condition from his hours of martial arts training.

"In that case, we need to be ready for all possibilities," said Mahatma, smiling. "That's what the sergeants keep telling us. It's impossible, of course."

"Sure, and so's FTL. Just ask any classical physicist," said Sushi. "Of course, you'd need time travel to go find one—they're all dead—and that's impossible too."

"*Impossible* is not a word I have heard Captain Clown use," said Flight Leftenant Qual. "Therefore you will not let it rule your speculations. 'The gryff sees only gryffish things, and therefore knows not the mountain,' or so my egg-mother always proclaimed. Of course, gryffs are very stupid."

"What's a gryff?" asked Double-X.

"A large, clumsy omnivore," said Qual. "They do not inhabit the desert, so we need not worry about them." He pointed his stun ray forward and depressed the firing button. "Come. I will clear the way for a while, and you will follow. When my weapon has used half its charge, another of you will take over."

He stepped to the front of the group and began sweeping his ray across the path. After a moment, he moved forward, and the team fell in behind him. They had no further trouble with hopper-biters.

* * *

There was nothing Major Botchup enjoyed quite as much as springing a surprise inspection. It gave him an exhilarating sense of power to see grown men and women cringing when he came unexpectedly into sight. They'd pretend they didn't see him, hoping he would go away. Sometimes he would just go about his business. But other times—just often enough to be unpredictable—he would pounce.

He didn't disguise the thrill he got from their panic as they realized they had no chance to conceal the things they'd let slide. And there were always things they'd let slide, things they wanted to conceal. That provided another thrill: finding all the evidence of their slacking off and wrongdoing and rubbing their noses in it, with ample punishment for every defect he found. Stern, unrelenting discipline was the best possible way to guarantee that the troops would live in fear of him, which was the only emotion the major wanted to inspire in his troops.

So there was a feral grin on his face as he emerged from the command entrance to the MBC first thing in the morning. This early, they wouldn't be expecting him. If he was lucky, they'd still be groggy from sleep. His eyes swung from side to side, his nose wrinkling as if he could sniff out his prey. He hadn't made up his mind just where he would strike today, but he knew he would eventually find a target. And then his aim would be unerring, and those who had earned his righteous wrath would tremble at the memory for years to come.

There, in the shade of a tool shed across the central parade ground of the camp, he spotted a likely target. It was one of the sorry pack of aliens that had been exiled to this pariah company because they couldn't cut the mustard in the real Legion. A Volton, reading a book. There shouldn't be any time for reading. He could give the creature a good chewing out just on general principles.

But it wouldn't do to charge across the parade ground directly at his victim. If the Volton had something to hide, he might slink off when he saw Botchup coming, and that would make the major exert himself for no purpose. Better to take a roundabout approach and lure the loafing sophont into complacency. There was a small knot of legionnaires to his left, so he chose that direction.

As Major Botchup's eyes focused on the group he was approaching, they began to grow wider—and wider still. The group ahead of him was even worse than anything his previous experience of Omega Company had led him to expect. They were lounging idly, clearly doing nothing in particular. Worse, they were *out of uniform*! Instead, they wore a hodgepodge of civilian clothes, mixed with bizarre purple garments of various sorts. Most were unkempt and unshaven; in his entire career in the Space Legion, Major Botchup had never seen anything to approach it.

He swooped on the group like a tactical hoverjet discovering an unprotected ammo dump. "What the devil do you people think you're doing?" he snapped. "This is an outrage! Where are your uniforms?"

"We done took 'em off, Major," said one human in an accent that straddled the boundary between Standard and incomprehensible jargon. "Lieutenant Snipe's orders."

"*What?*" Botchup's face turned the same color as the antirobot camouflage the troops were wearing. "If Snipe said any such thing, I'll see him cashiered out of the service! Exactly when did he issue this order?"

"Well, it was just yesterday, Major," said a young woman whose face seemed vaguely familiar. "A bunch of us asked him about which orders we had to obey, and he said—"

"Which orders to obey? Preposterous!" By now, the major had gone well past the boiling point. "A legionnaire obeys all orders, or I'll know the reason why! Where are your sergeants?"

"I dunno, Major," said the first legionnaire—*Street*, according to his name tag. "They don't usually bother us long as we doin' the job—"

"They'll answer to me, then!" the major fumed. "What makes you think you can dress this way?"

The legionnaires all began talking at once. "Well, Major, Sarge said we was likely to see action against robots …"

"It was the captain told us to wear the uniforms he got us, so we figured we shouldn't keep wearin' 'em, 'cause he's not the CO anymore …"

"The captain said not to worry about the robots, but we aren't supposed to obey him …"

"I didn't have any of my old uniforms …"

"I didn't have anything but civvies, 'cause of when I joined up …"

"*Quiet!*" Major Botchup shouted. The entire group—indeed, the entire camp—fell into complete silence, broken only by the faint hum of machinery and the steady gurgling of the company water pump, not far from where they stood. The major put his hands on his hips and said in a voice that could have air-cooled the entire camp, "I don't know what Lieutenant Snipe told you, but I'm not going to let that get in the way of proper Legion discipline. Every man jack of you is going to report yourselves to Lieutenant Snipe for conduct unbecoming a legionnaire, and then you are going to your quarters and get into proper uniform. And you are every one of you going to do extra punishment duty, and it will be damned hard duty, I promise you!"

"But Major—" came a voice from the back of the group.

"Oh, *shut up!*" said Major Botchup. He looked around the camp, ready to flay another victim. Much to his annoyance, the Volton he'd observed before had gone away. But he'd find somebody else. He was sure of that.

* * *

The search party had settled down after its first full night of desert travel. Soon the Zenobian sun would be rising, and when it did, they needed to be under shade. They'd set up in a pair of insulated tents on the north side of a small hill, where they'd get a bit more shade. They'd try to sleep through the daylight hours and get a fresh start when the sun had dipped low in the sky again.

Just before they'd halted, Garbo had surprised a small creature near the edge of a water hole, and she and Qual had run it down. Now she and Brick were stewing it, stretched out with Legion-ration dried vegetables, in a pot over a portable heating unit between the tents; it smelled delicious. Meanwhile, Flight Leftenant Qual, whose race preferred its food uncooked, had gone out into the desert to find a breakfast more to his liking.

In his tent, Sushi had set up his portable detector unit and strung out a few meters of antenna between the tent and a spiky plant a little distance away, trying to get a more precise fix on the signal they were homing in on.

"How much farther do we have to go, Soosh?" asked Mahatma, who was sharing the tent with Sushi and Double-X. "This desert travel is nowhere near as oppressive as Major Botchup, but it'll never be my idea of relaxation."

"Hard to get a precise reading," said Sushi, fiddling with the fine tuning. "If I knew how strong the signal is at its source, I'd have a better idea. At a guess, it's a couple more days of travel; but if the signal's an order of magnitude stronger than I think, it could be a lot farther."

"What do we do if it's halfway around the planet?" said Double-X, who lay on top of his sleeping bag, propped up on one elbow to play a handheld computer game. "I ain't walkin' all that far, even if it does get me out from under the major's nose for a while."

"That's for Qual to decide," said Sushi. "It's his people that are being invaded, and it's a fairly big priority for them, so I suspect he's not going to give up unless it's obviously hopeless."

"What if it ain't obvious to him?" said Double-X. "He can live off the land, but we're gonna run out of food sooner or later, even if we do catch one of these desert rats every now and then."

"After seeing Garbo hunt, I would think we'd catch one more often than that," said Mahatma. "She is very efficient once she spots a prey creature. And unless my nose is playing tricks on me, this one will make very good eating."

"Yeah, it does smell good," admitted Double-X. "That don't mean I wanna eat it every night for the rest of my life—"

Sushi raised a hand to cut him off. "Hold it a moment; I'm getting something," he said. The receiver had begun emitting a series of high-pitched squeals and beeps.

"Aww, give a guy a break, Soosh. That's just noise," said Double-X. "You been out in the sun too long if you expect that to make any sense."

"Soosh can't find out if it makes sense if you don't let him hear it," said Mahatma, with an expansive gesture. "Why not give *him* the break?"

Double-X had already opened his mouth to reply when he grasped Mahatma's point and closed it again, nodding silently. The beeps from the receiver continued, getting louder and softer as Sushi continued to play with the fine tuning. "I'd swear there's a repeating pattern, but I can't quite put my finger on it," he said. "I wish I had the captain's Port-a-Brain."

"I wish I had the money to buy one of those mothers and then go spend it on other stuff," said Double-X, but he kept his voice low.

"It's fading out," said Sushi, leaning closer to the receiver. "I'm losing the signal, damn it! No—quiet, it's getting stronger …" The others held their breath, but a moment later, the signal faded out entirely and was replaced by obviously random noise. Sushi pounded a fist into his thigh and said, "Well, it's gone again. We might as well eat."

"If these creatures are affected by the heat, they're probably getting ready to go to sleep, just as we are," Mahatma pointed out. "That could explain the signal fading in daytime."

"It doesn't fade every day," grumbled Sushi. "There must be some other explanation."

"And perhaps we will learn it," said Mahatma, getting to his feet. "But for now, I am interested mostly in learning how this stew will taste. Gambolt cookery will be a new experience."

"Hey, I helped cook it too," said Brick with mock indignation.

"Then we will blame you equally with Garbo if it is inedible," said Mahatma, deadpan. Before Brick could react, he added, "It does not smell inedible, though. I don't think there will be any blame to apportion."

"Continue in that vein, and we will forget to include you when we apportion the stew," said Garbo. While translators were not at all reliable on the subtler nuances of alien speech, the statement was accompanied by a very good simulation of laughter. Grinning, the legionnaires filled their mess kits with the stew and were soon enjoying a meal that even Escrima might have taken some pride in serving them.

* * *

Mess Sergeant Escrima lifted the lid of the soup pot and took a deep sniff. He wrinkled his nose, trying to decide how it was coming along. Captain Jester had found him a source for several herbs and spices he'd been running short of. The shipment had come in just before they'd departed Landoor, and he'd left them unopened until their arrival at the new base. Now he was beginning to work them into his recipes. So far, everything had been good quality, but Escrima wasn't a man to jump to conclusions—at least, not when it came to cookery.

This was the first time he'd used the bay leaves, touted as being from the same grower who supplied the Alliance Senate dining hall. Escrima had heard that kind of puffery before and knew better than to put much weight on it. The aroma coming from the pot wasn't bad, he had to admit … but how was it going to taste? There was only one way to find out.

He'd been scowling at the slowly simmering liquid, trying to decide whether it was time yet to dip in a spoon and taste it, when he became aware of someone entering his kitchen. He turned and glared. Whoever it was might have legitimate business here, but he didn't want them to start thinking it was a place just anyone could walk into whenever they felt like it. He had a reputation to maintain.

It was the new CO, Major Ketchup, or something like that. He waved a sheaf of printouts and growled, "Sergeant, I see from these purchase orders that you've been going outside the Legion commissary network for supplies. That's a violation of policy, and an unnecessary expense to boot. What the hell do you think you're doing?"

"What the hell you doing in my kitchen?" said Escrima, his eyes glowing like red-hot coals. "You got a problem with my food?" His tone of voice made it clear that any such statement would be taken as grounds for a preemptory strike.

At that point, any person with the slightest sense of self-preservation would have contented himself with a very polite "No" and quickly left the kitchen, apologizing profusely and being especially careful not to expose his back to this obvious madman who had a large supply of knives and cleavers within easy reach.

Major Botchup was evidently lacking a sense of self-preservation. "I've had a look at your menus," he said. "You're coddling the troops with all this gourmet stuff, and wasting money besides. I'd be surprised if they can tell—"

"Can't tell?" Escrima's eyes bulged out. "You want me to tell you something? I tell you get the hell out of my kitchen before I put you in the soup pot. No, I don't do that; nobody eating the soup then." He began stalking toward the major, his voice growing louder with each sentence. "Maybe you just fat enough to cook down for lard, though—"

"Are you threatening a superior officer?" sputtered Botchup, but he backed away. "I'll have you in the stockade—"

"I'll have you in the stock pot!" shouted Escrima, and he grabbed a cleaver off the counter.

Whether or not the mess sergeant would have used it, Botchup never learned, for he turned tail and ran.

* * *

Lieutenant Snipe was feeling very unfairly put upon. It was bad enough taking the blame for his own foul-ups—that was part of being an officer—but somehow, Major Botchup had taken the position that Snipe was responsible for everything that had been going wrong. And, as Snipe had learned in a very unpleasant meeting with the major, quite a few things had gone wrong so far today. The chewing out he had just gotten was far from the first of his Legion career—working for Botchup, getting raked over the coals was par for the course—but it was by a good distance the most memorable.

Snipe was willing to admit that the major could hold him partly responsible for the troops' willful misinterpretation of his remark that orders given by the former CO might not be valid. But how could anyone have foreseen that they would take that as license to disobey *all* orders predating Major Botchup's arrival? And the mess sergeant's ferocious territoriality about his kitchen was certainly none of Snipe's doing; in fact, previous experience with mess sergeants might have in some part prepared the major for it. Admittedly, threatening to throw a superior officer into the soup pot was a bit extreme …

The final straw had been when the major had bolted from the kitchen into the outdoor sunlight, still in fear for his life, to collide with an oversized female legionnaire wearing only a bikini: First Sergeant Brandy. Never mind that the first sergeant was officially off duty, or that the climate conditions at this base amply justified her choice of attire and her decision to "catch a few rays," as she explained it, or that her considerable padding and quick reflexes in catching the major before he could fall prevented injury to either party. What mattered was that several nearby legionnaires had witnessed the incident—and *laughed*. Major Botchup could not tolerate laughter—at least, not at his own expense. Lieutenant Snipe had been the first to pay for the major's humiliation, and he had paid a high price. His only recourse was to take it out on someone lower down the ladder. Luckily for him, there was a whole company of victims available.

Snipe emerged from the MBC with a fierce grimace on his face, looking around for someone to oppress. Any excuse would do. And knowing what he already knew about Omega Company, he would find plenty of excuses without having to search very far. Sure enough, there came a legionnaire; Snipe didn't know his name yet, but he recognized the face: dark greasy hair, sideburns that just stayed within the limits of regulations, thick lips that hinted at a sneer. He didn't like the fellow on general principles, but if memory served, he'd talked to this legionnaire yesterday. He'd been one of the group who'd gotten him into this trouble by taking his comments on orders literally. He owed this one a special reaming out. Snipe descended on the unfortunate victim like a ballistic missile on its target.

"You there. Didn't you get the major's orders?" the lieutenant barked. "Uniforms to be worn at all times when on duty!"

"Sir, I am wearing my uniform," said the legionnaire with a bewildered look. Good; he was already on the defensive.

"If it's not worn in the regulation manner, it's the same as not wearing it at all," said Snipe, pointing to the legionnaire's upper chest. "That top button's open!"

"Sir, in this heat, I thought—"

Snipe cut him off in midsentence. "I don't want to hear any of your excuses. You'll report for extra KP—on the double! And your regular job better get done as well, or you'll get yourself another round of extra duty! Go on, get out of my sight."

"Yes, sir!" said the legionnaire, and he quickly turned away in the direction of the kitchen.

Snipe smiled—not a pretty smile, but a sincere one nonetheless. Sending the offending legionnaire for KP was a stroke of genius. If Snipe could find half a dozen more to punish the same way, he'd have the kitchen filled with superfluous personnel, and that'd give the mess sergeant the headache of finding something for them to do that didn't interfere with his precious kitchen. He began a leisurely stroll around the compound, looking for more offenders to punish.

To his surprise, he'd barely gone a dozen paces before he ran into the same legionnaire! There was no mistaking that face, especially not the annoying sneer. "What do you think you're doing, legionnaire? Didn't I tell you to report for KP?"

"Sir, it's not my day," said the legionnaire, a puzzled look on his face. "I'm not on until tomorrow."

Snipe thought the fellow's voice sounded somehow different, but that didn't matter. It was obviously the same man. "Are you crazy or just stupid?" he barked. "I ordered you to extra duty less than two minutes ago. Now get down to the kitchen before I throw you in the stockade instead!"

The legionnaire spread his hands. "That wasn't me, sir; it must have been—"

"Get out of my sight!" shouted Snipe, his face turning red. The legionnaire, evidently deciding not to press his luck, saluted and went off quickly toward the kitchen.

Snipe was starting to get into his stride now. He found another legionnaire with a loose button, and one who hadn't polished his boots sufficiently for Snipe's taste, and he sent them both to KP. But his jaw nearly fell when he rounded a corner of the MBC and found the same legionnaire there again, sitting in a chair and reading!

"You!" he sputtered, walking over to the sideburned malefactor. "You …"

The legionnaire looked up at him and said with a smile, "Howdy, can I he'p you with anything, son?"

"That's *sir* to you," screamed the lieutenant. "And you'll stand at attention when you speak to an officer. You're in deep trouble now, if you don't know it …"

The legionnaire closed his book and stood up, more or less at attention. For some reason, he looked taller than before—and a bit older. "Why, sir, I didn't think we was standin' on protocol quite so much in this outfit. Captain Jester never did get around to decidin' jes' what my rank oughta be. But seein' as how you're new, I'm happy to oblige. Now, jes' what can I do for you today, Lieutenant?"

Snipe's jaw fell to his chest. The fellow was acting as if nothing at all had passed between them earlier, and yet it was no more than fifteen minutes since he'd last reprimanded him. The fellow must be mentally unsound; it wouldn't surprise him, having seen the kind of material this company was made up of. Perhaps he was even a multiple personality. How else to explain the complete change in his expression, even his voice and accent? In any other outfit, the fellow would doubtless have been discharged as unfit for military service.

Snipe was still trying to figure out what to say when another legionnaire strode up to them and said, "Excuse me, Rev, do you have a minute to talk?"

The man he'd caught reading turned to the newcomer and said, "Not right this second, son; the lieutenant has something he wants to talk about. But if you'll come back in maybe fifteen minutes, I'm sure I can spare the time."

The newcomer nodded, snapped off a very decent salute to Lieutenant Snipe, and turned to leave. The man who had been reading turned back to Snipe with an expectant smile. "Now, sir, what was it you wanted?"

But the lieutenant was speechless now. He rubbed his eyes and looked again at the man in front of him. The tag on his uniform said Reverend Jordan Ayres, and on his collar was some kind of badge Snipe did not recognize—an antique musical instrument, it appeared. But what gave Snipe pause was the fact that the man who'd just come up and saluted in perfect military form, said a few polite words, and turned to walk away *wore the exact same face as the man now in front of him.*

Snipe muttered something and walked away, shaking his head. Everybody in the company was starting to look the same to him. It must be the desert sun. Yes, that was it—the sun. He'd go back to his quarters, get a cool drink of water, and just lie down and rest a bit.

He managed to keep his composure reasonably well until he entered the MBC and found himself face-to-face with still another legionnaire, this one obviously female, with *that same sneering face.* That was when he lost it entirely.

* * *

Lieutenant Rembrandt was walking stiffly and a bit gingerly as she came into Comm Central. Her back injury was healing nicely, thanks to the pills she'd gotten from the autodoc, but even cutting-edge military medicine wasn't going to do much to speed up the process.

There was a vacant straight-backed chair behind the counter where Mother worked, and Rembrandt lowered herself into it with a sigh. Mother looked over at her with a raised eyebrow. In her quiet voice, she said, "Still hurting, Remmie?" She could sometimes speak to another woman without the incapacitating shyness of her face-to-face interactions with male humans.

"Yeah," admitted Rembrandt. "Best prognosis is that I'll be close to a hundred percent by the middle of next week. Right about now, it feels as if I'm somewhere under fifteen percent."

"A bad back's tough," said Mother, nodding. "My dad hurt his when I was a little girl, and he was never the same after that. Hope you don't have that to look forward to."

"Thanks, so do I," said Rembrandt. "I might have been better off just to let Louie run me down on that glide-board. He couldn't have done much more damage than I did trying to dodge him."

"Yeah, that's how it is sometimes," said Mother. Her eyes kept shifting back and forth from Rembrandt to the readouts on her comm equipment. "But if he'd hit you, you both might be hurt."

"That's what I tell myself," said Rembrandt. "Anyhow, I'm getting along, and I guess I'm getting better." She paused a moment and asked, "Any luck with that message I asked you to send?"

"Answer came through just before you got here," said Mother. "I didn't print it out because you said it was confidential. Printouts can get read by the wrong people. Not much to report anyhow.

They acknowledged receipt and said they'd see if anybody was available. No promises."

"You'd think they'd show more interest," said Rembrandt. "This company's been one of the hottest stories in the Alliance ever since the captain came on board."

"Sure, and that with a buck fifty will get you a one-minute local public comm call anywhere in the galaxy," said Mother. "Those people have attention spans in the nanosecond range, unless it's something they can use against you."

"Still, you'd think they'd be interested in what's happening to the company," said Rembrandt, her brows crinkling. "They wouldn't have to make any particular effort to get somebody here. Why, we're only a couple of days' sublight travel from Lorelei—"

"Couple of days probably seems like forever to them," said Mother, shrugging. "Don't get your hopes too high, Remmie. I know you're looking for some way to fight back against the brass hats, and I'm all for it. The captain would be fighting them, if he were himself. I keep hoping he'll snap out of it—"

"So do I, Mother," said Rembrandt. "Until then, we've got to try to guess what he'd be doing, and do the same ourselves. I just wish we were getting better results."

"You want results?" Mother scoffed. "Girl, those pills the autodoc gave you must be making you giddy. This is the Legion. They don't believe in results; they just say they do." She chuckled, but her face was serious.

"Except for Captain Jester," said Rembrandt, lifting her chin. "He not only believes in results, he gets them."

"I know what you mean," said Mother. "I just worry whether his luck's run out at last. I hope not, but I'm afraid to hope for too much."

"The captain wouldn't want us to give up," said Rembrandt. "He'd want us to start figuring out a way around the system, and that's what I'm doing."

"I know," said Mother. "More power to you, because I don't want to think about what happens if the brass hats win this one."

"Neither do I," said Rembrandt. "I'm doing what I can to keep the bastards from winning."

"And if it's not enough?"

Rembrandt stood up, wincing. She looked down at Mother and said in a resigned voice, "I don't know. I don't have much else to throw into the fight."

Mother sighed. "Well, let's just hope it's enough, then." Rembrandt just nodded and made her way slowly out of Comm Central. Mother watched her leave, then shook her head sadly and turned back to her comm screen.

CHAPTER FOURTEEN

Journal #573

One curious feature of life with a Legion company was that one was always being stationed in places where the normal amenities of civilization were rather thin on the ground. Of course, my employer had done what he could to alleviate this by moving his legionnaires into the best available accommodations on those worlds where he was assigned. For our stay on Zenobia, a planet with no human presence before ours, he had gotten a custom-made encampment module that supplied many of the essentials of the good life: running water, electricity, air-conditioning, comfortable beds, a thoroughly modern kitchen.

But some things could not be done simply by throwing money at them, and this turned out to be particularly true of the military aspect of our assignments. Like it or not, a decent system for the distant detection and identification of incoming spacecraft—something most real planets take for granted—was sadly lacking on Zenobia. And, to my employer's chagrin, neither the Legion commanders nor the Zenobian military seemed to think a single Legion company really needed one.

This was to have consequences.

* * *

"The major wants me?" Lieutenant Snipe looked up from the bed where he'd been hiding for several hours, covers over his head, until Major Botchup had sent a legionnaire to find out where his aide-de-camp had disappeared to. It was probably mere chance that the major hadn't sent one of the legionnaires who'd remade their faces "in the image of the King," as his followers called it. But it was definitely the right choice. If Snipe had looked up and seen *that face* again ...

"Yes, sir," said the legionnaire, Koko, one of the crop of recruits who'd joined the company on Lorelei, a gawky but very polite farm boy from an agrarian community on the planet Roosha. "He says it's very important."

"Everything the major wants is important to him," said Snipe. The lieutenant's attitude toward his commanding officer was somewhat less adulatory than it had been at the beginning of the day. "Let me just wash up and straighten my uniform, and I'll be right there."

Despite his sour mood, Snipe took less than five minutes to freshen up, and shortly thereafter he followed Koko into Major Botchup's office and saluted. "Lieutenant Snipe reporting, sir!"

Botchup glanced up at his aide-de-camp and nodded. "Good, Snipe, about time you got here. Tell me what you make of these printouts." He handed a sheaf of flimsies to the lieutenant and waited.

Snipe scanned the printouts and then looked up at the major. "When were these recorded, sir?"

"Within the hour," said Botchup. Then he glowered at Snipe and said, "But I asked you what you make of 'em."

"A ship in orbit around this planet, sir," said Snipe. "I assume it isn't one of ours."

"It's not Starfleet, anyway; it may belong to the natives," said the major. "I've had that woman in Comm Central trying to raise the native capital, but there's nothing but bloody interference. You'd think a race that has its own space fleet could get up a few comsats, make it easier to talk. Stupid lizards."

"Yes, sir," said Snipe, thinking. "What's our status?"

"It's not responding to attempts to hail it, so we're treating it as hostile," said Botchup. "The natives brought us in here because of aliens they'd found spying on them. Apparently, they briefed Jester about it, not that I can get much sense out of him. Any data they passed on to him probably went down with his hoverjeep. If things ever settle down, we ought to send a team out to look for it—try to recover the vehicle at least, if not the data. In the meantime, we don't know any more about these damned aliens than we did before we landed."

"Yes, sir," said Snipe again, nodding. "Your orders, sir?"

"I've put the base on full alert," said Major Botchup. "I want you to go out there and make sure these people are vigilant and totally prepared—no slacking off. I think this is the real thing, Snipe. Promotions could be at stake."

Snipe nodded, a grim expression on his face. If there was one thing about the Legion he understood, it was promotions. "There'll be no slacking off while I'm out there, sir!"

"Good man," said Botchup. "I'll be monitoring the situation from in here. Send me a report at once of anything you notice. Our remote systems are good, but a CO needs a trustworthy pair of eyes and ears, too. You'll give me that—and more. Jester's people are soft. They've never done anything more dangerous than riding roller coasters. Put them in a real firefight—and this might just be one, Snipe, it just might be one—and they're a good bet to crumple. I need you to put some steel in their spines. If you have to make examples of a few slackers, don't be afraid to do it."

"Yes, sir!" Lieutenant Snipe saluted sharply and left the command center. He was ready to put some steel in the Omega Mob's spines whether they needed it or not. He looked forward to making some examples. After the day he'd been through, he wouldn't mind making examples of the whole company.

*   *   *

"We're getting closer," said Sushi, looking at the dial of his detector.

"This is fine to hear, Sushi," said Flight Leftenant Qual. "Do you have a concept of how close the Hidden Ones may be?"

"Nothing precise," said Sushi. "But the signal's started to cover a wider angle, and that means we're getting closer. How close depends on just how big an area the signal sources are coming from. If it's a couple hundred feet across, we're *real* close; if it's a couple hundred miles, we're still a long way away."

Qual nodded, then asked, "And there is nothing to distinguish between those cases?"

Sushi looked up from his machine and said, "Nothing objective; the signal's growing stronger, which *could* mean a closer distance. But I assume that people only a few feet away from one another have some way more effective than radio signals to communicate."

"That is not an infallible assumption," said Qual. "One could postulate a race that sees radio frequencies the way we do visible light, and uses them to communicate. After all, Garbo and I see deeper into the infrared than you do."

"Yeah, and we humans can hear lower pitches than either of you," said Sushi. "I know it's possible, Qual, I'm just trying to keep the number of variables down to a bare minimum until something proves I need to look in other directions. Otherwise, we'll be spending so much time on woo-woo ideas that the serious probabilities will get lost."

"How could they get lost?" asked Qual. "They will still be there, even if we are looking at the boo-hoo ideas."

Sushi grinned in spite of himself. "You know, Qual, sometimes I think you speak our language better than you let on."

Qual returned the grin, showing a mouthful of predatory teeth. "I do not speak your language at all, Sushi; it is all done by the translator. Though I understand that the machine can learn from experience, so perhaps that is what you are hearing."

"Guess that could make sense," said Sushi. Then his brow wrinkled. "Say, that just gave me an idea. In fact, I feel like an idiot for not thinking of it earlier. If these signals we're getting are some sort of messages, the translator ought to be able to make sense out of them. Maybe when we stop, I can borrow yours, and we can hook it up to the receiver ..."

"That is a very interesting plan, Sushi," said Qual. "Of course you can borrow it. Although it will leave me temporarily powerless to communicate, I think the risk of learning something useful is paramount here. Or, now that I think of it, Garbo has a translator as well. Perhaps it would be better to use hers, so I can stay advised of what occurs."

"Sure, that ought to work just as well," said Sushi. "We'll give it a try when we stop again. It shouldn't take long to set up."

The search party set out again in the direction Sushi's detector indicated the signal was coming from. But it was only a short time when Sushi stopped and said, "Hold on, guys. This thing's going crazy."

"Crazy? How?" asked Brick. "Has it stopped picking up the signal?"

"No, the directional indicator's gone haywire," said Sushi. "It says the signal's coming from all directions. Wait a minute … That could only mean one thing. Except it doesn't make any sense."

"I see what you mean," said Qual. "If the signal comes from all directions, it means we are in the place where the signal comes from. Yet there is nothing but the desert here." He had taken a handheld spotlight off his belt and was shining its beam in all directions.

"Be damn," said Double-X. "Maybe them Hidden Ones really *are* invisible."

"I still don't believe that," said Sushi. "More likely, they're hiding underground."

"Then the signal would come from below us, would it not?" said Mahatma. "Does the detector indicate that?"

"No, it's from all directions including straight up," said Sushi. "Maybe it's time to hook up a translator to the detector—"

"Hey, what's that?" said Brick, pointing off into the desert.

Qual swung his spotlight beam back in the direction she was pointing, and the legionnaires saw the reflection of the beam from something metallic.

"We'd better go check it out," said Sushi. "What are your orders, Flight Leftenant?"

"Wait, I can see it well," said Garbo, the Gambolt. "It is a Legion hoverjeep!"

"It's gotta be the captain's jeep," said Double-X. "What's it doin' this far out? That's a hell of a hike for a guy without any supplies or protection."

"That's a good question," said Sushi. "I expect we're going to learn the answer to that, and to a lot of other questions, very soon now."

"Yes, I think we are," said Qual. "Here is the plan. Sushi and I will advance carefully and examine the jeep; the rest of you must take up positions whence you can observe and keep us covered in case of surprise; having the best night eyes, Garbo will command the covering party. Be certain to shout a warning if you see any movement other than ourselves. Is it understood?"

"Understood, Leftenant Qual," murmured Garbo. She directed her group to fan out to positions with clear sight lines toward the hoverjeep, while Qual and Sushi carefully made their way forward. Stunners on the ready, they waited breathlessly to see what would happen next. Around them, the sounds of the desert filled the air.

* * *

The camp was full of activity as Lieutenant Snipe emerged from the CO's office into the open area inside the perimeter—as active as he'd ever seen it. Brandy had the troops in their defensive emplacements, and everyone in sight was wearing a helmet and body armor. It made the lieutenant's blood sing to see it.

A short distance away, Snipe spotted Lieutenant Armstrong scanning the sky with a pair of high-powered stereoculars. Snipe hurried over and stood next to Armstrong. "What can you see?" he said.

"The ship's still below the horizon," said Armstrong with a casual air that Snipe wished he could emulate. "So far, no sign of missiles or landing craft."

"Keep a sharp eye out," said Snipe, not bothering to keep an edge out of his voice. "I'll need to know instantly if you spot any sign of activity."

Lieutenant Armstrong took the 'ocs away from his eyes and fixed Snipe with a look that would have made an oyster flinch. "Sure, *Lieutenant* Snipe, just as soon as I see anything worth reporting. I hope you don't mind if I use my judgment. It'll be a few minutes before the ship clears the horizon, so if you need to do anything urgent—"

"Good, good, keep your eyes peeled," said Snipe, oblivious to the chill in Armstrong's voice. He turned and headed toward the perimeter to check out the defenses.

To Snipe's surprise, there were only two legionnaires visible, sitting with their feet in the perimeter trench and quietly eating sandwiches, with their backs facing outward. One of them was looking at the centerfold of a men's magazine, while the other was nodding his head in time to the music in the earphones he wore. "What are you doing?" Snipe shrieked, his voice going up an octave in pitch. "There's an unidentified ship—probably an enemy—approaching the camp, and you've got nothing better to do than sit here reading a skin mag?"

"Chill, Lieutenant," said the one wearing earphones—Snipe recognized him as the one named Street. "We on lunch break, is all."

"*Lunch break!*" Snipe's jaw dropped. "I never heard such bullshit! This is a war zone, legionnaire, and we're under attack. Who told you to take a break?"

"Sergeant Brandy said it was OK," said the other legionnaire. Snipe saw that his name tag read Gears.

"'Sides, ain't no attack I can see," said Street. "Somebody starts attackin', we be there."

"And meanwhile you think you can go off and do as you please," snarled Snipe. "The major will hear of this, you know. Consider yourselves both on report!"

"You can go get yourself some vacuum," said Street. "I take my orders from Brandy." He reached down, turned up the volume control on his headset, and proceeded to act as if Snipe did not exist.

Furious, the lieutenant turned around and began to search for the first sergeant. To his surprise, she was nowhere near the two errant soldiers. Finally spotting her unmistakable figure across the camp, he marched over to her, stiff as an overwound toy soldier.

Brandy was standing on the parapet of the trench on this side, looking out over the desert. "Sergeant!" Snipe strode right up to her and put his hands on his hips. "Sergeant, I need to talk to you."

Brandy turned slowly and looked at him. "We're in the middle of a situation right now, Lieutenant Snipe. Is this important, or can you wait until we get it sorted out?"

"A situation! I should say so," said Snipe. "You've left the entire western perimeter undefended, except for a couple of men who say you told them to take a break!"

"That ship's coming from the east, Lieutenant," said Brandy. "If it's going to land west of us, we'll get plenty of notice. We don't even know if it's landing at all. If it does, I've got time to get those men back."

"That's not the point, Sergeant," said Snipe. "Discipline must be maintained—"

"Sure, sure," said Brandy, waving the lieutenant off with a huge hand. "You Headquarters types always think discipline's the whole game. But this is Omega Company—"

"Yes, and your headline-hogging Captain Jester thinks he can throw away centuries of Legion tradition," said Snipe. "Well, your little journey into unreality is over, Sergeant. We're going to do things the Legion way from here on out. And you're going to—"

"Here comes the ship," a voice behind him called suddenly. It added, dryly, "Looks like she's about to land."

"Oh my God!" said Snipe, turning white as a sheet. He turned to Brandy, but she was already moving along the line, giving terse orders to her people. The whole line tensed, looking at the dot of light that was now visible to everybody in the camp. Lower it came, and lower still. Snipe watched in helpless fascination. It seemed to descend agonizingly slowly, but at last it touched down.

* * *

After a careful approach, Qual and Sushi reached the hoverjeep only to discover that it was unoccupied. That was a disappointment, though hardly a surprise. Inside the vehicle's cab, the legionnaires found equipment belonging to both Phule and Beeker: notably, the captain's Port-a-Brain computer, an item that could put a serious dent in the budgets of most planetary governments.

"That's not something the captain would leave behind unless he was out of choices," said Sushi. "And if Beeker were in any position to protest, he'd have made him take it along anyway. I wonder why he didn't bring it back to camp with him."

"If I am not mistaken, it is still turned on," said Flight Leftenant Qual, pointing at the light glowing on the Port-a-Brain. "Captain Clown must have been in a great rush to leave the vehicle without closing down his brain."

"You're right," said Sushi, suddenly excited. He leaned in and peered more closely at the device. He blew a film of dust off the front panel and looked more closely at the readouts. "Look at that. The modem's operating. I wonder what it's connected to."

"No doubt to whatever the captain was accessing when he left it," said Qual.

"Let me see that computer," said Sushi suddenly. "It wouldn't stay connected to the web that long; the connection will automatically time-out unless there's activity on the user side. So either the captain left only a short while ago ... But that's impossible; he's been in camp since before we left. So it's still tuned in to whatever it was picking up when he left here. And my guess is that the something else is—"

"The signal you have been following to here!" Qual finished the sentence. His mouth fell open in a broad grin. "Great Gazma! The Hidden Ones attempt to communicate with the computer!"

Sushi grinned back at him. "It's probably a pretty one-sided conversation, but yeah, I think that's exactly what's going on. I bet they're sending different test signals, trying to get it to respond to them."

Qual's translator emitted a sound the legionnaires had learned to recognize as laughter. "Can they not tell the difference between a sophont and a machine?"

Sushi's expression turned serious. "Funny you should ask. There's a famous experiment some old Earth computer scientist invented. And if the Port-a-Brain has the Hidden Ones fooled into thinking it's a sophont, it's passed the Turing test. Which I guess it ought to, considering the price tag."

"Your machines are designed differently from ours," said Qual. "We know directly whether we are confronting a machine or an intelligent being. Confusion is not wanted."

"I guess machine intelligence is so useful, we humans are willing to put up with a bit of confusion," said Sushi. "Who needs stupid machines when we have so many stupid people? Besides, this Port-a-Brain may be smarter than all of us put together, but it doesn't look like any living creature I've ever seen. The Hidden Ones must be very strange if they can't tell it's a machine they're trying to talk to … Hey, wait a minute."

"I suppose I can," said Qual with a reptilian shrug. "But I think it would better utilize our time searching for the captain's butler."

Sushi laughed. "No, I mean I've got an idea what could have happened. Those strange signals we've been receiving—they're all around us here, but we don't see any sign of civilization, except for the hoverjeep and the things in it."

"That is manifestly true," said Qual. "It is a jigsaw."

Sushi frowned, then shrugged and said, "I think maybe the Hidden Ones haven't hidden on purpose. They're just too small for us to notice. And that may prevent them from noticing us—or at least, from recognizing what we are—as much as it prevents us from seeing them."

"Too small?" Qual turned and looked in all directions. "Even very small creatures would need machines and buildings, and we do not see those, either."

"No," admitted Sushi. "But I suddenly feel very confident in this idea. I think it's time to try that experiment I've been talking about. Didn't the captain and Beeker take along translators on their visit to your capital?"

"I think they did," said Qual. "No doubt they would be in the baggage compartments."

The baggage compartment was locked, but that deterred Sushi only a few moments. Sure enough, there were a pair of translators there, neatly packed in their neoplastic carrying cases. By the time Sushi got them out, Qual had signaled the rest of the squad to join them, and (at the Zenobian officer's direction) they began looking around the area for signs of the jeep's occupants.

"With two translators to play with, I've got another idea," said Sushi. "If the Hidden Ones are trying to communicate with this Port-a-Brain, I want to see if there's some way we can hook a translator into it."

Brick, who'd helped Sushi unload the baggage compartment, said, "Sounds like your kind of fun. But why don't you hook it up to your own gizmo first? I mean, the captain's fancy computer's got more brainpower than the Alliance Senate. If it hasn't cracked the language on its own by now—how long's it been working at it, a week?—maybe us sophonts deserve a shot at it."

Sushi laughed. "Maybe you're right," he said. "I'll give that a try first. If nothing else, I've been thinking about it long enough, so I have some idea where to start." He set down the translators and headed back to retrieve his receiver and his tool kit.

*　*　*

Perhaps an hour later, Flight Leftenant Qual wandered over to the hoverjeep, where Sushi had set up a makeshift workbench on the tailgate. He took off his dark sunglasses and peered at the electronic tangle. "How functions it, young one?" asked the Zenobian.

Sushi leaned back and sighed. "These things were never meant to fit together," he said. "If I had a parts shop handy, I could probably find something off the shelf to make the job easier. Out here in the field, I've got to kludge it up pretty much from scratch."

"So this signifies it will not perform?" said Qual.

"Oh, I think I can make it work," admitted Sushi. "I've probably voided the captain's warranty on his computer, and it'll never win any beauty contests. But I think he'd approve the project, just on general principles."

"Since you're doing it to save his butler, I guess he *would*," said Brick. "He can buy another computer, but Beeker's not going to be easy to replace."

"I just hope Beeker's still in condition to save," said Sushi quietly. "He's been out in the desert for a long time, and all the emergency rations are still in the jeep. Unless he's got some other source of food and water …"

"If the Hidden Ones have seized him, they ought to nourish him," said Qual.

"I hope so," said Sushi. "Problem is, until we can communicate with them, we don't know whether they even know where Beeker is. For all we know, he tried to get back to base with the captain and didn't make it. He's not a young man—"

"I do not think something has happened to Beeker," said Qual. "Captain Clown would surely have talked about it."

"You'd think so, wouldn't you?" said Sushi. "But something must have happened to him on that trek back to the base. He's not acting anything like himself. Brick, you said he acted like he couldn't even see you when you talked to him."

"Yeah, it was weird," she said solemnly. "He heard my voice and answered my questions, but he kept looking around for me, like I was hiding from him or something. And now that I think about it, some of his answers didn't, like, totally add up."

"Yes, they did not totally total," said Qual. "I spoke to him, and it was as if we were of different species."

"Weird," said Sushi without looking up from his work. He twisted two wires together, then said, "Let's see if I've got it right."

He turned on the translator's power switch, leaned close to hear if the speaker was on, then booted up the Port-a-Brain. Nothing happened.

"Aaah, bad luck," said Brick. "Back to the blank screen, huh?"

Sushi was unperturbed. "Nah, I turned it off when I made the modifications. Now I've got to go back to the program that was up when we found it. I saved the settings. Let's see …" The display changed rapidly as he entered a series of commands. "OK, let's see what we get here," said Sushi, and hit a key.

The translator's speaker emitted a low warming-up buzz, then broke into articulate sounds. "Intersystem Sklern—two thousand at nineteen. *Please instruct concerning exercise of pets.* Research P/E on Pickup Pizza Ltd. Common. *Do you receive signals?* Trantor Entertainment Preferred—hold until forty-five, then sell five hundred. *We will take five hundred.* Mark Pickup Pizza Ltd. Common to buy below ten ..."

The legionnaires listened for a moment, then Sushi turned to his companions and grinned. "Hey, guess I know what I'm doing after all."

"Acclamations, Sushi," said Qual, showing all his teeth. "At long last, the Hidden Ones speak to us!"

"Triff," said Brick. "But what the hell are they talking about?"

"The captain had the computer automatically checking and trading his stocks on the net," said Sushi. "It's sending out commands, and the Hidden Ones obviously thought it was trying to communicate to them. I'd guess they've been trying to get it to respond to them, and it's been carrying on the original program, of course. Now that we've got the communication channel open, we can try to start them talking to us instead of to the Port-a-Brain." He turned to Qual. "Leftenant, you're the officer in charge. What do we want to say to them?"

"Why, that is obvious," said Qual. "Where is the human known as Beeker?"

"OK, you've got it," said Sushi, and he began entering commands as the rest of them looked on expectantly.

* * *

The unidentified ship was dropping rapidly, and the legionnaires in their defensive positions kept a wary eye out for possible hostile action on its part. "If it was gonna launch missiles, it woulda done it 'fore it cleared the horizon," said one private.

"Yeah, but laser beams are line-of-sight," Brandy reminded him. "Stay low, and be ready to move when I tell you."

"Can you make out what model it is?" Lieutenant Snipe asked Armstrong, who was still tracking it with his stereoculars. From the corner of his eye, Snipe saw one of the Synthians whiz down the defensive line on a glide-board, wearing a bizarre helmet and carrying some kind of huge weapon.

"Not yet; still too much atmospheric distortion," said Armstrong. "She's midsized is all I can really tell." He looked at Snipe and said, "If you went over to Comm Central, Mother may have been able to raise them. Maybe they called for authorization to land or something sensible like that."

Snipe nodded, trying to decide what to do. He skipped aside as Chocolate Harry roared by on his hovercycle, leaning over the handlebars with an expression that meant business. Major Botchup had been monitoring the electronic traffic, so he should have picked up any such communication—and the major had not changed his orders. Snipe shook his head and said, "The CO will tell us if there's any word on that front. For now, stay ready for anything."

"In case you hadn't noticed, Lieutenant, that's what we were doing," said Armstrong. He picked up the stereoculars and looked at the approaching ship again, pointedly turning his back to Snipe.

After a few moments, while the noise of the approaching ship got progressively louder, Snipe turned to Brandy. "Sergeant, what plan do you have if the ship opens hostilities?"

Brandy snorted. "Depends a whole lot on what they throw at us, Lieutenant. Landing this close, I don't think they're going to be using any nukes, do you?"

"Nukes?" Snipe gulped. He hadn't even considered that possibility.

"Course, this could be some kind of fanatical suicide mission," Brandy continued. "Maybe they'll try a quick push with conventional force, and then blow the ship's core if we're too tough a nut to crack. Been done before. Not much we can do if that's what we're looking at, is there?"

"Uh, I suppose not," said Snipe. His face was growing pale.

Brandy continued in a voice that carried over the sound of space drives throttling down. "More likely what we get is some softening up with whatever heavy armament the ship's carrying. Something that size could have Class 4 UV lasers, I'd say.

Shouldn't hurt as long as you're behind about six inches of lead shielding, or maybe ten feet of packed earth."

"Ten feet?" Snipe looked around, trying to determine where in the trenches he'd have that much cover.

"Yeah, ten feet oughta do," said Brandy. "Once they've got us keeping our heads down, they turn loose whatever they've got in the way of infantry—and then it gets nasty."

"Nasty?" Snipe gulped.

"Yeah, nothing worse than close-quarters combat," said Brandy at top volume. "But you've probably seen it all before, being a second lieutenant and all that."

Snipe had his mouth open, gulping air, when Armstrong called out, "Ship's touching down. Look alive there."

"Look alive!" repeated Brandy at the top of her voice, turning to look at the dust cloud rising around the ship. "Once that dust settles, they can cut loose with any rays they have, so be ready to get down."

The infernal racket of the ship's engines abruptly ceased, and there was a long moment of expectant silence. The dust began to thin out, and Snipe cringed at the notion that death rays might even now be warming up to fry him. He looked around for something to crouch behind and finally settled for a nearby hoverjeep. It wasn't perfect cover, but perhaps it was thick enough to protect against the Class 4 UV that Brandy had warned of. From somewhere out of sight, he heard Armstrong say, "Hatches opening."

Snipe stuck his head around a corner, only to fall almost instantly backward as something large came roaring directly at him. From a position flat on his butt he watched Chocolate Harry rush past on his "hawg," and heard the shouted warning, "Yo, man, heads up!" as the supply sergeant whipped on past at incredible speed.

Another more cautious peek around the corner showed him shadowy figures in the dust cloud by the mysterious ship. Several of them were busy catching and stacking unidentifiable equipment being tossed to them from an open cargo bay. Now some kind of vehicle emerged from the ship, followed by several more figures (were they humans?) on foot.

Deciding that it was, for the moment, safe to expose himself to possible fire, Snipe ran quickly to join Armstrong, who stood behind a waist-high pile of crates, surveying the action through the stereoculars. "What's going on?" Snipe asked, panting a bit from the exertion. He crouched behind the crates, admiring Armstrong's coolness in the face of the enemy.

"They're unloading their equipment," said Armstrong helpfully. He looked down at the cowering Snipe and added, "Here they come."

Snipe risked a peek over the crates. Here came the vehicle, slowly advancing toward the Legion position. It had the look of a hoverjeep, and several of the figures seated in it were carrying what might be beam projectors—or almost anything else, Snipe realized. A small group of invaders trudged along behind it. In the defensive line, Snipe could hear Brandy talking to her troops: "Steady now, steady."

Seeing that the invaders had so far done nothing that could be taken as a hostile move, Snipe decided it was safe to stand up. The dust had settled enough for him to make out that the hoverjeep was painted a bright yellow. *That's not a military color,* he realized. There appeared to be some sort of writing on the side, although from this angle Snipe couldn't make it out. A figure in the front of the jeep was standing up, exposed to the Legion defenders. "This doesn't look like an invasion force," he muttered.

"No, it doesn't, does it?" said Armstrong. "But if they're who I suspect they are, you and the major may wish they had been."

"What?" said Snipe. He peered at the approaching jeep. Now it was close enough for him to discern the figure standing up: a woman, smiling and waving to the Legion camp. "I've seen that face somewhere," he said, frowning.

"I bet you have," said Armstrong, lowering the stereoculars and waving back. The troops in the front line were also standing and waving. What was going on?

Then the jeep turned to avoid a spot of rough terrain, and at last Snipe could clearly see what was painted on its side: Interstellar News Service. The woman standing in the jeep was none other than Jennie Higgins, the reporter who had made Captain Jester a media darling.

They'd been invaded, all right—by the intergalactic press corps.

* * *

Being confined in a dimly lit enclosure, even with companionship, was boring. There was no other term for it. It was quite some time since Phule and Beeker had run out of useful observations to make on their current condition, and no other topic of conversation got very far. It was incredibly boring.

At one point, Phule had gotten so bored he'd tried bouncing the gravball their captors had given them against the opposite wall of their cell, but the bell inside jingled every time the ball moved. That got on his nerves—and on Beeker's, as well—after about three bounces, and he went back to slouching against the wall, trying to think of a way to escape—or to communicate with their captors. So far, Beeker had relentlessly shot holes in all his good ideas.

Even so, every once in a while, when he was starting to get really bored, he'd cast an eye over at the ball again. Maybe there was some way to get the bell out ... but trying it would undoubtedly make more noise, and then he'd have to put up with more of Beeker's baleful looks and sarcastic comments. Compared to that ... well, he thought he could put up with the boredom a little while longer, anyhow.

Maybe it was starting to get to him, though. He hadn't touched the ball, and yet he could swear he'd heard the bell jingling again very softly. The ball wasn't visibly moving. His nerves must be starting to fray. They said that solitary confinement could drive a person mad. They didn't say anything about confinement with one's butler, but Phule was beginning to think it must be at least as bad.

"Sir, would you please stop that?" snapped Beeker, as if to reinforce Phule's thoughts.

"Stop what?" said Phule. "Can't a fellow sit and think without you complaining?"

"You're doing something to the ball, sir," said Beeker, glaring at him. "I hear the bell ringing."

Phule sat up straight. "Do you hear it too? I thought it was my imagination."

"No—look, sir, it's moving," said Beeker, pointing. Sure enough, the ball was wobbling slightly, as if the floor below it were shaking.

They both stood, instinctively moving away from the vibrating gravball; whatever was happening, it was something new. The previous changes in their cell, when their captors had delivered food or the ball, had been accompanied by almost no noise or vibration. As they looked, the wall at the far end of the cell began to change color—or rather, its color seemed to become more diffuse, almost like paint being diluted by a colorless liquid.

After the phenomenon continued for a few moments, shapes could be seen through the wall. Phule clapped his hands and said, "I think they're going to let us out, Beek."

"You may be right, sir," said Beeker. "Equally possible is that they intend to come in here and interrogate us."

"There's not enough room in here," said Phule. "Well, maybe if they're the size of Synthians ..."

"Yes," said Beeker. "They've done very little so far to indicate what race they are—if, in fact, they are any race we know."

Phule put a hand on Beeker's arm. "I think we're about to find out," he said. The opening was almost transparent now, and the shapes outside seemed to be moving closer.

To their surprise, one of the figures bent over to look through the opening and said, "Hey, Beeker! Is that you in there?"

"I know that voice!" said Phule, leaning forward. "Sushi, what are you doing here?"

"Captain!" said Sushi, now plainly visible through the opening. "What are *you* doing here? Or maybe I should ask, if you're here, who's that back at the camp?"

"I haven't the vaguest idea what you're talking about," said Phule. He and Beeker scrambled quickly out of their prison. They found themselves in the shade of a small hill, just outside a sort of cave dug into the sandy soil. In front of them were Sushi, Flight

Leftenant Qual, and a group of other legionnaires. But as glad as they were to see their comrades, Phule and Beeker's gaze inevitably turned to the other figure standing there.

Phule's first impression was that he was seeing a mechanical man born of an illicit union between a hoverjeep and a portable computer ... with a very bad hangover thrown on top of it.

On second impression, the thing looked even *more* like the offspring of an illicit union between a hoverjeep and a portable computer—although it had a curious shimmer about it, as if it were a badly focused holo. But he had a strong suspicion he'd have plenty of other things to worry about, and for the moment he was enjoying just being out of his cell.

Harsh reality would undoubtedly assert itself before he got too comfortable.

CHAPTER FIFTEEN

Journal #580

Unpleasant as our confinement had been, my employer and I had never entirely lost confidence in our eventual rescue. Still, when we learned the amount of time that had actually passed, we were surprised at how short it had been. Time inside a closed space, without clues to events in the external world, goes much more slowly than outside. This might account for the unusual trepidation with which even hardened criminals regard solitary confinement. In fact, even with each other as companions, my employer and I were quite relieved to learn that our captivity was at an end.

As attentive readers will have anticipated, once we were released into the light of day, we were thoroughly astonished to learn the nature of our captors.

* * *

"I don't understand it," said Phule, pointing to the robot-like being standing next to Sushi. "If this creature is what captured us, why didn't we ever see it?"

Sushi shrugged. "I wasn't here, Captain, but I don't think it existed in this form before we started talking to it."

"It didn't exist?" said Beeker. "How, then, Mr. Sushi, did it manage to take us captive?"

"I said, 'in this form,' Beeker," said Sushi. "The creatures that captured you are nanotech intelligences: tiny machines that can combine into various larger units to accomplish specific tasks. Until we started talking to them, they didn't have any reason to make themselves visible to us."

"This explains much," said Flight Leftenant Qual. "Not only why our instruments could not detect them but why they thought that your machines were the intelligent creatures, and you some sort of captive animal companions."

Phule's jaw dropped so far it looked for a moment as if it had been dislocated. "What?" he blurted out. "They think that Beeker and I are ... *pets*?"

Sushi managed to keep from grinning. "Yeah, that's about as close as I can describe what seems to be their basic assumption. As far as I can tell, when they saw you two leaving the hoverjeep, they thought you were running away, and so they captured you and took care of you until they could find out what your master—the jeep or the computer—wanted done with you. Apparently, Sir, they have a hard time imagining intelligent animal life ..."

"Machines?" Beeker interrupted. "I beg your pardon, young Sir, but I cannot accept the notion of a machine intelligence evolving independently of some original organic creator."

"I'm with you on that, believe me," said Sushi. Then he shrugged. "Maybe they evolved from mechanical junk left behind by some off-world visitors. But that's just a guess. Bottom line is, we're dealing with a civilization of nanomachines. Individually, they're general-purpose units with fairly low intelligence, but when they combine, the larger unit—the macro, I'd call it—can have a total intelligence as high as ours."

"Theoretically higher, if your premise is correct," said Beeker grudgingly. "But I've never heard of such a thing evolving independently."

"Neither have I," said Sushi. "First time for everything, isn't there?"

"Sushi's right," said Phule. "We've got to accept the situation as we find it. And I think he was about to tell us just what that situation is." He turned to Sushi with an expectant smile.

"OK, like Qual was saying, they thought the hoverjeep and the Port-a-Brain were the intelligent beings, and they've been spending their time trying to communicate with them. If you'd been wearing your translators, you might have been able to make sense of the noise on the jeep's communicator. But once you were out of the jeep, not even that would've helped."

"And so they took us prisoner and tried to negotiate with the jeep," said Phule. "I imagine they didn't get very far with that."

"Well, they kept getting back a signal from the Port-a-Brain' s modem trying to download your stock quotes," said Sushi. "They could tell it was intelligent, but they couldn't get any useful response from it. And of course they had no way to know that you guys were really in charge of the machines. They apparently had you in some sort of holding pen, being kept alive and healthy but not really getting much of their attention."

"That's not very flattering, I must say," grumbled Beeker.

"It could've been worse," said Phule. "Remember, for a while we were worried that they might decide to have us for lunch."

"I don't think they're interested in organics anyway," said Sushi. "They were more likely just to turn you loose in the desert to go fend for yourselves."

Beeker scoffed. "Not interested in organics? What do they use for fuel? For lubricants?"

Sushi shrugged, but there was a smile on his face. "We don't know, but it's worth finding out, isn't it? Maybe they could use another supplier ..."

Phule sat up straight and clapped his hands. "Now, there's the kind of thinking the Legion can use! There's always an opportunity to make a few dollars, if you just ask the right questions. Sushi, I thank you for starting the ball rolling. We'll definitely want to explore that issue further."

"Think nothing of it, Captain," said Sushi, buffing his fingernails. "In fact, they seem to have played the stock market very successfully. They've got a *lot* of money to spend, once we can figure out what they're likely customers for. I wonder if a finder's fee might not be in order …"

"You'll be in on the ground floor," said Phule.

"Thanks, Captain. I knew you'd do the right thing," said Sushi. "But for now, let's concentrate on getting this situation untangled. I've set the modem to a kiddie Internet channel, and we're running a Roger Robot marathon, but the nanomachines will probably get tired of trying to talk back to it before long. Still, it'll give us some time to figure out how to get you out of here and back to camp—and what to do once you're there."

Phule laughed. "What to do? That doesn't seem too difficult to figure out. A nice, long shower, a change of clothes, a cool drink, and then I'll settle down to solving whatever problems have come up since I left. Although now that we've found the Hidden Ones, we've got to get them and the Zenobians talking—figure out what their interests are, what common ground there might be. That's obviously our main priority. I can't imagine anything more important that'd have come up—"

"Captain, you don't know the half of it," said Sushi, shaking his head. "You don't know the half of it."

* * *

Major Botchup was *not* happy about dealing with the press. It wasn't that he saw publicity as a bad thing; indeed, he had a small file of clippings of his own, carefully gathered and organized to show the highlights (such as they were) of his career to date. Nor was he at all averse to standing in front of cameras and answering reporters' questions at length, often at greater length than the reporters were interested in devoting to him. He well understood the power of positive press.

No, what annoyed Botchup was that the reporters were here not because of him but because of his deposed predecessor. That stuck in his craw. These media vultures ought to be focusing on the winners, not defeated second-raters like that mountebank, Captain Jester. *He* was the commanding officer of Omega Company. It shouldn't matter that he hadn't done anything so far …

"Major, you don't seem to realize what the story is," said Jennie Higgins. "Captain Jester was responsible for putting this company into the public consciousness, and now he's suddenly been replaced in command. People want to know why this has happened, and they want to hear what he has to say about it."

"Miss Higgins, I'll remind you that this is a war zone," said Botchup, sweating despite the excellent climate control system Phule had installed in what had become his successor's office. Jennie's cameraman was lurking right behind her, and he had to measure his words carefully to avoid looking a fool on holoscreens half the galaxy away. His career could be ruined by a careless slip in front of billions of primetime viewers. "As much as we in the Space Legion understand the public's interest in what we're doing here, at the same time, we have to be on constant guard against our enemies learning something that could compromise our mission here—"

"Of course we understand that, Major," said Jennie with a dazzling smile. "And I know none of our viewers want these brave legionnaires to be put in harm's way by a careless word or holo image." The smile broadened, and she leaned forward over the major's desk. "That's why I've come to you before talking to your people. We've found that the closer we work with the officers in charge of a given operation, the better we can walk that fine line between security and the public's need to know. So what I want from you now is background—off the record, if you'd prefer—and once I know that, we can work out ground rules for the rest of my stay here. Is that OK?"

Botchup found the room getting even warmer; he'd have to check the air-conditioning. But the pretty young reporter—she certainly *was* pretty—seemed to be making sense, after all. It might be his best chance to get his own name attached to the company's growing reputation, supplanting Jester in public esteem as well as in fact. Jester had played the media the way a trained musician plays a fine synth-organ; now it would be his turn.

Botchup looked into Jennie's eyes and murmured, "Why, Miss Higgins, I think we can work together after all. Now, just what did you need to know?"

"Tell us about yourself, Major," she said, almost cooing. "What brought you to a military career? How did you end up as commanding officer of this company?"

Major Botchup took a deep breath, and a self-satisfied smile came onto his lips. Now he would tell the story his way. And, for the first time, people all over the Galaxy would understand what made Elmer Botchup the man he was. A man of some importance, a man worthy of respect. He looked straight at the holocam. "It all began when I was a small boy," he said. "That was when I first realized I had the gift of command ..."

The holocam purred quietly, recording every word.

* * *

"A new CO," said Phule, shaking his head after Sushi had brought him up to date on the situation back at their base. "That's going to be trouble, all right. And you say there's somebody who's impersonating me as well?"

"That's right, Captain," said Sushi. "He walked in from the desert one night; Garbo and Brick were on guard, then. They can tell you the story. But the main thing is, he was acting very strange, as if he didn't quite know where he was. They all just thought you'd gotten heat stroke in the desert. Now that I think back on it, though, there were plenty of clues that it wasn't you after all. Who do you think it could be? Do you think Headquarters sent somebody to replace you and play crazy so you could be discredited?"

"I doubt most of us would notice a difference, to tell the truth," said Beeker.

"I don't think Headquarters would try that," said Phule, ignoring the butler's jab. "They might be that devious, but they aren't that smart. I've got a pretty good idea what's happened back at base, though, and if I'm right, I won't have much trouble establishing who's who. I'm more worried about this Major Botchup, if he's as bad as you describe."

"Oh, man, he sure is," said Sushi. "Worse—he's like all the Legion horror stories about bad COs rolled up in one. Even the sergeants are acting worried. I've never seen that before."

"That's a bad sign," agreed Phule. "I didn't think there was anything in the galaxy that could faze a sergeant—well, not until the Renegades came after Chocolate Harry, anyhow. And I'll be really worried if the major's got Brandy off her usual track."

"You can judge for yourself when you get back," said Sushi. "And if you're lucky, you can convince the major not to have you cashiered for being AWOL along with the rest of us in the search party. Or maybe he'll throw you in irons for impersonating yourself. He's that kind of hardnose."

"I can get the search party off the hook," said Phule. "You'll claim I ordered you to look for the Hidden Ones before he got on base. Since I wasn't there, I couldn't tell him or the other officers about your mission. He can try to call me on that, but he won't get anywhere if we all stick to the story. I was the legal commander at the time I gave the order."

"Well, I appreciate your taking the heat on it," said Sushi. "He's still likely to try to come after us, but with you on our side, we ought to be all right. Thanks, Captain."

"No problem, Sushi," said Phule. "Remember, that was our main mission when we came here—to help Qual's people find the Hidden Ones, and now that you've found them, it'd look pretty bad not to give you credit for it."

"We're going to have to come up with some name other than Hidden Ones," said Sushi. "They aren't hiding, they're just very small—"

"Nanoids," suggested Mahatma. "From nanotech—"

"Well, that's catchy enough," said Sushi. "Nanoids—"

"A barbarism," sniffed Beeker. But the name stuck.

* * *

Jennie Higgins smiled. Her return to Omega Company—once she'd gotten past the new CO—had been like a reunion with old friends. When she stepped into the mess hall, Sergeant Escrima had made a point of filling her tray himself, proudly pointing out his new gourmet creations. Grinning broadly, Chocolate Harry had given her a purple camouflage T-shirt and fatigue cap with Omega Company insignia to wear—an instant icebreaker when she sat down to chat with the legionnaires. Brandy had thrown her arm around her like a kid sister and taken her on a personal tour of the modular base camp that was the company's field headquarters on Zenobia.

In fact, except for Major Botchup's snotty adjutant, Lieutenant Snipe, everyone in the company had been eager to make her welcome. And—except for one subject—they'd been more than willing to talk to her. But the minute she mentioned the captain, their expressions turned serious. "You gotta talk to him yourself," said Chocolate Harry, and everyone else had given her some version or another on the same line, without responding to her attempts to pump them for more information. Jennie was very good at pumping interview subjects, and to hit such a pronounced dry spell was in itself unusual.

The problem was, she'd been unable to find Captain Jester— or Willard Phule, to give him the name he'd gone by before he'd joined the Legion. Immediately after her arrival, she'd spotted him sitting under a sort of awning with a pile of paperwork on a table in front of him while everyone else in the company acted as if an invasion was imminent. But Lieutenant Snipe had whisked her off to the command center before her old friend noticed her. When she returned, he'd disappeared, and nobody seemed able to tell her where he was. In fact, when she asked where his actual quarters were, nobody could tell her. They weren't trying to hide it from her—she was too good a reporter to miss the signs of that. They just didn't know.

The other area she'd been unable to learn anything useful about was their mission here on Zenobia. Oh, everybody agreed that the Zenobians had called the company in to advise them how to deal with some mysterious problem. But, while everybody had an opinion, nobody seemed to know for sure just what the problem was. Even the Zenobians themselves had apparently never seen the mysterious invaders who were causing all the fuss. And the only one on the base who might have some more detailed information on the subject was none other than Captain Jester— the one man she couldn't find to talk to.

It had begun to gnaw at her. She'd racked her brain for reasons. Perhaps Phule was ill (she'd already heard the story of how he'd walked in from the desert from far enough away that his hoverjeep hadn't been found yet). Perhaps the new major's arrival had been such a blow to his normally very healthy ego that he couldn't bear to talk to her. Perhaps it was some kind of conspiracy by top Legion brass to keep him from talking to the press. Perhaps it was something *she* had unwittingly done.

So it was almost a shock to come out of her tent—Major Botchup had allowed the press corps to set up its own little enclave within the legion perimeter—and see the captain sitting under the awning on a camp stool, riffling through a pile of papers. His expression was good-natured as always, but his body language said "Man Working—Do Not Disturb" as plainly as if he'd hung out a sign.

Jennie hadn't gotten to where she was in her profession without being willing to ignore that kind of message, even from people she didn't know. Willard Phule had taken her out wining and dining and dancing in first-class restaurants on two planets and one luxury space resort. More to the point, he'd given her blanket permission to interview any and every member of his company, with holocams running. He had been her best contact for one of the biggest stories of her career. She sensed that whatever was going on right now might be the single most fascinating twist in the entire story to date. And she certainly wasn't going to let the fact that he was busy get in her way of talking to him.

"Hey, there you are at last! How are you doing?" she called, waving heartily and striding purposefully over to where he sat. She straightened her new purple camouflage hat and smiled her best smile.

Phule raised his head at the sound of her voice *and looked right through her.* Jennie stopped dead in her tracks. She was used to being looked *at*—with appreciation by the male lookers, often with envy by the females. On any given day, several billion pairs of eyes might be scanning her face on holo sets all across the Galaxy. And when she walked into a place, it was a given that she'd be the center of attention.

To be looked at with a complete lack of interest—to be looked at as if she didn't even exist—and by someone with whom she'd shared good times and helped in bad times, that was beyond the pale. Jennie couldn't even begin to understand it. She tried to meet Phule's eyes for a moment, but she might as well have been trying to stare down a statue. After a moment, she averted her gaze. This wasn't the man she knew, and whatever had happened to him, she wanted nothing to do with it. She turned away and stumbled off in utter defeat for the first time in her long career.

Under the awning, the captain looked around in puzzlement, and muttered, "I could have sworn somebody was calling me." Then he shrugged and turned back to the pile of papers.

Journal #593

Our return journey to the Legion camp was slower than originally planned, since not all the legionnaires were able to ride in the hoverjeep. Since my employer thought it useful for the party to arrive all at once, he devised a shuttle system, whereby a part of the party would ride to a point within walking distance of camp and wait while the jeep returned for the balance of the party. Eventually, after three trips, all the personnel and equipment were within striking distance of the destination.

Now, though, my employer paused to consider how to go about entering the camp. With a new commanding officer in place, it was not going to be the triumphant homecoming he had envisioned. In fact, it might bear uncomfortable resemblances to attending a hanging—as guest of honor.

* * *

"Very well, Captain Clown, we are here," said Flight Leftenant Qual. The party had paused in a thick pack of scrub trees, just within sight of the Legion camp. "Now our difficulty is to bring you into the camp lacking any incident."

"I fear a bigger problem is going to be smuggling out that robot without the new commanding officer learning of it," said Beeker. He turned to Phule and said, "I told you it was a risky idea to depend on it, sir."

"Oh, I'm not worried about the robot," said Phule. "We'll have Sushi bring it out of camp. It's attuned to my vocal patterns, so I can reprogram it verbally. Beeker, you'll put the robot in the hoverjeep and transport it back to the Nanoids' base. When you get there, you'll take the translator off the Port-a-Brain and connect it to the robot so it can communicate with the Nanoids. Then you come back with the jeep, and don't forget the Port-a-Brain! I'll put out the story that I left you behind on some private mission. If everything goes right, they'll never even suspect there was more than one of me here."

"Seems a shame to waste the potential for creative chaos," said Sushi. "We could play some interesting games with the major's head if we had both you and the robot here."

"Don't even think about it," said Phule. "It's much more important for the robot to serve as a liaison to the Nanoids. We need to set up a permanent communications link with them. If what we've seen of their capabilities is any evidence, they'd be an incredibly valuable addition to the Alliance as a whole. But I guess the diplomats will have to settle that question. I wonder if the Nanoids have diplomats."

"If they don't, I suspect they soon will. Their adaptability is their most impressive trait," said Beeker. He paused a moment, then added, "With proper instruction, I believe they could learn to be quite adequate butlers."

For a moment, Phule was speechless. Then he shook his head and said, "Let's just hope they don't try it. Civilization in this Galaxy has withstood everything from supernovas to clouds of dark matter, but a race of Beekers would be the final straw."

"To the contrary, sir," said Beeker, pulling himself up to his full height. "It would be the first opportunity for a real civilization to exist."

"You two could probably go on about this all night long," said Sushi with a crooked grin. "But I think we'd better get everything else taken care of before you get started on it—if you know what I mean, Captain."

"You're right," said Phule, chuckling. "All right, Beeker, you wait here with the hoverjeep until we bring the robot back. If anybody from the camp comes out looking for you, do what you have to do to lose them. Call me on our private frequency, and we'll figure out an alternate rendezvous point if we need to."

Beeker settled into the hoverjeep's cockpit, and the rest of the party began a careful approach to the perimeter. Not knowing what security measures Major Botchup had put in place since their departure, they couldn't assume they'd be able to walk in unchallenged. For all they knew, the major had ordered the camp guards to shoot any intruders on sight. And while odds were fairly good that the shooting would be done with Zenobian stun rays, being immobilized and brought in for questioning would put a serious crimp in their plans. All of them were technically AWOL, and even before that, all the legionnaires had been ordered confined to the base. The major would most likely throw the book at them without bothering to listen to explanations.

Closer they crept, making use of what little cover remained in the area around the camp. Unfortunately, Phule had chosen the campsite with some awareness of security, which meant that cover was sparse along the approaches to the camp, and thus the returnees were exposed to the eyes of any reasonably vigilant sentries within. Fortunately, this *was* Omega Company, so there was a fair chance that the sentries were somewhat less vigilant than their new CO might hope.

Suddenly, a voice rang out. "Yo, who that out there? You got half a second 'fore I fry your ass."

"I know that voice," said Sushi. Before Phule could say anything, he stood up and waved his arms. "Hey, Street, it's me," he called. "Keep it down before somebody hears you."

"Stay right there," said Street, somewhat more quietly. He and another figure were silhouetted against the dim lights of the camp, and the group of returnees heard a few lines of muttered conversation between the two before Street called out. "How I know you who you say?"

"Keep it down, OK?" said Sushi. "I'll come right in where you can see me—"

"No way, you stay there 'less you wan' get shot," said Street. "What the password?"

"Password?" Sushi said softly. "There wasn't any password before, was there?"

"Yeah, the major made us start using them," whispered Brick, who was closest to him in the group. "You must not have been on guard duty before you left."

"Who's the other one with him?" said Sushi. "Maybe they'll listen to me."

"Can't tell," said Brick. "They haven't said anything yet. Get 'em to talk, and maybe I can figure it out."

"No need for that," said Garbo's translated voice. "The wind comes from behind them, so I can identify his scent from here. That is the one called Gears."

"Good, he's not one of the major's brown-nosers," said Sushi. "If nobody else has been alerted, we may be in luck. I just have to convince 'em who we are. He lifted his voice again. Yo, Street, is that Gears with you?"

"You gots to have the password, Soosh," said Street. "Major's busting chops somethin' fierce."

"Take it easy. The major doesn't need to know about this," said Sushi. "Just be cool." He turned to Phule and said, "If the major's got Street asking for passwords, he's really got people scared. What do we do now, Captain?"

"Time to take the bull by the horns," said Phule. "Brick, you go to the left, and Garbo to the right, and move in on the perimeter. We'll keep Street and Gears busy until you're closer." The two legionnaires leaned closer as he outlined his plan, their heads nodding as he told them their roles.

"We can do it, Captain!" said Brick with quiet confidence. She and the Gambolt began creeping carefully away from Phule's position.

Meanwhile, Sushi was keeping up a stream of talk. "Look here, Street, you know I've been off base for a while—on a secret mission, you know. The major must have forgotten I was away, because he didn't tell me what the password was gonna be. But now I'm back, and I have to report. How do I get back in without you shooting me?"

Robert Asprin and Peter J. Heck

"Man, I dunno," said Street, obviously confused. "We gotta send somebody to ask the major."

"No, no, no," said Sushi quickly. "We don't want to wake him up. You know how cheesed off he gets. Just let me come in so I can clean up and get a little rest before I have to report to him. I don't want him giving me the eyeball about my uniform when I'm giving him bad news."

"Bad news?" It was Gears's voice this time, sounding concerned. "What kind of bad news?"

His answer was the soft buzz of Zenobian stun rays, wielded by Garbo and Brick. "Bad news for you," said Sushi softly. The returning group waited a moment, then began to move quietly forward. They were inside the perimeter well before the stunned sentries awoke.

* * *

At this time of night, Comm Central was the only place in Omega Company's camp with much activity, and for the most part, it was pretty much a dead zone. Not even the officer of the day usually bothered to spend the late-night hours at the cluttered desk provided in one corner of the comm area. Thanks to Phule's introduction of the wrist communicators, it was normally a matter of moments for Mother to contact the OD—or the CO himself— if something required an officer's attention.

But Lieutenant Snipe had not trained with Omega Company. In his eyes, the company's officers were unpardonably slack in their duties; he'd been sent here to put things right again. So when the rotation came around to him, he spent his OD duty exactly as the Legion academy had taught him: at the desk, alert and prepared for any emergency. After all, as the major kept pointing out (not that anybody seemed to pay attention), this planet was technically a war zone. Anything could happen, and somebody had better be ready to deal with it. According to the books, tonight that somebody was Snipe.

The only other human in Comm Central was Mother, hunched behind her console, keeping tabs on the minimal late-night comm traffic: mostly routine messages from off-planet mixed with perfunctory "all's well" reports from the unlucky legionnaires who'd drawn late-night sentry duty. She steadfastly refused to acknowledge Snipe's presence. At the other desk sat Tusk-anini. So far, Lieutenant Snipe's disapproving glances had drawn no response whatsoever from the Volton, who was steaming along at high speed through the second volume of Gibbon's *Decline and Fall of the Roman Empire*. The night was starting to look like another of those deadly dull intervals that had been the primary feature of Snipe's military career to date.

Having finally abandoned his futile attempts to intimidate Tusk-anini, Snipe found a challenge more worthy of his efforts: keeping himself from dozing off. He was well on his way to losing that battle, as well, when something in the faint buzz of comm traffic brought him to full alertness.

"What was that?" he said, staring in Mother's direction. "I could have sworn I heard something about intruders."

"ᵢmperthnthnthn," explained Mother, sinking lower behind her console.

"I hear it, too," said Tusk-anini. He marked his place and set the book down on the desk, then stood up and walked over behind Mother, looking over her shoulder at the readouts on her console. His piggish countenance took on even more of a frown than it usually wore.

Lieutenant Snipe stood and made as if to join him, but the Volton raised a huge paw and shook his head with unmistakable meaning. Snipe managed to resist the impulse to point out that, as an officer, he should be giving the orders. Instead, he asked in a somewhat timorous voice, "What's going on?"

"Don't know yet," said Tusk-anini. "Snipe be quiet; Mother listening."

Snipe opened his mouth to protest, but before he could say a word, all hell broke loose.

CHAPTER SIXTEEN

Journal #600

My employer had thought that getting inside the Legion camp would put him in position to untangle all his remaining problems. He would find the robot and reprogram it verbally to act as liaison to the Nanoids, then take its place—his own proper place—as a Legion officer. From there, he could present his solution to the Zenobians' problems and possibly use the prestige of that accomplishment to regain command of his company. It would take some politicking and an end run around the Legion brass, but with patience—and the liberal use of a Dilithium Express card—it ought to be possible.

Little did he realize just how fast events were already moving.

* * *

"Where you want to go now, Captain Clown?" Flight Leftenant Qual asked in a reptilian whisper. Once inside the Legion camp's perimeter, the group had taken cover behind Chocolate Harry's supply depot, a Legion-issue prefabricated metal shed across the compound from the MBC, where most of the company were undoubtedly sleeping.

"I'm not sure," said Phule. Then, after a pause, he said, "I should probably try to find the robot so I can reprogram it and take its place. Does anybody have any idea where it's quartered?"

"Officer's quarters, I'd think," said Sushi, peering around a corner the shed. "You don't want to go there. You're likely to run into the major."

"That's no problem," said Phule. "He'll just think I'm the robot. No, he doesn't know about the robot, does he?"

"None of us knew about the robot until you told us," said Sushi. He chuckled. "I know a few people who're going to feel pretty weird when they find out it wasn't really you they were talking to. I heard a couple of funny stories before I left—"

"Shhh! Something's happening," said Brick, who'd been keeping lookout for the party.

"What?" said Phule, instantly alert. But the answer came not from Brick but from the MBC, where a Klaxon began to blow. The legionnaires looked at one another. That signal had been drummed into their nerves by drill after drill. It was the battle stations alarm. Either it was an extremely ill-timed drill, or someone thought the camp was under attack!

"What do we do, Captain?" asked Sushi. Already, armed legionnaires were beginning to emerge from the MBC, headed for their assigned places.

Phule didn't miss a beat. "You know what you're supposed to do, all of you. You've all got your equipment. Now get to your battle stations and be ready for action."

"But ... we just snuck into the camp," said Brick. "They must have us all listed as AWOL."

"They aren't going to argue with you as long as you're where you're supposed to be," said Phule. "Go ahead, it's the one place nobody'll pay any attention to you."

"He's right," said Sushi, giving Brick a shove. "If we stay here, we'll stick out like half a dozen sore thumbs. Come on, everybody head for your stations. Captain, you know where to find us when you need us."

"Right," said Phule. "Now, hurry up before somebody notices we didn't all come from the same place as everybody else."

The legionnaires didn't argue. The group split up as they each headed toward their assigned place. But Flight Leftenant Qual had no assigned place. He watched the others for a moment, then turned and said to Phule, "This is very good, but where does Captain Clown go?"

"First thing I have to do is let Beeker know what's up so he can get under cover," said Phule. "If the camp's on alert, somebody's likely to pick up the hoverjeep on the sensors and assume he's a hostile. I'm sure Beek can talk his way out of almost any kind of trouble, but I have a hunch he'd be willing to forgo the added excitement of people shooting at him while he's doing it."

"Yes, that would be congruent," said Qual. "What might I do to assist you?"

"Maybe you can find out where my robot duplicate is," said Phule. "I ought to reprogram it before anybody figures out there are two of me. And if you can keep the new CO off my back, that'll be even better."

"I do not think he will get on your back," said Qual with his reptilian grin. "But in case he attempts it, I will repel him."

"Good man," said Phule absently, and he began trotting toward the MBC. He hadn't decided exactly what course of action to take, but he knew things would begin falling into place before long. They always did. For now, he just headed for the one place where, unless he was very unlucky, nobody should bother him until he was ready.

* * *

Jennie Higgins had not slept well. It wasn't like her. She'd slept in rougher accommodations on a dozen worlds, out on assignment. It wasn't even that uncomfortable; hot as the desert air was in full sunlight, it quickly cooled to something quite pleasant at night. There was even a bit of a breeze stirring. And while the desert creatures of this world made sounds unlike the soft night music the flenders and oloxi sang on her home planet, they were hardly the kind of thing to keep her awake. Her cot and sleeping bag were the best money could buy.

No, she knew very well what was keeping her awake. She was worried about Willard Phule—or, to give him his Legion name, Captain Jester. She hadn't realized she cared quite so much. Tough, spunky Jennie Higgins didn't let things bother her, did she? In the news business, you learned not to get too close to a story. Maybe it was time for her to back off from this one.

Except that backing off was turning out to be a lot easier to say than to do.

She *liked* Phule. Liked the men and women in Omega Company, too. And she was angry that they'd evidently become pawns in the political games of Legion brass. But she'd never thought Phule would just knuckle under and submit to having a new CO sent in over his head. The Captain Jester she'd known would have found some way to fight back, and his legionnaires would have gleefully joined in the fight.

The man she'd seen sorting papers this morning hadn't shown even a hint of fighting spirit. He hadn't even had enough spirit to look her in the eye.

She knew what she ought to do. She ought to put together a story that showed the Legion brass in their true colors, a story that would have generals quaking in their boots when she came on their holoscreens. But she couldn't muster the energy to do it all, not without Phule's help. And from what she'd seen of him, he had nothing left to bring to the fight.

Maybe coming to Zenobia had been a mistake after all. She hated to think of herself letting down the Omega Mob—men and women she'd come to think of as her friends—but a reporter had to choose her fights. And this one didn't look like one she could win. Not unless—

The sound of a Klaxon made her sit bolt upright on her cot. Something was happening out there in the camp. Already she could hear voices raised, the sound of men and women in a hurry.

She leapt from the cot and quickly threw on a set of Legion-issue fatigues, a gift from Omega Company in the old days. Maybe this was her chance to salvage some kind of story from this miserable trip.

She ran her fingers quickly through her hair, not even bothering to turn on a light to check her appearance. She was confident enough to take her chances with a camera. If the story was good enough, the viewers would forgive her for coming on-camera without fixing her face. She ducked through the tent flap and went to roust her cameraman out of his sleeping bag while there was still a chance to get some action shots. In the distance, the Klaxon kept up its urgent call.

* * *

The Andromatic robot aroused itself from the semidormant state it assumed to recharge its batteries and repair any minor wear and tear its mechanical components had sustained during its last active period. Its delicate sensors had detected the sound of people moving about, and that meant it had a job to do.

Its internal monitors ran through a quick system check; everything was in perfect working order. After checking the chronometer to determine local time, it adjusted its external appearance from the "Legion uniform" configuration that seemed to be most common hereabouts to the "Evening formal" that it had been programmed to wear at night, as the hours between 2100 and 0600 were officially designated. It had not observed any of the humans in this area adopting that appearance, but it had its orders. It was very good at following orders … at least, as long as the orders came from an authorized source.

It waited until the sounds in the corridor immediately outside its hiding place died down. That didn't take long. But no unauthorized humans could be allowed to learn its location when it was in a dormant state, and if it were observed leaving its hiding place, it would have to find a new one … not to forget the effect of alerting someone that it might not be what its external appearance said it was. It did not know exactly what a Legion officer was, but it knew that Legion officers did not spend their nights in broom closets.

Satisfied that it could emerge unobserved, the robot quickly moved into the corridor and began walking toward the nearest exit. The humans were apparently all gathering outside. Time for it to go to work.

* * *

"What *is* this shit, man?" Chocolate Harry came stumbling out into the night, a Legion fatigue cap on his head and a purple camo vest thrown hastily on over his size-XXXXL pajamas. He was clearly unhappy at being rousted out of bed.

"I bet it's another drill," said another legionnaire, blocked by Harry's considerable bulk in the doorway he was trying to get out of. "The CO's real big on farkin' drills." Then, after a pause, "Yo, Sarge, you wanna let me past? Brandy's gonna chew my ass off if I'm the last one on the crew to get there."

"Yeah, sure," grumbled Chocolate Harry, scowling as he stepped aside. He was starting to get tired of drills in the wee hours, but the major hadn't consulted him on whether or not it was a good idea. He consoled himself with the thought that he didn't have to run out to the perimeter and act as if he were repelling an invasion of heavily armed nasties. He began ambling toward the supply depot, where he'd be on call if any of the frontline troops turned out to have a dead battery in their laser rifles. It was a dirty job, but somebody had to do it.

He was halfway to his destination when a familiar figure came toward him, jogging. "Hey, Cap'n!" he called out. "They got you up and scramblin' too, huh?"

The captain stopped and gave him a friendly punch to the biceps. "Good to see you, Harry. Any idea what's happening?"

Harry scoffed. "Man, if they ain't tellin' the cap'ns, what makes you think they be tellin' the sergeants?" Then he stopped and squinted. "'Scuse me askin', Cap'n, but maybe I oughta ask *you*—and if it ain't my business, just say so—but is there somethin' goin' on I oughta know about? I didn't know you was into hangin' out behind the supply depot late at night."

Phule leaned closer and lowered his voice. "There's a new top-secret operation starting up," he said. He put his hand on the supply sergeant's elbow. "In fact, it's a good thing I ran into you here. We need a man with a good head on his shoulders, and I think you're right for it. Can you keep this completely to yourself?"

"Top-secret?" echoed Chocolate Harry. He looked over his shoulder, then nodded. "You know I can keep things quiet, Cap'n," he rasped. "What's the poop?"

Phule looked around with an exaggerated air of conspiracy. "You know that Beeker and I were away from the base, talking to the Zenobian leaders," he said. "Well, the Zenobians have got a lot of advanced military gear the Alliance hadn't known about before, and we were trying to get an agreement to try it out—just like the stun rays, you know."

"Cool," said Harry, nodding eagerly. The Zenobian stun rays had made a big impression on him. And, as supply sergeant, he'd be the first to get his hands on any new goodies coming to the company. "What kind of stuff are we getting?"

"That's the secret part," said Phule, still whispering. "I left Beeker behind to make arrangements for the delivery, and now he's finished with that part. But we can't let anybody see him returning to camp, or the enemy is likely to guess that something big is about to happen. You know what I mean ..." He let his voice trail off.

"I get it," said the supply sergeant eagerly. "We got to smuggle him in so nobody spots him. Ain't no need to ask twice. If that's your business, Chocolate Harry's your man! What you want me to do, Cap'n?"

"Here's the plan," said Phule, and he whispered into Chocolate Harry's ear.

After a few moments, the supply sergeant began to nod enthusiastically. By the time Phule was finished, he was grinning from ear to ear. "You got it, Cap'n," he said. "You got every bit of it."

"Good," said Phule. "Now, let's go do it!"

* * *

Major Botchup's first reaction upon being wakened from a sound sleep by the Klaxon was annoyance. *I didn't schedule another*

255

drill, he thought to himself. *Snipe's going to pay for this.* Then he heard another noise under the racket of the horn: the beep of his wrist communicator's alarm, a few feet away on his nightstand. Something was going on.

He sat up and grabbed the communicator. "Botchup here," he growled. "What's going on?"

"Trouble, sir," came Lieutenant Snipe's whining voice.

"I know that, you twit!" roared Botchup. "What kind of trouble?"

"We've got an alarm in Sector Blue, sir," said Snipe, whining even more annoyingly. "The guards on that part of the perimeter aren't responding to signals. Considering that we're in hostile territory, I've called a full alert, just to be on the safe side. What are your orders, sir?"

Botchup nodded; he'd been expecting something like this. "Stay on top of it, Snipe," he barked. "Keep me informed of anything that happens—anything at all. I'm on my way to the command center." He cut the connection before Snipe could answer.

The MBC's command center was, logically enough, immediately adjacent to the CO's sleeping quarters, a setup that Botchup would have been surprised to learn had been designed by Phule himself. But it showed in the details: the soundproofing between the work area and the sleeping area and the quick and easy access to every part of the encampment. Unlikely as it was that the CO's personal presence was required at a given point on the perimeter, he could get there in under five minutes if he was seriously determined to do so.

Botchup pulled on his uniform, ran a comb through his hair, and quickly ducked through the metal sliding door into the command area. A legionnaire was already on duty, a young human with long sideburns and a hint of a smart-assed expression. There was something about him that Botchup instinctively didn't like, but he couldn't quite put his finger on it. Was there a hint of insolence, perhaps, in that little half smile?

"You," said Botchup. "What's the situation?"

"Uh, we have a possible intruder, sir," said the legionnaire. From the voice it might have been a woman, thought the Major, though he could have sworn this legionnaire was male. Those sideburns certainly gave that impression.

The answer would just have to wait, he decided; there were more important problems right now. "Where's the encroachment, and what's being done about it?" he snapped, leaning over to peer at the readout the legionnaire had been consulting.

"Uh, it was over behind Chocolate Harry's, sir," said the legionnaire, gesturing vaguely.

"Was?" said Botchup. "*Was?* Are you telling me that it's already over?"

"Uh, no, sir," said the legionnaire. "It's just that—"

He was interrupted by a cheerful new voice. "Good evening, how's everybody doing? Is everybody feeling lucky tonight?" It was Captain Jester, wearing a freshly ironed tuxedo. A broad smile was on his face as he sauntered into the command center, and he swirled a martini glass in his left hand.

"Jester! Are you out of your mind?" barked the major. "The base is under attack—"

"Security will take care of it," said Jester, dismissing it with a wave of his hand. "Why don't we let them handle it? It's nothing you need to worry about, is it? You're here to forget your worries. And you've come to the right place, let me tell you." He lifted the martini glass in a salute, then lifted it to his lips.

"Damn you!" shouted Botchup, and took a swipe at the glass, trying to dash it from Jester's hand. "You're drunk! And out of uniform! I'll have you cashiered from the Legion—"

"The cashiers are on the first floor, right by the casino entrance," said Jester, nimbly protecting the glass from Botchup's clumsy swing. "Remember, you're here to forget your troubles. Have a drink, play a few games, and you'll find yourself looking at the world with a new attitude. Remember, though, play *with* your head, not over it. Well, got to move along. The place is really jumping tonight!" He spun around and was out the door without waiting for an answer.

Botchup was still trying to make sense of what Captain Jester had just said, and coming up short, when the legionnaire on duty said, "Uh, Major, you've got a call from Lieutenant Snipe."

The major snatched the comm set from the legionnaire's hand. "Snipe! What the hell is going on in this crazy place?"

"Excuse me, sir?" said Snipe. "As I reported before, we've had an alarm in Blue Sector—"

"I know that, you nincompoop," said Botchup. "Have you sent anybody out to see what's actually going on there?"

To Snipe's credit, he only stammered for a moment before answering, "Uh, sir, I'll take care of it at once, sir."

"If it takes any longer, the damned base is going to be overrun," barked the major. "I needed that report five minutes ago, you understand? Now do it!"

"Yes, s—" Botchup cut the connection before Snipe could finish and turned to the command center's sensors to try to make sense of them. As he quickly discovered, that was a lot easier to try than to accomplish.

*　*　*

The camp was full of black-uniformed legionnaires running headlong toward positions on the defensive perimeter. Jennie Higgins stopped to try to get her bearings; without the night vision goggles the legionnaires would be wearing, it was hard to make out details. She ought to ask the captain for a pair. No, she wouldn't. She'd accepted her last favor from him.

"Where do you want me to set up, Jen?" asked a familiar voice nearby. It was her cameraman, Sydney, ready for action despite being rousted out of bed on a moment's notice; there was a dark mass perched on his right shoulder that had to be his holo equipment.

Jennie looked around. "I'm not sure yet, Sydney," she said. "Can you get anything in this light?"

"Light? There's light out here?"

"OK, that answers the question," said Jennie resignedly. "I don't think the Legion would appreciate your turning on a floodlight just to get a few action shots. In fact, if there's really an attack under way, *I* might not appreciate it."

"I wasn't about to offer, if you want to know the truth," said Sydney. "Maybe we should just wait and see if there's any action. Maybe there'll be a few explosions. That'd make good footage, I think."

"I like good footage as much as anybody, but if there are any explosions, I hope they're *way* out in the desert," said Jennie. "I've got a lot of friends here in the camp."

"Hey, I didn't say I wanted *close-ups* of explosions," protested Sydney. "Out in the desert's fine with me."

Jennie said, "Good. Let's see what we can find out, then. This whole scramble might be just a drill, in which case I want to go back and get some sleep. Maybe one of the officers will let us in on the scoop."

"OK, just don't hold your breath expecting the time of day from Major Botchup," said Sydney. "He's about as helpful as snot on a doorknob."

"If that," agreed Jennie. "Let's see if they'll let us into Comm Central. Somebody there'll know what's happening. And if something is going on, there'll be enough light there for you to get some footage." She turned and headed toward the MBC with Sydney close behind.

* * *

"Yo, Mother!" Chocolate Harry burst into Comm Central, sweeping past the startled Lieutenant Snipe as if he were invisible. "Cap'n needs a message sent."

"Sergeant, aren't you forgetting something?" said Snipe, frowning. He drew himself up to his full height, still nearly a foot shorter than the supply sergeant and not even in the same arm of the bell curve in terms of sheer bulk.

"No, man, it's cool. I got it all," said Chocolate Harry, paying about as much deference to the lieutenant as a battle cruiser would to a garbage scow. "Now listen, Mother, here's the deal—"

"Sergeant, this base is in a state of emergency," Snipe said, in a nagging tone of voice. "The equipment has to be reserved for essential military communications, and as officer on duty, that is my decision to make."

"Look here, the cap'n told me to send this," said Harry, turning for the first time to face Snipe. "You got a problem, go talk to him, OK? Better yet, go—"

Before Harry could complete the sentence, the door burst open again, and in came Jennie Higgins and her holocam operator. "Hi!" said Jennie, with her best professional smile. "Can anybody tell me whether this is a drill or not? If it's the real thing, I've got to put together a story."

"Honey, this is some *serious* shit goin' down," said Chocolate Harry with a wink. "I can't tell you nothin' now, but you come talk to me when it's over, and I'll tell you stuff make your hair curl."

"Her hair already curling," said Tusk-anini, looking up from his book.

Lieutenant Snipe raised his voice. "I want this area cleared at once," he shouted. "The major has put the base on full alert status—"

"He didn't do that," interrupted Tusk-anini. "You do that, just a few minutes ago."

"Can I get your statement?" said Jennie, stepping up to the lieutenant and turning on her microphone. Sydney hovered behind her, his holocam humming almost inaudibly. "I'm speaking to Lieutenant Erwin Snipe of Omega Company. Can you tell my viewers whether the base is under attack?"

"Yo, Jennie, don't go botherin' Snipe with questions," said Chocolate Harry, waving his hand. "You'll just get him worse confused. Nobody tells baby lieutenants what's happenin'."

"That's not true!" said Snipe, his voice going up an octave. "I have reports from the front line—"

He was interrupted again as the door swung open and a new voice boomed out, "Hi, it looks as if I've finally found the party!" It was Phule, wearing a perfectly tailored tuxedo and holding a martini glass in one hand.

"Cap'n!" said Chocolate Harry. "I thought you was goin'—"

"Change of plans," said Phule with a wink. "You know, there's very little in life that's so important that a fellow can't afford to stop and smell the roses, is there?"

"Captain, I have reason to believe that this base is under attack!" said Lieutenant Snipe. "If I could get the comm center clear of unauthorized personnel ..."

Jennie stepped forward. "Captain, can you confirm the lieutenant's rumor of an attack?"

Snipe tried again, a little bit louder. "All unauthorized personnel will leave the comm room at once, or I will have security clear it!"

"Oh, *man*, will you get off that jive?"

"Tgfrblt ..."

"I don't know about you, but I'm going to go attack the free lunch buffet over by the dollar slots. It's the best deal in the casino!"

"Captain, can you confirm or deny the rumor?"

"Tgfrblt!"

"I'm calling security right now, do you hear me?"

"Who you calling security?"

"Come on, let's go see the action at the roulette tables!"

"*Will everybody please shut up for one freaking minute?*" The voice booming through the loudspeaker behind the comm console made everyone in the room jump and turn to look. There was Mother, standing at the console with a mic in her hand, glaring at the room. Suddenly realizing that six pairs of eyes and one Galaxy-wide network holocam were pointing at her, she gave a little shriek and ducked back behind the console almost as if someone had grabbed the collar of her jumpsuit and yanked her down.

In the silence came Phule's voice: "Well, time to go see about that free lunch," and before anyone could respond, he was out the door. Not that anyone was paying particular attention to anything except Mother's uncharacteristic outburst.

"Uh, did you wanna say somethin', Mother?" said Chocolate Harry very sheepishly.

"She say it already, but people weren't listening," said Tuskanini, shrugging. "Now it too late."

"Too late for what?" said Lieutenant Snipe, making one more try to control the rapidly deteriorating situation.

"Yes, too late for what?" said Phule, slipping quietly into the room. He was wearing a legion jumpsuit that, for the first time in anyone's memory, seemed not to have been cleaned and pressed within the last twenty-four hours.

"Cap'n!" said Chocolate Harry. He stared for a moment, then shook his head. "That's two of the fastest clothes changes I've *ever* seen, dude. You gonna have to tell me how you did that."

"Oh, good, you back," said Tusk-anini. "Mother have message for you from Beeker, but she thought you gone already."

"From Beeker!" said Phule, surprise on his face. He lifted up his communicator and pressed a button. "If Beeker's breaking comm silence, it's got to be a serious emergency. Patch him through on a secure channel, Mother. I'm ready to receive him." He lifted the communicator close to his ear.

Silence reigned in Comm Central as everyone present strained to hear what Beeker was saying, but with Phule holding his wrist communicator inches from his ear, only an undifferentiated buzz was audible.

Phule's replies were singularly unhelpful: "Yes?" "Really!" "I'll get someone on that at once," and "Good man, Beeker!"

When he lowered the communicator, every pair of eyes in the room was staring at him. He looked back at them and grinned. "Well, I guess we've all got jobs to do, don't we?" he said, and turned and went out the door again.

It was Chocolate Harry who broke the silence. "Man, he flies lower than any dude I ever seen." Then he shook his head and turned to Mother. "That reminds me. Orders from the Cap'n—he didn't say nothin' to change 'em, so get this out to all personnel ASAP."

"Excuse me, Sergeant," said Lieutenant Snipe. "We *are* in an emergency situation, and I am the OD. I am responsible for all communications until further notice."

Chocolate Harry stared at him for a long moment. "Dude, you just got further notice. Mother, send this out, and if any jive-ass Lieutenant wants to put his mark on it, he's gonna have to do it on the fly."

"Chocolate Harry right," said Tusk-anini, and he folded his arms, adding his stare to Chocolate Harry's. After a moment, Snipe blinked. He stood up hastily and made a rapid exit from Comm Central. Nobody watching had any doubt where he was going, but nobody bothered to stop him. The only question was whether he and the major had any way to stop *them*.

* * *

"Hey, Brandy, is this a drill or not?" said one of the legionnaires in the trenches looking out into the night. "I got a nice, soft bunk back in the air-conditioning if we ain't doin' anything in particular out here."

"You think I'm out here trying to get a date?" said Brandy. "All I know is, if this ain't a drill, some nasty BEM's likely to hear you jawin' and put a laser hole through your butt. And if the BEM don't do it, you got a top sergeant right here that'll kick it halfway back to Lorelei. Either way, you lose. So maybe you ought to act like it's the real thing and keep your mouth shut."

"Aw, gimme a break, Brandy," said the legionnaire, but he kept his voice low and his eyes toward the desert beyond the perimeter. If anything was happening out there, it was too subtle to be visible, even with the help of night vision goggles. But Brandy wasn't in the habit of issuing idle threats, and if she wanted the troops to treat the situation as a genuine emergency, that was what she'd get. After an indeterminate length of time, Brandy's wrist communicator buzzed. She sighed and reached out to touch the miniature control that would let her hear the incoming message, undoubtedly the recall signal, ending tonight's drill. Another pointless exercise. That seemed to be Major Botchup's stock in trade. At least Captain Jester's exercises usually had some objective she could understand. It wasn't until she realized that she had also heard the buzz from all the other communicators within earshot that she began to wonder whether this might be something other than an ordinary drill after all.

CHAPTER SEVENTEEN

Journal #605

The one thing that consistently allowed my employer to triumph over his adversaries was their utter inability to escape their preconceived notions. In business, this ability to "think out of the box" was at least given lip service, although a true innovator often met more obstacles than rewards. But in the Space Legion, especially among the officer corps, any notion that hadn't been held by generations upon generations of legionnaires was suspect. So the reaction of a typical Legion officer to one of my employer's schemes was completely predictable.

I am informed that within military circles this inflexibility is considered an asset. Perhaps it is just as well that I was never tempted to follow that career myself. It was all I could stomach to watch the operation of the military mind at a safe and comfortable distance ... preferably several kilometers away.

* * *

"Major, we have a mutiny on our hands," said Lieutenant Snipe, bursting into the command center.

"Mutiny?" Botchup snarled. "These damned incompetents couldn't organize a barroom brawl, let alone a mutiny." Then he frowned. "What are you doing away from your post?"

"The supply sergeant sent out a message, and he wouldn't let me look at it first!"

"Huh. I just got that damned message," said the major. He handed Snipe a printout. "What the hell do you make of this?"

Snipe squinted at the printout for a moment, then said, "I don't understand. This says that all full members of the Church of the New Revelation are to report to the supply shed at once, orders of Captain Jester. What in the world does he want with them in the middle of an attack?"

"Uh, that'll be me," said the legionnaire behind the console.

"You'll stay right where you are," Major Botchup grunted. He turned to Snipe and said, "I want to know what he's doing sending the supply sergeant to transmit the message when he ought to be bringing it here in person. Maybe you're right. We just might be looking at a conspiracy, Snipe."

Snipe rubbed his jaw, thinking fiercely. "That makes sense, Major; he might be trying to open a door to the very invaders we're digging in to repel. What other motive could he have for pulling essential personnel out of our defensive lines?"

"Exactly," said Botchup. "It looks as if our friend Jester is about to sell us out to the very enemy he was sent here to suppress. I'm not surprised that he's doing it, but it is a bit of a shock that he'd be fool enough to put it on record. This'll be all the grounds we need to expel him from the Legion—and clap him into prison for a good long term as well."

"It'll serve him right!" agreed Snipe. "In fact, I wish they'd … What's that?"

"It's the distant motion detector alarm, sir," said the legionnaire at the command console. "Something really big seems to be approaching the perimeter."

"Seems to be?" said Botchup. "*Seems* to be? Is it approaching, or isn't it?"

"I dunno, sir," said the legionnaire, pouting. "Why'n't you take a look if you think you can tell any more than I can?"

"I'll do just that," snarled Botchup, and he elbowed the legionnaire out of the seat and slid in. The legionnaire said nothing but began sidling toward the exit.

Botchup fiddled with a control, muttered something foul-sounding under his breath, switched to a different control, hit a couple of buttons, cursed under his breath, fiddled some more, and then fell silent. Gradually, his mouth began to fall open, and his hands began trembling. After a long silence, he gave a low whistle and said, "Great Ghu, how can anything that big not show up on visual?"

"I don't know," said Snipe. "But it sure is moving fast—"

"Told you so," said the legionnaire, smirking, just before he dodged out the door. But Major Botchup sat staring at the console, not even noticing the young man's departure. That was when Snipe really began to worry.

*   *   *

"What's the story, C.H.?" Rev looked at the supply sergeant, then at the group of legionnaires, all with variations on the same face—the sideburned, full-lipped face with the Grecian nose that he himself wore. By his quick calculation, every member of the Church of the New Revelation—the Church of the King, as it was also known—was here by the supply shed in response to the cryptic message calling them all together at this tense moment.

"I'm just the dude carryin' the message, Rev," said Chocolate Harry. "The cap'n's the only one knows the whole story, and he said he'd be here to fill y'all in as soon as he got one other bit of work taken care of. So be cool, and I reckon he'll be along when whatever's happenin' is ready to happen."

"I can wait, sure 'nuff," said Rev. "Only thing that worries me is, I don't see where the major's signed off on whatever we're doing. That could get mighty touchy if the major decides we're away from our posts in the middle of an emergency—"

"Let me worry about that," said a familiar voice.

"Cap'n!" said Chocolate Harry. "Glad you're here. Looks like we got everybody you asked for—"

"That's right," said Rev. "Every single one of my flock is here, waitin' t' hear what you've got in mind."

"Good work, both of you," said Phule. "Now, here's what I want all of you to do …"

* * *

"What are we going to do, sir?" Snipe peered over Major Botchup's shoulder at the command center's combat situation screen. "What are we going to do?" The screen showed a large, amorphous blip sitting in the desert immediately outside the camp. But reports from the lookouts on that section of the perimeter reported nothing unusual.

"I still can't believe that none of those idiots can see anything out there," muttered Botchup. "Instruments don't lie, damn it." The major sat, staring at the screen and rubbing his chin a moment, then turned and looked at his adjutant. "Snipe," he said.

"Yes, sir?" said the adjutant. Then he saw Botchup's expression and said, "No, sir! You can't be thinking—"

"Don't *you* let me down, too, Snipe," said Botchup, a growl in his voice. "There's something fishy going on here, and I don't dare take any chances. Either these moronic Omega Company clowns are even more grossly incompetent than they've been up to now, or Jester's talked them into deliberately refusing to report a hostile incursion. I need somebody out there, Snipe, and you're the only one I've got."

"Sir," said Snipe resignedly. "What do you want me to do?"

Botchup put a hand on Snipe's shoulder. "Get out to the perimeter in Blue Sector," he rumbled. "That's where the trouble seems to be—and tell me what's going on. And be ready for anything, Snipe, *anything.* When in doubt, assume the worst. Do you hear me?"

"Yes, sir," said Snipe, his face a mask of discontent. He patted his hip, where a sidearm rested in its holster. "I'll be ready, sir." He came to attention and saluted smartly, then turned and headed for the door. It would have been a very smart exit had he not misjudged his step and tripped over a heavy power cable on the floor. He landed flat on his face and lay there a second, then pulled himself up, saluted again, and headed for the door.

He almost made it this time, except for colliding with a legionnaire coming in as he went out. The legionnaire managed to get an arm around Snipe and prevent him from falling again.

"Sorry, Lieutenant," she said. "Ah'll be mo' careful next time."

Snipe stared at her—an oval face with thick dark hair in a high pompadour, with locks combed into sideburns. Her thick lips had an expression somewhere between a sneer and a pout. "Didn't you just leave?" he said. He stared at her name tag, which read "Tupelo."

"No, suh, ah'm just at the start of mah shift," said Tupelo. "That must've been Private Sandbag."

"Oh, yes, I guess you're right," said Snipe. "Well, sir, I'm off." He turned abruptly and made a dash for the door, and this time he managed to find the way out.

* * *

It took Lieutenant Snipe a moment to get his bearings in the dark; too late, he remembered that he had a pair of night vision goggles back in the Comm Center. But the major was in a hurry for answers; no time to get the goggles now. His eyes would just have to adjust.

Now, which way was Blue Sector? Snipe remembered that the incursion had reportedly begun somewhere near the supply depot, which was to the ... to the left of the exit he'd taken from the MBC? Yes, that must be right. He'd looked at the screen before leaving the command center but wasn't sure just how it was oriented in relation to his present position. Well, the encampment wasn't *that* large. He'd find it soon enough.

He jumped as a voice behind him said, "Excuse me, sir, can I help you?"

He turned to see a legionnaire with a dark pompadour, sideburns, and night vision goggles hanging around the neck. "Aren't you supposed to be on duty in the command center?" he asked.

The legionnaire grinned. "No, I wish I was. Working there's got to be a lot more fun than running around in these stupid drills."

From the voice, Snipe realized that this one was a male. Obviously not the same as the one he'd just seen ... except the

Robert Asprin and Peter J. Heck

face was uncannily close. Snipe shivered, then said, "I need to inspect the perimeter in Blue Sector. And don't assume it's a drill, either. This is a war zone, you know."

"Uh—yeah," said the legionnaire, whose nameplate Snipe couldn't make out in the dark. "Blue is over that way, sir"—he gestured to the left—"just past the supply depot, if you know where that is. I'd take you there, but I've got to get to my post."

"That's good enough," said Snipe, and he set off in the direction indicated. His eyes were beginning to adjust to the dark. Above him, the desert sky was full of brilliant stars in unfamiliar constellations—not quite enough light to see by, but perhaps enough to help him avoid crashing into objects the size of a hoverjeep. He made his way gingerly, wondering just what he was supposed to be looking for.

After a short distance, he made out a vague shape ahead of him: the supply depot, he assumed. He moved purposefully toward it, but barely had he covered half the distance when a hulking figure loomed in front of him and said softly, "Who goes there?"

Snipe drew back a pace, noting even in the dark that his challenger was aiming a large weapon toward him. "Point that thing the other way," he said. "It's Lieutenant Snipe, on orders from the major."

"Oh, sorry, sir," said the legionnaire. A small red light appeared in his hand, briefly illuminating Snipe's face—and his own. Snipe got a momentary glimpse of a dark pompadour, long sideburns ...

"I thought you had to go the other way," said Snipe, beginning to wonder if this legionnaire was following him for some reason.

"No, sir, this is my post," said the legionnaire, just loud enough to be heard. Then he drew closer and whispered, "Say, if you don't mind telling me, sir, are we going to see action tonight? Seems awful long for a drill."

"I'm damned if I know what's going on anymore," said Snipe. "That's why I'm out here. Have *you* seen any sign of action?"

"No, sir," said the legionnaire. "Quiet as a mouse, right here. You're the first person I've seen."

"I see," said Snipe. "Wait a minute. I hear something over there!" He pointed toward the dark shadow he assumed was the supply depot.

Before they could react, a group of dark figures dashed up to them. Snipe felt what had to be the muzzle of a weapon pressed against his midsection. "What are you doing here?" growled a low voice.

"L-l-lieutenant Snipe," he managed to stammer. "M-major's orders."

"Snipe? Not bloody likely," said one of the newcomers. "He's probably sitting in his soft bunk while the real legionnaires run the show. Give me a light here."

Again a soft red light gleamed, and in its brief flare Snipe saw the legionnaires around him. After the first instant of shocked recognition, he gave a terrified shriek and fainted dead away.

* * *

Major Botchup paced, stopping occasionally to look at the Command Center console over the shoulder of the legionnaire on duty. What was taking Snipe so long? The approaching ... *entity* that showed, now larger than the Legion camp itself, on the Command Center's screens, surely must be visible from the defensive perimeter. Even Snipe must be able to see it.

He'd tried paging the lieutenant on the communicator, but the interference that had plagued communications ever since he'd arrived on this planet had suddenly increased again. He suspected sabotage. It *had* to be sabotage. Not even Omega Company could rise to this level of incompetence. The camp was in a state of siege, the enemy was gathering its strength for a final assault, and now the enemies were boring from within.

"Try him again," he snapped.

Obediently, the legionnaire at the console went through the routine of trying to hail Botchup's adjutant, but the speakers kept up an unrelenting rumble and rattle of white noise. Or was it noise? Botchup could swear there were patterns in it, but the cryptological analysis devices in the company's arsenal could

Robert Asprin and Peter J. Heck

detect no meaning in them. Either the code was subtler than anyone expected, or ... He didn't want to think about what the alternatives might be.

Suddenly the door to the outside burst open. He turned to glare at the intruder. But his heart sank when he saw Captain Jester come through the door along with Lieutenant Armstrong. Supported between them was the limp, pale form of Lieutenant Snipe.

"What the hell?" said Botchup, as Jester and Armstrong maneuvered the unconscious Snipe to a seat.

"Stand back, sir; let him have some air," said Armstrong. He stepped over to the water cooler and filled a disposable cup and brought it back to Snipe. "We think he'll be all right, but he's got to get a few moments to breathe."

"Yes, yes, but what the hell happened?"

"He appears to have passed out," said Phule. At least now he was in proper uniform, Botchup noted absently. "He was found on the ground out in Blue Sector. It could have been the heat, or it could have been sheer terror ..."

"Terror?" Botchup asked, his brows going upward at least an inch. "Terror? The man's a Legion officer. What in the world could have frightened him?"

"There's something uncanny going on out there," said Phule. "Something's lurking just beyond the perimeter. Look at your readouts! It's there, all right, but nobody can see it. It's the reason the Zenobians called us here."

"I don't believe one word of it," said Botchup, jaw firmly clenched. "Invisible menaces are the stuff of bad holodramas— something to scare babies with. Whatever's out there—"

"He's waking up," said Armstrong, hovering near Lieutenant Snipe. "Here, try to drink some of this water," he urged, holding out the cup he'd filled.

"Good, maybe now we can get some sense out of him," said Botchup. He walked over to Snipe and barked, "Wake up, man! What did you see out there?"

"Dark," muttered Snipe, his eyelids half-open. "*Dark.* That face ... looking at me ..."

"Face?" said Botchup. "What's he talking about?"

"I haven't the foggiest idea," said Phule. "Or perhaps … No, that can't be. It's just a native superstition."

"What native superstition?" growled Botchup. "Out with it, man! There may be lives at stake."

"Captain Clown!" The door burst open again, and a diminutive lizardlike creature came scrambling in, dressed in what was obviously a uniform. It stopped when it noticed the major and made a complex gesture—a salute, apparently. "Major Snafu! It is my onerous duty to report to you!"

"Who the hell is this?" said Botchup.

"It's our native liaison, Flight Leftenant Qual of the Zenobian military," said Phule. "He'll know what's going on, if anyone does. What's happening, Qual? Our instruments show *something* out there, but nobody can see anything."

"Ah-hhh," the Zenobian hissed. "It is as I feared, Captain Clown. The Hidden Ones come, and we shall be powerless against them."

"Powerless?" Major Botchup smirked. "You underestimate us, Flight Leftenant. A Space Legion company is nothing to sneeze at, and even considering the sorry shape they were in when I came on board, I fancy I've got these fellows in pretty decent fighting trim by now."

"With all respectability, it is not so effortless, Major Snafu," said Qual. "The Hidden Ones appear to be where one can strike at them, but when one strikes, the effect is as of nothing. I have seen it. We Zenobians have concentrated the fire of an entire Swamplurkers battalion on them, without consequence except the expenditure of munitions. And when they become agitated, they begin to play tricks on the mind."

"Tricks on the mind?" Botchup scoffed. "Now you're really telling fairy tales. Invisible bogeymen that you can't shoot and that play tricks on the mind when you annoy 'em—go tell it to the Regular Army!"

"It is quite true," insisted Qual. "They cause the victim to become unable to distinguish between persons. It is as if everyone in the world were hatched from the same egg."

Botchup laughed, a harsh braying laugh that conveyed no warmth. "Pardon my Vegan, Flight Leftenant, but that's bullshit, plain and simple. If I had a plot of tomatoes to fertilize I might buy some, but until then, I'll pass."

"Hey, it looks as if I've found the party," came a jaunty voice from the doorway. It was Phule, dressed for a night on the town, with a half-full martini glass in one hand.

Major Botchup turned and stared. "*You!*" he snarled. Then his eyes flicked back to Phule, standing there in Legion uniform, cool and correct as a recruiting poster, and a sudden doubt crossed his face. "Two of you?"

"Excuse me, Major?" said the Phule in uniform, with a carefully neutral expression.

"We could use a few babes to liven things up," said the Phule in the tuxedo. "I know the answer to that. It's ladies' night in the hotel disco. How about we go down there and check out the action?" He whirled and was out the door before anyone could stop him.

Oblivious to the entire episode, Armstrong had been helping Lieutenant Snipe get down a glass of water. Now, at last, Snipe managed to sit up straight and to look around. "How did I get back inside?" he said. "Thank goodness for the light—and for a friendly face. I was beginning to think—"

"Easy, now," said Armstrong. "Why don't you tell the major what happened?"

"Excuse me, Major, we've got somethin' new on the screen," said the legionnaire sitting at the console. He swung around to look over his shoulder.

In that instant Snipe saw his face. "Oh my God!" he screamed. "He's everywhere! He's everywhere!" His eyes rolled up into his head, and he fell back unconscious yet again.

* * *

There were four officers in the command center now. Major Botchup, Phule, Lieutenant Armstrong, and Flight Leftenant Qual. Snipe was back in his own quarters, under sedation, with a large, sympathetic legionnaire outside the door to make certain nobody disturbed him. Externally, Botchup remained calm, but he kept casting a suspicious eye toward the other three officers, as if expecting them to metamorphose into identical triplets.

"The Hidden Ones are upon us," said Qual mournfully. "It remains to be seen whether we can escape utter madness."

"I know what you mean. Damn it, my adjutant's already close to the edge," said Botchup. "For a while there, I was beginning to think I was seeing things myself."

"Well, sir, it's a good thing that didn't happen," said Armstrong. "We need a sound mind at the helm, if you'll pardon a naval metaphor, sir."

"Yes, I suppose so," said Botchup glumly. He turned to Qual and asked, "The thing is, if these, uh, Hidden Ones keep up the pressure, how long can we, uh, hold out against them?"

"That alters according to the specific, Major Snafu," said Qual. "They do tend to focus their attention on the leaders. But a strong-headed sophont such as you ... There is no reason to believe you could not withstand it for hundreds of hours." He flashed a toothy grimace and waved a foreclaw toward the console, which still showed the mysterious presence beyond the camp's perimeter. "In any case, they are present, and we shall undoubtedly learn the answer."

"Yes, I suppose we will," said Botchup glumly.

"Yes, sir," said Armstrong. "Omega Company is lucky to have a commander who's willing to take these risks for his people."

"Not as if I have much choice," said Botchup. "The only way I have to get off-world is the landing shuttle. That'd get me up to orbit with some power to spare, but there's no way to get me to an inhabited world. I'd starve waiting for another ship to come."

"Oh, it is not so difficult as that," said Qual. "You may not be aware—in this same system your Alliance has a large space station, easily reached in one of your landers. Lorelei, I believe your name is for it. But of course that does not signify, since you intend to stay and fight the Hidden Ones."

Botchup raised his brows. "Lorelei? The resort station? You mean Zenobia is in the same system as Lorelei?"

"Yes, we were very surprised to learn that," said Phule. "Of course, nobody had any notion this world was inhabited. It's not one we'd have settled for ourselves. It wasn't until after the Alliance signed a treaty with the Zenobians that we found out where their home world was located."

"A sensible precaution, with the other party's intentions unknown to us," said Qual. "Of course, now we are allies together, and we trust you to know these things."

"Lorelei," mused Botchup. "You know, poor Snipe might need to be evacuated—"

"That's a very humanitarian thought," said Armstrong. "Of course, he couldn't pilot the lander himself. Somebody would have to go with him. "I'd be glad to—"

"Let me think about it," said Botchup. "This isn't the kind of decision that should be made on the spur of the moment. If Snipe recovers, it wouldn't be necessary. On the other hand—"

The door opened and in came Phule, dressed in a tuxedo. "Just a reminder," he said. "Free breakfast on the casino floor!" He waved his martini glass and ducked back out.

Botchup turned several shades paler. "You know, I think I have the most experience piloting that particular shuttle model. We really need to get Snipe to safety."

"Sir, that's a dangerous voyage," said Armstrong. "Shouldn't you let one of your subordinates take the risk?"

"Major, I think you should send the most expendable officer," said Phule. "That's obviously me ..."

"Oh, no, you don't!" said Botchup. "I happen to know that you own the biggest casino on Lorelei! You'll run off and check into a luxury hotel suite and live the life of leisure. We're wise to your tricks, Jester. You're not taking that shuttle, not on your life."

"Very well, Major. I'm sorry you trust me so little," said Phule. "But if we're going to evacuate poor Lieutenant Snipe, who's to take him?"

The door opened to admit Chaplain Jordan Ayres, better known to Omega Company as Rev. "'Scuse me, gen'lemen, I reckon we got to talk about the morale problem here ..."

Major Botchup's jaw dropped. He stared at Rev for fifteen seconds, then abruptly said, "Get Snipe ready to travel! And send a man to my quarters to pack up my personal belongings! I'm taking him to Lorelei myself!"

Armstrong said, "Sir, I admire your courage, but you need to designate someone to command in your absence—"

"Jester can do it," snarled Botchup on his way out the door. "He's half-crazy already. Let the Hidden Ones have their way with him! I'm going to get off this crazy planet while I still have a few brain cells left!" He stormed out and left the other four staring at the doorway.

It was Flight Leftenant Qual who finally broke the silence. "It is a pity he was not more adamant. We did not even get to deploy our most interesting effects."

"That's all right," said Armstrong. "We can save 'em in case General Blitzkrieg ever visits."

But Rev stood there with a puzzled expression. "I guess y'all are gonna have to let me in on the secret sometime," he said. "I could swear that feller took one look at me and jes' flat out lost his cool. I didn't think there was anything that disturbin' about my face."

Phule grinned. "Rev, I'm not going to explain it until later, but I will say that I've never been gladder to see your face than right now." Armstrong and Qual joined in the laughter.

CHAPTER EIGHTEEN

Journal #611

Having regained de facto command of Omega Company, my employer moved quickly to solidify his gains. First of all, he made certain that Major Botchup and Lieutenant Snipe were able to leave the planet without undue difficulty or delay. He had no personal animus toward them, although many of his legionnaires seemed to. Besides, getting them to their destination with all due speed and safety would work more in his favor than otherwise.

His next priority was to reprogram the Andromatic robot; it had finally remained in his vicinity long enough for him to give it the verbal command that deactivated it. He had been tempted to return it to Lorelei in the same shuttle as the major, but that would have been unnecessarily cruel; there was little enough room in the ship. He had more useful tasks planned for the robot in any case.

His most important task was to pass along to the Zenobians the full details of his encounter with the Nanoids and his suggestion for a codification of the relationship of the two races: both, as he had reason to believe, were authentic natives of this world. Flight Leftenant Qual was useful as a go-between in this matter, and we soon had a broad-based approval of the general terms of the agreement from the Zenobian side. Now all that remained was to *bring the two races together and consolidate this diplomatic victory.*

Oddly enough, while there were a hundred details to check and loose ends to tie together, everything moved extraordinarily swiftly once things were set in motion. After waiting outside the camp during most of the action, I drove the hoverjeep in at dawn and found I barely had time for a proper bath and change of uniform before I was up to my ears in work. But by late afternoon, everything was in readiness.

* * *

The command cadre of Omega Company stood facing Phule near the perimeter of the camp. While many of them were smiling, there were also several dazed expressions; the pace of events over the last twenty-four hours had been too much for almost anyone to keep track of without a script. Phule himself was not quite sure he understood everything that had happened, and he *was* sure that most of the things that had happened were best kept from the Legion's high command.

Next to him stood the Andromatic robot that had been his stand-in at the Fat Chance Casino on Lorelei and, after its kidnapping and escape, his unofficial double here in camp. Even now, several of the legionnaires kept looking back and forth between him and the robot, as if they weren't entirely sure which was which.

Lieutenant Armstrong spoke for all of them. "It's really uncanny," he said. "Even when it stands there, entirely motionless, it's hard to tell you apart."

"It would be even more difficult if he hadn't engaged the robot's override protocols," said Beeker.

"What's that?" asked Chocolate Harry.

"They prevent it from doing anything other than what I give it a specific order to do," said Phule. "But when I have it set to impersonate me, it'll follow a general program of doing things I might be doing, and it'll respond appropriately to events around it, subject to the robotic laws."

"Respond appropriately is an understatement," said Rembrandt with a nervous laugh. "If you hadn't come back, I guess we would have figured out it wasn't really you, but it would have taken a good while longer. And somebody like the major, who didn't know you from before—I don't think he ever had a chance."

Phule grimaced. "I suppose I ought to be glad I got my money's worth from the manufacturer," he said wryly. "But I can't help feeling a bit miffed that none of my officers noticed any difference between me and the robot."

"Yo, if folks paid attention, they'd a spotted it pretty quick," said Chocolate Harry. "Every time somebody came up to it wearing my purple camo, it couldn't see 'em. If somebody had tipped me to that, I'd have spotted that sucker for a bot in no time flat."

"At least, I'm glad it wasn't you ignoring me like that," said Jennie Higgins. Then she stopped and peered at Phule more closely. "It *wasn't* you, now, was it?"

"On my word as a gentleman and an officer," said Phule, holding up his hand as if taking a pledge.

Jennie feigned a pout. "Coming from you, I'm not sure how much that's worth."

"Oh, coming from me, it's worth a great deal," said Phule.

"And he's got the Dilithium Express card to prove it," said Rembrandt, winking.

Before anyone could reply to that, Brandy pointed out into the desert and said, "Something's coming, Captain."

"Ah, that may be what we're waiting for," said Phule. "The Nanoids coming to finalize their agreement."

"Movin' mighty fast," said Chocolate Harry. "They on a bike or somethin'?"

"Conceivably, yes," said Beeker. "They evidently have the ability to form themselves into aggregations for special purposes, so perhaps they've adopted a form not dissimilar to one of your hovercycles."

"Whatever you say, man," said Chocolate Harry, shading his eyes with a huge hand. "Still comin' in fast. Are y'sure this is all cool, Cap'n? We can still get a couple antitank lasers zeroed in on it 'fore it gets too close."

"I doubt they'd hurt it any," said Sushi. "It'd do about as much damage as shooting a rifle at a swarm of ripners."

"I just hope it has good brakes," said Armstrong. "Shouldn't we stand out of its direct line of approach?"

"That's actually not a bad idea," said Phule, stepping off a half dozen paces to one side. The group of legionnaires followed him and watched as the cloud of dust came closer, eerily quiet for something so fast-moving. At last, just as it seemed it would inevitably crash into the camp, the oncoming entity came to a pinpoint stop a few meters away from the group of officers who, observing Phule's cool unconcern, stood quietly waiting for it. Only when the dust began to settle did anyone react to what had arrived in their midst.

"Sheeee-*it*! It's the renegade robots!" cried Chocolate Harry, and he fell flat to the ground, reaching for a weapon.

"Looks like it, doesn't it?" said Sushi. "We've been showing them kids' adventure holos, and they must have decided they want to look like Roger Robot. You can get up, Harry. Meet the Nanoids."

"Nanoids? What the hell is that?" said Harry, slowly getting to his feet. He eyed the new arrival suspiciously.

"They're the whole reason we came to this planet," said Phule. "They share Zenobia with the Zenobians, and now we've got to arrange it so the two species can coexist in peace. And as it happens, I've got the perfect ambassador in mind."

"Ambassador? Who's that?" said Armstrong.

"Yours truly, of course," said an uncannily familiar voice. The voice came from the Andromatic robot, which they now saw was dressed in a tuxedo, carrying an impressive-looking portfolio under one arm.

"The robot?" said Jennie Higgins.

"That's right," said Phule. "The Zenobians will accept it because it looks like me, and they already think of me as a human of unusual integrity and leadership—"

"I can't imagine where they got that notion," said Beeker dryly.

Phule ignored him. "And the Nanoids will respond to its robotic logic in a way they couldn't to any organic ambassador. So both sides will trust it, and meanwhile, it'll remain completely loyal to the Alliance because it can't conceive of any other course of action."

"Man, are you sure about that?" asked Chocolate Harry, squinting carefully at the Andromatic robot.

"Absolutely, Sergeant," said the robot. It gave a very passable imitation of a wink. "And, by the way, it's a pleasure finally to see you without all that silly purple. Awkward for me to pretend I didn't see you."

"Say what?" said Harry. "You mean you could see me all along, even with the camo? I be damn—"

"That is exactly right, Sergeant," said the robot.

"Why did you pretend you couldn't see us, then?" said Jennie, her eyes beginning to smolder.

"Very simple, Miss Higgins," said the robot. "That purple antirobot camouflage is distributed by Phule-Proof Industries. For me to reveal that it was ineffective would be to damage my owner's interests, which, of course, I am programmed to protect. So until he reprogrammed me, I had to pretend that it did, in fact, work as advertised."

Chocolate Harry let out a long, low whistle. "Man, that's way too fast for my speed. I got to tell you, Cap'n, I'm glad this sucker *is* on our side."

"So am I, Harry," said Phule, chuckling. "So am I."

Journal #612

General Blitzkrieg was not at all happy when he received the news from Zenobia. To begin with, he was forced to pay off his thousand-dollar bet with Colonel Battleax when the arbiters—General Havoc, Ambassador Gottesman, and the third judge chosen by them, Chief Potentary Korg of Zenobia—declared that Omega Company had successfully achieved the mission's stated objectives. And that was only the beginning.

Next, the Alliance Senate had called him in to testify on the treaty that my employer had concluded between the Zenobians and the Nanoids, who had turned out to have great potential as trading partners for the Alliance, once communications channels had been opened up. Having gone on record as opposing Omega Company's being given the Zenobia assignment, he was caught completely off guard by this development. It was particularly aggravating that he was forced to depend almost entirely on Captain Jester's reports to prepare himself for the Senate hearings.

Most annoying of all, the man he'd hand-picked as CO of Omega Company had evidently turned tail and run away just as the new race was arriving to make its overtures to the Legion company. There was very little the general could do to make his choice of Major Botchup look like anything but a blunder.

He didn't understand how so many things could have gone wrong at once. Still, if there was a way to make himself into the hero of the day, he intended to find it.

* * *

General Blitzkrieg gripped the bridge of his nose between thumb and forefinger. There was the beginning of a headache lurking just behind his sinuses. He wanted nothing more than to go lie down, but he had to appear before the Alliance Senate in half an hour, and he didn't dare go in there without some kind of coherent story—not unless he wanted to be even more a laughingstock than he already was.

"All right, tell me again how we're going to explain this," he said. "Not only did Major Botchup and his aide desert from Omega Company in the face of what they thought was an enemy incursion; they ran away to Lorelei. *Lorelei!* Why the hell did they have to pick the plushest resort station in the sector to escape to?"

Major Sparrowhawk looked at her superior, tight-lipped. She'd hitched her career to Blitzkrieg's, and she'd always been careful to tell him what he wanted to hear. But it was beginning to look as if her best bet for survival was to start telling him what he *needed* to hear. And there was no better time to start than right now. She drew a star on her notepad and said, "Sir, Lorelei was the closest Alliance outpost. You need to keep emphasizing that fact, General."

"I just hope the senators buy this bill of goods," said Blitzkrieg. He opened his eyes and glared. "It looks bad, damn it, very bad."

"It doesn't help a bit that it was *your* picked commanding officer who ran off," snarled Colonel Battleax, pausing in her pacing back and forth around the anteroom to which the Legion delegation had been sent to wait until the Senate was ready for them. "The Legion's lucky Jester was there to pick up the pieces. *If* you were smart, you'd make the most of that point. He's the Legion's golden boy, as far as the civilians are concerned, and that includes the Senate. Our best chance to profit from this episode is to give him full credit for it."

"It galls the hell out of me," said the general. "That son of a bitch is leading a charmed life, Colonel. If it weren't for the good of the Legion—"

"The next time you give a damn about the good of the Legion will be the first time," said Battleax. "You didn't have the sense to leave Jester alone to take care of a situation he was perfectly suited to handle, and you've ended up saddling Botchup with a failure he may never get off his record. Not that anybody expected much of him to begin with."

"We don't want the senators to focus on any of that, ma'am," said Major Sparrowhawk quietly. "General, you are going to tell them we had an important mission that required Botchup's presence on Lorelei. And to make the most capital out of Jester's diplomatic coup—"

"Diplomatic farking coup!" moaned Blitzkrieg. "How the hell does a complete idiot keep coming up with diplomatic coups?"

"Idiot or not, he keeps doing it," growled Battleax. "His company did everything they were asked to do, and more. By my count, this is the third time he's saved our bacon." Her expression made it very clear who *she* thought was the idiot.

"Don't rub it in, Colonel," growled Blitzkrieg. "You've won your damned bet, thanks to Jester and his rabble—and those half-blind judges. I don't need your gloating—"

Sparrowhawk cleared her throat. This wasn't going to be easy to say, but somebody had to say it. "As I was suggesting, General,

285

Colonel, the Legion will look a lot better if you claim that Captain Jester was acting in furtherance of your orders instead of letting everybody know he did it in spite of you. And the best way to make capital out of his accomplishments would be to return him to official command of Omega Company and promote him to—"

General Blitzkrieg sat bolt upright. "*Promote* him! I'd sooner promote the devil!"

"Have it your own way, sir," said Sparrowhawk with a shrug. "I suspect the senators will have their own ideas of what Captain Jester deserves, though."

As it turned out, she was right again.

About the Author

Robert Lynn Asprin was an American science fiction and fantasy author, best known for his MythAdventures and Phule's Company series. As an active fan of the genres, he was a member of the Society for Creative Anachronism, a co-founder of the Great Dark Horde, and founder of the Dorsai Irregulars. He was nominated for the Hugo Award for Best Dramtic Presentation for The Capture in 1976.

Asprin died in 2008 at the age of 61 having published over fifty novels and several short stories.

Peter Jewell Heck is an American science fiction and mystery author, best known for his "Mark Twain Mysteries" and Phule's Company series. He was an editor for Ace Books and is a regular reviewer for Asimov's Science Fiction and Kirkus Reviews.

If You Liked ...

If you liked *Phule Me Twice*, you might also enjoy:

No Phule Like an Old Phule
Robert Asprin

The Magic Touch
Jody Lynn Nye

Lights in the Deep
Brad Torgersen

Other WordFire Press Titles

Phule's Company

Phule's Paradise

A Phule and his Money

No Phule Like an Old Phule

Phule's Errand

Our list of other WordFire Press authors and titles is always growing. To find out more and to see our selection of titles, visit us at:

wordfirepress.com

CPSIA information can be obtained
at www.ICGtesting.com
Printed in the USA
LVHW092255150319
610881LV00001B/53/P

9 781614 755753